"What a wonderful, delightful read! Jennifer Probst never disappoints, and here she's outdone herself. The story of these three wonderful sisters is the perfect book to fall into and forget about your world. Moving, absorbing, compelling, and heartfelt. Not to mention the luscious setting! You can almost smell the sea air and taste the food."

—*New York Times* bestselling author M. J. Rose

"Hidden love and a rediscovered sisterhood await readers in Probst's latest. . . . Probst once again proves her talent at writing female relationships that will resonate with readers of contemporary women's fiction."

—*Booklist*

PRAISE FOR
Our Italian Summer

"The novel is carried by the rich interactions between the women, as well as the lush Italian landscape, city descriptions, and culinary pleasures. Probst consistently charms."

—*Publishers Weekly*

"*Under the Tuscan Sun* meets *Divine Secrets of the Ya-Ya Sisterhood* as Probst (*Searching for Someday*, 2013) explores the dynamics of womanhood between three generations against a picturesque Italian backdrop. . . . Filled with family drama amidst a lush setting, plus a touch of romance, *Our Italian Summer* will provide a delicious escape for readers."

—*Booklist*

"I never wanted this story to end! Jennifer Probst has a knack for writing characters I truly care about—I want these people as *my* friends!"

—*New York Times* bestselling author Alice Clayton

"For a . . . fun-filled, warmhearted read, look no further than Jennifer Probst!"

—*New York Times* bestselling author Jill Shalvis

"Jennifer Probst never fails to delight."

—*New York Times* bestselling author Lauren Layne

TITLES BY JENNIFER PROBST

Our Italian Summer

The Secret Love Letters of Olivia Moretti

A Wedding in Lake Como

THE TWIST OF FATE SERIES

Meant to Be

So It Goes

Save the Best for Last

THE SUNSHINE SISTERS SERIES

Love on Beach Avenue

Temptation on Ocean Drive

Forever in Cape May

STAY SERIES

The Start of Something Good

A Brand New Ending

All Roads Lead to You

Something Just Like This

Begin Again

BILLIONAIRE BUILDERS SERIES

Everywhere and Every Way

Any Time, Any Place

Somehow, Some Way

All or Nothing at All

SEARCHING FOR . . . SERIES

Searching for Someday

Searching for Perfect

Searching for Beautiful

Searching for Always

Searching for You

Searching for Mine

Searching for Disaster

MARRIAGE TO A BILLIONAIRE SERIES

The Marriage Bargain

The Marriage Trap

The Marriage Mistake

The Book of Spells

The Marriage Merger

The Marriage Arrangement

NONFICTION

Write Naked

Write True

Writers Inspiring Writers: What I Wish I'd Known

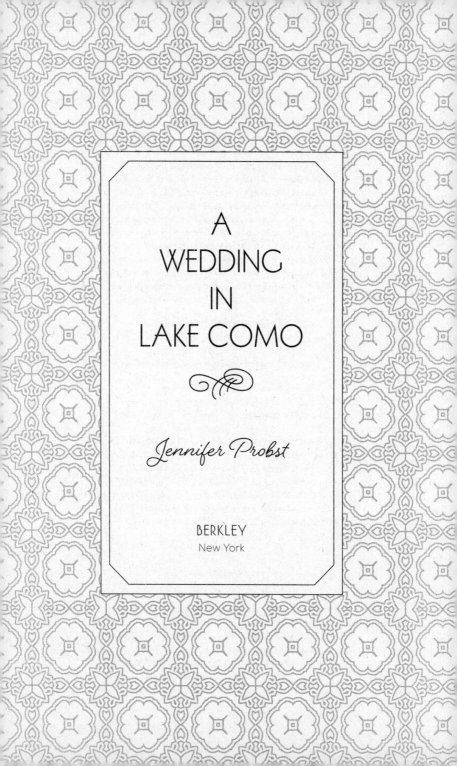

A
WEDDING
IN
LAKE COMO

Jennifer Probst

BERKLEY
New York

BERKLEY
An imprint of Penguin Random House LLC
penguinrandomhouse.com

Copyright © 2024 by Triple J Publishing Inc.
Readers Guide copyright © 2024 by Triple J Publishing Inc.
Excerpt from *The Secret Love Letters of Olivia Moretti*
by Jennifer Probst copyright © 2022 by Triple J Publishing Inc.
Penguin Random House supports copyright. Copyright fuels creativity,
encourages diverse voices, promotes free speech, and creates a vibrant
culture. Thank you for buying an authorized edition of this book and
for complying with copyright laws by not reproducing, scanning,
or distributing any part of it in any form without permission.
You are supporting writers and allowing Penguin Random
House to continue to publish books for every reader.

BERKLEY and the BERKLEY & B colophon are
registered trademarks of Penguin Random House LLC.

Library of Congress Cataloging-in-Publication Data

Names: Probst, Jennifer, author.
Title: A wedding in Lake Como / Jennifer Probst.
Description: First Edition. | New York: Berkley, 2024. |
Series: Meet me in Italy
Identifiers: LCCN 2023036906 (print) | LCCN 2023036907 (ebook) |
ISBN 9780593546048 (trade paperback) | ISBN 9780593546055 (ebook)
Subjects: LCGFT: Romance fiction. | Novels.
Classification: LCC PS3616.R624 W44 2024 (print) |
LCC PS3616.R624 (ebook) | DDC 813/.6—dc23/eng/20231013
LC record available at https://lccn.loc.gov/2023036906
LC ebook record available at https://lccn.loc.gov/2023036907

First Edition: May 2024

Printed in the United States of America
1st Printing

BOOK DESIGN BY KATY RIEGEL

For the ones who saw me,
chose me,
and loved me anyway.

To friendship.

Everyone thinks of changing the world, but no one thinks of changing himself.

—Leo Tolstoy

There is one friend in the life of each of us who seems not a separate person, however dear and beloved, but an expansion, an interpretation, of one's self, the very meaning of one's soul.

—Edith Wharton

A WEDDING
IN LAKE COMO

1

AFTER

stared at the embossed envelope, fingers gripping the sharp edges with such force, indentations cut into my tender flesh. The wedding invitation blurred before me, my name like a mockery in its perfect gold scrawled font.

Ava was getting married.

The breath left my lungs in a whoosh, so I allowed myself to drop into the kitchen chair. It was a long time before I decided to open the envelope. When I did, my French-manicured nail sliced through the wax seal, but I was beyond caring if the paint chipped. Like doing anything unpleasant in life, I learned to do it fast. Much better to take the hit of pain full force rather than in steady doses over time. I prefer a fast death.

In Ava's usual fashion, the invite was elegant, timeless, and spoke of her signature grace. The heavy stock paper was the color of rich butter, painted in thick gold-leaf brush-strokes that glittered. I skimmed the card.

You are cordially invited to the wedding of Ms. Ava Anastasia Aldaine to Mr. Theodore Roberto Barone . . .
  The family invites you to a weekend of festivities at the Aldaine estate in Lake Como . . .

My gaze skipped over the words with greed. I didn't recognize the name of the man she'd finally decided to marry and wondered if it was a whirlwind affair, or if Ava had given in to her father's wishes and chosen a proper husband. Of course, it had been five years since we'd spoken, and I'd been ruthless in my denial of any information. Keeping her name off my social media search bar had been a coping mechanism, though there'd been many nights I wanted to drunken search for any nugget of information about her life. But I'd stayed disciplined. Too bad the success still rang hollow, but the years had taught me not to question the empty space. Better to keep it unfilled and have a life of truth than lies.

Even though lies felt so much sweeter.

I dropped the invitation on the table, but my gaze snagged on a small white card nestled within wispy golden tissue. Picking it up, I noticed it wasn't the usual RSVP card. Black marker bled into the fabric threads with a familiar, bold style I'd memorized long ago. This time, my heart paused in my chest.

Maddie—

    Come to my wedding. I need to talk to you.
    Please. It's important.
    You made a promise.

Ava

I closed my eyes and fought back the whimper of pain that clutched my insides. Memories rushed through me like a stampede—of me and Ava and Chelsea drunken dancing under a full yellow moon with our arms linked; crowded in our dorm room with Harry Styles blasting on repeat, sharing secrets while painting our nails and recording silly Tik-Tok videos, heads mashed together, smiles stretching our lips, the gleam and vigor of youth amid a bubble of love and trust that can only be found in the purest of friendships. Of Ava teaching me how to be brave when the doubts struck. Of Ava choosing me from the group that clamored to be in her magic circle, showering me with long hugs and whispers against my ear in the dark; of the familiar scent of rosemary and mint from her shampoo; of the clasp of her tapered fingers and joyous laughter and dazzling beauty that always made my heart stutter in appreciation and fierce pride that she belonged to me; to us. Ava was ours.

Until she wasn't.

I read the words again, hearing her lilting voice in my ear as if she was whispering to me. And for the first time in five years, the foundation of the wall I'd shored up and carefully built shook. The crack let in just enough of the past to make me question the decision to run and cut Ava out of my life forever.

A silly word, really. *Forever.* What really lasted forever? Certainly not love. Or youth. Not beauty or lust; dreams or certainty; not even friendship—the only thing I believed would never fail.

What about broken promises? Would this one steal a piece of my soul? Because there wasn't much left. I needed to salvage every bit that remained.

Dammit, why now? When I was so vulnerable?

I dropped the note on the table and got up, heading to the wine rack to grab a bottle even though it was only three in the afternoon. The expensive cabernet was bold and rich with burgundy and earth tones, so I sipped it slow, and paced, pondering my options.

The quiet space around me that had once been my fortress felt like it was closing in on me. The expensive loft in Midtown Manhattan had been an indulgence, but I treasured privacy and, instead of hiring a decorator, decided to do most of the interior design myself.

Ebony black wood floors and vaulted ceilings gave the space breath, and the open-concept rooms allowed the furniture to delineate barriers. A spiral staircase led to my bedroom, and massive custom closets were transformed to house my social media shoots. I kept the eggshell-colored walls mostly bare, allowing a few retro art pieces from fashion history. Coco Chanel, Christian Dior, Cristóbal Balenciaga, and Donatella Versace all kept my secrets. The furniture was white and lush; accented with fluffy throw rugs, stuffed pillows, elegant candles, and hand-knit blankets. My kitchen was a trendy dream of clean white—cabinets, marbled granite, subway tile, and tiled floor in black and white invited cooking and lingering, one of my favorite activities since I'd become mostly a loner.

It was a feminine retreat now. I'd made sure after moving back to New York that I'd wiped away any last vestige of the life I'd had before.

I winced and took another sip.

Ava had always had an incredible sense of timing. Almost as if she sensed my weakening and decided to strike. I remembered how she always seemed to anticipate when I'd had enough of the madness—the sucking energy of her need for attention and love—and it was then she transformed into my favorite part of her: the joyful, free spirit filled with a warmth I'd never met in anyone else. She'd always been a mass of contradictions, ranging from drama to a heartfelt supportive mentor that knew exactly what was needed in the moment.

Another reason it was so easy to fall in love with her. But being friends with Ava had consequences. I just hadn't known how big a debt I'd need to pay until it was too late.

Scowling at my dark thoughts, I nursed my wine and eased out on the balcony. New York City was already hot and muggy, the air unable to take flight and breathe, so it stuck on my skin and clothes and clogged my lungs, refusing to budge. I used to love everything about summer in the city. When everyone ran off to the Catskills or Hudson Valley, to beach trips and cool mountains, I'd hunker down and crawl deeper into the city I adored. Walk its streets for hours, explore hidden cafés and art shops, finding fashion treasures that rewarded only perseverance and patience. Getting lost amid strangers was oddly freeing, a balance of anonymity and crowds. It was here I'd first come alive and grown into my real self. Fresh from graduation, drunk on possibilities and dreaming of fame, I was at my most pure before reality hit and threw me onto a different path. One I wanted. One I paid for.

I lifted my head up and stared at the scatter of tall buildings that jammed the sky, housing both power and poverty, depending on who lived inside. How many times had I wondered if I never left for LA if everything would be different? It used to torture me, teasing my sanity, all those what-ifs. I tried to focus on all the wonderful things happening in my career, but I guess I was one of those crappy people who focused on what they didn't have rather than what they did.

One late night, I stumbled on a Tony Robbins seminar and was told life happens FOR me, not TO me. I'd tried to change my viewpoint because it made things easier, but it was hard to keep the momentum up. Daily life and tasks eroded away the positivity, until I found myself waking up at 5 a.m. too many mornings in the same hopeless mood I'd started with.

My mind churned and I drank more wine and the memories pulled me back. I used to think my greatest loss would be my first love.

I should've realized Ava always had more power than him.

2

BEFORE

The first time my gaze landed on Ava Aldaine, I sensed my life would change.

She was sitting on the steps to the lecture hall, surrounded by a crew of laughing girls, all looking similar in subtle designer labels. Small leather crossbody bags, silky T-shirts with theme-driven mottos scrawled across the front, matched with low-heeled ankle boots with strappy gold buckles and heels. Even their carefully ripped jeans held an intention I'd never been able to inject into my own persona, one that screamed significance.

But Ava seemed more than a leader, more important than the typical high school prom queen. She practically glowed from within, pumping out energy to the surrounding crowd the way a guru offers energy shocks to a chanting audience. I paused before the steps, not knowing where to walk, and she looked up at me with extraordinary cobalt blue eyes, a deep dark blue that made you want to look closer. Rich, glossy waves of chestnut hair spilled down her back, and her heart-shaped face tilted upward, her lips stretching into a big smile, as if she'd met a good friend rather than a stranger staring stupidly at the blocked pathway. "Hey, you're in my English class. Madison, right?"

I nodded, still held mute by the strange feelings that rose up within me, a mix of longing and knowing, as if we had known each other before. Later on, I'd remember Ava said the same, and called it kismet. Soul-sisters. I always loved the thought and would pull it tight to my chest when I found it hard to breathe. A reminder I was special.

"Love your outfit."

I tried not to gape. I had no money for top-rated brands, and I was obsessed with fashion. I'd mastered the art of finding cool vintage items or luxury fabrics and putting them together with flair. Unfortunately, my high school classmates mocked me for my crafty wardrobe. This was the first time I'd gotten a compliment. I wondered if she was joking, but her face was bright and open and . . . honest.

"Thanks."

Her crew had grown quiet, looking at me with the familiar judgment I was used to, but Ava only laughed and began to scoot her butt to the side. "Sorry—we're in your way. Procrastinating so we don't have to go in there yet, right, Chels?"

The girl sitting next to her nodded, curly blond hair bobbing at the motion. A slight gap between her front teeth stole my attention when she spoke. "How are we supposed to study poetry, for God's sake? Do I really care what the poet's intention was? All I care about is what we need to know to pass the test." Her big brown eyes rolled. "Why can't I just skip to my finance classes? No one gets a liberal arts education anymore. It's so old-school."

I couldn't help the words that sprang out. "I like liberal arts. It's like going to a buffet, a little bit of everything. Then I can figure out what I want more of."

Some of the girls snickered and I felt myself turning red. Ugh, why did I have to be so awkward? She wasn't looking for an actual answer!

Ava laughed, a bold, robust sound that commanded attention. "Love it. Havisham is really the Golden Corral of universities instead of the steak house it wants to be."

Chelsea laughed with her, and suddenly, everyone was laughing and I didn't feel like such an idiot.

I'd begun to relax, wondering if I could get myself to talk a bit more, when the sharp slap sounded against my eardrums. "I'm glad to see all of you have so much time to socialize and relax before my class. I'll be sure the questions for Friday's exam are hard enough to equal your confidence." Professor Lithman taught English and was known to be tough. She didn't pause, and the girls scrambled to give her a wide pathway, her smart black heels clicking on each of the steps like a countdown to doom. The overall groan made her chuckle just a bit as she entered the double doors.

"Better head in," Ava declared, standing up with an innate grace. Her bulky knit red sweater stopped just a few inches above the waist, flashing her flat belly. Dark wash ripped jeans clung to her curves, then flared out at the ankle.

Red flat-heeled boots added the perfect dash of style. I tried not to drool over her ensemble, and her body as she shifted to grab her bag.

Her admirers pressed in around her like a protective layer, and I hurried past, head down. Sliding into my seat in the back row, I watched as students shuffled in, chatting and laughing with ease before Professor Lithman began class. I tried not to stare at Ava and her friends, wondering what it would be like to fit in and make friends easily.

Soon, I got caught up in the professor's lecture regarding Emily Dickinson, losing myself in the words that detailed the poet's struggle and deep emotion. I'd always loved dabbling in writing, finding it cathartic to spill all the crap from my mind onto paper.

"Ms. Davenport, I'd be interested to hear your thoughts on Dickinson's poem 'I'm Nobody! Who are you?'"

The attractive brunette who was one of Ava's sidekicks gave an audible sigh. I winced. There was one thing Professor Lithman hated, and it was attitude in her class. "It was a bit confusing to me," the girl offered. "I think she was angry that no one really recognized her since she stayed home all the time. So she was mad she was a nobody and mocked the ones who had fame and fortune since she was jealous."

"I see. Did you like the poem?" Professor Lithman asked.

Ava's friend tittered. "Not really. I find her works boring and stuffy. I wish she'd just say what she meant."

Professor Lithman nodded, though I could tell she wasn't too keen on the girl's answer. "Remember, Dickinson was commonly termed the poet of paradox. Any other ideas on Dickinson's intent or frame of reference for this popular poem?"

A few students offered shallow throwaway ideas. I knew this was an unpopular class, but I secretly liked it, along with Dickinson. Suddenly, Professor Lithman was gazing at me with intent. "Ms. Heart. I'd like your take on all of this. What did you get from the poem?"

Half of the class swung around to stare at me. I felt my cheeks flush and damned my fair, freckled skin for the betrayal. Oh, God, I always hated being put on the spot. Ava was looking at me curiously. I rarely spoke up.

"I liked the poem. It contained layers of wit many people don't see in her work."

The professor nodded. "Go on."

"I believe Dickinson actually enjoyed her solitude and had no wish to be out in society. She was happy to be a nobody, and the poem's tone seemed to be poking fun at others who want to chase attention or to look to be a someone in the world. I think she liked being whoever she wanted in the comfort of her room, even though we pity her."

"Interesting angle. What do you think she'd make of today's society?"

I couldn't help but laugh. "She'd despise social media. She'd probably think chasing likes is an asinine thing to be concerned about."

The class laughed, but I caught Ava's friends rolling their eyes at me. Ugh, why did she have to call me out? I wanted to be Dickinson right now and be left alone.

Professor Lithman nodded. "Excellent observation. Let's drill into the mechanics of the poem."

She went on, and I was blessedly ignored the rest of class.

After, I packed up and headed out. Ava fell into step with me. "I liked your answer in class," she said with a warm smile. "It's cool you like her poems."

I tried to ignore the glare from Ava's friends. "Oh, thanks."

"We're heading to the library to study for the exam." I was suddenly trapped by her piercing gaze. "Wanna study with us?"

A lump settled in my throat. I'd been having a hard time making friends my first semester. I hadn't attended any of the popular parties, and my roommate seemed to want nothing to do with me. All my visions of being different in college crumbled within the first two weeks. I nodded. "Sure. Thanks."

Most of the girls didn't seem thrilled. "We don't really have room for another person in our study group, Ava," Patricia Davenport said. "Sorry." Her tight smile was mocking and I wanted to slink away.

Ava's voice chilled. "Then maybe we should create another group."

Everyone froze. Chelsea broke the tension by bounding over and linking her arm with mine. "There's always room for one more. Please tell me you know more secrets you can help me with to understand that chick. I try but I don't have a clue."

I grinned, my muscles relaxing into the casual embrace. "Actually, I do. You just need to look beyond the surface and think about what type of life she led. She struggled with depression for a reason."

"What do you think it was?" one of the girls challenged. "Being too weird for society?"

I acted on pure impulse. "A life with no orgasms," I said.

Ava and Chelsea broke into laughter.

Patricia looked pissed off.

Ava drifted to our side and linked her arm with Chelsea's. "You're funny," Ava declared. "Come on, let's go."

I couldn't help feeling pleased, glad I'd gone for the dramatic punch line. I loved to banter, but I was usually too shy to show my real personality. The rest of Ava's crowd hung back, and the three of us marched down the hallway to the library. For the first time, I felt I was part of something special. Giddiness fizzed in my veins like uncorked champagne.

Ava had chosen me.

3

We all passed the test with A's.

Freshman year rolled through fall as the leaves turned crisp on the sidewalks and woodsmoke hung in the air even though there were no fires around. By the holidays, we'd formed a tight threesome that everyone began to recognize, though we always invited girls to join us at parties or study lessons or barhopping. Nights regularly ended with us naturally finding our way back to one another, to share a last drink and go over the evening—who looked or spoke to who; what gossip was tearing around the campus—and finishing up entangled together, limbs loose with alcohol and laughter.

Usually, I played the role of wing woman, making sure Ava and Chelsea didn't get too drunk and go home with some asshole and get hurt. New York wasn't kind, and I'd read about women needing to protect themselves from becoming drugged or kidnapped for sex slaves. Most of the time we went out, I was too nervous to really let go, but watching my friends run free and know I had their back gave me the same type of happiness. It was nice to feel responsible for people who appreciated it, even though they teased me constantly about being the oldest living virgin on the planet.

Ava was lucky enough to have her own place close to campus, so instead of dealing with my roommate and squishing into one of our small dorms, we ended up at her house. Most of the time, we slept over, the hours rolling over too late to walk or cab it back.

At first, Ava's friends treated me like crap, obviously not seeing why she'd give me the time of day, but soon it didn't matter because the crowd thinned to the three of us, leaving no room for others. Ava told me they'd never been true friends anyway, just people to hang out with. She and Chelsea had met earlier in the summer during their scheduled tours, and clicked immediately. They spent the months leading up to school growing closer, but said when I appeared they were finally complete. I called them witches recruiting for their third member in a coven, and they cracked up.

I don't think any of us remember the exact moment we realized we didn't want anyone else in our circle. Maybe no one really needed to figure it out because we were all happy. We'd found our home within one another.

One Thursday night, we were gathered in Ava's bedroom. I loved the generous king-size bed, silk sheets, and fluffy aqua blankets. Chelsea and I always claimed the bed, stretching out against the bubble gum–colored pillows, while Ava liked to sit on the teal blue rug, legs crossed. She was into yoga and was just as graceful on the floor as she was walking in stacked platform heels. The television blared in the background. Mini white lights were wrapped around the headboard. A massive makeup vanity set took up one corner, with a velvet plush chair, light-up mirrors, and bags of cosmetics strewn on every surface. A stuffed sloth was smooshed into a bookcase filled with textbooks, framed achievement certificates, and mini photos. A desk with a laptop seemed like an afterthought, rather than anything that Ava used regularly.

Ava passed around some White Claws as we discussed the newest sorority that we all decided not to pledge with.

"Sororities are limiting and push the exclusivity," Chelsea stated, propping her cheek in her palm and investigating the box of Lucky Charms for the marshmallow bits. "I refuse to be a cog in the wheel of their world."

Ava laughed as she shook the bottle of OPI Bubble Bath nail polish. Her feet were propped up in front of her with cotton separating her toes. "We're all cogs in the world," she pointed out. "It just depends on which one you decide to be part of."

I thought over her words, realizing how right she was. "I don't like many of the girls there," I said honestly. "The guys they invite are pretty awful, too."

"Agreed," Chelsea said, lighting up as she unearthed a pink four-leaf clover. "We need something better. Should we start our own club?"

I wrinkled my nose and stuffed my hand in the cereal box, happy to take the leftovers. "I like things the way they are. Just us."

Ava grinned. "Yeah. Just us. Our own threesome."

Chelsea snorted. "Not that type of threesome."

"I'd do you two anytime," Ava said, and we all burst into laughter.

Ava began painting her nails with slow, even strokes. "Do you ever wonder where we'll be a few years from now?"

"Nope, I have it all planned out." Chelsea gave up on her marshmallow hunt and wiped her hands with a napkin. "I'm going to set up my own financial firm that caters to women and working-class families. It's about time someone helps them get rich, too."

I stared at my friend in admiration. Chelsea was the earth element of our group. She was always practical, was good at making quick decisions, and burned to make things better in the world. She recycled, stuffed money into jars of the homeless, and volunteered at the local food kitchen. She tried to make us better even though Ava and I preferred sleeping in and binging Netflix.

"Why does it seem so easy for you?" I asked curiously. "Have you always known your goals?"

Chelsea nodded. "Yep. My parents are do-gooders. Raised me on volunteer work and giving back. I look up to them. Unfortunately, a few years ago, they got taken by a Ponzi scheme and lost all of their retirement money." Her dark eyes flickered with anger. "Now they're stuck working non-stop when they'd always dreamed of traveling the world. It changed them. They're . . ." She trailed off, and I unconsciously reached over to squeeze her hand. "Sad."

Ava muttered a curse. "The real problem is there's no

punishment for any of it. I hate that your family is going through that, Chels. It sucks."

Chelsea gave a weak smile, obviously trying to shake it off. "Yeah, well, I made a decision I'd make a difference. Too many people don't educate themselves on finances, especially women. My agency is going to change that."

I gave her a high five, loving her goals.

"God, I wish I had your ambition," Ava said, frowning at her toes. "My father wanted me to go to college at the university in Italy to get a more worldly view, but I always wanted to be in New York. He thinks this whole liberal arts thing is a waste but gave me four years to figure stuff out." Her nose wrinkled. "So far, nothing here has interested me. I don't have a brain for numbers, or art, or history. I thought maybe I could do something with languages, but other than Italian, I suck."

We laughed but her confession took me by surprise. Ava was always confident, always the leader. She rarely showed doubt in any aspect of her life.

"We're still freshmen," I pointed out. "We got stuck with a bunch of core classes—how are we supposed to know yet? We have our whole lives to decide what we want to do."

Ava sighed. "Yeah, I know, but my dad expects me to bring some type of value to the family name. And I despise being thought of as some poor little rich girl whose daddy takes care of everything."

Chelsea shook her head. "Impossible. You'd never look to someone else to make your own choices. You're too kick-ass for that."

"Or a pain in the ass?" Ava asked with a teasing grin.

"Definitely that one," I deadpanned, while Chelsea chucked some cereal at me. I ducked and fell halfway off the bed, bringing more giggles. Too many White Claws eventually had caught up with me, but I loved the bubbly sensation in my veins.

I leaned my head against the headboard. "Do you get mad at your dad?"

Ava usually spoke about her father with affection, but I wondered since he was such a financial bigwig internationally, and had homes around the world, if she resented not getting to have much time together. I knew she'd lost her mom when she was young. I wondered if it would be better to have a memory of a perfect mom I could love forever, or a real one who didn't care. The thought gave me an unpleasant jolt, and I took another sip of my drink to wash it away.

"Sometimes. He's stubborn and we fight a lot, but we both respect each other. I also know no matter how mad I get, he acts like a jerk because he loves me." She shrugged. "Maybe if my mom was around, I'd hate him more, but he's everything I have. Guess I missed the normal teen rebellions."

"I think it's nice," I said softly. Both Ava and Chelsea looked up to their parents even if it was uncool—half of the time anyone mentioned their parents at Havisham it was with a shudder and roll of the eyes. An ache throbbed in my chest and I recognized the envy, even if I was happy my friends had different experiences.

Ava started on her other foot, a frown creasing her brow as she judged her painting skills. "What about you, Maddie?"

I stiffened at the question and tried to ignore the clench low in my gut. It happened every time I thought of my parents, and how to explain our screwed-up relationship.

How to explain to someone that when I was five years old, my mother told me I was a mistake.

Even the memory made me cringe. She explained that she and my father had decided early on not to get tied down with children, but she got pregnant and didn't believe in abortion. I remember her face when she told me—like she was reciting a speech she'd rehearsed, her taut face like stone, not caring that those words would change who I'd become. She said they took their responsibilities seriously, but at age eighteen, I'd be on my own. Their duty would be complete.

As I grew, I realized my birth stripped them of their dreams to get out of the small upstate town that imprisoned them. Mom worked as a waitress at the local diner. Dad worked in a warehouse loading boxes. Neither seemed happy with their lot in life because of me.

I learned to take care of myself early on, making my own meals, doing laundry, and basically getting what I needed for school. If I asked for a certain item, they paid for it without comment. But it was the silence that was worse than anything. I would have preferred if they raged at me for fucking up their life rather than the endless, chilly, polite silence that permeated our small house.

I kept my grades up, kissed my teachers' asses, and scored high on the SATs, knowing it was my only exit out of hell. I'd applied to the Fashion Institute of Technology and got rejected, which stung. Havisham University was not as much for the rich as it was for the exclusive. It was hard to get into, focused on liberal arts as a foundation of success, and courted some of the best teachers in the world. It was a school that didn't pressure students to declare a major right away but encouraged experimentation in a wide variety of classes to help fit the needs of all students.

When Havisham University offered me a full ride, I packed my stuff and never looked back. Now that I was over eighteen, I knew I was on my own.

But I didn't want to tell my friends the truth. I hated the idea of them pitying me, or acting different. So, I shrugged and tried to sound casual. "Oh, you know, we never got along. Couldn't wait to leave. We fight and they don't respect me."

Chelsea murmured in sympathy. "Parents can be the worst."

"Hey, if you don't want to go back for holiday break, come stay with me," Ava said, stretching out her feet. Her toes glowed with the soft, glossy pink polish. "I'd love the company. Daddy always has to take off early for work, so then I'm bored and stuck in the house. Same for you, Chels."

"Thanks, but my parents would freak if I didn't get home," Chelsea said.

I smiled at Ava's invitation. I needed to work every spare

moment but had to keep my grades up to maintain my scholarship. I'd scored a decent job waitressing in an Irish pub that gave adequate pay with fair tips. The owners were nice and always offered me free food. "Thanks but I'm working."

"Not on Christmas. You have to come for dinner! Dad would love to meet you."

The cold spot in my heart warmed from her passionate invite. "I'm doing a double shift to cover for people going home. I need the money."

Ava's face morphed into her stubborn expression, but I could tell she was tabling the argument for later. I hated that Ava paid for everything, knowing Chelsea and I were always short on cash. Even though she got mad when I challenged her, citing her family wealth, it felt wrong to lean on her for entertainment. I never wanted to be like the others in her life, the ones who clung and expected her to pay, so I'd begun making excuses to avoid pricey outings and stick with dive bars and fast food.

Chelsea saved me by changing the subject. "Any idea of what you want to do, Maddie? You said you liked the digital media classes. Are you thinking of doing something like photography?"

Ava looked up with interest. I chewed on my inner cheek. I'd tried convincing myself a decent college degree would open up plenty of opportunities, but I was consistently drawn back to fashion and modeling. It was a silly dream, of course. I was just a small-town girl with a lanky body and an awkward manner.

I learned early I'd never be able to afford an expensive

wardrobe, and the kids at school wore basic, boring clothes anyone can find in a catalog or the lone local mall.

Not me. I was obsessed with studying high fashion on social media, then finding cheaper ways to put an outfit together. I learned to sew, though it wasn't my passion. The result was. I'd take pictures of my creations, modeling them in the house, while my mother shook her head with disapproval and my father ignored me. Even when I got teased about my fashion choices, I knew I was onto something. Why couldn't there be better options for girls like me, who wanted to dress in high style but couldn't afford it? Girls who refused to wear the same cookie-cutter clothes sold at department stores?

I'd dreamed of more since the moment I binge-watched *America's Next Top Model* and opened my first *Vogue*. Unfortunately, it was like wanting to be a Broadway dancer but not being able to touch her toes. A model needed to stand out and own the room. Make people take notice with a memorable personality and certain look.

I had none of that.

There wasn't money for professional photographs or building a portfolio. My only option was using social media and trying to share my stuff and gain followers. That would help me build traction and get some exposure.

Except, I was too shy. Too ungainly, with my stick-thin legs and freckled, pale skin, and strange green-gold eyes. I wasn't what the mainstream wanted. I'd posted a few things but never did much more.

God, I couldn't tell them the truth. They'd give me that

awful look of shock and sympathy while Ava volunteered to help, and it would break me even more if I dragged my dream into the light.

"Not sure. Still figuring it out."

Ava frowned. My heart beat madly in my chest. Her eyes narrowed, and it was as if she suddenly saw all I was hiding, and even though it scared the hell out of me, it was also a rush of relief. "You're lying. Why are you afraid to tell us?"

"I'm not!" I tried to keep the color from rushing into my cheeks. Damn pale skin showed everything. "It's too early for me to figure it out."

Ava narrowed her gaze. I felt as if she was probing underneath my surface for the messy stuff. "If you got to pick to be anything, what would it be?"

I grabbed a hot-pink blanket and pulled it around me, suddenly chilled. "Are we five?"

Chelsea giggled but Ava kept pushing. "For real. We've been hanging out nonstop, but sometimes it's like I don't really know you."

Stung, I did my usual and tried to retreat. "I share with you both. I don't know, okay? What's wrong with that—you don't know."

Chelsea glanced back and forth between us, as if sensing something bigger going on.

"Because I'm telling the truth and you're trying to hide. What's the big deal, Maddie? If we're as close as I thought, you'd trust us."

Suddenly, the alcohol turned my stomach. I didn't feel

so lighthearted anymore, with the only two people I ever bonded with staring at me like I was lying.

And I was. But how could I tell them something so pathetic?

Suddenly, Ava put the nail polish brush in the bottle and, risking her pedicure, slid across the room until she was next to me. The fragrance of sandalwood from her favorite skin cream drifted to my nostrils, and she took my hand, squeezing tight as if she knew how much I needed it. "We're not going to laugh. Just own it."

Own it.

The words stirred something inside me and poked at the underbrush I'd carefully hidden after years of being alone and shoring up my defenses. I met her gaze, and those beautiful blue eyes were filled with encouragement and a silent support that almost made me cry.

When I spoke, my voice came out in barely a whisper. "I want to do something in fashion. Modeling. Or become a social media influencer."

I waited for the sympathy or fake motivational speech, but Ava just tilted her head. "That's the big secret?"

I blinked. "Yeah. Stupid, right? I have no followers, and most of the time I want to hide in a corner so no one looks at me. Some supermodel."

Ava laughed, but it was a sound of delight, not mockery. "I can't believe you've been hiding this from us! It's not stupid. You were made to be a model, Maddie."

I snorted. "Sure. I'm so far from that world, it's a joke. I'm not the type. I have no content, and no idea how to even start." Despair edged into my voice. "Can we just drop it?"

"No," Ava said. A zealous light sparked from her gaze, and she suddenly looked at me differently. Like she was sizing me up. "This makes perfect sense! I'm always saying your outfits are dope. You make clothes pop in a unique way. That denim jumpsuit with patchwork you wore the other day? I would have never given that a second look, but the moment I saw you in it, I realized I wanted the damn thing."

Chelsea jumped in, grabbing my other hand. "Ava's right. Plus, your height and coloring are crack to a camera. You just need help getting started."

Ava continued. "Influencing isn't something you can study or get a degree in. But you can learn." She ticked off each item. "You need connections. Fresh content. Direction on branding. All of that stuff can be built with some time and the right people. You have two things going for you nobody else does."

Curiosity forced me to ask. "What?"

She grinned. "Your best friends who know how to help you. And your look. Do you have any idea how gorg you are? In a totally different way, which is exactly what the industry needs. Completely natural and untouched. Farm girl meets big city. Your red hair will be legend. I have just the right person to text—"

"No." I shook my head with venom. "Listen to me, I don't want any favors called in or friends contacted. I mean it. I didn't tell you for that type of help."

Chelsea and Ava shared a look. "Everyone does it," Chelsea finally said. "It's part of the business. Don't let silly pride or stubbornness stop you from your dream."

"We can't get you the jobs," Ava said. "Only introduce you to people in the field."

"No. I need to find my own way or I'll always wonder if anything I achieve is real."

Ava sighed. "You're such a pain in the ass."

I licked my lips and took the leap. "No outside help, but I'd love your help on growing my feed. And doing videos. Each time I practice and try to post, I chicken out." With anyone else, I'd die of shame at confessing my secret, but already my chest had loosened, as if I'd dropped a weighted vest off it. Hope flowed sweet and bright at the excitement in my friends' eyes. Even if they secretly thought it was silly, they wanted to help. With Ava's social expertise and Chelsea's smart business skills, maybe I'd build a foundation. At least it'd be a start.

"We can help," Ava said quickly, her face flushed with excitement. "There's so much stuff we can do on campus, and cater to the New York crowd."

"What I really want to showcase is ways to find great fashion by looking outside the box," I said tentatively. "It was hard for me. I'd like to make it better for other girls who dream big but don't have money."

"Brilliant," Ava said. "Everyone can relate to that type of mission. Social media will love it."

Chelsea was already reaching for her phone and typing furiously. "She'll need a plan to build followers and get sponsors."

They began going back and forth, coming up with ideas and steps to get me noticed. Panic licked at my nerves. Dreaming it was one thing; I was safe with that. But actually trying to put myself out there and facing rejection and ridicule? I didn't know if I was strong enough to handle it. Sure, I'd done research, but each time I tried to step forward, I backed down. What if I disappointed them, too?

"Wait—slow down. I can't believe you're going to help me. I've never told that to anyone before."

Ava gave a long sigh. "Maddie, the problem with you is you don't see yourself like we do. We're going to make sure the world notices you!"

Chelsea gave a whoop and then we were all laughing, and the joy came back, the possibilities flowing through me so fast, it was like I'd taken a huge hit from a bong and was riding it out, free-falling.

And I knew right then and there, Ava and Chelsea had saved my life from the worst thing I'd been suffering from.

Loneliness.

No wonder I'd fallen so hard. Female friendships are like a first love affair—filled with wild joy, excitement, and passion.

Unfortunately, they can also turn and fan the flames of rage and jealousy. They can rip your heart out and steal a piece of your soul, so you spend the rest of your life looking for it to put back.

But I wasn't at that point.

Not yet.

4

Freshman year ended and Ava and Chelsea began a new period in my life that marked BU and AU.

Before us and after us.

Before us, I'd been alone. Most kids I spoke with were used to their parents being the center of their lives, furiously scheduling around every important or minor event. I wondered what that would feel like to be paid attention to in such a manner. Imagined being tucked in at night and read to; shopping with my mom and rolling my eyes as she picked out hopelessly fashionless clothes for me to try on; being photographed on the staircase for prom while my father tossed threatening looks at my date and Mom forced us to pose for pictures.

I never questioned my upbringing until being surrounded by others who seemed to think attention was an automatic right, and not a gift. Maybe that's why I was so taken by Ava at first glance. She was the first one who seemed to recognize I was special. She'd chosen me from the crowd clamoring for her attention and friendship. It was a heady feeling.

Sophomore year rolled into spring. The biting March wind turned to tentative sunshine, as trees began to bud and birds returned to nests. I worked nonstop to sock away money, kept my grades high, and began to slowly transform my social media accounts. At first, posting was painful. But Ava suggested I look into the camera and speak to the specific woman I wanted to inspire—my perfect consumer. It made the whole thing easier, and I began to loosen up and let my personality shine. I kept to a schedule of regular posts and focused on the niche I wanted to carve out.

New York City fashion finds.

As someone who knew how to stretch a dollar, one of my favorite things to do was explore pockets of New York. I'd grab the subway and delve into hidden parts of SoHo, Hell's Kitchen, the Fashion District, Chelsea, Chinatown, and Little Italy. I stayed away from the big designer stores and concentrated on shots of me scoring amazing finds. Then I'd style my new clothes and post the entire look, using various hashtags and tagging big influencers for more views.

All those hours spent alone in my room, scrolling through beautiful pictures of people I longed to be, spun into an asset. I scoured vintage stores and newly launched businesses from talents that hadn't taken off yet. My instinct to spot a certain piece and immediately know how to spin it was my superpower, from the simple maxi dress to a funky jacket or even custom jewelry. Rachel Zoe had flourished into a multimillion-dollar brand from a stylist background due to her ability to grab a statement piece and make it the main show. I also knew how to pull apart luxurious fabric from sale items and transform it into something beautiful.

I lasered in on my brand and targeted a certain niche. The college girl who didn't have the funds yet to indulge but craved to step in the ring with the power crowd. A working woman at the ground floor who had to impress the executives but demanded her own style. As time passed, Ava and Chelsea offered me the emotional support I'd always been lacking, and I began to grow into my dreams. To trust that maybe I was good enough.

I spent my free time engaging with growing influencers and fashion-forward accounts, making sure I shared and commented. My followers began to steadily increase, and I started to see strong engagement in my posts.

One night, we decided to get tanked at a popular dive bar, the Hard Swallow, in the East Village. The beers were cheap, the dark interior with red lights gave a cool vibe, and the wall art was entertaining. We'd just been approached by some NYU students who'd been a bit too loud and clingy, adopting a casualness that wasn't reflected in their lusty, glassy eyes. With her usual effortlessness, Ava managed to redirect them by gushing nonstop about our amazing boyfriends, until the guys moved on to fresh prey. I practically shuddered with relief once they trotted off, leaving us blissfully alone.

"I'm so tired of sloppy college boys," Chelsea groaned, sipping her tequila and Coke. "Why can't I meet a sexy CEO?"

"Have you been reading those romances again?" Ava teased.

"Smart women read romance," Chelsea said, brows drawn in a frown. "I'm ready for an intelligent conversation that has nothing to do with a hookup."

I couldn't help but laugh. "You seemed to like hooking up last weekend with that actor guy," I pointed out.

Ava snorted. Chelsea shot me a look. "That was different. He's auditioning for a pilot and wanted to go over his lines. One thing led to another."

I couldn't resist. "Was it his audition or yours?"

Chelsea grinned. "His. And he failed. In bed and out. I have to stay away from creative people. They're too whiny."

We cracked up. Chelsea was a straight shooter. Whether it was academics, work, friends, or sex, she hated the empty chatter or polite routines that seemed like window dressing. She dated men with a purpose, and had no issues dumping whoever didn't come up to her standards. I wished I had that much belief in myself, to be brave enough to move on without the need to get people to like me. It was impossible for me to turn down men's invitations, or say no to an extra shift, or even my last partner in psychology class who stuck me with most of the work because I was so good at writing papers.

"I think the real problem here isn't Chels's bad hookups. It's Maddie still holding on to her V card."

I rolled my eyes at Ava's statement. "I don't need to be in love, but not one guy has inspired me to want to lose it."

"That's because you haven't given anyone a real chance! Plenty of cute guys have approached us the last few months, but you always turn them down."

I opened my mouth to tell Ava the truth—most of the time they were using me to get to her. Being in Ava's circle was like rotating around a beautiful butterfly while I was the moth. She stole the light from a room the moment she walked in, and I knew most of the men would do anything to get closer to her. Including acting interested in me.

The first few times it happened, I'd felt stung and embarrassed. When Ava asked what had gone wrong when I ended up alone, I shrugged and cited my noninterest. Telling her the truth would only make her feel bad and me look jealous. Chelsea seemed to attract a certain type with her strong personality, so I think men realized they wouldn't get away with that behavior.

I was definitely pegged as a bit naive. But in another way, I didn't care. I was happy to focus on school, work, and my growing platform. I was telling the truth when I said there hadn't been a guy who interested me enough to want to have sex. I felt like I could be a sexual person with the right guy, but it wasn't my driving force like it was for my friends.

Chelsea must've sensed something was off and I needed help, because she waved her hand in the air. "She's just picky. Can't blame her. My first time sucked and so did yours. She wants better."

Ava opened her mouth to protest then clamped it shut. "Yeah, my first time did suck," she said with a sigh. "He didn't know how to find anything, poor man. But I liked the cuddling."

"Ugh, that was the worst part," Chelsea said. "I rolled over and got dressed right away, but he freaked out so much. Wanted a scorecard."

"What'd you tell him?" I asked.

"Good effort. Solid potential. Little results."

We shared a look and burst into laughter. "You're cruel," I gasped, but I laughed harder, imagining Chelsea in that exact situation and the poor guy's expression.

We were about to order another round when Ava grabbed my arm. "Maddie, look over there," she whispered against my ear, motioning toward a tall guy sitting at the end of the bar. "He's totally your type."

A mop of blond hair gave him a surfer-type look, and as he spoke to his friends, his wide smile flashed white teeth. He was dressed in faded jeans, a baby blue crewneck with the logo *Cape May* sprawled across it, and old sneakers. Somehow, his very lack of style made him stand out. I squinted my gaze to study him more closely, noting the easy clasp of his beer within his fingers, his broad shoulders, and his olive-toned skin.

Chelsea stuck her nose into our tight circle. "Where? That guy? Oh, Maddie, he's cute! Definitely your type—a non-arrogant Malibu dude who just wants to live life free. Go talk to him."

I took a sip of cheap beer, now used to the taste. Ava was always trying to buy rounds and encouraged us to get whatever we want, but I hated taking advantage of her. Too many people did because of her generosity—another thing I tried to look out for when her bar tab suddenly exploded in a room full of poachers. I didn't have much, but paying my own way was important. "No way. He's out of my league."

I knew I'd made a mistake the moment the words escaped. Chelsea gasped and Ava got that dangerous look on her face. "He'd be lucky to breathe your same air," Ava said fiercely, as if the poor guy had rejected me. "Why do you keep saying crap like that? You're gorgeous and smart and funny—"

"With a perfect bod," Chelsea added, bumping me with her elbow.

I groaned, hating that I sounded like I'd been fishing for compliments. "Stop, you know that's not what I meant. He's obviously a player and I'd get tongue-tied like I always do and say something ridiculous and I just want to avoid all of it, okay?"

"Not okay," Ava sang. "I think we'll need to fix it." As she turned her head, I noticed the weighty stares of the men in the bar, as if they were watching every move to time their opening. I didn't blame them. Ava wore sleek black pants that hugged her curvy frame and a lace top that accented her perfect breasts. Her hair tumbled down her back in glossy chestnut waves, and her lips were painted a dark red, like a poison apple begging for a bite. I ignored the tiny flare of envy locked deep inside me. Ava didn't deserve it, but it was hard not to compare. Everything seemed to come easy to her.

Chelsea giggled, revving Ava up. "Let's send him a beer."

Horror washed over me. "No, I mean it, guys. I'm not interested."

But Ava was already waving to the bartender, ignoring my pleas. Of course, he came right over past the crowded line of people begging for attention. "Whatcha need?"

Ava shared a quick glance with Chelsea. "IPA on draft. Can you send it to the guy over there?" She pointed. "Blue shirt."

Even though the place was packed, the bartender took a moment to flirt. "Sure? You can buy me a beer, sweetheart."

I winced at the awful line, but Ava smiled. "Next time."

"You got it."

"I hate both of you," I muttered, knowing no matter how I protested they were too focused on me loosening up. "I don't want him to come over here because he's polite. Plus, he'd probably be interested in you both instead of me." I struggled to be cool but get my point across. "It's no big deal if he's not into me, but I don't want to put him on the spot when he'd rather date you."

"Let's test it," Ava suggested. "We won't tell him who sent the beer and let him choose. If he comes over."

Chelsea gave a squeal. "I love it! Yes, Maddie, you can't say no. It's fair."

I knew I didn't have a choice when they thought they

were helping me. God, I was going to die when he rejected me, even when I was used to it. Most men weren't interested in an overly tall, freckled, small-chested redhead who had a hard time being confident. It was as if I emanated a desperate air they could sense and decided to stay far away from me.

"Fine. But I doubt he'll leave his friends. It's obviously boys' night."

"No such thing as a boys' night without picking up women," Chelsea said. "Here we go!"

I watched as the bartender leaned over the bar to say a few words, sliding the beer across in one graceful swoop. The guy frowned and looked over. My breath caught in my chest when I noticed his eyes were a light sea green—like a cove in the Caribbean, beckoning someone to swim deep. I almost blushed at my poetic thoughts, they were so lame.

It didn't take long. The guy pushed off his barstool without pause, holding his hand up to his friends as if to say he'd be right back. Gaze lasered in on the three of us, he strode over. His hips kind of rolled a bit as he walked, making me want to watch him more closely. He stopped in front of us, easing forward to take up the precious inches of space between the stool and bar.

"Thanks for the drink," he said easily, his full lips curved in a smile. "I'm Riggs."

Ava glanced at me but my tongue tripped and I remained silent. His name was as sexy as he was. Ava ended up answering. "Hi. I'm Ava, and this is Chelsea and Madison."

"Nice to meet you. Are you all from around here?"

I liked the way he posed his question—like he was interested in the answer and didn't just want to throw us a pickup line.

"We're from Havisham University," Chelsea said, nudging me with her elbow. I had to say something or I'd look like a complete idiot. "How about you?"

"NYU. Figured we'd blow off some steam after a tough week." He gave a quick jerk of his head toward his friends. "Can I return the favor? Would you like a drink? You can join us."

Ava and Chelsea stayed silent, forcing me to either engage in dialogue or deal with awkward silence. My heart beat madly in my chest, but I managed to meet his gaze head-on. "You can buy one of us a drink."

He blinked. His lower lip twitched in amusement. "Just one?"

Not knowing where my sudden boldness came from, I nodded. "Just one. The drink came from one of us—not all."

His blond brow lifted. "What if I choose wrong?"

I couldn't help smiling back at his question. "There is no wrong choice. Just yours."

"May the odds be ever in my favor?"

We all laughed at that. Any guy who could quote *The Hunger Games* deserved mad respect. A prickle of excitement raced down my spine, but I reminded myself he'd never choose me. No need to get myself stirred up for nothing—I didn't know him enough to feel bad.

Yet I did want him to choose me, I recognized. Badly.

Chelsea linked arms with us, laughing at the game. "Go ahead. We're ready."

He crossed his arms in front of his chest, stretching the fabric of his T-shirt. I wondered if it smelled like Bounce dryer sheets. I wondered what his hands would feel like clasped in mine. I wondered how it would feel to be the one gazed at with adoration, like I'd seen Ava and Chelsea experience when they chose their boys for the night.

I pushed this all aside and waited, pretending not to care.

His gaze lingered on Ava, and my breath tripped in my lungs. For one long moment, the air held heavy amid the laughing chatter of customers and the music blaring through the speakers. Then I was suddenly caught in his hot stare, those jeweled eyes piercing into mine and making my insides jump and shiver.

"Can I buy you a drink, Madison?"

I knew in that moment, like the time I'd met Ava, my life would never be the same.

I said yes.

5

AFTER

scooped up my phone and dialed the number.

"Maddie?"

The familiar voice made me catch my breath. Crisp around the edges and matter-of-fact. I jumped straight to the point. "Did you get the invite?"

There was a loud, raucous noise in the background, low chatter, the slam of pots and pans. I pictured her cooking dinner for her family, curly hair pinned up, a no-nonsense look on her face as she directed her boys to keep quiet as she talked. "Yeah, I did."

"Did you know she was going to send me one?"

The pause told me the truth. Chelsea let out a breath filled with unspoken emotion. "It's been five years," she said quietly. "We've changed so much. You need to stop running from this. From Ava. I think you need to go to this wedding."

Pain exploded low in my gut at her words. "It was easy for you to forgive her."

"No, it wasn't. We took a long time to heal our friendship. But we made a pact, Maddie."

"I made a pact with someone I believed was my friend." Bitterness edged out my usual neutral tone.

"You can't wipe away the past. But that means both the good and bad, doesn't it?"

Chelsea always knew how to hit hard and straight. I closed my eyes, wishing it was all black and white, that I could wipe everything else out except for that one betrayal. But Chelsea was right. There was so much more, and I'd been trying to forget for too long.

"I'm not sure I can go."

Chelsea snorted. "Are you kidding me? There's never been a better time to get out of the city. Let things blow over." A moment of silence fell over the line as we both acknowledged my life had shredded into tatters that I still didn't know how to piece back together. "Are you doing okay?"

I swallowed back the lump in my throat and lied. "Sure. I'm handling things. Won't be going out for a while. Good thing I'm in New York. People don't venture out for anything anymore. I'm embracing my hermit ways."

"You can't do that forever, Maddie. It was just a mistake. One bad moment. Everyone will realize that soon."

I thought over how I'd been hiding from the press. Hunkering in my apartment, letting texts and voice mails and messages pile up, from both friends and people who gleefully watched me get what they thought I deserved. I'd always known the public was fickle. They adored an influencer, but they loved it more when they fell, especially in dramatic fashion.

"Maybe. Maybe not. But I knew the stakes in this profession and took the risk anyway."

"What are you going to do?"

I shrugged even though she couldn't see it. "Wait it out? Try to figure out what else I can do in the meantime."

"Come to Italy with me. We'll be together again, like the old days. We can talk things out, and maybe have a chance to heal. Have you thought about what it's costing to keep up this silence?"

"She made that decision. Not me."

"Yes, but now you're the one making it. And at what cost? Has it helped freezing us both out of your life?"

"Not you," I said automatically. "We talk."

"No, not like we used to." I heard another clatter, the hiss of steam, then a door being slammed. "I remind you too much of Ava, so you like to avoid me, too. Sure, we chat casually on the phone and you check me off your list, but when was the last time you tried to come out to see me or the boys? Do you know Brady is turning four and Carter is almost two?"

I hadn't. Guilt pricked. I knew she was right. It was impossible to separate Chelsea from Ava, and even though I'd tried, it was easier to let her fade away, too. I'd hoped with time I'd build my own life and not need them anymore. But even when my career exploded like I'd dreamed of, my relationships always skated above the surface. I'd tried with

Levi, but there'd been too much for us to overcome. My other romantic relationships never lasted long, and casual acquaintances never became real friends.

Here I was, years later, still empty inside. Nothing seemed to fill me. Not handsome men, or adoring fans, or money. Not wine, or drugs. I'd been living half a life since Ava had destroyed mine.

"I'm sorry. I didn't meant to hurt you, Chels. It's just . . . hard."

My friend's voice softened. "I know. But we all have to move forward somehow. We've been stuck in time—and the past—and I want us to either move on in a new way, or cut the ties. Because it's too painful for me. Not to be all together."

I understood even when I didn't want to. We were all bonded in such a way that separate relationships couldn't form. In our quest to create a meaningful, deep friendship, we lost the ability to ever have distinct identities outside of the group.

Chelsea sighed. "Think about it. I'm going to the wedding alone—Ed's going to stay home with the kids. I'm staying the full three nights to attend all the festivities."

"Okay."

"Gotta go. I have dinner on the table."

"Thanks. I'll let you know."

She hung up. I pondered her words in the silence, then turned the phone around in my hands. Heart beating madly in my chest, I hit the Instagram app.

My news feed was immediately clogged with my face.

Various tags, notifications, and messages seemed to jump from the screen in an effort to strangle me with the sheer need for a response. My silence only fed the media frenzy, and sure enough, I scrolled straight to my agent's message, begging me to let her offer a statement—anything to keep the public informed about my headspace on an event that should have been nothing.

I paused on the now infamous video of me on-screen, drunk, sneering with an anger I didn't realize I held, my words dripping with disdain and privilege.

"You think I need you?" I snarled at the camera, stumbling slightly in my designer stacked red Gucci heels as paparazzi followed me down the street outside the brand-new RAGIN club. "Because I don't. I never did. I got my success on my own and didn't get it handed to me by marrying some guy, or a rich daddy, or family connections." My green eyes were sheened by a mad gleam as I laughed, sticking my face close so the viewer caught my painted lips, and white teeth, and well-known freckles, but it was the hate that made the clip go viral, a hate directed outside of myself and straight at whoever was looking. "I feel sorry for you. Build your own life and stop trying to steal mine. I refuse to help you—help yourself." I pushed my long white-tipped nails at the screen and tossed my head away, continuing to stumble toward my car, too late for anyone to save me.

Shudders wracked my body like being overtaken by fever. The comments kept scrolling, and I was helpless to tear my gaze away.

This bitch is so into herself she makes the Kardashians look selfless.

Cancel #maddieheart for ads! No one wants her fakeness anymore. #unfollow

It's time to expose these influencers for who they really are. #stopthehate

I thought women were supposed to lift other women. Unless you're #maddieheart #unfollow #cancelmaddie

I'm unsure how long I allowed myself to look. For the past few days, I'd been holed up, trying to find a way to deal with putting myself back in the world. My agent had constructed an apology that read like that of everyone else who got caught exposing their own monsters, but every time I tried to post, something held me back. I knew I had to respond on my own about what drove that tirade, and I wasn't ready to truly face it yet.

I picked up the invitation again along with a pen.

And wrote out my RSVP.

I was going to Lake Como for a wedding.

6

BEFORE

"You're coming with me on spring break," Ava announced.
We'd just spent a grueling week completing projects and research papers, and I felt drained. Everyone was talking about going home or embarking on a vacation, but I was stuck in the city, working nonstop. The only thing that excited me was seeing Riggs. Since the night we met, he'd been calling and texting regularly, and we planned to see each other.

I stopped walking toward the coffee shop and faced Ava. "What do you mean?"

Her face glowed with satisfaction. "Dad rented a cabin for us in the Catskills. We're going upstate for the week!"

Chelsea gasped. "But I told my parents I'd visit. Why didn't you warn me ahead of time?"

A frown creased Ava's brow. "Because then it wouldn't

be a surprise. You'll see your parents all summer—they're not going to bitch about you going with me on an amazing getaway. Look, we've been through a lot this semester. I almost failed Principles of Finance and you saved my ass, Chels." She turned to me. "And Maddie, I have so many ideas of where we can shoot for you and shops we can explore. You're stuck at that pub way too much. We need some fun, guys. It'll be awesome."

I opened my mouth to tell her I had planned to cover extra shifts, but she was already shaking her head hard. "Don't say it! No work. This is my treat; I'm paying for everything. We all deserve it, and I'm not taking no for an answer. I need you there. Dad is away and I'm not getting trapped bored and alone."

"I'd have to talk to my boss," I said. "Plus, Riggs and I were going to get together."

Her deep blue eyes gleamed with irritation. "You haven't taken any time off in months, and Riggs will wait. It'll be good for him not to see you jump so fast. Guys love the chase."

A ripple of frustration took me off guard. Ava could go anywhere she wanted for spring break—she didn't have the responsibilities I had paying my way through school and having no help from my family. She was also big on staying tight and not letting any guys break up our circle. When Chelsea tried to cancel on a party to meet a guy she was interested in, Ava gave her such a guilt trip, she ended up standing him up. As we'd gotten closer, Ava became more controlling, claiming she knew what was best for all of us.

Whenever I tried to explain to Ava, though, she got pissy, as if I was the one being ungrateful when she wanted to pay for everything and tell me what to do. I know she had good intentions, so it made things even harder.

She seemed to sense my hesitancy, because she suddenly linked her arms through ours and pulled us close in the middle of the busy sidewalk. "Come on, guys, do this with me. We'll swim in the lake and go antiquing and even horse-back riding. We have the cabin all to ourselves. I need you."

It was the last statement that got me, and obviously Chelsea. We both gave in and she let out a happy shriek. "I have everything planned out. We leave early Saturday morning. It's this cute place by Saratoga Springs. We'll go to the spa, shop, do day trips—I'm so excited!"

I swallowed past my doubt and relaxed. Ava was insistent, so why shouldn't I enjoy a getaway with my besties? I'd text Riggs and see if we could meet when I got back, and tell my boss I needed to go see my family. That would go over better than a trip with the girls.

Later on, Riggs called me after I let him know I wanted to push out our date. "Hey, spring break trip with the girls?" he asked, teasing in his rumbly voice.

I let out a breath, happy he didn't seem to care. "Yeah, it just came up. Ava has a cabin in Saratoga, so we're spending a few days together. Sorry I'm letting you know last minute."

"That's fine—I get it. What are you doing tonight?"

I blinked. "Umm, nothing. Just packing for the trip."

"Wanna grab a drink?"

My heart raced. The idea of seeing him again, one-on-one, caused excitement to flare. "Sure."

"Cool. Meet you at seven? Bryant Park? I'm in the library doing some research."

I did a quick calculation in my head and figured I could save on cab fare and take the subway. "Sounds good."

We hung up and I immediately tore apart my closet for the perfect casual cocktail date outfit. I settled on distressed, flared jeans and a sexy black tank with a bow in the back. I paired it with high wedges in powder blue. My bag was dark denim with a bloodred script that screamed *Love Hurts* by Ed Hardy. I left my hair loose and ran a straightener through the strands, making sure they lay perfectly flat. Giant silver hoops and a stack of tricolor inspirational bracelets pulled the outfit together. I took a few pics with the hashtags #datenight #firstdate #becool and posted.

I held my breath as I always did after a post, my nerves shredded, but the likes began to pour in. Tucking my phone in my purse, I promised not to check any social media until the end of the evening. I wanted to concentrate on Riggs and see if I still liked him at the end of our date.

By the time I strolled up the steps at Bryant Park, I was so nervous my breath was coming fast. I quickly swiped my palms down my jeans and pulled myself together. I was too old to be acting like this on a date. I had to remind myself it was no big deal.

He came toward me with a big grin, and I loved that he wasn't trying to act cool and seemed happy to see me. We did a half hug kind of greeting, both of us laughing, and I tried not to gape at his good looks. His hair was thick and blond, curling around his nape and ears in a messy way that made me want to run my fingers through the strands. His eyes were as beautiful as I remembered, a pale sea green, with thickly fringed lashes that should have been wasted on a guy, but I appreciated them. Like me, he wore jeans, and a button-down Henley in heather gray. He looked at ease and comfortable in his skin, with an aura of knowing who he was, even though he was only a year older than me. Suddenly, I burned with questions, wanting to know all of his secrets. I almost blushed at the thought, surprised by my neediness, which I'd never experienced before. I shifted my weight and we smiled at each other, probably looking like two big dorks.

"Do you want to go somewhere specific?" he finally asked.

I looked around at the park, buzzing with people and chatter and that innate energy that was unique to New York City. "Someplace quiet?"

He nodded. "Perfect. I've been looking forward to seeing you and don't need to hear anyone else's conversation."

We settled at a small bistro with pizzas, sandwiches, and a low-key bar. I ordered wine and he got an IPA—reminding me of what Ava had sent him the night we met—and I rested my elbows on the too-small table, clasping my hands together. He did the same. Our arms bumped. His gaze drilled into mine.

"How was your week?"

His casual question contradicted his stare. We'd kept

our text and chats lighthearted, getting to know the basics. He was in his junior year, studying business management, and had always lived in New York. He liked baseball, basketball, and video games. I got the impression he was well-mannered, charming, and too good-looking to have had many struggles. I also wondered if he craved to go deeper like I did. The very thought startled me. "Hard. It's like the professors knew we'd have too much fun on break and needed to punish us. You?"

"Same. I feel like I could sleep the whole week."

"Do you have any plans for break?"

He flashed that lopsided smile that heated my blood. "Wait for you to get back."

I couldn't help but laugh at the outrageous statement, but my cheeks still warmed. "Oh, sure, like you have nothing else to do."

He gave a half shrug. "Get ahead of some studying. Hang with my friends. I'm lucky enough I don't have to work until summer, so I better indulge in some R & R now."

He reminded me of Ava, and how nice it would be not to have constant pressure to keep afloat. I took a sip of wine. "Do you know what you want to do yet?"

"Manage people, I guess."

I shook my head. "You don't seem worried about not knowing."

"I'm comfortable with doubt. Everyone stresses too much about where they'll be at a certain age, but I think we all end up the same in the end."

"What do you mean?"

"Well, when I was a toddler, I guess I had a hard time getting potty-trained." He pulled a face, making me laugh again. "At least, that's what my mother always said. She worried about it all the time. She read books and listened to experts and tried all sorts of ways to get me to fall in line, but I was still having accidents in pre-K regularly. Then one of her friends told her something that changed her perspective. She said no kid ends up in first grade wearing a diaper."

I pressed my lips together. "That was the big light bulb moment?"

"Yep. And she was right. A few weeks into kindergarten and I never had another accident. I just needed to get to the next stage in my own time. Mom could've saved herself so much stress if she just let me do that."

"So, that's your life motto now? No one gets to tell you when to stop peeing your pants?"

He chuckled, reaching across the table to grab my hand. He did it so naturally I never thought to question the move or pull away. "You're funny."

I wrinkled my nose. "Not really. Humor's not one of my prime assets."

"What is?"

I fell into the easy banter, surprised when the answer popped out. "Loyalty."

He leaned in with fascination. His fingers rubbed over mine, bringing chills. "I like that."

I liked him. Liked his easy manner and sexy smile. We ordered two pizzas and spent the next hour talking about everything and nothing. By the time he grabbed the bill and walked me back to the subway, we were holding hands like we'd known each other longer than a first date. I stood against the dirty concrete building on the corner of 42nd, pressed against his chest while pedestrians bumped into us, and fell into his gorgeous green gaze.

"I'll see you next week?"

It was more of a statement than a question. I nodded. Something shifted between us; an awareness that could have been strictly physical but felt like more. He bent his head and kissed me, gently, just a peck, but his firm, warm lips against mine made my belly tumble and heat gather between my thighs.

He was gone before I could make sense of what happened. The kiss was like no other. I was already out of my element and had no idea what could transpire.

But it was already too late for me.

I fell hard for Riggs, and that changed everything.

AVA RENTED A white convertible with red leather seats for the drive upstate. We cranked up the music, sang loud, and watched concrete and traffic give way to open roads and vibrant green hills. The weather was still fickle in March, so the wind whipped at our faces, but our butts were toasty warm from the seat heaters. Though my mind still flashed to Riggs and our kiss, I was excited for the week ahead with my friends and a break from work.

We pulled up the circular drive, cresting the hill, and I gasped at my first look at the house. The gorgeous log cabin gave off a rustic air, but nothing about it screamed simple. The wood was polished and gleamed with richness. The wraparound deck offered swings and carved benches, and the landscaping was a mix of wildflowers and pruned bushes, with various stone paths leading around the back. A hot tub and pool were off to the right.

We jumped out of the car with excitement. "This is sick," Chelsea said in a low voice, eyes wide at the oversize windows and multilevel decks set up with rocking chairs. "Like glamping."

Ava laughed and led us inside. "Girl, this is better than glamping because we're not sleeping in a tent and there's a full bar and hot tub."

"Yeah, Chels, what are you thinking?" I teased, walking through the rooms with my jaw unhinged. The stairs were carved out of timber so it almost looked like you climbed up to a tree house. Each bedroom had a queen- or king-size bed fit with comfy blankets and fluffy pillows. A private bathroom held a soaking tub, crazy glass shower with multiple jets, and giant lighted mirrors. A gorgeous bar boasted an onyx granite table with various bottles lined up on the back shelves. Throw rugs in thick white fur and rustic chandeliers added elegance.

"Ava, I never want to leave this place," I said, opening my arms and spinning around.

Ava grinned. "Wait till you see the private dock and lake! We can go on a boat ride, hike, or just sunbathe without anyone bothering us. I told you it'd be awesome!"

"I never doubted it," Chelsea said, giving her a hug. "Wait till my mom sees pictures! She'll go crazy."

"At least she didn't give you a hard time for coming with me," Ava said, grabbing bottled waters from the refrigerator. "What about you, Maddie? Any blowback?"

I tried not to wince. I hadn't spoken to my parents since the polite holiday well-wishes. "Nope, they understood."

"Good. Now, let's get settled in and we can go to dinner in town. I already made reservations."

I dragged in my suitcase and fell onto the four-poster bed with a sigh. Already, my mind clicked to my outfit and what I'd post. I thought of some cute hashtags, deciding to focus on bonding with friends on a girls' trip, and the cabin-by-the-lake element. My followers would adore the glamour of the house with the balance of woodsy atmosphere.

We all decided to dress up for dinner. While we waited for our Uber, I did a quick video, breaking down my choices and linking the store purchases. Ava stunned in a short beaded dress the color of pale lemons, and white boots. Chelsea went with a classic black body-con dress cinched with a Gucci gold belt that hugged her curves shamelessly. I decided to go bolder than usual and did the unthinkable for redheads—dramatic, bright pink. It had originally been a two-piece pantsuit that looked like a frumpy office nightmare, but I had a different vision. I cut the pants into shorts, tailored the jacket, and slashed the sleeves. With a black halter top and ankle boots, it was now a chic, fresh type of outfit that no one would find in stores.

I was still looking at my feed on the drive over, and when I clicked on a message, I gasped.

"I told you to ignore the haters," Ava said, assuming it was one of my many cringeworthy moments when a follower would say something crappy about how I looked. I was trying to thicken my skin since I knew if I wanted to make it in this industry, I couldn't keep taking things to heart.

"No, it's not that. Oh my God, I'm being asked to sell a brand! They want to book a paid advertising spot!"

My friends gave a whoop. "We told you this would happen," Chelsea said. "Your follower count has been doubling steadily, and companies take notice. Who wants you?"

"Lovely Ts. You know those cute shirts with the quotes on them? I can't believe this—what should I do?"

Ava snatched my phone and tucked it in her Louis Vuitton purse. "Nothing now. We'll discuss it at dinner over champagne."

"Will they check my ID?" I asked lowly. It held up pretty well at most bars, but I wasn't sure if this fancy restaurant would take one look at me and throw me out. I didn't seem like the champagne type.

Ava patted my arm. "When you order champagne, they don't check ID. They just want to be paid."

"Got it. Making a mental note for when I'm rich and famous before twenty-one."

Chelsea snorted.

The place was lit up with white lights from the outside and gave off a cozy, luxurious feel. We had a small corner table set with crisp white linens, a crystal pitcher of water, and fancy silverware. Candles were lit everywhere and the accents were all deep wood, from the large booths and floors to lantern-type chandeliers hanging overhead. Ava immediately ordered champagne and an array of appetizers as we sat back and enjoyed the view.

"It's small-town upscale," Chelsea said in a hushed voice. "I love towns like these. Maddie, how far upstate are your parents?"

I tried not to stiffen. "Oh, I'm all the way up north several hours from here. Blink and you'll drive past the place."

Ava shuddered. "No offense, but I bet you couldn't wait to get out of there. Especially with a goal in modeling. You need to be in the big cities to get anyplace."

"Which is another reason I wanted to go to Havisham," I said. The waiter came back, expertly uncorked the bottle, and poured the sparkling liquid into flutes. "Sometimes I felt like I literally couldn't breathe."

The confession came out easily enough, but before my friends could offer sympathy, I was raising my glass with a smile. "A toast to Ava, for spoiling us rotten and being the best friend ever."

We cheered and I took a sip, the bubbles dancing crisply on my tongue. I could get used to this kind of life. As much as I hated the idea of taking advantage of Ava's generosity, there was also a thrill that I finally got to experience such pleasures. I thought of my parents and what they would think. Probably that I had no pride to let someone pay my way.

I pushed the darkness aside. My parents made their choices and now I got to make mine. I'd choose differently. To care about all the people in my life and never treat them like they were dispensable. They'd taught me the cost too well.

"Now, let's see what type of offer you got," Ava said, returning my phone. Her scarlet nail tapped against the delicate flute, and for a moment, I was thrown off by how well she fit in anywhere we went. From expensive restaurants and dive bars, to frat parties or the dean's holiday party, she seemed to mesmerize anyone she deigned to speak with. I wondered what it would feel like to have life be so easy. To own the gift of not only fitting in, but being admired in any circumstance. She was the one who was meant to be famous and before the camera.

Not me.

But Ava didn't want it, so I needed to do my best to level up and make it happen.

I read the message aloud. "Free T-shirts for one post! Pretty good, huh?"

Chelsea agreed but Ava frowned. "Absolutely not," she clipped out. "You need to get paid in cash, not product."

I blinked. "But everyone starts that way."

Her stunning blue eyes narrowed. "Not you. You need to be different, Maddie. Not some chick chasing free crap. Tell them two hundred fifty dollars for the one post and the shirts."

"What? They'll say no."

Ava gave a half shrug. "Then it's not worth the work. You need to learn one lesson if this is going to be a career. If you don't value yourself, no one else will, either."

Chelsea shook her head. "Not a bad plan. I agree with

Ava. If they say no, you'll get another sponsor later. Even bigger."

I chewed at my lip. It scared me to turn an offer down, but I sensed they were right. I needed to be willing to hold out for the right offers, or I'd end up chasing everything and not getting the big stuff. "Okay, I trust you both. I'll message back."

"What about the portfolio? Are you working on that?" Ava asked.

I nodded. "I saved up enough to hire a photographer. I'm still deciding which one to use, and then I'll start approaching agencies."

The bread basket came, along with tiny dishes of Brie puff pastries, crab-stuffed mushrooms, and calamari. We filled our plates and I moaned with delight at the food. I was lucky I could pretty much eat anything and never gain a pound. Not that I thought the skinny models were right to get so many of the jobs. I'd seen more diversity in sizes and shapes, which was needed in the industry. I always wished for curves and a more feminine shape, but I was stuck with my body type and it still did well in fashion so I didn't complain.

Chelsea forked up a mushroom. "What's the end goal, though?"

I cocked my head. "To make money with fashion."

"Yeah, but other than building your social media presence, where do you see yourself? As a huge influencer making money with ads? Modeling? Working in the fashion industry?"

I swallowed back the tightness in my throat. Chelsea got right to the heart of my fears. I didn't know what I wanted. It was still muddled in my head, and I lacked the moxie too many other girls had with their looks. I couldn't imagine myself walking into an agency with a kick-ass attitude and selling myself. But how did I gain that type of bravado? Ava and Chelsea had it naturally. Frustration nipped at my voice. "I don't know. When I dream about it, I see myself modeling stuff online and having people come to me for the newest look. I love the pics that are almost high art—they've carved more than a regular catalog or runway career. But then I can also see myself doing photo shoots for magazines or brands." I stared at my champagne like it held the answers. "I lack the right skills. I don't know how to walk, or show off clothes in the right way. I'm not bold or brash. Is it even realistic to think I could have success at this?"

"Yes," Ava said forcefully. "The entire reason it will work is because you *are* different. I've never seen a look like yours, Maddie. Your bone structure and coloring make someone want to study you. You're an original. The stuff you wear not only flatters you, it speaks to your personality, but I think you'd give that off with any outfit, like you own it. You may not be the usual definition of bold, but that doesn't mean it won't work. Bring the bold to how you envision yourself."

Chelsea nodded. "Exactly. For the other stuff, you can learn. Don't they have modeling classes you can take?"

Ava snorted. "They're useless. Better to walk with a plate on her head for good posture than spend a fortune on basic

101 steps she can learn along the way. Listen, there's this amazing friend of Dad's who works with Italian designers. I can get him to jump on a call and—"

"No." My friends shared a suffering look. "I mean it—I don't want any help even though I appreciate the offer."

"Why? Pride doesn't get you what you want." Ava glared. "Being bold is going after opportunities."

"If I never met either of you, I'd be on my own, trying to figure this whole thing out. I was alone for so long, you have no idea how lonely I was." Emotion clogged my throat. "Now, I have the support I always wanted, but I still have to do the steps myself or I'd always wonder if I got my career from a connection rather than merit." I leaned in, trying to get them to understand how badly I had to succeed on my own. "It won't mean the same if I get easy access to someone through you, Ava. I have crappy confidence anyway. But if I do this, and get the results, I'll finally believe in myself."

"And if you don't?" Chelsea challenged. "Are you going to call yourself a failure just because you can't get to the top of a billion-dollar business in a few years?"

"Yes."

Chelsea and Ava gasped, ready to blister me with a lecture, when I began laughing. "Just kidding. I'll just keep trying different approaches. Maybe it will be another way than I imagined, but I won't quit."

Ava hit my shoulder. "You scared me for a minute. There are no quitters in our coven."

"I knew you'd turn me into a witch eventually."

"Maybe you need a love spell for Riggs," Chelsea teased,

swinging her fork in the air. "That kiss sounded hot. And dirty."

I hated the easy way I blushed. Ava was known to give us blow-by-blow accounts of her sexual activities and I never got uncomfortable, but sharing anything myself was embarrassing. "Well, the wall was definitely dirty."

They laughed. "Maybe I should be a dating coach," Ava said. "I knew he was perfect for you. I seem to have this inner talent for sensing two people meant to be together."

Chelsea snickered. "Sorry, girl, but I have to disagree. You pushed me to go out with drummer guy, remember? Total disaster."

"Hey, he was hot."

"Until he opened his mouth."

I cracked up at Ava's frown. "Well, it was a first date, but I'm excited to see what happens when we get back. I'd hire you anytime, Ava."

Ava stuck out her tongue and Chelsea giggled.

We feasted on thick, rare filets, garlic mashed potatoes, and crispy green beans. Dessert was a trio course of chocolate mousse, blackberry tart, and coconut sorbet. By the time we got back to the house, I felt like collapsing, but Ava insisted we go in the hot tub.

More drinks were brought out, and we sank ourselves into bubbly, steamy water while the chilly night air snapped around us. Crickets chirped and the moon hung golden in the sky. We chatted nonstop like always, and I relaxed further into the water, bliss overtaking my muscles.

"Maddie, I was thinking of what you said before," Ava said. "About feeling alone. Was school hard for you?"

I'd lied to them because it was too hard to face the truth, but I didn't want to run away from it anymore. I stared at my friends' faces and knew I'd finally found a safe space. "Yeah, but it started at home. My relationship with my parents isn't what you think."

Chelsea squeezed my arm. "Tell us."

"They didn't want me. Never have. I grew up knowing I was a burden, and they told me I'd be on my own when I turned eighteen." I explained how my mother had said I was a mistake, and how cold they were; how I had to learn to live independently without much guidance.

Ava's blue eyes went wide. "That's terrible. I can't imagine how hard that was for you."

"Did you really go home over break?" Chelsea asked softly.

I shook my head. "I stayed at the dorms and worked double shifts. They don't want to see me. Hell, I wouldn't be surprised if I found out they moved without a forwarding address."

Ava shimmered with anger. "No more of that bullshit. From now on, you stay with me. No wonder you don't have confidence in yourself. Maddie, that must've messed with your head. Do you have any other family to lean on?"

"No. Mom has no siblings, and Dad doesn't talk to his brothers. I hated my school. It was very small and closed-minded. Pretty much everyone ends up working locally or disappearing after graduation without a look back. I met a few girls I thought I could bond with, but they ended up heavy into drugs and that just wasn't me." A humorless laugh escaped. "Maybe that's why I got obsessed with fashion. It was such a glamorous world, and I could pick up my phone and be transported. It gave me hope of something bigger."

"You're out of there now and never going back," Chelsea said. "Plus, you have us."

"We're your family," Ava said, leaning her head against mine. Her wet hair brushed my cheek and brought the scent of rosemary and mint. I sighed against her, feeling lean strength and love that I'd always dreamed of. Chelsea floated over and completed the circle. The tightness in my chest loosened and breath flowed more freely in my lungs. It was as if releasing my secrets allowed me to be truly me, not afraid anymore of what others thought. My friends accepted me wholeheartedly and didn't think I was broken.

So, maybe I wasn't.

7

The week flew by and we all became closer.

We indulged in mud baths and massages at the Saratoga Spa, eating healthy beet salads with lemon juice, only to stop at a café later and order a platter of french fries. We discovered a magical boutique that sold designer dresses, and Ava bought a wraparound Halston in emerald green while I snatched up a crop top in delicate white lace with tiny beads embroidered in the fabric. One night, we hit the bars and drank our way through, and Ava fell for a beautiful boy with soulful brown eyes and long, floppy dark hair. He quoted her Walt Whitman poetry and they made out in a dark corner. Even though he begged her to go home with him, Ava refused, telling us she knew he'd break her heart because he was a Scorpio and destined to hurt her. And at night, we lounged in the hot tub, played silly games like Truth or Dare? and Fuck, Marry, Kill, and confessed our deepest secrets.

On our last evening, Ava and I sat outside on the wrap-around deck, watching the sunset. Chelsea had fallen asleep on the couch, so we'd taken our wine and sunk into the pillows of the glider, rocking back and forth. In the distance, the fiery disc slowly sank over the lush green tree line. An air of stillness hung in the air.

"I don't want to go back to school," Ava said.

I sighed. "I know. But we're almost done with the semester and then we have the whole summer to look forward to."

She shifted in her chair and pulled at her sleeve. Even in her fleece sweat suit, she gave off an air of glamour. Dark hair fell in loose waves over her shoulders, and her naturally red lips were pursed in thought. "No, I mean I don't want to go back at all. I've been thinking of dropping out."

A gasp escaped. "Wait—what? I don't understand. Your grades are solid, and I thought you liked Havisham."

"I do. Some of the time." She gazed out at the dying sun, and melancholy skittered over her face. She pulled up her knees and wrapped her long arms around them. "Then I wonder if this is a waste. Clocking in to classes that mean nothing. Going through the motions to gain some useless piece of paper. What will it really prove? I still have no idea what I want to do or any type of direction. Maybe I was hoping I'd know more about myself than I do. That school would help give me some ambition."

I'd rarely heard her express doubts other than the occasional throwaway remark about still not having a major. "Is your dad pressuring you?"

She shook her head. "He's fine with me using this time to get my degree."

"Then take it, Ava, and stop being hard on yourself. We're only twenty years old! Chelsea may know what she wants, but most of us are figuring things out. You can't leave half-way through. What would you do?"

Her shoulders lifted in a shrug. "Travel. Intern at a few of Daddy's businesses to see if anything interests me." She fell silent, and I didn't push her, sensing she was going to tell me something important. "I don't have any passions like you and Chels. Other than my parents, I wonder if I've ever really loved something or someone that made my life worthy."

She gave a humorless laugh, and I saw another part of her, the dark side we all seem to hide and stuff deep down so no one can find it. Not even ourselves. "I wonder all the time what my mother would think of me. If she'd be disappointed in my very averageness.

"What if I'm destined to do nothing but marry some rich guy and pretend I'm important by volunteering at a bunch of foundations? What if I'm just a trophy wife? What if I end up being nothing?"

I grabbed her hand and squeezed. "You're getting tripped up by things that have never happened. What if you fall madly in love and open up an amazing business and change the world? Ava, you're special. You could never be nothing. When you walk into a room, people are drawn to you. They want to be near you."

She began to laugh, taking me off guard, then swiveled her head to drill her gaze into mine. Her voice was a husky whisper carried by the gentle breeze. "No, Maddie. Don't you know? That's you—not me."

I stared at her speechless. She had no idea how wrong she was, and I tried to tell her but she kept talking.

"You see people for who they are. You listen. You glow from within. And one day, you're going to be a huge star and the world will adore you for the simple reason you never thought you deserved it. They're going to fall in love with you."

I realized then that Ava didn't know her power and I may not be able to convince her. All this time, I assumed she knew the world would kneel at her feet without question, yet she believed it was me. Sympathy flickered inside. I made a vow to be the best friend possible, and maybe one day she'd look in the mirror and see what I did.

For now, I smiled at her words and touched her cheek. Her olive skin was smooth under my hand. "Thank you for seeing those things. When I look at you, I see so much, Ava. You're beautiful and smart and generous. You have so much to give and have only scratched the surface. You need to believe that."

A ghost of a smile curved her plump lips. "If you believe it, Maddie, I guess I can."

"Good. For now, I'm not letting you drop out of school and leave us. You're stuck with me for two more years, and we'll figure shit out together. Got it?"

She smiled back and the mood lightened. "Fine. I'll stick it out."

"Good."

"Got your phone?"

"Always." I picked it up. "Why?"

"I think we should record this historic moment. Plus, your outfit is adorbs. It screams pajama day and accessibility. TikTok loves that."

I rolled my eyes, but we squeezed in close and made funny faces at the camera. My fingers flew and I posted it, quickly showing it to her.

#friendshiprules #girlsrock #springbreakfashion

She stared at the picture for a while, a funny look on her face. Then she looked up.

"Send it to me. I want to remember it forever."

I did, but I already knew it was a moment carved in my memory. We sat in comfortable silence for a bit, shoulders pressed together.

"Sorry for the melodrama," she finally said.

"What melodrama?"

Chelsea walked into the room, rubbing her head and yawning. "What'd I miss?"

I waited for Ava to answer.

"Oh, nothing. Just talking about what we should do for our final night. Who's up for pizza and a movie? We can braid one another's hair and make popcorn."

Chelsea flopped down in the rocker next to us. "Sounds perfect."

"I think so, too."

We didn't mention anything else and moved on.

Later on, I realized two important things occurred from our conversation.

One, Ava ended up reposting the pic on her feed, and within twenty-four hours, my followers had exploded. I also got an answer from Lovely Ts brand, who agreed to my fee and promised to ship out my merchandise.

The second was the knowledge a deeper bond had formed between us that almost felt wrong because Chelsea wasn't included. I knew Ava wouldn't repeat or linger on what she'd expressed to me, so it became a secret. Our secret. That secret changed things. Looking back, I pegged the moment as a turning point between us; cementing our relationship on a deeper scale. Chelsea never had the chance to catch up.

I also know I liked it. That Ava had trusted only me. My vow to be there for her wasn't the normal promise made by best friends who end up growing apart after graduation. She'd saved me from myself. Offered me a glimpse of a life I always dreamed of. Offered me safety.

I'd die before I let her down in any way. I wonder if she knew it. Knew I'd take her confession and offer myself up as her savior. I cherished the role, and she stepped fully into hers.

That's when the real story began.

8

When I got back to school and resettled into my routine, I had another date with Riggs. I was even more nervous the second time because the first had given me such high expectations. I prepped myself to feel differently, to have lost that intense connection that burned between us, but the moment our eyes met my whole body shuddered with longing. My heart beat madly in my chest, and we floated close together like in one of those rom-coms, falling into each other like we'd been dating for years.

"I missed you."

He wrapped his arms around me for a hug. His thighs bumped into mine. My hands clutched at his hips. "I missed you, too. Which is weird."

He laughed. "Flatterer."

"No, I mean I've never thought about someone so much after one date."

"Me, either."

I couldn't help but snort. "Sure."

He tipped my chin up with his finger. I expected teasing, but his green eyes were serious, drilling into mine. "I mean it, Maddie. It's like since we met and you dared me to pick which one sent my drink, I can't stop thinking about you."

I blushed. I didn't know if I should believe him, but he made it feel real. I refused to deny the happiness that bubbled up inside me. There'd be room for doubts later. "I'm glad."

We spent the day enjoying the city and the vast amount of culture freely offered. We spent hours in the Strand bookstore—a booklover's haven with thirteen miles of stuffed shelves in every genre, and even had vinyl, stationery, gifts, and brand merchandise. We got lost amid the dusty aisles and cozied up in a dark corner with our stack of finds. I learned he had a weakness for old-school classics like Fitzgerald and Hemingway, and I called him a "man's man," which made him laugh. I was an Austen girl, devoured every Taylor Jenkins Reid book written, but also loved books and memoirs on fashion. When he asked questions, I found my normal shyness slipping away as I explained about how Hepburn changed life with the little black dress and Billy Porter broke through barriers for a whole new audience and Zendaya made everything she wore cool.

He bought all my books and then we grabbed mocha lattes and headed to the Metropolitan Museum of Art. Both of us admitted we sucked at recognizing famous art or artists but liked the galleries. We played games to guess each other's favorites and held hands as we wandered through the hushed rooms with walls filled with priceless works that had once been someone's misty dream and a blank canvas.

I tried not to use my phone much, afraid he'd think I was addicted to social media, which most guys didn't like. I snapped a few selfies with paintings, tagging #afternoonculture #artfashion, and watched as my new fans poured in with comments, including many with blue badges who were well-known in the influencer fashion world.

I tried not to get too excited, tucking my phone away for the rest of the day. I hoped Riggs wouldn't end up becoming annoyed at my focus on building a platform but reminded myself it was my business and it was only our second date.

A reminder of how much I already liked him.

By the end of the day, we both seemed reluctant to leave. "What are you doing tomorrow night?" he asked, his lip quirking in a half grin. "Or will that freak you out and peg me a stalker?"

I laughed and leaned in. He smelled like fresh-laundered cotton and mocha. "I'm going out with Ava and Chelsea to a club."

"What if I met you there with some of my friends?"

I thought it over. My instinct was to jump at it, but I was worried what Ava would think. She kept mentioning to me she'd lost friends who gave her up after some guy turned their head. I didn't want her to think I'd ever be like that. "Let me double-check and see if they're cool with it."

"Good. Text me. My friends are all single. Maybe we can hook them up."

"I love it. We're already recruiting other couples because we're so happy."

He grinned and kissed me. I was so different with Riggs. I felt comfortable being a bit of a smart-ass—and it was a side of me I never explored. The way he responded gave me a rush of power and confidence, and I kissed him back full on, wishing we were in private instead of on another street corner.

"Maybe next time you can come see my place."

My breath caught. I liked how he said it a bit hesitantly, as if wondering if it was okay. I nodded. "Yeah. I think I'd like that."

We clung to each other, kissing one last time, and I headed home. On the train back to campus, I tried a few drafts of texts to my friends, trying to strike the right breezy tone. Finally, I sent one, asking if they'd like to hang with Riggs and meet his friends who were hot and available.

Chelsea texted right back with an enthusiastic thumbs-up.

But it was Ava I was holding my breath for.

I kept checking, but it took a while. Finally, the text popped up.

I'm in.

Relieved, I fell back into the hard seat. I needed to tread carefully, for both Ava's sake and my own. No need to fall head over heels and find out he was a jerk. Or untruthful. Maybe he just wanted to get me into bed. Maybe he had a bunch of girls at NYU and was entertaining himself for a little while. Maybe . . .

I knew it wasn't true. My very soul cried out he was meant for me.

The real question was what I was going to do about it.

WE MET SATURDAY night at the club, which was a perfect mix of good music, a decent dance floor, and multilevel tiers where you could actually talk without the pounding speakers stealing your voice. Riggs had already scored a table and introduced his friends—Brian, Patrick, and Sergio. I immediately zeroed in on Patrick as a possibility, pegging him as Ava's type. She loved guys who towered over her, with a touch of the intellectual, and his hot nerd vibe seemed to interest her immediately. He had wavy dark hair, a goatee, and nice eyes behind black glasses. His outfit was also perfect—a chill but cool look with khakis, a classic white shirt, and leather shoes with no socks. He was fit and had a great smile, and he shook her hand and repeated her name rather than the usual slurring and slobber near the ear from too many frat boys we'd met.

Chelsea and Brian also hit it off, but I got the friendship vibe instead of romance. Sergio was the perfect middle player, fetching some drinks, chatting casually, and hitting the floor to dance with a few of the women looking over. He was also cute, with a shaved head, huge muscles, and a sharp pink shirt paired with jeans. Riggs said he got a football scholarship and vowed he'd be famous one day. The mix of personalities worked perfectly, and before long, we were hosting some other girls at our table Sergio had recruited, doing shots, and dancing our asses off. I noticed Ava and Patrick already grinding against each other, and grinned.

Riggs noticed, too. "We're good at this matchmaking stuff," he whispered in my ear, swaying back and forth as I pressed against him. It was a sexy hip-hop song where anything went, so I used the anonymity of the crowd and looped my arms around him, letting my body melt into his. My limbs and tongue were loose with sexual tension, giddiness, and alcohol.

"Why didn't you choose Ava?" I asked.

He looked down at me with surprise. Our gazes crashed and stayed tight. "Did you think I would?"

It was as if I was staring down at myself, free to confess my true thoughts amid the pounding music and crush of sweaty bodies and Riggs holding me close. "Yes. I would have."

His hips swiveled and my body shuddered. His hands slid down my back and cupped my rear. "Would you have been upset if I had? Would you have fought for me?"

I blinked, keeping him in focus. "No. I would have told myself I didn't want Ava's leftovers."

"But you wanted me to choose you, right?" He bit my earlobe. "Right, Maddie?"

I let out a whoosh of breath, a bit dizzy. "Yes, I did. I wanted you."

Satisfaction carved out the lines of his face. His green

eyes gleamed. "Good. The truth is, I never even saw Ava. She was just someone standing next to you. It was you from the start."

I sucked in my breath, wondering if he was telling the truth, but the rawness of his tone told me he wasn't lying. The idea he chose me when he could have had Ava made my head spin, as if confirming I was special, like Ava had told me on spring break. But I only cared about Riggs and the fact that I was the one from the beginning.

I smiled big and wide. "That was a really good answer."

He laughed and we kissed, making out as we pretended to dance. Then Chelsea crashed into us, throwing her arms out, and Ava drifted over and we began to dance in a big group, wild and free, young and happy, with everything good ahead of us.

"Girls' trip!" Ava finally shouted, grabbing our hands and leading us away. We stood in the bathroom line, wiping sweat off our faces and talking over one another.

"Do you like him?"

". . . saw you out there all over each other . . ."

"Oh my God, his friend is hot but it was too awkward to ask for an intro!"

"I think I'm going to Riggs's place tonight."

That statement made everyone shut up and stare at me. Ava gave a smug grin. "Knew it. Time to give up the virginity, huh?"

The group in front of us turned around, laughing. "You go, girl!" one said drunkenly, raising her thumb in the air. "Virgins are now overrated!"

We laughed and I turned red.

"Do you trust him?" Chelsea asked low, suddenly looking serious. "This is only the third time you've seen each other. I just want to make sure you feel safe."

I nodded. "I do. I can't explain how I feel—it's so weird! Like we've always known each other. I never wanted to before."

"Aww!" Chelsea said, throwing her arms around me. Her curls bounced and tickled my face. "I love this so much."

"Me, too," Ava said. She was smiling, but there was a flicker of something in her eyes, an uneasiness that made my stomach suddenly cramp. "We just want you to be happy, and if Riggs does it, I say go for it."

We moved up in the line and took our turns. After washing our hands, Chelsea pointed across to the bar. "Oh, I know her—it's Maisy from accounting class—I'll be back!"

She took off and left us alone.

I turned to Ava. "Looks like you and Patrick are into each other. What do you think?"

A mysterious smile played upon her plump lips. "He's not only hot, he's smart. If his brain is any indication, I'd say we could have a good time."

I cracked up. "Wouldn't it be amazing if you became a couple? We could double-date and hang out all the time?"

Her face tightened for a moment, and I worried I'd said something wrong—that she was being nice to Patrick because of me and I was pushing her. Then her expression smoothed out and there was only an intense curiosity burning from her blue eyes. She grabbed my hand, her fingers entangling with mine, and leaned in close. "Would that make you happy, Maddie? If I had a boyfriend, too?"

I jerked back, unsure of her question. "Of course, I'd be happy. But only if you were. Ava, I don't want to force you to do anything you don't want, and if you're not into Patrick that's totally fine!"

"But if I was, would you be happy? That we'd all be hanging together if things worked out with both of us?"

Unease flared, but she was looking at me with such urgency, and her hands were warm and firm, making me feel safe, so I told the truth. "I think that'd be lit. Everything is better with you, Ava. But it's no big deal if you're not into Patrick. I don't care. Don't feel like you need to stick with him if there's another guy in the club you're into."

I held my breath as the moment stretched between us; almost as if there was a decision about to be made but I had no idea if it was good or bad or if I'd said the right thing. And then Ava smiled slow and bright and I was mesmerized by her beauty, the powerful aura that seemed to pulse around her and make everyone in her orbit feel . . . *more*.

"Come on, let's go. You've got a big night ahead of you."

She kept my hand in her grip and led me into the crowd and back to our table. Ava stopped in front of Riggs, who looked up and met her gaze. I stayed quietly at her side, waiting to see what she was doing, and then she leaned in and said something. He nodded. She tilted her head, regarding him, and then she took my hand and put it in his.

He pulled me close to his chest.

Ava spun on her heel and walked to Patrick, her hips swaying, while he stared at her with the usual hungry expression most men wore around her. She grabbed at his fancy shirt, bunching up the fabric, and dragged him to her for a kiss. I watched, fascinated by the female power she put out when she had a guy in her space. In a matter of seconds, I knew Ava had decided she wanted him. The outcome wasn't even in question.

"Do you want to come home with me tonight?"

I tore my gaze away from Ava and refocused. "Yeah."

He grinned. "Ready to go?"

I laughed. "In a bit. Want to dance some more?"

He agreed, and I grabbed Ava and we began another round of dancing. The four of us pressed together, jumping up and down while we sang the lyrics at the top of our lungs, and everything felt right.

We left around 2 a.m.

Riggs's apartment was dark and quiet. Patrick had gone to Ava's, and his other roommate wasn't home.

We went to his room, kissing and undressing each other. I felt safe under the gentle gleam of moonlight through the window and the deep shadows that lent me courage.

"This is my first time," I whispered in his ear, as his hands ran over my body, bringing me to a hot fever I craved more of.

He stopped, tipping up my chin to look into my eyes. "Are you sure? We can just sleep."

I grinned and kissed him. "I don't want to sleep."

He made love with a control and tenderness that I'd always craved; respect and hunger; a perfect balance that allowed me to surrender to my body and bloom under his words and touch, knowing I was enough.

After, we lay together, our naked bodies twisted on the damp sheets.

"I'm not seeing anyone else," he said.

Relief and joy unfurled. "Me, either."

"So, we'll just see each other? I know it's early. I know—"

"I only want to see you."

We were quiet, but I know we were both smiling.

9

AFTER

I waited awhile before I felt ready to record my apology.

My agent, Sierra, had already posted a formal statement that had gone to all the news feeds, but I faced even bigger backlash by disappearing from social media without further explanation. I know I'd built my career on opening up my life to anyone who wanted to walk through. Of course the world would get pissed off when I suddenly shut and locked the doors after such a spectacle.

I left for Italy at the end of the week. When I suddenly realized Ava's wedding invite had come with such a short window, I texted Chelsea. Weren't big weddings usually planned out at least a year in advance?

Chelsea tried to deflect, then told me the truth. Ava had deliberately sent mine late. She'd told Chelsea if I had too much time to think and plan, I'd never come.

I couldn't help laughing. Ava still knew me so well. If I'd

received the invite even a few months beforehand, I would have had plenty of time to stack up my excuses and keep my anger simmering. I'd always reacted on an emotional basis. She'd used the knowledge to her advantage.

I was more surprised I didn't sink back into my familiar rage. Maybe there really was an expiration date on how long you can hold on to hate. Of course, I'd been told many times hate was the flip side of love. I'd prayed for indifference toward Ava, but the relief never came. Now that my career was on the line, there was only so much I could take. Italy was both an escape from my present and a plea for my future.

If I could finally find peace with the past.

My fingers shook a bit, but I set up the camera and lighting, falling into the routine I'd perfected from years of practice. I put on little makeup and kept my outfit simple: silk T-shirt and loose matching slacks. My hair was in a ponytail with no fancy clips. I was going for personal chat, stripped-down vulnerability.

I closed my eyes and took a few deep breaths before hitting record. Resentment leaked through me at being forced to beg forgiveness for something the world would never understand. Yet, this was the position I'd put myself in by running away from my emotion. Stuff things down long enough and eventually they explode in messy, epic proportions.

Besides my drunken rant, I'd been bitchy to the newest hot-girl influencer on the block, Kameron Divinity. A few misplaced comments came off snotty, and suddenly fans demanded I make nice. They couldn't understand why I refused.

As if I could tell the truth.

My lids flew open and I hit the button.

"I know it's been a while since I went live with everyone, and I know you've all been looking for answers. I could sit here and feed you a bunch of excuses as to why I behaved so badly, but I don't think anyone is looking for that. Neither is Kameron Divinity." I took a timed breath, allowing my lips to relax into a nonsmile without resting bitch face. "I can only apologize from the bottom of my heart for my actions. They were hurtful and uncalled for. I had too much to drink, and I've been struggling with an identity crisis lately." I shook my head slightly. "I'm questioning my purpose. I'm at a crossroads and I'm scared, so I took it out on that reporter and Kameron, and all of you. That's the truth. I screwed up."

I looked directly into the camera and let the world see my pain. "I'm going offline for a while to figure things out. To take a step back and do some inner work. Some may say I'm running away, or trying to gain sympathy, but I only want to share my truth. I've lost myself and I need to find her again. I'll be back when I do. All I can ask for now is your patience and your support. Love to you all."

I clicked off.

Sierra would go apeshit. I hadn't cleared my speech with her because she would have convinced me to rework it. I had no idea if I made things worse or better, but it was time I began to do something to change my life.

I laughed without humor and fell back into the chair.

Go to Italy. See Ava again.

Find myself.

An easy task list to complete. If only I didn't feel poised on the threshold of complete terror and fear, peering over the cliff to see what was next, and having no clue what was down there if I jumped.

A shrill noise pierced my thoughts, and I glanced down to see who was calling.

My agent practically screamed silently at me to pick up.

I clicked the button and put her through, steeling myself for the fallout.

10

BEFORE

Love is a funny thing. You see movies and read books and hear stories and imagine how it should be, or at least how you think it can be. But the reality for me wasn't even close. It was so much more than what I could dream up, and as I entered my junior year of Havisham, I began to grow into layers of myself I never even knew existed.

Riggs and I fell in love with an ease that contradicted angsty college romance. There was little drama, or fighting, or even struggle to figure out who we were to each other. Every day we learned a bit more, and made space for the other. Ava and Chelsea repeated how disgusting we were, from our shared looks, the way we agreed on too many subjects, to the obvious way we couldn't keep our hands off each other.

Chelsea, Ava, and I also made some shifts. The tight friendship flourished under our watchful eyes, as we made sure we spent plenty of time away from the boys. Chelsea began dating a hotshot Wall Street guy who dressed in sharp suits, had a slick haircut, and liked to scatter financial advice to us like he was further along in his career than he was. Ava and I were not fans, especially since it was his first year as an intern and he was basically fetching coffee and doing crappy jobs for the bigwigs, but Chelsea had fallen hard and we supported her. Thank God, he didn't join us too much due to his work schedule, but we made sure she was always taken care of and never felt like an outsider.

Ava and Patrick were an item, following the path Riggs and I were on. I loved seeing them together, how cute they were when they teased each other or I caught Patrick staring at Ava with stars in his eyes. It was obvious he was crazy about her, and Riggs said he'd literally do anything Ava asked. Sometimes, Ava rolled her eyes and told me she wished he had a bit more backbone, but when I got worried, she'd wave her hand in the air and tell me she was just being pissy. She said Patrick was great and one of the few men who could handle her moods. We became a fierce foursome, pushing through our final years of college while setting the city on fire. Patrick and Riggs were going after internships at a small law firm for the spring. I was still waitressing, but my TikTok and IG had grown to offer a good supplement of income. I gained a ton of experience about what posts people liked the most, and what brands fit my style. When I tried to peddle health shakes, everything fell flat, so I hurriedly backed off that segment and went back to fashion, where most of my audience was. I posed and sold T-shirts, makeup, and small homegrown businesses run by women who liked my approach.

I finished my portfolio and found a decent photographer for reasonable rates, but got no response from agencies I queried. I took a class on how to go viral on social media, and signed up for a few electives in photography to learn how to do more myself. I couldn't afford to pay anyone yet, but Ava and Chelsea were always there to help.

Once Riggs realized my dreams for fashion, he began to support me in ways that made me fall even harder. He marked sites of interest, helped me with posts, and rallied everyone he knew to follow me and share. He never gave me a hard time when my phone was out, understanding it was more work than my fevered, egotistical dream of being loved by the world.

But if I was honest with myself? The comments and likes fed me. Somehow, the work to be a fashion model and make a difference for my audience began getting tangled up with how much the world liked my content. I began to feel a bit out of control, chasing bigger numbers and trying to elevate my brand to meet it. For now, things were still manageable, though, so I figured I could handle it.

One Sunday, Ava recruited Chelsea and me to join her at brunch. We sat outside with a charcuterie board on a table filled with pancakes, bacon, fresh fruit, and Greek yogurt, sipping mimosas. I tried not to feel guilty about another extravagant bill, but I could tell she was a bit down and I wanted to be able to talk.

"How's it going with Wall Street guy?" Ava asked, inciting Chelsea's eye roll at his nickname. "Are you going to invest your money with him to fund your business?"

"Stop! I know he's a bit much, but I'm only interested in a guy who's razor focused on the future. I can't help it. Ambition turns me on."

I laughed. "Nothing wrong with money and ambition. Hey, as long as he makes you happy, I've got you, boo."

She blew me an air-kiss. "Thanks. Plus, classes are hard this year with all statistics and finance management. He's not on me all the time to hang out. Not like your guys."

The waiter appeared, refilling our coffee, his gaze stuck on Ava with male appreciation. He directed his question to her. "Can I get you anything else?"

She tossed him one of her famous looks, her lips turning slightly up in an engaging pout, her cerulean blue eyes squinting with appreciation, making him feel like he was the only one on the planet. "Maybe," she purred.

I tried not to jerk in shock at her bold answer.

He smiled and cocked his hip out. He was cute, with curly dark red hair that had a bed head vibe, a strong jawline, and big brown eyes. "I was hoping for that. But for now, how about another round of mimosas?"

"Perfect."

He left the table with some extra cockiness in his step. It was weird, because I assumed Ava was only seeing Patrick, but maybe I was wrong? And if so, did Patrick realize it? The four of us had gotten so close, it was as if both our relationships overlapped.

Chelsea whistled. "He's cute. Are you still into Patrick?"

Ava smirked. "Of course. But he's so predictable. I literally asked Patrick to come over at 2 a.m. because I had a bad dream. He was there in under twenty flat."

I shifted in my seat. Her comment made me uncomfortable. "I hope you're not taking advantage of the guy. He's crazy about you."

Suddenly, her gaze swiveled and drilled into me. A coldness I'd never heard before seeped into her voice. "Are you questioning if I treat him right?"

I blinked. "No. I'm just saying it's obvious he's in love. What about you?"

"You mean, am I in love with Patrick?"

I didn't know what I'd missed, but there was a strange edge to the question, like I was being tested. "Yeah."

"Why? If I'm not, will you be on his side?"

Chelsea looked back and forth curiously. I frowned. "Ava, it doesn't matter to me whether you are or not. You're the one I care about."

Her body relaxed and she was back to her old self. "Sorry, I guess I'm still not sure. For now, I'm happy being with him and we'll see where it goes."

I spoke gently, sensing something else was bothering her. "I always have your back, okay? What's wrong? Is everything with your dad good?"

She sighed and fiddled with her mimosa flute. "Dad's been seeing someone. He's dated plenty of women before, but this is the first time he specifically wants me to fly to Italy to meet her for Thanksgiving. I think he may marry her."

Chelsea sighed. "I'm sorry, babe, that sucks. I can't imagine wanting to share your dad with anyone, but maybe he's lonely?"

"Yeah, maybe. I want him to be happy, I don't want to deny him that, but it's always been us. A team. Now, he won't need me the same. He'll have her."

My heart broke for her. Ava was always self-confident with a huge presence, but now she seemed to shrink into herself with doubt. "This person will never replace your mom or you," I said firmly. "I'm sure he wants a companion as you build your own life, but you're the one who will always come first. I guarantee it."

She bit her lip and nodded. "I hope so. Ugh, the last thing I want to do is fly out there and spend the weekend feeling awkward. I'll die. But I don't want to hurt him, either."

"Make up an excuse so you only have to spend two nights," Chelsea suggested.

"I guess." She picked at her blueberry pancake. "Unless . . ."

"What?" I asked.

She looked up and the familiar sparkle was back. "You come with me to Italy."

Chelsea groaned. "Ava! You know how my parents are about Thanksgiving. They'd kill me."

"But it's Italy! What if we left Wednesday and came back early Saturday? You can go straight to your parents and still have the weekend with them."

"Oh, crap, that is tempting."

"Right! The three of us together in Italy? It's exactly what I need to face this—I'll have you with me. Maddie, you're in, right? I know you usually work, but you'd be back for Saturday and Sunday night, and you got that new sponsorship, and I'll pay for the airline tickets and travel arrangements. Guys! Are we doing this?"

My heart pounded and my palms sweat. Conflicting emotions warred inside me. The idea of going to Italy with my best friend filled me with excitement, but I'd already made a promise to Riggs. I planned to meet his parents and spend time with his family. When he asked me, I was nervous and excited but hopeful. I hadn't been included in any family celebrations, and he told me about his sisters and how his parents were looking forward to meeting me.

But how could I say no to Ava? Her face was glowing again, and she'd be heartbroken to think I chose Riggs over her, especially since the relationship was still relatively new. I hesitated, caught between two worlds, wanting them both but knowing I had to choose.

"Of course, I'm in." I forced a laugh, knowing I was committed. "Come on, Chelsea, when will we have another opportunity like this? You have to come."

Chelsea sighed, but I could tell she'd already given in. "Fine. I'll go."

Ava gave a whoop and lifted her glass, clinking it to ours. "To Italy, and the best friends I could ever have!"

We toasted and laughed and talked about the things we'd do in those three days together. And though I was happy, and loved how Ava needed me, the flicker of guilt over Riggs kept me from being fully engaged. I told myself it was for the best. Maybe I should wait to meet his family anyway, after we'd been together longer. Riggs didn't need me like Ava did.

The waiter came back and dropped the check. "I'm Cris, by the way," he said, nodding his head at us. "I hope you enjoyed your brunch."

"We did." Ava cocked her head. "Thank you so much."

"No. It was my pleasure. I've never been so happy to work on a Sunday before."

Ava laughed, and I watched as her gaze assessed, deciding if he was worthy of her time. He left without asking her out, but then Ava picked up the check and waved it in the air. In red, there was a smiley face and his number. I smiled and kept my mouth shut.

But I noticed after Ava paid, she tucked the check in her purse.

11

The first moment I arrived in Lake Como, I experienced a sharp sense of déjà vu, as if I'd visited in some long ago dream and was returning home.

We flew into Malpensa Airport in Milan, then drove, and finished with a boat that would sail directly to Ava's villa. The boat floated on the eerily quiet lake that looked like clear glass, masking the deep, dark depths. Mist shrouded the skyline, floating above the spill of rock. Luxurious mansions lined the lake among the cliffs, painted in mustard yellow, soft pink, and terra-cotta. With elaborate decks, massive windows, and cultivated landscaping, each villa competed for attention as we sailed toward Ava's home.

"This is sick," Chelsea whispered, both of us sitting in stunned silence at the postcard scenery we'd only imagined.

Ava smiled at us. "It's off-season so we won't have to fight the tourists. But Dad said it's been pretty warm lately, so maybe we can squeeze in a swim."

I shivered at the thought, staring at the water. "Not sure if I'd want to go in. This isn't where the Loch Ness monster is, right?"

Chelsea bumped my shoulder. "That's Scotland, silly."

"Oh, right." I turned to Ava. "Umm, why did you want to come to New York again?"

A longing flickered over Ava's face as she stared at the home slowly growing bigger at our approach. "Because I needed to find myself. New York is the perfect place to do it."

"I can find myself here, no problem," Chelsea quipped.

We pulled up to a private dock, climbed out, and I stared up at Ava's childhood home.

It was a magnificent three-story in pale lemon, reminding me of a sorbet. Dual arched windows and decks gave off a welcome charm, and I walked up the steps past a low stone wall to the pathway, which wound around manicured trees and multiple shrubs, as if guarding the sloping green hills in the background. I took in the side deck outfitted with furniture and tables big enough to host a small wedding. Moss clung to the far left wall, climbing halfway up and giving the place an old-world charm.

I'd stepped into a Disney tale, and right now, Ava was my fairy godmother.

Ava studied our faces as we took it all in, and pleasure shone in her bright blue eyes. "Wait till you see the inside. You'll—"

"Ava!"

The deep, booming voice cut through the air with an authority that would make me snap to attention, but Ava gave a yelp and ran hard, right into her father's arms.

My throat tightened with emotion and a touch of sheer envy.

He swung her around and she laughed, her dark hair flying in the wind, and I wondered how it would feel to have someone love me that much; to welcome me back home, proving I'd been missed. For one horrible moment, I regretted coming with her. It was too much to witness something I'd never had and never would, but then the moment passed and she was dragging him over toward us.

"Dad, this is Chelsea and Madison. We call her Maddie. This is my father, Antonio."

I caught my breath at the similarities between them. I'd seen the pictures of Ava's mother she had displayed in her room, but it was obvious she'd gotten her dad's strong facial features and hypnotic eyes. The matched blue of their gazes was startling, and I could tell his hair had once been thick and black, but was now an elegant silver, brushed back from his high brow. He wore a dark gray suit with a navy tie and leather shoes that shone with polish. A jeweled watch encircled his wrist, but I caught a flash of gold and noticed he wore a thin gold band on his pinky with a dull green stone. It looked cheap and piqued my curiosity, as I wondered why he'd chosen it.

He immediately stepped forward, but as I held out my hand, he pulled me into a warm hug. "Maddie, welcome, I feel as if I know you." He did the same to Chelsea, then stepped back and beamed. "It is my pleasure to welcome you. Ava has told me so many wonderful things. I am honored you are here."

I blinked with unexpected emotion at the welcome.

"Thank you so much for having us. I'm in awe—your home is gorgeous."

"Yes, we're so happy to meet you! I can't believe we're here—I feel like a princess in a castle!" Chelsea said.

Antonio gave another deep laugh, eyes shining with pleasure. I was entranced by the strong sense of presence he radiated, just like Ava. It was as if he owned the space around him with ease, while the rest of the world seemed to apologize for taking up room. No wonder he was a force in the business world. "Ava will show you around the house and to your rooms. I need to take care of a few things for work, and then we will all enjoy dinner together. *Va bene?*"

Ava nodded. For now, happiness radiated from her. I'm sure for a little while she'd forgotten about the woman she came to meet, but I vowed to help her through it. Maybe we'd all be surprised and Ava would end up really liking her. Or maybe their relationship wasn't as serious as Ava feared.

We followed her through the house, which was even more impressive than the outside. The foyer was like entering an art museum, with high ceilings, a circular staircase with scrolled wrought iron rails, and a giant arched doorway with stained glass on the top. As we walked around, we oohed and aahed over the gold embossed antique lamps; the rich tapestry throw rugs; the gleam of polished marble and deep wood. Glass doors opened up to the terrace, which housed a long banquet table and velvet plush chairs and loungers. We stood at the edge of the balcony and looked over the gorgeous sprawl of the lake, still misty from the drifting fog. I breathed in the scent of dampness and floral and lemon polish, feeling my head spin.

My room was a spa oasis, with a four-poster bed, vintage furniture in cherrywood, and doors that led out to my own private deck. The attached bath was modernized, with a tiled shower and a soaking tub in aquamarine blue.

"We have six bedrooms and five baths," Ava said, ticking off the features of the house as we explored. "Formal dining room, piano room, four decks, two terraces, a pool, and private gardens."

"What was it like growing up here?" I asked. "As wonderful as I imagine?"

She smiled at me a bit sadly. "Yes. I wish I remembered more, though. We lived here until I was five. I had no siblings and my memories are fuzzy. Of course, most of them revolve around my mom." She pointed to the mantelpiece in the elegant space that held a grand piano and was decorated in rich reds. "That's my favorite pic of her. I have a copy on my phone, but there's nothing like the canvas up close."

I caught my breath as I studied Ava's mom. She had Ava's long dark hair, but her eyes were a light brown. Her smile was gentler, and she seemed to have a quieter presence in the picture, looking out as if searching for something. Her small smile reminded me of Mona Lisa. She was wearing a blue dress, standing outside with the lake behind her. Her feet were bare.

"How old were you when she passed?" Chelsea asked, voice full of empathy.

"Ten. Mom was from New York and met my dad on vacation in Bellagio. They went back and forth for a while before getting married and settling here. This house was passed down by Dad's great-grandfather, so it's important to our family." A little sigh escaped her as she looked caught up in memory. "But Mom always wanted to go back to the city, so Dad bought a company and condo and we stayed there till I was ten years old. I remember all of us being so happy. Until she got sick." She paused and my heart ached for her. Pain splintered from her very pores. "We moved back to Italy—Dad thought it was best. And though it's beautiful, I've always connected more to New York. Not sure why."

Ava was stunning even in her grief. I studied her chiseled profile, lush lashes lowered, as if trying to hide her agony. "Maybe because you remember your mom better," I said. "You must feel closer to her when you're in the city."

"Yeah, I think you're right." Ava shook her head and began walking again down the hall, toward the bedrooms. "But this is where my dad's the happiest. He really wants me to settle in Italy when I'm done with school."

The idea of losing Ava made my heart stop. But of course, what did I think? That we'd be together forever?

Maybe. I pictured us rooming together with Chelsea, all of us working in the city, building our careers. The details were blurry, but I never imagined she'd want to go back to Europe.

Chelsea spoke up and distracted me. "Well, if you insist on coming back, you'll need to take us with you. This will be my permanent bedroom." She flopped on the gold bedspread, flinging her arms wide above her head, staring up at the beaded chandelier that dripped crystals and flickered back bright prisms of sunlight.

We laughed, climbing on the bed with her, falling into a short silence as we settled into this place together.

"I didn't think Italians celebrated Thanksgiving," I said after a while.

Ava snorted. "They really don't, but Mom always celebrated it, so we took on the tradition. Dad loves a good party, so it became one of his favorite holidays. Wait till you see the spread."

"Yum, I can't wait. Is there apple pie?" Chelsea asked.

"Girlfriend, there'll be more than that. It would be an insult to serve less than five desserts."

I quirked my brow. "How many other people are coming?"

"Just us and Dad's friend." As if remembering the point of the visit, Ava stiffened. "I hate that she'll be here. Is that crappy of me? I haven't even met her."

"No, it's being human," I quickly said. "Who wants to share their parents?"

"Maybe we'll love her and all this worry will be for nothing," Chelsea said in an upbeat tone.

"Let's hope." Ava shot off the bed. "For now, let's get some rest. I'm exhausted. Dinner's at seven and then we can go over plans for the next two days."

We agreed and headed to our respective rooms. I quickly unpacked, set my stuff up in the bathroom, and slipped under the covers. The pillows were soft and smelled like lavender. I could look out the window from here and see glimpses of the cliffs and houses through the sheer curtain. I closed my eyes and thought of Riggs. I'd texted him I arrived safely. He was already home with his parents in Poughkeepsie, and going out for a few hours with his siblings to the local bar where they always partied on the night before Thanksgiving. He sounded happy. I missed him, but I focused on my beautiful surroundings and new adventure, then tumbled into sleep.

WHEN I WALKED into the formal dining room with Chelsea at my side, Ava and her dad were already there, heads together, talking low in Italian. I was struck again by their close resemblance. Ava had changed into loose flowy pants in silver with a simple white V-neck T-shirt, and Antonio was in the same suit he wore earlier, but without his jacket, white sleeves rolled up to the elbows. Antonio cupped his daughter's cheeks, kissing her on the cheek, and the adoration in his gaze made me understand why Ava would be afraid to lose his attention. It must be like a drug, to be loved by someone so much, such that the thought of becoming secondary was too much to bear. Suddenly, he looked up and gave us his full attention.

"Ladies!" Antonio greeted, opening his arms with invitation. "Come in. Can I get you some wine? If you like red, I have a local blend that I think you'd enjoy."

We agreed, and he poured us all a glass. I sipped the ruby liquid, loving the fruity taste of blackberries on my tongue. I had to try not to gulp it down like a shot. No wonder Italians drank wine at a young age. It was better than fruit punch.

"We're having some pasta and salad tonight, if that's

---

acceptable?" Antonio asked, refilling his own glass and joining us at the table. "Simple tonight, no? Tomorrow we shall have course after course! I've hired a wonderful chef for the day."

"Where's Lucia?" Ava asked. "With her family?"

"Yes, she deserves a day off." Antonio turned toward us. "Lucia has been with us for years; she takes care of the house and me, of course. Mario will not disappoint us, though." A knock echoed through the house, and Antonio rose to his feet. "There is our final guest. Someone I cannot wait for you to meet."

I looked at Ava, who'd tensed up and regarded the door like a gate to the lion's den. Chelsea and I immediately switched chairs so we flanked her. She gave us a grateful smile and dragged in a breath. Heels clattered on the floor, and low murmurs drifted in Italian.

"Ava, this is Gabriella. And these are Ava's friends, Maddie and Chelsea."

I was surprised that Ava looked half-frozen, which wasn't like her, but I stood up and she followed. Her smile was forced, but she walked over and greeted Gabriella with poise. We all shook hands.

"I've been excited to meet you," Gabriella said, her hand lightly touching Ava's arm. "Your father talks about you nonstop. I feel as if I know you well already."

"I wish I could say the same."

I stilled at the barb, but Ava gave a laugh, as if she was joking, and Gabriella joined in. Soon, we were all chatting casually, and I took the time to study Antonio's girlfriend.

Her straight cocoa brown hair was pulled back in a casual knot. Tailored black pants fit well on her trim frame, and she'd paired them with a jeweled cashmere sweater that looked soft and ridiculously expensive. Her large, dark eyes were accented with smoky shadow. She had a long face, tapered fingers, and a graceful neck, reminding me of a ballerina. Her lips were thin and painted red. Her voice was a bit low and clipped, but I had to say she looked genuinely pleased to be here and talk with Ava, so if she was pretending, she was a good actress. Antonio reached over to take her hand with a naturalness that told me they'd been with each other awhile. Sympathy flared for Ava. Her father should have warned her before it got this serious, but maybe he hadn't wanted to introduce his daughter until he felt positive the relationship would last.

Dinner was easier than I thought. We feasted on ravioli with a light, tangy sauce, and the salad was filled with everything I loved: olives, cucumbers, artichokes, roasted red peppers, and arugula dressed in a fragrant olive oil dressing with a tang of garlic. The wine poured freely. Ava seemed happy, asking Gabriella an array of questions, and Antonio's face lit up with joy, obviously over the moon these two women were getting along.

Gelato and cappuccino finished up the meal. I took my cue from Ava, and we all got up when she announced she wanted to show us the grounds. Ava's father and Gabriella said goodbye with a kiss and hug, and I relaxed in relief when we headed outside. It had gone well. Ava must've understood how happy her father was, and Gabriella seemed really nice, not bitchy at all.

Ava was silent as we walked into the gardens, lit by a trail of fancy lanterns, and stopped at the stone wall that overlooked the lake. I caught my breath at the beauty of the scene: villas scattered throughout the cliff, glowing softly in the darkness. The stars twinkled above and it was almost a full moon. The water gently lapped against the dock. My nose twitched with the scents of earth and flowers and Ava's fragrant perfume.

"You good?" Chelsea finally asked, staring at Ava worriedly.

"She was pretty cool, right?" I asked.

Ava let out a deep breath. "I hate her."

I barely covered my gasp. "But—why? You didn't think she was nice?"

Ava turned, and I caught the vicious glitter in her eyes, the firm set of her jaw. "No. Oh, sure, she acted nice in front of my father. What else was she going to do? She was probably planning this coup forever. I guarantee she convinced my dad not to tell me anything because she knew I'd put a stop to it and cause trouble. Now, I'm too late."

I met Chelsea's stare, which looked just as confused as mine. "What made you get all this?" she asked. "Did she say or do something in particular?"

"Nope. I know the type. I've seen these women go after my father before, but he always saw through the game. Did you see her clothes? The way she spoke, almost like she was entitled? She wants Dad's money and lifestyle. She certainly doesn't have her own career."

I bit my lip, trying to find a way to support Ava but still

play devil's advocate. "She mentioned her work in translations."

"Yeah, she works for my father! She has nothing of her own."

Chelsea spoke up. "I liked her, Ava. Maybe you just need more time to get to know each other. Your dad seemed happy."

Ava practically hissed like a pissed-off cat. "Are you kidding me right now? I'm telling you I will never support this—not with her. Dad was probably lonely with me gone and she took advantage."

I didn't know how to respond. Half of me wanted to challenge her on giving Gabriella a chance, but the other half sensed Ava needed my full support, no questions asked. Besides, I had no experience with losing a mom and protecting a valued relationship. I was starting from the beginning, and Ava had been the first one to show me about true loyalty.

"Maybe you can talk to your father," I suggested. "Tell him your suspicions about her?"

Ava shook her head. "I don't think he'll listen, especially this weekend. God, she's going to be here all day tomorrow, too! Did you see her in the kitchen? How she knew where everything was? How she got Dad his special Scotch after dessert when he specifically asked me for it? She was showing me I was being replaced."

Chelsea looked hesitant to say anything after she'd gotten snapped at.

I tried to think what I'd need if this was my problem.

"Okay, so we get through tomorrow and then you make a plan. Maybe do some research on her?"

Ava gasped. "Yes! I can hire a PI to find out about her past! After I get proof she's hiding something, I can talk to Dad."

Chelsea opened her mouth, then shut it. "You know a PI?"

"My dad does, but I can't use him. I can find one, though." A smile wreathed her face. The usual zest of energy returned, and relief loosened my shoulders. Good. I'd helped. "Thanks, Maddie, that was a brilliant idea."

Chelsea looked worried. "Umm, what if nothing shows up?"

"It will." Ava patted Chelsea's shoulder. "Trust me, I've seen this before. I know she seemed great, but that was the point. We'll just pretend tomorrow everything is good and I'll deal with Dad later, with proof."

I didn't know what Ava expected to find, but I figured she'd handle it. I'd be here if she needed me. The mood lightened, and Ava threw her arms around us. "Sorry for being such a downer. Come on, let's go for our walk and I'll show you the rest of the grounds. Tomorrow, I'll take you out on the boat and we'll go exploring."

Happy the crisis was averted, I pushed all other thoughts away but enjoying our time together.

THANKSGIVING WAS EXACTLY what Ava warned it would be: a food fest. My parents used to make a small chicken breast, with canned creamed corn and overdone potatoes, and call it a day. But this was a celebration with all the trimmings I'd always imagined.

The chef began with square portions of lasagna. The pasta was firm—called al dente—and the cheese was gooey and plentiful. I gobbled it up, soaking up the sauce with a slice of Italian bread, and then the antipasti were served. Platters of meat, cheeses, crackers, and condiments, but my favorite was the salty prosciutto wrapped around sweet melon. The flavors complemented each other and made an explosion of happiness. The turkey came like I'd seen in movies, golden brown and perfectly cooked. Antonio carved it with expert ease—Ava said he was actually a wonderful cook when he wanted to be—and I enjoyed the white meat with an array of sides: stuffing with sausage and cranberry; stuffed artichokes; mashed potatoes with Gruyère cheese; green beans with almonds; and a vegetable frittata with fresh herbs. We drank prosecco in tiny delicate flutes, and spoke of easy topics: city culture, our classes, and some of our greatest hits from the past year highlighting our friendship.

Ava mentioned Patrick but downplayed their relationship. I didn't say anything.

Afterward, we indulged in apple and pumpkin pies, chocolate tarts, pears with brandy flambé, and fresh figs with nuts.

By the time the meal was over, I could barely walk. I pretty much rolled into my room to change into jeans. I'd photographed us in our holiday best, posting various pics with hashtags, and noticed my stats were off the charts. I also found a message from a boot company who wanted to send me a few pairs and asked me to do sponsored posts. I quickly responded with my pay rate, smiling smugly now that I knew how to handle myself thanks to Ava's advice.

But I also got a rejection from another agency in my email, which deflated me a bit. I tucked my phone away and refused to think about it for now.

We said goodbye to Gabriella and headed to the dock. Ava was taking us out on the boat for an expedition before evening rolled on. I asked her how she thought the day went, this time not even bothering to try and put a positive spin on the situation.

"It was fine. I'm afraid she thinks she'll manipulate him into an engagement. I'll have to stop it."

I felt bad for Antonio. He was obviously smitten, and kept shooting eager looks at Ava over dinner, as if reassuring himself they really liked each other. But I didn't know how these things worked. What if Ava was right and she was saving her dad from manipulation?

"You know the worst part?" Ava continued. "He took off his wedding ring. All this time he never would have thought of it. I guarantee she made him."

The stark pain in her face hurt my heart. "I noticed he wears a pinkie ring that's unusual. Was that from your mom?"

Ava shook her head. "I gave that to him when I was in elementary school at one of the Father's Day fairs. He's always worn it." A smile stole her lips. "Even when his finger turns green."

"See? It shows how important you are to him."

"He has to pick me over her," Ava whispered to herself.

An image of Gabriella flickered in my mind; the loving expression on her face as she laughed at something Antonio said. The gentle way he touched her hand. They looked happy together. Why would Ava despise him getting a second chance at love?

I ignored the thought.

"Is this a wooden boat?" Chelsea asked, changing the subject.

I studied the highly polished, gleaming wooden boat that curved gracefully to points at the front and back. Three semicircles sprang from each side, joined together by two thick wooden beams. I stared at the strange contraption. There were two large paddles, bench seats, and not much else. Ava nodded. "Yep. It's called a Lucia, and they're pretty common on the lake. Mostly used by fishermen." Ava tapped on the wooden circles. "The net would be strung up here. Come on."

I looked at the vessel doubtfully. "Is it safe?"

"Of course, silly."

We climbed in, and I grabbed at the sides when it tilted. Ava laughed, and Chelsea looked like we were about to embark on a yacht cruise instead of a narrow vessel with old-fashioned oars.

"This is so cool," Chelsea yelped, sitting comfortably on the seat. "I read about these in a blog post on Lake Como."

"They're very popular for tourists, but most have an engine and are bigger. I like being able to row myself and how quiet it is. I use it for an escape. I'd come out here on the lake by myself and think." Her eyes sparkled wickedly. "Or I'd meet boys."

"Bet you did," I said with a laugh.

She pushed us off and expertly cut through the water with smooth, firm strokes. It took me a while to get comfortable and relax in my seat rather than gripping the edges in fear, but eventually, I realized we were seaworthy and began to enjoy the experience.

The wind tugged at my hair and caressed my face. The sun danced on the water. The sky was a stretch of blue-gray above. The scenery was breathtaking—a long line of clustered mansions guarding the massive lake, sprawled up and down the cliffs in a spectacular display of earthy color. It was like being in a dream or a movie, and I had to pinch myself to understand I was really here, and this was my life.

Ava pointed out different landmarks—George and Amal Clooney's house, the famous hotel and place where one of the James Bond movies was filmed, and various spots we'd seen in magazines or movies. "There's not a lot of people out because it's Thanksgiving," Ava said, her arm muscles bunching as she rolled the oars. "Off-season is my favorite—we have the place to ourselves. I'll take you shopping tomorrow in Bellagio. And to the beach, of course. Did you bring suits?"

My eyes widened. "It's too cold to swim!"

Ava laughed. "The water is warm here in November, so we're still good. You can borrow one of mine. Or not."

"Skinny-dipping!" Chelsea shouted.

"Trust me, that's not how I want to get famous," I said. But on cue, I took my phone out and snapped pics, managing a selfie with Ava at the helm.

We sailed around the lake until Ava docked the boat

and led us into a tiny town called Lenno. Ava explained it was less touristy, pointing out the Villa del Balbianello, an incredible estate where *Casino Royale* and *Star Wars: Episode II—Attack of the Clones* were filmed. The lush foliage and gardens stole my breath. Many shops were closed, but Ava took us to a small place that made olive oil, and we spent time picking out our favorite to bring home with us. We poked around and explored an array of crooked side streets, and my spirits soared, still not believing I was able to experience Italy with my best friends.

My phone buzzed and I read the text from Riggs.

Thinking of you. Hope you're having a blast.

I smiled and tucked it back away, but Ava had caught me. "Riggs?" she asked, tilting her head. I nodded. "It's sweet— you guys are really into each other."

I looked for nuances in her voice that would convey judgment, but she seemed relaxed. "Yeah, we are. I'm not sure why, but it's like I've known him forever."

Chelsea sighed with longing. "Soulmates. Maddie, I'm really happy for you. You went from virgin to sex queen this year."

We all cracked up.

"He's good in bed, right?" Ava asked.

Ugh, my cheeks flamed, which was ridiculous because I had nothing to be ashamed about. "Very."

Chelsea whistled, but Ava gave a slight frown. "Not that I'm ripping off blinders, but how do you know? He's your first. I mean, maybe somebody else would rock your world even more."

I tensed up, automatically springing into defense mode. "Sometimes, you don't need to experiment. Personally, I prefer quality over quantity."

"But you have no comparison," Ava said.

I shrugged, annoyed at her pushiness. "Don't care. Riggs makes me happy."

"Then that's all that matters," Chelsea jumped in. "Just be in the moment. It's not like you guys are making crazy plans."

I thought of our whispers at night, wrapped in each other's arms. How we seemed to be a natural extension of the other. The future didn't scare me; I couldn't see myself with anyone but Riggs. I tried to see how it looked from the outside, and understood they didn't get the feelings involved.

The energy shifted when Ava grabbed my hand with easy affection, swinging her long arms back and forth. "Don't be mad, Maddie. I'm just looking out for you, but I agree with Chels—enjoy Riggs and be happy. Maybe it's because I've been through this before a few times, and I see how easy it is to start giving up on things once a guy takes over. If you're not careful, he becomes your whole world and controls it. Not on purpose. It's just the way society still is, and how women compromise all the time when men don't have to."

"Agree with that," Chelsea said.

"Like this thing with Patrick. We've been having a blast, and I'm into him. But he was hinting he wanted to be in-

vited to Italy with me for Thanksgiving! Can you imagine?"
Ava maneuvered gracefully over the cobblestones in her
heeled boots as she laughed. "When I said no, it got a bit
intense. I think we need some space."

"Did you guys ever talk about not dating any other people?" I asked tentatively.

Ava gave a shrug. "Kind of. We both decided not to see
anyone else for now."

I hated the idea of them breaking up, but that was selfish. I wanted Ava to be happy, just like I was with Riggs. I
kept thinking of her pocketing the waiter's phone number,
and tried to keep a positive tone. "Yeah, that's probably a
good idea."

"God, he told me Riggs invited you to meet his parents
for Thanksgiving! I bet you were so happy when I invited
you to Italy. How were you getting out of that one?"

I hesitated. "Umm, I wasn't sure."

"Next time tell me and I'll be your wing woman. Why
are guys so weirdly intense? We're in college for God's
sake—no one's ready to settle down yet. Especially you, with
so much to accomplish. I saw your follower count shoot up,
and you're booking regular sponsors. It's all going to happen
for you, Maddie."

Keeping quiet felt like a betrayal to Riggs, but I had no
words. In a way, Ava was right, I'd thought about how things
were going so fast, even if it didn't feel forced. But I did have
big goals, and losing my focus over a guy might be a huge
mistake. My belly knotted at the thought.

"Hey, what about me?" Chelsea asked. "Why aren't you

worried Wall Street won't charm me into forgetting about my goals?"

Ava snorted. "As if that were possible. I can't wait to invest in your business, Chels. You're going to kick ass."

Chelsea beamed. "Thanks. You're forgiven now."

"I may have figured out what I should do after all!" Ava beamed right back at us. "I'll be an angel investor for both of you. A financial firm focused on helping women, and a famous fashion model that will sell any brand I give her. I set you both up, I get a cut, and I'll compete with Kris Jenner's mega skills. What do you think?"

I looked at Ava and saw she was serious. A wave of fierce love and loyalty crashed through me. She meant it. She'd easily sink her money into us because she believed. Who else did? Not even my own parents cared. Ava may be intense at times, but it was because she was so passionate. Overcome, I stopped walking and threw my arms around her. "I love you," I said in her ear, her perfume surrounding me, her warm arms hugging me back and making me feel safe.

"I love you, too."

Her voice was muffled against my hair, and a thrill coursed through me, knowing she belonged to me in some special way. And then Chelsea jumped into our circle, smothering us with kisses, and we collapsed into laughter in the middle of the street in Italy.

When we broke apart, my cheeks hurt from smiling, and all troubled thoughts had floated away.

12

We started out early Friday, knowing we had one precious day to see and experience everything.

This time, Ava took out the luxury boat for us. Bruno, one of the people on staff at the villa, drove us around so we could see Lake Como from all angles, beginning with the water. The boat had cushy leather seats, dark, sleek wood, and a deck perfect for sunbathing. We nibbled on fresh figs, sweet melon, and crusty pastries stuffed with cheese. It was all washed down with strong, slightly bitter coffee served in small white cups, which I quickly became addicted to.

I caught my breath at the dizzying sights and smells from the water—the majestic Alps shimmering like a king in the distance, dusted with white clinging to the ragged peaks. Vivid greens and dusty browns melded together along the shoreline. The lake sparkled like glass, reflecting the sun. We waved to other boats we passed, while Ava stood out on the far deck, dark hair blowing in the wind, her perfect figure clad in a crop top and jeans, balanced expertly on the smooth surface, head tilted up to the sun. She was the woman everyone secretly longed to be: poised, elegant, sexy. Free.

I quickly snapped a picture.

We climbed the mountain via the Como-Brunate funicular while the city of Como dropped farther beneath us. I studied the patchwork of red roofs growing smaller, dazzled by the views as the entire lake sprawled below us, squeezed in by magnificent villas and ragged shorelines and miles of lush green trees. The air was snappy and cool, and I breathed in a lungful, holding it deep, feeling the dizzying rush of oxygen hit my bloodstream.

"This is Brunate. It's small but charming—only houses about two thousand people. It's known for its architecture and laid-back vibe, so I thought you'd like to explore. Ready to walk?"

Chelsea and I eagerly agreed, and we spent the next hour exploring the charming town. We stopped at the Chiesa di Sant'Andrea Apostolo, a church perched in the center of town. We studied the gorgeous hand-painted murals and ceiling in reverent silence. We were the only people there for now. Though I wasn't religious, I found myself longing to believe in something more than I did. As I stood in front of the carved statue of Jesus, the altar seemed to glow from a gentle light that had nothing to do with the sun or lamps. Goose bumps broke out on my arms. I bowed my head and asked for all the things I dreamed of besides succeeding in the fashion world.

Peace. Knowing. Happiness.

Were they even gifts to give from someone higher like God? Or were they things I had to find on my own, within myself? And if so, would I ever reach them?

My friends appeared to sense my sudden turbulent thoughts and stepped away, giving me privacy by the altar. When we left, there seemed to be a bit more space inside my chest.

Ava pointed out various residences, and I drank in the sights of wrought iron balconies crammed together, exploding with vibrant-colored blooms of plants. Peeling painted doors in gorgeous pastels surprised me around each sharp corner. People were out and about walking, greeting us with *ciao*s and warm smiles. I felt a million miles from New York and the rushed chaos I'd learned to embrace. Time grew sluggish here, more liquid than the crisp black and white of the city's demanding schedule and how we fit ourselves in.

Here, Italy wrapped around me in an embrace, allowing me to fill the hours on my own terms. I loved the patience and beauty of Ava's home, and felt as if a part of me might always long for it now that I had a taste.

"I'm assuming you want to skip the three-mile hike to the Volta Lighthouse," Ava said with a grin, knowing we hated exercise and looked upon it as a necessary evil. I was used to endless miles in uncomfortable shoes since I'd always rather save money than grab a cab, but it didn't mean I loved walking just to do it.

"How about we eat instead?" Chelsea suggested.

I gave her a high five.

Instead of taking us to a fancy restaurant on top of a cliff, we ate at a tiny place with a few tables situated outside on a back terrace. "We'll have dinner in Bellagio, but I'd recommend the lasagna here. It's pretty sick."

Chelsea and I had no issues with the recommendation, and soon we were moaning over the layers of melty cheese and firm bite of pasta we knew was homemade. We paired it with a nice red wine called Grumello, and dipped chunks of bread into the leftover sauce. Right before we got back on the boat, we bought some gelato. I got coconut, Chelsea had black cherry, and Ava did boring chocolate, yet hers actually looked the best.

Back on the water, I digested and enjoyed the breathtaking view. When we arrived in Bellagio, I was struck by the character of the town, a gorgeous little place bursting with shops, food, and local color. The musical stream of Italian rose in the air along with the delicious scents of fresh bread. We zigzagged down narrow cobblestone streets and got serious in the shops.

"Why aren't you videoing this?" Ava asked with a shake of her head. "This trip will be enough juice to get you some bigger endorsements. Italy was made for social media."

I hesitated. "I know. It's just . . ." I trailed off, trying to find the words to explain.

Chelsea cocked her head. Her curls bounced in the breeze. "What?"

"I don't want to be that girl who loses all the good moments trying to capture them for someone else."

It was the closest way to phrase my reservations about this career I wanted so badly. I was a walking contradiction, shy and awkward inside, yet dying to be seen and recognized by others. But I also didn't want my friends to think I was using them for a photo op, either.

Chelsea and Ava shared a look, then began laughing.

I frowned. "What? I mean it, I'm trying to be honest with you!"

"No, it's kind of sweet, but Maddie, we love this shit. You're always respectful, but you need to be bold in order to stand out. Tell us what you want, or how to pose, or demand we tag you. We're here to help," Ava said.

"Because when you get famous, we get to come for the ride!" Chelsea finished.

I grinned, then looked up. The boutique we'd stopped in front of was full of handbags and dresses and looked as good as a candy store used to. Or Toys "R" Us. I still missed that chain. "Okay. But you asked for it. Let's go."

We dived into the shop and barely surfaced for the next few hours.

I knew Ava's and Chelsea's shopping habits like my own. Ava was patient and could flip through a rack forever in order to score the perfect piece. Chelsea was too distracted in a store. She floated everywhere, grabbing items off hangers, trying them on, discarding, and starting the round all over. It was a little bit like a visiting shopping tornado. I was a decent balance, depending on the vibe. If I didn't feel it, I quickly got in and got out. But if it was a store I scented possibilities in, I could spend ages, combing through the racks, searching out a perfect accessory, and taking pics of my outfits along the way.

Some stores didn't allow photos, but I found the smaller shops rarely told me no.

Ava held the camera while I posed, talking to my followers about rare finds in Bellagio, and how to take separate accessories or items and stack them together to create the perfect outfit. I decided to have a treasure hunt and wear the outfit I pulled together live tonight. Ava and Chelsea got excited, and we all agreed to do the challenge together.

From the Corner Shop Bellagio I grabbed a gorgeous ruby and onyx evil eye necklace. The sexy tapered black pants that had a wet shine to them clung to my body and were on sale at Boutique Patrizia. A gorgeous magenta scarf and perfect white T-shirt brought it all together, but we hit Rolando's for my first pair of real leather Italian shoes. Buttery soft, with a perfect wedge heel, they were sexy and grown-up.

Ava insisted on buying the three of us the same shoes in different colors, throwing her credit card on the table and talking rapidly in Italian before we could argue. Then she went to the manager or owner and convinced them to let us change in the dressing rooms, giving us bags to pack our old clothes in. Ava whipped out her purse of miracles that held a ton of her expensive makeup, and we giggled and made ourselves up in the back room of the shop to get ready for dinner.

I noticed Riggs texted and tried to call, but I didn't get back to him.

As we headed to the restaurant, bags in hand, shoes clicking on the pavement, there was a loud whistle behind us. A group of men called out to us, waving, and Ava responded with a laugh and shake of her head. "What did they say?" I asked. I'd heard the word *bella* so I figured they were complimenting us.

"Basically that we're beautiful and do we want to join them tonight." She gave a naughty wink. "I told them to keep dreaming."

"Good answer. Oh, let's go over there and film. The background is perfect."

They followed me to the small alcove with a bench and the lake behind. The rolling mountains rose up in glory. I held up my phone and took a deep breath. Hitting the live button was easier now, but my stomach still fluttered with nerves. Putting myself out there on a regular basis for comments or insults challenged my natural shyness, but this last year, I'd learned to push past my barriers.

I launched into my spiel, showing off each piece of my outfit, mentioning stores and brands and cost. I noticed within minutes I had over five hundred people viewing me, and the numbers kept increasing as I continued. Ava and Chelsea modeled for me, and with the background of Lake Como spread behind us, comments and hashtags poured in.

#whyrusogorgeous
#badassbitches
#iwanttobeu

Finally, I wrapped up. Excitement flicked through my body. Ava had been right—this trip was taking my online presence to new heights. I knew part of the social media image was to show glamour and make viewers want to be you. It seemed like I'd finally cracked that part, even though my purpose was to share how girls who feel like me inside, who may be trapped in their own rooms, with their own demons, can watch me and feel alive. To feel hope they can do the same, too.

Chelsea looked at me with admiration. "Wow, you're really killing it. Do you remember when you hardly had anything posted and said you were afraid?"

I nodded. "You were the ones who helped me. I'd probably be the same scared girl if I hadn't met you."

"No, you wouldn't." Ava stared at me, her deep blue eyes shining with a myriad of emotions. "You'd find a way. Don't do that, Maddie."

"Do what?"

"Limit yourself. Let your parents set your value. Fuck that."

I widened my eyes at her fierce tone. Basked in the aura of protection that vibrated from her; stepped into the magic circle and knew I'd never be alone again to face the world. "Okay."

Chelsea laughed and bumped Ava's shoulder. "Forget investor. You need to be a motivational speaker. *Fuck* that."

The mood lightened and we continued to dinner. "I can't believe we're eating at a Michelin-starred restaurant," I said in a hushed voice. We arrived at the Grand Hotel and I caught my breath at the elegant atmosphere of Mistral.

Ava gave a snort. "Just don't embarrass me by screaming if we get served something with the head still on."

"Oh, hell to the no," Chelsea said. "I'll stick with pasta. Will they serve us wine here?"

Ava shot her an amused look and spoke to the hostess, who led us outside. A square table with white linens and sparkling crystal was set on the terrace, overlooking the glamour of the Alps in the distance, and the still, glassy water of the lake. It was a bit chillier with the sun going down, so I opened my scarf and wrapped it around myself, breathing in the scents of flowers, lake water, and herbs.

"They have a seven-course tasting menu that's a game changer, but I'm not sure if you're feeling that ambitious after Thanksgiving dinner last night," Ava said.

I blinked. "Seven courses? How do you eat so much?"

"They're tiny. Plated for not only taste, but vision. It's like art on a plate."

"Have you always eaten like this?" Chelsea asked, spreading her napkin primly on her lap.

"Yes. Mom and Dad raised me to try everything they give me. If I didn't like it, they respected my decision, but Dad always said an adventurous palate is the key to a deeper understanding of people."

"Wow. That's deep," I said, processing the statement. "No wonder I don't understand many people. I grew up on chicken fingers and fries."

That cracked up Chelsea, who began telling us stories about when her mom tried to sneak healthy veggies into her food after reading some cookbook. "She spent hours in the kitchen, making these secret sauces with sweet potato and spinach, then tried to serve it to me and my brother, saying it was just mac and cheese, or just baked chicken." Chelsea shook her head. "Of course, we both sensed a rat and refused to eat it."

"What did she do?" Ava asked.

"Had a breakdown in the kitchen. Cried so hard, my father begged us to try it, so we each had a bite. Then my poor brother threw up."

I laughed, imagining the happy, chaotic home she grew up in. Chelsea never seemed to emanate any dark edges like Ava, or quiet broodiness like me. She was the sunshine of the group, always pulling us together as if she truly believed things would all end up okay. I loved the way she viewed the world.

The waiter appeared, dressed smartly in black, his voice low and hypnotic as he deftly explained the menu, switching easily to English once he caught Chelsea and me squinting with concentration as we tried to understand.

I ordered the champagne risotto. Chelsea was going with the tortellini but freaked out when she heard it was stuffed with peacock breast. Ava rolled her eyes, probably embarrassed by our food naivete, and went with the risotto also. Ava shared a few words in Italian with the waiter, and his robotic face turned soft, his dark eyes drinking her in like she was on the menu.

When he left, I snickered. "Dayum. Even old men fall hard for you."

She pursed her lips. "He's not old. He's distinguished."

Chelsea leaned in. "Would you consider dating a guy that much older?"

"Maybe. Depends on if he interests me. And I've always been attracted to older men."

I thought of Patrick, who was a bit juvenile sometimes. I'd caught Ava's disapproval when he acted like a frat boy, getting drunk and sloppy at a party or playing *Jackass* jokes for YouTube. Maybe I was silly to believe Ava could ever fall long term for someone like Patrick. It was just that the four of us fit so well together as a group, I hated to lose it.

"Has Riggs texted? I have a bunch of messages from Patrick, but I haven't had time to answer."

I shifted in my seat. "Yeah, he left me a message, too, but we were shopping."

Ava turned to Chelsea. "What about Wall Street guy?"

She sighed. "Nada. But he had a big family thing and then work. Trust me, he's made me aware I'm not a top priority."

"Does it hurt your feelings?" I asked softly.

"No, like I said before, I kind of like it. I can do me."

Ava suddenly swiveled her gaze to me, locking me in. "At least we can count on each other. Right?"

Unease slithered through me. "Umm, sure, but are you talking about anything specific?"

A slow smile curved her red lips. "I'll always have your back if you want to explore other options. Without Riggs knowing, of course. And the same for me. Why should we have to completely give up on one relationship just to experiment with another, right?"

I swallowed. "But, isn't that technically cheating?"

Her gaze narrowed. "Not really. Unless you vow you'll never sleep with or date anyone else, there's a lot of gray area. I think we've gotten out of control with this idea you can't even flirt or share a small kiss with someone without it being labeled cheating. We're young, we're living in New York City, and we're not allowed to explore any other options?" She seemed to warm up to her topic, hands gesturing in true typical Italian fashion. "Why are women always held to a higher standard? We're termed whores or sluts because we don't promise monogamy right away? Ugh, I hate it. I just think it's too easy for us to be manipulated into being good. Which is bullshit."

Our waiter brought our champagne. Uncorked it and poured three glasses. It was the interruption I desperately needed, because my mind was racing like crazy, trying to understand what Ava was really saying. I had no desire to ever cheat on Riggs, but was she right? Had I dropped into a comfort zone, seeing security as love? I thought over our conversation in bed, when we both admitted we weren't interested in anyone else. Would he tell me if he suddenly was, though? Or just act upon it, hoping I'd never find out?

He was friends with a lot of girls. He'd introduced me to many, citing classes or parties where they'd hang out. What if he messed up after drinking and ended up kissing or fooling around with someone? Yes, it was technically cheating, but Ava had a point. We hadn't confessed our love or made serious promises to each other.

I knew I'd be heartbroken and angry if Riggs stepped out

on me, but did I really have the right? And even more importantly, would I be willing to give up the entire relationship over it?

Ava was staring at me, waiting for my response, so I said the most honest thing I could. "I don't want anyone to get hurt."

Her face softened. "And we don't intend to hurt anyone. If we protect each other, we'll never have that issue. Right?"

I didn't want to agree—my body said something wasn't right in saying those words. But it was Ava. "Right."

She raised her glass. "To us. To Italy. To friendship."

We clinked the flutes together. I drank mine in one gulp rather than delicate sips.

I needed my stomach to settle.

We devoured the food, and I tasted caviar for the first time. It was delicate, salty, and perfectly paired with the risotto. Ava ordered the frog leg appetizer with snails, daring us to try it. Chelsea refused but I went for it, admitting the flavorful, crispy crunch did not taste like chicken, and the potato sour cream pushed it all to the next level.

I tried not to think of Kermit.

Each plate was presented like high art, drizzled sauces over delicately stacked layers topped with sprigs of herbs. We ordered a second bottle of champagne, and moaned over the chocolate soufflé with hazelnut ice cream. When we stumbled out, pleasantly buzzed, Ava announced we were going to her special spot down by the beach.

"Isn't Bruno waiting for us by the boat?" Chelsea asked, grabbing my arm to steady herself in her new heels.

"No, I told him I'd call to pick us up when we were ready. Come on, let's go."

The wandering alleys were quieter at this hour, but Ava said during high season the town buzzed with liveliness till late. Giddiness bubbled up in my veins like the champagne. The moon was full tonight, ripe and heavy and glowing goldish orange. We clung to one another and walked awhile, until we got down to a small strip of rocky beach, shadowed in privacy and deserted.

"This is it! I used to have make-out sessions here," Ava said, flinging her arms wide as if to encompass the night. "Isn't it beautiful?"

I caught my breath. My heart hurt with the stunning view of mountains and moon and lake laid naked before me. "I feel like I'm somebody else," I whispered. "Like in a dream."

Chelsea hiccupped and bent down to unbuckle her shoes. She walked in, toes in the water, yelping a bit as the chill hit her skin. "Look at the moon—it's glowing. Like in a movie. I bet we could wish for anything tonight and get it."

"What would you wish for, Chels?" Ava asked.

She closed her eyes with a sigh. "I want to create my own successful business on my own terms. Take care of my family. That would be my dream."

I loved her generous heart and gave her a hug. "You will."

"Maddie?"

I turned to Ava and pondered my answer, reaching deep to tell the truth. "I want to be known in the fashion industry as someone important."

"Why?"

I cocked my head at Ava's question. It didn't strike me as a challenge but more of a gentle inquiry. "Because I've felt like nothing before. And I never want to feel like that again. I want everyone to *see* me."

The words escaped into the quiet night and I flinched, wondering if I'd made a mistake. My wish seemed to catch on the breeze and lift up to the moon, and for one heart-stopping second, I realized I may have messed up.

But my friends both nodded, as if I'd asked for something worthy. My breath released from my lungs.

"Ava? What about you?" Chelsea asked.

She stood in front of us, facing the lake. The water lapped gently against the rocks. The moon beckoned like a wild goddess urging her to confess her secrets. I studied her profile, the pursed red lips, the fall of her silky dark hair, the smooth angle of cut cheekbone, all combining to reflect an eerie beauty that was its own gift to the world. She flung her head back and whispered something, bathed in shimmers of moonlight.

"Everything. More of . . . everything."

Before I could process, she let out a wild cry and swung around. Her husky voice became fierce with demand. "Let's go swimming."

My jaw dropped. "What? It's freezing!"

"The water is warm once we get in. Come on, we'll never have this night again. We need to grab it so we won't forget. Together."

Ava began pulling off her clothes with a madness that

made me laugh. Discarding her black lace bra and panties, she spun around gloriously naked, and I was struck once again by her body, curved in all the right places, olive skin smooth and flawless, limbs long and graceful, like she was offering herself as a gift to Mother Earth.

I caught her urgency and the need to experience that wildness myself. Without a second thought, I shook off my clothes and joined her on the shoreline. She reached out for my hand and our fingers interlocked. A rush of power washed through me. My toes curled over the rocks, gritty with sand, and my skin prickled with goose bumps.

"Chelsea. We need you," Ava said.

A curse word split the air, but soon Chelsea was also undressed, taking Ava's other hand, and with a whoop, we raced into the water.

The shock of cold burst through me, but I gritted my teeth against the pain and dived deep. Soon, warmth began easing into my limbs, and the silky water closed around me in protection. I heard Chelsea scream and Ava laugh, and I swam through the lake, turning on my back to a dead float, gazing up at the moon.

A splash came near me, and then we were in a circle, floating together. Once again, we clasped hands, and I gave myself up to the moment, finding a peace deep in my soul I didn't know existed.

The silence was more powerful than words. Energy snapped between us, like we really were witches casting a spell, and the whisper of the earth rose around me in all its elements: air, water, earth, and the fire of the moon.

"You're my sisters," Ava finally said. "Stronger than any blood ties because we chose one another."

A surge of knowing flooded through me. "Yes. I swear to you both, I will always be here for you."

Chelsea's voice was choked with emotion. "Me, too. Through everything."

"I won't ever get married without you both by my side."

"I agree with Ava. I couldn't do anything that important without you both," I said.

Chelsea agreed, and then Ava flipped over, treading water. "Let's make a pact. A pact under the full moon swearing on our friendship."

"We can't swear we'll be together forever," Chelsea said. "We may get separated by our careers, or families, or relationships. The pact needs to be doable."

Ava spoke. "We swear we'll be in one another's weddings. No matter what happens, or where we are in our lives. We show up for one another during the biggest days of our lives."

I turned and looked at Ava's face. Resolution carved out her features. Her blue eyes gleamed with raw demand, as if our agreement was essential to her next breath.

I didn't hesitate. I couldn't imagine being without my two friends in any scenario, but missing their weddings would be a betrayal to what we'd formed. "I swear it, to both of you. No matter what, I'll be by your side during your weddings."

Chelsea kicked to get closer to us. "I swear, too. I'd never miss either of your weddings."

Ava broke out into a joyous smile. "Good. Now let's seal the pact."

We swam back to shore and shivered in the cool air. Ava padded barefoot into the small flock of trees to the side, spending a few minutes searching about while Chelsea and I jumped up and down, calling out her name.

She returned with a small, sharp branch narrowed to a point. "Here we go. We're reciting a blood pact."

Chelsea raised a brow. "Umm, isn't that a bit retro? With all the diseases and stuff going on today?"

I giggled, still buzzing even after the midnight swim. "Oh my God, I always wanted to do this! I never had any real friends before."

Ava's wet hair spilled down her back. Her breasts gleamed in the moonlight. She held out the branch with the ceremonial air of a chief ready to begin. "Break the skin with this. Then we all join together and recite the pact. Ready?"

Chelsea still looked doubtful, but I could tell she was in. Ava gave a quick jerky motion to her thumb and squeezed out the drop of blood. I took the branch from her and repeated the gesture. The swift bite of pain only added to the excitement of the ritual. Chelsea followed and then we pressed our thumbs together, one by one, each mixing our blood with that of the others.

"I swear no matter what, I'll be at both of your weddings and support you always," Ava said.

I drew in a breath and met each of my friend's gazes. "I swear no matter what, I'll be at both of your weddings and support you always."

Chelsea winced but her voice was clear and firm. "I swear no matter what, I'll be at both of your weddings and support you always."

Then we all broke into laughter, high-fiving with our injured thumbs, clumsily re-dressing. Material stuck to my damp skin. Rivulets of water trickled down my back from my hair. My head spun with an explosion of emotion and alcohol and adrenaline.

When we got picked up, Bruno asked no questions. We returned to the villa and quietly walked to our rooms. Ava paused with her hand on the doorknob.

"Maddie?"

I turned. "Yeah?"

"I'll never forget tonight."

Her whisper caressed my ears, my skin, my heart. Our gazes met and melded together, and I spoke past the lump in my throat. "Me, neither."

I went to bed, dreaming of a full moon and our pact.

13

Months passed.

Senior year both threatened and beckoned.

Chelsea broke up with Wall Street and began dating an artist, telling us she needed to switch up her type. He wore a man bun and long white shirts, and scored a show at a local gallery, making him a mini sensation in Chelsea's eyes. Ava and I supported her wholeheartedly even as we both knew it'd never last past three months. His feet were too high off the ground to ever give Chels the security she craved, but I agreed she needed to get a little wild.

Riggs and Patrick graduated. They both scored jobs at the place they interned, getting hired in the legal department in entry-level positions.

Ava and Patrick continued dating, and our foursome kept strong. Ava stopped talking about wanting to date other men, and seemed to settle in to her relationship. Riggs and I fell harder for each other every day, until it became natural to spend more time at his place than my dorm. We began talking seriously about our future. It was as if all of my doubts that night in Italy disappeared the more time we spent together. Ava stopped warning me and seemed to support my choices. I counted that summer as a turning point, before everything began to shift and speed up momentum.

Before things began to fall apart.

One late Friday night, Riggs and I and Patrick went out to a bar. Ava canceled due to a migraine, insisting I go out without her. We ate tacos and drank margaritas in the back booth while a band set up. The place was already packed, and crowds pressed onto the small dance floor to get close to the modest stage.

"We should've stayed with our original plan," Patrick said. "Beer and axe throwing is my jam."

I rolled my eyes. "No wonder Ava got a migraine. Besides, it's way across town. This band is good."

"I guess." Patrick studied his margarita moodily. I shared a glance with Riggs, who admitted his friend had been off lately.

"What's up, dude?" Riggs asked, leaning in. "You have a fight with Ava?"

I knew Patrick used her moods to dictate his own, which I thought was unhealthy, but Ava shrugged it off and said it was just their thing. They had high ups and deep lows, but

I guess that's what kept them coming back to each other. Patrick was crazy jealous, which turned Ava on. Riggs and I were now used to their fights and the makeups but I was glad we were more on a slow, steady burn and rarely argued.

"Nah, we're good. Too good, maybe. I'm sensing she's not as into me anymore, and I'm not sure what to do."

It was always a slippery slope for me when Riggs and I hung out alone with Patrick because he liked to pepper me with questions about Ava, which I rarely answered. I left Riggs to deal with it. I refused to spill any of Ava's secrets. "I'm sure you'll work it out," I said lamely, shifting my attention to the band.

"I'm thinking of asking her to move in with me."

I jerked back and stared at him. Riggs and I spoke about the future, but I had no idea Ava and Patrick were that serious. "But you just said she seems distant?" I pointed out.

He gave a surly look. "Yeah, but I think it's because we're not moving forward. It's been a year. Women want goals. I have them, and Ava's the one for me. I'm talking real commitment here."

Riggs shifted in his seat. I could tell he was uncomfortable and didn't know what to say. "Did you ever mention moving in together? Or even use the *love* word?"

"We say we love each other all the time. In private. I've been taking things slow, but I'm ready to step it up." His dark eyes lit up with eagerness. "I got it all planned out. Now that I have a steady job and she's a senior, we should begin the next steps."

Riggs cocked his head. "Umm, you're rooming with me now. Am I supposed to move out?"

"Nah, I make enough to afford a studio outside the city. I'll just commute."

I thought of Ava listening to this plan and laughing. I couldn't imagine my friend commuting in on the subway and shacking up in a tiny one-room place while she waited for Patrick to work his way up the ladder. But Patrick's face was bright with hope for the future, and hell if I was going to tear him down.

I glanced at Riggs, who nodded, as if he understood. He cleared his throat. "Dude, I think you should have a serious talk with Ava. See where her head's at."

"But you think it can work, right?"

"Yeah. Sure, if you both want this, anything can work."

Patrick finished his margarita and slapped the table. "We do. Ava is unlike any other woman I've ever met. I just want to be with her, you know? Give her anything she wants."

I popped up from the table. The band began to start their set, so I had to shout. "Gotta hit the ladies' room."

I squeezed my way through the crowds and toward the back near the bar. When I got home, I had to talk to Ava and give her a warning. That way, she could think about what to say so she didn't hurt Patrick's feelings.

Unless she did want to move in with him?

These past few months, she seemed happier. There was a bounce in her step and she seemed content with Patrick. I could be missing something, and all that talk during

Thanksgiving was just her being restless. My mind spun as I got in line. Maybe I'd have a chat with her and see if she'd open up. See if she saw anything long term with Patrick. I didn't want my relationship with Riggs to affect her ability to confide in me. It was a tricky line to balance.

It took a while for my turn. I washed my hands, reapplied my lipstick, and made my way out.

That's when I saw her.

The tumble of her chestnut hair and heart-shaped face flashed in my vision, and I squinted, trying to focus. She was laughing up at some guy. He bent down and kissed her, tugging her forward until they were swallowed up by the crowd heading outside.

Was that Ava? Or my imagination?

Automatically, I began pushing toward the exit door, trying to make my way past the dancing, drunken partyers.

My heart pounded as I stumbled past the bouncer and outside. Groups of smokers lined the sidewalk, and the smell of tobacco and weed drifted in the air. I glanced up and down the street, looking for her familiar figure.

She wasn't there.

Unease slithered in my gut. Of course it wasn't her. She was home sick with a migraine.

I bit my lip, pondering. Then I grabbed my phone and sent a text.

Hey, I'm worried about you. Leaving early and coming over. Need anything?

I waited, feeling ridiculous and slightly guilty at even imagining she'd lie to me to be with some other guy.

Her response pinged.

> Aww, you're the best! Took some pills and
> going to sleep. Stay with Riggs and have fun.
> Love you. ☺

I stared at the phone. And knew I had a choice. I could push back and test things, or I could trust my best friend. I had no real proof that was her. I was tipsy and had only gotten a quick glance. Plus, I'd been thinking of her, so it was normal to imagine I saw her.

Of course it wasn't Ava.

I made the decision and worked my way back into the pub, refusing to second-guess myself. Or her.

LATER THAT NIGHT, wrapped in Riggs's arms, he turned over and stroked my cheek. "I've been thinking about what Patrick said tonight. About Ava."

I tried not to stiffen, cradling into the warmth of his body. My leg tangled with his. "What do you think is going to happen?"

"I think he's nuts about her. The guy has never committed to more than a third date—I've never seen him like this. But I'm not sure about Ava. Did she say something to you?"

My heart beat madly in my chest. "Like what?"

"About how she feels. I know Patrick puts on a front, but he really loves her and I don't want to see him hurt." His eyes flickered with doubt. "There's something about Ava I worry about. Like she's putting on an act with him, but that doesn't make sense, right? If she wasn't interested, she'd just break it off."

The words kicked into my memory and haunted me. How Ava expressed she wanted to be part of the group and be around me. I thought over our group dates and trips and hangouts. How the four of us had created a bond but how rarely Ava went out with Patrick alone. It was always with us.

I thought of tonight and what I imagined, but it felt wrong to confide in Riggs. I chose my words carefully. "I think Patrick is more focused on the future than Ava. She's not ready to settle down yet."

"I get it. But she's into him, right? There's no one else?"

My hand curled into his chest. I thought of her taking that waiter's card and wondered if she'd ever called him. But how could I confess those fears to Riggs? I had no proof, and it would only cause problems for all of us. Besides, Ava was my best friend. My tongue stumbled on the words, even though I had no proof I was wrong. "Yeah. Definitely."

His muscles relaxed. "Good. I guess we're all on the same page, then."

"What page?"

He smiled and kissed me, long and slow and sweet. "I'm seriously into you."

"How serious?" I whispered against his lips, half teasing.

His gaze delved deep and held. "I'm seriously in love with you, Maddie."

My insides shivered, and the hard shell around my heart cracked open like an M&M. Since the moment we met, I'd sensed we were completing each other, but it was too scary to hope for. Other than Ava and Maddie, no one had ever cared about me, and I worried something inside me was too broken. But Riggs wasn't running away, and all the emotions I'd been holding tight to burst free. I smiled so big my cheeks hurt. "I love you, too."

He was gentle, and kind, and funny. He was smart and handsome and he loved me.

Me.

We kissed and laughed and tumbled together, tangled in the sheets, and it was one of the best moments of my life.

Except for the lie.

I wondered what lies were forgivable in order to protect someone you love.

I was about to find out.

14

It was girls' night and we were at Ava's.

Legally Blonde played on the TV, and we sat on the couch with our feet up, wearing seaweed face masks and spa robes. The coffee table was littered with limes, tequila shots, and Ranch Water cans. Chelsea had come up with our new plan of sticking to one drink all night so no one got sick. I had to agree; when I mixed wine with any type of liquor, I got a headache in the morning. She said tequila was our new go-to, and we easily fell in line.

"Hey, are we still heading to the Hamptons next month?" Ava asked. "I got a new bikini and can't wait to wear it."

It was the summer before senior year began, and Ava had booked us a house for a long weekend. Chelsea and I stayed at the dorms so I could work and she could take a summer class. Chelsea bounced up and down on the couch. "I can't wait! Jeremy and I need some quality time. He's dropped into an artistic tunnel and barely comes out. When he does, he's all moody. I guess that temperamental artist crap is for real."

"Well, once he spots you in your bikini, he'll only have eyes for you," I teased.

"Hope so. Anyone else coming?"

"Just the usual gang. Brian will be there. He's bringing his new girlfriend. So it'll be the eight of us," Ava said.

"Perfect." I was still uneasy about Ava and Patrick's relationship, but I really wanted to have fun this weekend. I never questioned Ava about that night I thought I saw her, but I did notice things with her and Patrick seemed better. I'd warned her that Patrick was going to ask her to move in, and she'd only bitten her lip, nodding thoughtfully. Maybe I should just mind my own business and let Ava work it out. Once classes began, things would get serious. I still hadn't signed with an agency, and though my feeds were growing and I had a decent number of sponsorships, I wasn't where I needed to be. I had to somehow transition from social media to actual modeling with a paycheck. My degree would be in Digital Media, but I still wasn't sure what type of job I wanted in the industry.

"How are things with Riggs?" Chelsea asked.

Happiness bubbled up inside of me. I hadn't told them yet about our official declaration. "Really good. In fact, he said he loved me last weekend!"

They both gasped. "You waited this long to tell us?" Ava asked. "Wow, this is intense."

I tried not to get irritated with her remark and turned

to Chelsea. "It was romantic. He was all serious and sweet in bed and—"

"He told you in bed?" Ava blew out a breath. "Ugh, Maddie, you can never trust what guys say during sex!"

I pressed my lips together. "It was after sex. We were just talking. It was natural and I trust him."

Chelsea shot me a sympathetic look. "I think it's wonderful. Riggs is an awesome guy. Did you talk about after graduation?"

I nodded. "We're moving in together. Just have to figure some stuff out."

"Too bad. I was hoping the three of us could get a place."

Guilt cut through me at Ava's remark. "Well, you two could and we can live super close."

Ava smiled but it was tight. I told myself it was the seaweed mask. I knew she didn't approve of getting caught up in a relationship this young, but I was different. I was ready to be with someone who loved me and who'd be there for me. I didn't have magnificent villas or a great dad to help me. Riggs had become an important part of my life that I hadn't even believed I could get.

"What about modeling?" Ava asked. "You're not going to give up, are you?"

"Of course not. But I keep getting rejections—no agency wants me, even the smaller ones. I don't have the right look and I'm not young enough. One actually said they have a model in house with red hair! Like there can only be one."

Ava waved her hands in the air. "I can set you up for

an interview right now. At least let me help you get in the door."

"No, I can't. Thanks, but you know how I feel about this."

"Everyone networks, babe," Chelsea said gently.

"Maybe my IG or TikTok will pop. Or a clothing line will contact me about a bigger deal. I know there's a way I can do this on my own. You both help me all the time. I need to draw the line at this."

"You're so stubborn," Ava muttered. "I hope Riggs knows what he's getting into."

I grinned. "Nah, but it's good to keep him off-balance." I took a sip of Ranch Water. "How's your dad doing?"

"Great. He's flying in next week and we're seeing a Broadway show. You guys should come."

"Your dad is so cool," Chelsea said. "Is he bringing Gabriella?"

A slow smile crept over her lips. A tingle shot down my spine. "No, that's over."

I stared at her. "What happened?"

The smile grew. "It took a while, but I finally got him to see the truth. She was never worthy to be with Dad, anyway. I just needed to show him."

"Ava, what did you do?"

My question was met with an arched brow. "God, whose side are you on? All I did was talk to him. I explained my feelings and how I could never accept her as part of our family. I said I didn't care if he dated her, as long as I never had to spend a holiday or any time with her."

I knew there was more. So did Chelsea, but no one wanted to push. I studied Ava's face, her features hidden behind the mask, and wondered how far she'd go to get rid of a threat.

A threat to one of her own.

Uncomfortable with my train of thought, I took a big gulp of my drink and tried to settle. Chelsea spoke up. "Did you ever hire a PI?"

"No. Never got around to it." She sprang up from the couch. "We have to rinse these off! Come on."

She disappeared into the bathroom. I trailed behind her with Chelsea and lowered my voice to a whisper. "Don't you think something else happened she's not sharing? I can't believe her dad just stopped seeing Gabriella because she asked him to."

Chelsea shrugged. "I know, but they're super close and maybe her father didn't want to mess up their relationship? Ava's his only daughter. Maybe Gabriella wasn't important enough to upset Ava?"

"Maybe."

But my gut said there was more to the story I'd probably never know.

THE HAMPTONS WERE created for the rich. Luxury mansions, designer stores, and cool, trendy, sexy people littering the beaches and clubs. When I took in a deep breath, I smelled salt water, sunshine, and money.

Our place was an obnoxious white and black colonial

with a pool, a hot tub, and ten bedrooms. The back deck was sick and outfitted with loungers, patio furniture, grills, and a pizza oven. I wondered if anyone here planned to cook.

We'd driven up in two cars, and the girls split from the boys, so I was ready to spend some quality time with Riggs. Our schedules were so busy, this weekend gave us the opportunity not only to cut loose but to gain precious alone time. We'd already talked about sneaking out for our own date night, even though I was sure the group would disapprove.

We ordered in Mexican food, deciding to eat outside together and then hit the bars. Chelsea and I prepped the table, whooping when we discovered the professional margarita machine in the kitchen. We got to work and handed out drinks. Ava gave us a high five after one sip. "Maddie, why don't you move to bartender instead of server? You can make so much more money."

"I actually asked about it, but they don't have any openings yet. I was thinking I should take a course and be prepared when I can jump in."

"It sucks you have to be in the server industry," Patrick said. "Working nights and weekends is a lot, especially when Riggs has an office job. How will you ever see each other?"

Ava tilted her head. "Is she supposed to find some admin job so their schedules line up?"

Patrick wrapped his arms around her, but I could tell Ava was pissed at the comment. "Babe, I'm just saying it's hard. I'm lucky we don't have that problem."

"We may. Because I think I'm going to Italy for a few weeks this summer. To be with my dad."

Patrick stiffened, craning his head around to stare at her. "I thought we were going to do some traveling together?"

Ava broke away, tossing him a smile. "We'll see. I'm sure we'll take a trip or two with the four of us. Let's talk about it later."

"Sure. Maybe I can come with you if I can get the time off," Patrick said hopefully.

Ava didn't answer. She took her drink out on the patio and began chatting with Chelsea and Jeremy, the artist. I kept my attention on making the next margarita, noting Patrick's frustrated expression from the corner of my eye. He muttered something and followed Ava. I hoped he wouldn't act like a kicked puppy dog. Ava hated that crap.

The scent of soap and citrus hit me, and then Riggs was grabbing me from behind, pressing a kiss to my neck. "Pre-gaming?"

"Yep. Want one?"

"Absolutely." He took the drink, sipped, and whistled. "You got talent."

"Ava just mentioned I should bartend."

"Good idea, you'd make more money."

I put my drink down and linked my arms around his neck. "You wouldn't be mad about me working weekends and nights?"

"Of course not. I'll hang with you at the pub."

I smiled and gave him a kiss. "I knew you'd say that. You're the best boyfriend."

The flush of red on his cheeks delighted me. I took in his messy surfer hair, defined jaw, and sexy stubble. I couldn't seem to get enough of him, always needing to be touching or standing close to him, and I loved that he felt the same. Riggs wasn't the type to act cool around his friends, or pretend he wasn't totally into me, but it was different from Patrick. Riggs wasn't as clingy.

Maybe because he was secure in the relationship.

We all had dinner then got dressed for the night. I picked a short emerald green knit dress that brought out my eyes, and slicked my hair back tight, secured at my nape. Chandelier earrings were my only jewelry. I took out the shoebox JoJo's sent me—a new brand trying to gain traction—and put the shoes on. The stacked heel and gold straps had just the right amount of bling to stand out without looking cheap. Might as well do my sponsored post when I looked like this.

Ava and Chelsea bounced in. "Oh, are you filming?" Chelsea squealed. "Can we help?"

"Of course!"

Ava whistled. "Girl, you're smoking. Love the dress."

"Thanks! I can't wait to dig around and find sales this weekend."

Ava laughed. "If anyone can, it's you, Maddie. I think the light will look better away from the window."

"Good idea." My friends were the best assistants, knowing exactly what was needed to make the picture look glamorous without overreaching.

"Wait—you should shoot it while you're putting the shoes on, getting ready to go out. Women will love it."

I heard my name being shouted from downstairs and frowned. I opened up the door and responded, "I'm filming! Give me fifteen more minutes!"

Grumpy mutters drifted up the stairs, but I just rolled my eyes and shut the door. "They're waiting."

"Who cares? This is more important," Ava said.

A surge of confidence hit me. Ava and Chelsea never made me feel like this stuff was a hobby, or silly. Their belief drove my own, and I reminded myself that I needed to stop relying on others' opinions of my worth. Eventually, that inner weakness would come to bite me in the ass.

I removed one of the shoes and perched on the chair, showing off the length of my bare leg. I spoke to the camera like a friend, stating confidence is a girl's best friend, and the right pair of shoes is key. Ava directed and we did one run-through, then I was ready.

We got it in one shot. When we watched the video back, everyone agreed it was one of my best. I quickly typed in all the hashtags and posted.

"You're really good," Ava said quietly. "Don't forget that, Maddie. Just promise me you won't . . . settle."

I felt torn between unease by her warning and the fierce devotion she gave unmatched by anyone I'd ever met before. I smiled back, focusing on her positivity. "I won't. In the meantime, I can pay you both in shoes. They're sending me a few more pairs."

Chelsea gave a whoop. "Best job ever! Now, let's go out and get drunk."

The guys teased us about being late, but I could tell they

appreciated our appearance. Ava was in black tonight, a formfitting jumpsuit that clung to every inch of her curvy body, and Patrick's tongue hit the floor. I couldn't help noticing every guy snuck a peek at her. She reminded me a bit of Kim Kardashian when she walked into a room—the immediate hush and hot stares of the crowd were not only anticipated, they were expected. Ava held her audience well, never edging over the line from light flirting with anyone's boyfriends. Down deep, she was a girl's girl, turning her nose up at the ones who begged for attention.

The tiki bar was loud, crowded, and fun. Everyone was in the party spirit, and we started with shots of tequila, furiously sucking lime wedges, swaying our hips to the DJ's hip-hop music. Riggs pulled me out to the floor and we danced, bodies pressed together, arms wrapped tight, swaying to the dirty rhythm while we stared into each other's eyes. My body was already on fire, and I melted against him helplessly.

His voice was rough against my ear. "You're so damn hot. I can't get enough of you."

Feminine power coursed through me. Bubbles of giddiness danced in my veins. "Good. I always want you to feel that way."

His grip tightened with possession. "Is it fucked-up that I can already see a future with you? You haven't even graduated and I'm making plans for us."

I caught the raw emotion in his gaze; understood the passion and confusion mixed together, because it was exactly what I experienced. I slid my hands into his hair. "No. I see it, too. So we're both fucked-up."

He gave a half laugh, his lips brushing my cheek. "Good. I'm not into fairy tales or fake promises. But I've never felt more like myself than when I'm with you."

I fell apart at his words and opened my mouth to tell him my own truths, but someone bumped into me hard, knocking me to the side.

Ava threw her arms around us, smiling drunkenly. "Come on, guys, you already got a room! Give her some space to breathe, dude. We're here to party."

Riggs frowned, obviously annoyed, but she was already tearing me from him, and I let myself go, knowing she was too drunk to be aware she was interrupting. I shot him an apologetic smile and began dancing with Chels and Ava, falling back into our usual routine. I'd have plenty of time alone when we got back to the house. We'd have all weekend together.

Tonight, I'd just have fun with my friends.

15

❧

The weekend was a jigsaw of pieces in bright flashes of color. Friday night, we stumbled home and ended up falling asleep in the living room after Brian's idea to play drunken Twister. After a few contorted moves, we dropped one by one into exhaustion and woke up to a mess.

Saturday, the group split up—the guys went to a brewery and we hit the stores. It was a day of true retail therapy, and I ended up finding a secondhand shop that resold designer wear. My treasures were all posted on my social media, and I freaked out to find a bunch of my followers were tagging me from the Hamptons, asking to meet me in person. Chelsea called me a celebrity. It was the first time what I was doing felt real and that I was reaching actual followers. Ava insisted I tell them we'd meet at another popular nightspot so we could hang together. I hesitated, since

Riggs and I had planned to go to dinner alone tonight, but I figured he'd understand. It was a rare opportunity for me.

The evening went even better than I thought. There were three girls there who treated me like a star, asking my opinions on fashion and begging me to do a series of posts on using makeup to emphasize particular outfits. We spent hours crushed into a corner, comparing media feeds, recommending other influencers, and drinking lemon drop martinis.

By the time I got home, I was buzzing not only from the alcohol but from the high of finally feeling I was making headway. Riggs asked to go to the hot tub, and even though I wanted to collapse, I agreed. We needed some quiet time together and no one was out back.

I dressed in my bikini, grabbed a towel, and snuck out. Most of the group was in the kitchen warming up leftover pizza and discussing what bingeable series was the best. I slipped into the hot, bubbly water with a sigh and slid over near Riggs. "This feels so good," I said, relaxing my head against him.

He grunted but didn't answer. I craned my head to look at him. "You okay?"

"Yeah." A pause. "It's just we haven't spent more than a few minutes alone together."

Guilt pricked. "I know, I'm sorry. It feels like everything is going so fast. But I really wanted to meet my followers, and it was amazing."

"No, I'm glad you did that. It's . . ." He trailed off with a deep sigh. "Forget it. You're here now."

He pulled me in and I wrapped my arms around his broad shoulders. Our foreheads touched. His damp skin was hot and rough sliding against mine. In minutes, I was breathless, and desperate to get back to our room. "I missed you today," I murmured, kissing him.

"Hmm. We'll make up for it tonight. You looked happy at the club. What did they say?"

I filled him in on the details. "They gave me a great idea for a new segment, and they're mentioning me on all of these other influencer pages. It was so cool, Riggs. They were actually excited to meet me."

"Babe, they should be. You've been working hard on building your audience. I may not be into fashion, but I've watched the stuff you put out and it's damn good. Not that I'm surprised."

"Stop."

"No, I mean it." He squeezed me tight, cupping my cheek, his gaze intense. "I don't know how it's going to happen, but I think one day you're going to be a big deal. Just don't trade me in for a newer model."

I laughed. "Why get a new car when I own a vintage Cadillac?"

He groaned. "That was awful."

We burst into laughter, and then we were kissing.

"There they are!"

I looked up as our friends surged into the hot tub, carrying drinks and talking loudly. Riggs and I shared a look, but we didn't want to excuse ourselves right away. Already, Patrick was hitting him in the arm, handing him a beer. Ava looked drop-dead gorgeous in her tiny red bikini. Chelsea and Jeremy perched on the edge, nibbling on pizza. Brian and his girlfriend had stayed in their room, which seemed par for the course since they hadn't been able to keep their hands off each other.

Everyone began sharing jokes and good-natured ribbing, and soon we were all hysterically laughing. I'm not sure how much time passed before I noticed Ava getting a bit sloppy. She slurred her words and clung to me, even though Patrick kept trying to kiss her. Chelsea and Jeremy left first, and I was getting ready to make my own excuses, craving some time alone with Riggs.

Ava wrapped her arms around my neck and whispered, "Don't feel good, Maddie. Help me out."

"Here, I got you," Patrick said, trying to guide her out, but she threw back her head and laughed a bit hysterically.

"No, I want Maddie!"

"I'll take her." I knew Ava didn't like to be out of control. She rarely drank to where she passed out, so this wasn't like her. I shot an apologetic look at both the guys and talked her out of the tub, wrapped a towel around her. She stood docile like a child as I dried her off, blotting her wet hair, then walked with her into her bedroom.

"Feel spinny. Don't like it."

I shook my head. "Why did you open up that last bottle of champagne? Poor thing, lie down and I'll get you water."

She giggled and curled up on the bed, legs tucked in a fetal position. I brought her a large cup of water with ice and two aspirin. "Here, I need you to drink this. Your headache will be legendary tomorrow."

Ava managed to sit up and obediently drank, taking the pills. "Tonight fun."

I smiled and stroked her hair back from her face. "It was. Thanks for pushing me to meet those followers. They were awesome."

"You need me, right?"

I frowned. The way she said the words didn't sound like a joke. Shadows seemed to reflect in her glassy blue eyes. "Of course I need you."

"But you're gonna leave," she sang off-key, laughing but without humor. "Everyone leaves."

Ava rarely confessed her vulnerabilities. Most of the time, I wondered if she had any, other than trying to figure out her career. "What do you mean? I'm not leaving you, Ava."

"Y'wll. No one stays with me."

I sat beside her. My heart broke at her obvious pain, expressed in a drunken state when her walls were lowered. Maybe even I was guilty of thinking Ava to be removed from the rest of us; so confident and poised with the world at her feet. Maybe, even as much as I knew her, she kept her fears and insecurities locked up tight. "I'm not going anywhere. You will have Chelsea and me forever. You have your dad. You have Patrick."

She looked at me mournfully. "No. Mom died. Dad is back with Gabriella, and he's going to get engaged. I'm not enough."

I sucked in my breath. Her dad had looked a bit sad when we went to see *Hadestown* on Broadway, staring at Ava as if he wanted to tell her something but didn't know how. "They got back together?"

Ava nodded and gulped. "I told him the bad things I found, but it didn't matter. Now, nothing will ever be the same. He has her. Doesn't need me."

I ignored the truth that told me she'd done something specific to try and break them up and focused on what she needed from me now. "Sweetie, that's not true. Your dad loves you. He's probably lonely because he can't build a life waiting for you to visit. This could be a good thing, so you don't feel guilty for not staying home. Gabriella could never ever replace you."

Ava stared back, obviously not believing me. I sighed and pulled her into a hug, and she tucked her head underneath my chin, letting out a ragged breath. "Riggs wants to take you away, too. He doesn't like me."

I froze. Finally, the truth was out. Ava felt threatened by Riggs, just as I'd feared. I spoke carefully. "Of course he likes you! He's just a guy, and if he doesn't get enough attention, he gets a little pissy." I hated the way I was betraying Riggs when I was just as frustrated, but Ava needed reassurance. "You have nothing to worry about. You're my best friend and I'm going nowhere."

"Promise? You'll pick me?"

I squeezed my eyes shut. What type of question was that? I didn't have to choose, but she was drunk and emotional and not making sense. "Yes, always. Now, why don't you go to sleep?"

"'Kay." She sighed and I helped her get situated under the blankets. "Love you, Maddie."

I smiled. "Love you, too."

I closed the door gently behind me. Patrick was in the living room hanging out with Riggs. "Patrick, she's passed out. I'm heading to bed."

Riggs got up. "Me, too. Night, buddy."

We locked ourselves into the bedroom and I faced him. "I'm sorry we keep getting interrupted."

"It's okay, I knew it was a group weekend. I just think Ava depends on you too much."

I sighed. "She's going through some stuff. And she counts on me because we're not just friends—we're family. I don't know how to explain how much she's done for me."

He muttered something and cupped my cheek. "Baby, you give her just as much. Anytime she asks, you drop everything to be with her. I'm not trying to split you up. I'm asking to give us a little more time. Maybe it will force her to figure things out with Patrick and not hide behind our foursome."

I nodded, agreeing with him. I'd been thinking the same thing. By trying to make things easier, maybe I was only encouraging her to ignore her issues with Patrick. We were becoming a distraction to her relationship. "Yeah, I see your point. I'll try to be firmer about our boundaries."

"Thank you."

He picked me up and we kissed. The physical connection between us exploded, and I surrendered to his body claiming mine, pushing thoughts of Ava away for a little while.

EVERYTHING CHANGED SENIOR year.

Chelsea broke up with Jeremy after finding him screwing his nude model. She spent a week in rage, a week revenge dating, and ended up agreeing to a date with the guy she was paired up with for her final financial project. He'd been asking her out for a while, but she labeled him a bit too nerdy for her.

They slept together on the third date, and Chelsea declared herself in love.

Ava solved her issues with Patrick and said she was all in. They seemed happier, and Patrick gave her more breathing space now that she'd made the full commitment. The four of us grew even closer, talking about moving into dual apartments after Ava and I graduated. Ava was graduating with a marketing degree after changing her major twice, and she talked about starting her own business. I finally scored the elusive check mark that classified me as a person of influence. My YouTube videos and reels became more mainstream, and I gained sponsors. But no agencies seemed interested in another pretty girl trying to make it big on the Internet. I brainstormed ways to make a living, but the money still wasn't there. Sure, I got tons of free products, but the income was too fluid—sometimes I'd have a great month, and then another I'd have zero dollars coming in. I

finally switched to bartending to make a bit more money
and kept trying new things.

I was at the pub one late afternoon and the crowd was
thin. I spent some time wiping down the bar and refilling my condiment trays, when a familiar good-looking
guy walked in. He was dressed in a sharp suit—a deep blue
with a pink shirt—and smelled of money. Thick black hair
was long in the front and shaved in the back. Black trendy
frames were perched on the bridge of his nose. He sat at the
bar and smiled at me, showing straight white teeth. "What's
on tap?"

I smiled back, my mind trying to figure out where I saw
him last. I gave him the spiel and he ordered a Juice Bomb
IPA. I slid the glass over.

"Madison, right?"

I blinked. "Yeah." I didn't wear a name tag. "Have
we met?"

He tapped his finger against the glass. Up close, his features held a bit of elegance, from his patrician nose and
high forehead, to a sharp-cut jaw. Dark eyes gleamed with
intelligence. I noticed a gold ring on his index finger but no
wedding band. "No, but I've been here a few times. Checking you out."

My face stiffened. "Sorry, I have a boyfriend," I said,
turning away.

His husky laugh halted me. "No, sorry, didn't mean it
that way. Here." He slid a business card across the bar. I
picked it up.

The Trendsetter Agency.

"What's this?"

"Your lucky day, I hope." I frowned, but his expression was a bit mischievous and nonthreatening. He stuck out his hand. "Sorry, I'm Levi. I'm one of the scouts for the agency. I've been following your socials, and you've managed to impress us."

I shook his hand, trying to still my beating heart and remain calm. There were so many scam artists, I needed to be prepared. "I've never even heard of this place."

He didn't look offended. "We're only a year old. Hit up our website to see our clients and what we do. Trendsetter isn't your usual modeling agency. We're not looking to put our clients in catalog shoots or go on constant booking appointments to compete. We have a bigger vision and think you'd fit perfectly. Do you have time to talk?"

I glanced at the clock and nodded. It'd be slow for the next hour. "One minute." I grabbed Angie from the kitchen and asked her to cover for a bit, then we went to one of the back tables.

"How did you find me?" I asked.

"You mean here? You're on social media, Madison. It was pretty easy to find the tags from the pub and then I asked one of your staff members when your next shift was. May need to be more careful in the future when you get stalkers. I'll help you with that."

I quirked a brow at the assumption. "Why don't you tell me why you're here?"

"I'm on the lookout for up-and-coming influencers who can do more with their platform, especially in modeling.

We work for a variety of well-known brands who don't just want a model for a catalog or billboard—they're looking for a personality who can also sell. I've watched your accounts grow and the way you connect with your fans." He drummed his fingers on the table absently, as if it was a habit he wasn't conscious of. "Too many times, an influencer is great with connection but can't model the clothes. Or the look isn't unique enough. But then I found you." He smiled, brown eyes filled with banked excitement. "It's been a long time since I've been this eager about a prospect. Usually, age would be a factor—you're a little older than where we typically start, but your face is fresh and young. You're not only gorgeous, but interesting to look at. You can sell. And the camera makes you come alive."

I tried desperately to mask my reaction and reminded myself this was business, not some adoring fan paying me compliments. I needed to be smart. "Tell me about the agency and what to expect if you represent me."

"Our clients pay us to find them the right fit, so you're already presold to represent the product. We handle all the expenses. You'd be doing video, photo shoots, and social media campaigns. I'd like to set you up with an appointment with one of the partners to discuss details and contracts. What do you think?"

I didn't know what to think. I felt halfway numb because things like this just didn't happen to me. I prepped to be disappointed by a scam and knew I couldn't go to this place alone. Not until I did some hard research. "Yes, we can schedule a meeting."

"Great." He took a silver pen out of his suit pocket and scrawled something on the back of the business card. "Here's my cell phone number if you need it. You can call the main number and ask for Brianna, then tell her Levi sent you." He handed it back. "I know you're suspicious, as you should be. Look up our website and our clients. We're legit." Levi stood up and shook my hand again. "Nice to meet you, Madison."

I watched him walk out of the pub, then stared down at the card. Holding it in my fingers, I flipped it around. My ears roared and my palms grew damp. I was still wary, but something told me my life was about to change drastically, and nothing would be the same.

And I was right.

16

Within weeks, I signed with Trendsetter Agency and began the career I'd always dreamed of.

Brianna was a smart, savvy businesswoman who was also a former top model. With the changing landscape of social media and influencers, she wanted to start a company that would address the new media and offer personalized recommendations to brands who had little time to do hours of scouting and booking appointments. I loved her vision.

I'd warned Brianna I had only months left before graduation, and she promised we could be flexible with my schedule. If this whole thing went bust, I didn't want to miss out on my degree. I switched to online classes to make things easier, and began my first campaign.

Riggs took me out to a fancy steak pub to celebrate. I decided to eat obnoxiously since I had a feeling my diet would be strict from then on, even though I didn't easily gain weight. I sipped my lemon drop martini and admired him in the candlelight of the dim restaurant. He'd tamed his thick waves of hair back from his face, which emphasized the gorgeous sea green of his eyes. Sexy stubble clung to his chin—he was growing a goatee and I loved it. He wore a black shirt with paisley pink cuffs rolled up, dark wash jeans, and leather shoes. The scent of clean, ocean air cologne drifted from his skin, and I had to fight the urge when he held me not to bury my nose in his neck and take a whiff. I only found him more attractive as time went by, sinking deeper into how he made me feel when we were together. All my walls were gone, and I wasn't even scared anymore. I loved him with everything I was. I knew he felt the same.

"All that hard work you did paid off," Riggs said, clasping my hand across the table. "Babe, this is amazing. I knew you'd succeed, but this is like the movies! I mean, a guy walks into a bar . . . and you get famous."

I laughed. "That's an awful line. But it's weird Levi was stalking my social media, right? I kept sending queries to all these agencies without a response, and didn't even realize Trendsetters existed. I should have researched better."

"Yeah, but they're new and you said they didn't show up under modeling. Anyway, who cares? He found you." Riggs split open a roll, and the steam rose from the fresh bread. He slathered on butter, then handed it to me before working on his own. He was always making sweet little gestures that meant more than he imagined—showing me he cared.

I bit into the bread and moaned. I'd miss carbs the most. "Yeah, you're right. I start filming next week."

"Jeans, right?"

I practically jumped in my seat with excitement. "Yes, but these are the Betty Blues that are blowing up! You actually commented on them last week when I wore them, remember?"

"The ones that made your ass look fire?"

I laughed. "Yes, those. They're in smaller shops, but you can't find them in the department stores yet. The campaign is a way to get more eyes on the brand and hopefully get to the next level."

He cocked his head with interest. "Tell me the plan again. What will you need to do?"

Nerves mixed with anticipation of the intense work ahead of me. "Everything. I'll be modeling the jeans in a photo shoot, then we'll do a video for Reelz and YouTube and I'll put up sponsored posts. It's going to be intense, but I'm ready. I've been waiting for this opportunity, and I'm not going to blow it."

My words sounded braver than I felt. I was scared out of my mind. I had no real experience, and after a few meetings with the Betty Blues brand ambassador and hours of pre-shooting to make sure I got the look they wanted, we were finally moving forward. I knew this was my turning point. I had to succeed no matter what. I'd been leaning heavily on Ava, Chelsea, and Riggs to keep me supported and sane.

"You're not. What did your parents say? I bet they were proud."

Sadness hovered but I fought it off. "Not really."

A tiny frown creased his brow. "Maddie, I know you said

you weren't close, but they have to be excited. This is a huge opportunity."

I hesitated. I'd told Riggs about my past, but it was hard to understand the dynamics of my family when you took a loving mother and father for granted. He couldn't really imagine not being accepted or loved, so I tried to understand where he was coming from instead of getting frustrated. "They said they were happy I was able to make a living on my own. And wished me luck." The pain simmered low in my gut where I managed it. "Then they thanked me for calling."

Riggs's look of horror made me feel worse. "Babe, I'm so sorry." He entwined his fingers with mine, his voice low with sympathy. "That's awful. Fuck them."

I gave a half laugh. "Yeah, it doesn't matter anymore. I'm tired of hoping for one shred of emotion from them. I'm done. I don't know why I thought this time it would be different."

"Because you have a heart. A beautiful, kind heart that stole mine in minutes."

I melted like a pile of goo and then we were leaning over the table and kissing. My entire being lit up from the inside, and I realized I had everything I ever wanted or needed. A dream-worthy career. The best friends I could imagine. And Riggs.

I swore to enjoy every moment while things were perfect.

I WALKED INTO the studio where the shoot was set up and tried not to throw up.

Cameras and lights and people crowded the space. A petite brunette with her hair twisted on top of her head and a pile of papers clutched in her hand darted right over. "Madison? Welcome, I'm Cecil, your assistant. I'm here to help with anything you need or to answer questions. Come this way—your stylist is waiting for you."

She chattered nonstop, her energy almost a physical presence. In her other hand, she held a Red Bull, and I wondered how many she drank in a day. I was introduced to the team, and my brain whirled to keep up. My stylist, Dionne, was thin, gracious, and dressed in a burlap-type dress with combat boots and pink hair in thick braids. We immediately clicked and talked about some of our favorite designers while various pieces were pulled from the rack for me to change into. It was hard at first to get used to being naked in front of strangers, but I soon learned everyone saw me as more of a structure than a nude female. Fabric was manipulated and hands tugged and maneuvered over my nipples and my ass, until I stopped being stiff and just went with the flow. Ava warned me that's how it would be, so I'd prepared myself mentally, but it wasn't as bad as I imagined.

Hours passed as I was worked on like a painting, my face and body a blank canvas. The first look was the skinny acid-washed jeans with a simple white button-down shirt open in the front. I was naked underneath, my breasts taped to expose the perfect amount of cleavage. I was barefoot, my toes painted a bright sunshine yellow to match my fingernails. My hair was styled long with loose curls tumbling over my shoulders. A blue couch and chair were the only props.

It took me a while to relax. I expected the photographer to yell and get nasty with me when I kept getting corrected, but he was really patient and kept saying positive stuff that helped me get in the right mindset. Soon, I was lounging on the couch, pretending to be at my house, and nailing the expressions he wanted. He got pumped up when I straddled the chair and propped my hands on the top, staring moodily at the camera with my lips open. The sheer energy in the room was like a live wire, crackling with intensity and zapping me with adrenaline. The click of the camera and hot bulb of the lights became secondary. I concentrated on my photographer's voice and instructions, burrowing into myself like I used to in my room, playing dress-up for the camera and imagining my audience watching me, adoring me, seeing me.

We did it again. And again. And again.

I'd heard modeling was hell on the body, and now I knew why. There were few breaks, and you needed to be comfortable with people picking at you and treating you like an object, and with being able to come alive on cue. I fumbled with a few of them—I could tell I wasn't giving the shots needed—but the photographer kept pushing and I eventually rose to the occasion. By the end, he looked pleased and told me I'd done a great job.

My calendar began to fill up with appointments, fittings, and various shoots as the campaign was built from scratch.

I loved every moment. I began to bloom under the attention I'd always craved. I didn't examine the reasons being in the spotlight satisfied a part of me, because I didn't want to know. I just wanted to keep doing it. I wanted more.

It was the beginning of a new me I didn't plan on. But it was too late to go back.

And I didn't want to.

Soon, I began courting big-name influencers and celebrities on my account. I knew the agency had sown many connections to get my account viral worthy, and the combination did what we all hoped. The full campaign went live.

And I blew up.

In the weeks leading up to graduation, I worked around the clock, trying to balance the new aspects of my life. I made sure to carve out time for Ava and Chelsea. My friends were my family, and I treated them with a responsibility my parents had never given me. I'd never be like them.

I left the dorm early and moved in with Riggs, even though Patrick and Brian were still there. Ava had suggested it would be easier to see each other since I could be there when she came to visit Patrick, though it was a challenge around boys who weren't too clean and partied late in the night. Ava ended up at the house with Patrick a lot, so we crashed together, many times sharing a blanket in front of the television. Riggs still had issues with the way Ava demanded my time, but he didn't complain. I could just tell from his look toward her when she pushed his buttons. But I was grateful he didn't challenge me and accepted it was part of our friendship.

One night, Chelsea and I gathered at Ava's for a girls' night. It was rare I didn't have to get up early, and even though I craved being in Riggs's arms for a lazy Sunday morning, it had been too long since I saw my friends alone. Instead of going out, we had an old-fashioned sleepover like our freshman year. We lounged around in our pj's with *Bridesmaids* on the TV, an empty box of pizza, and a carton of White Claws in Tropical Fruit on the table. This time, our face masks were charcoal and we giggled at one another for looking like creatures from the Black Lagoon.

"I can't believe college is officially over next week," Chelsea said with a sigh. "Is it screwed up I'm actually more nervous than excited?"

I shook my head. "Nope. Even though I was only halfway here for this semester, Havisham is my safe place. It's like real life won't start until you're kicked out. Plus, I'll miss this. Especially us."

Ava's voice hit like a whiplash. "Don't say that. We'll always be together; it will just be a new chapter. Remember our pact."

"We'll never forget the pact," Chelsea said. "I know what Maddie means. We won't be in the same school or dorm together. We have no idea of our future anymore, and it freaks me out."

Ava threw her hands up in the air. "Are you guys serious? Both of you have nothing to worry about. Chels, you're going to open up your own business, and Maddie is already on her way to fame. What am I doing? Graduating with a marketing degree that will get me nowhere."

"Stop. You already know what you have to do, Ava. Create your own business managing media for up-and-coming influencers. You know everyone, and you're amazing at it. I would never have followers if you hadn't helped me create my page."

Chelsea jabbed her finger in the air. "Agreed. You're a genius and will get clients immediately."

"Dad wants me to come back to Italy for a while. He said I can start in one of his businesses and work in the marketing department."

I nibbled my lip, worried. The idea of losing Ava hurt my insides, but I didn't want to be selfish. "Are you thinking about it?"

A pained sigh escaped her. "No. I can't. Not with Gabriella there all the time. I warned him I wouldn't move home if he continued this. Plus, I want to stay in New York. It's more of a home here and there're better opportunities."

Relief coursed through me. "I'm glad. I don't know what I'd do without you. What about Patrick? Are you guys moving in together?"

Her features tightened and she avoided my gaze, sipping her White Claw. "Actually, I wanted to talk to you about Patrick. I decided to break up with him."

Chelsea and I gasped. I hadn't seen this coming. They'd been seemingly happy together, and Riggs told me his friend had already found a place for them. "Ava, what happened? Why didn't you tell me?" I asked.

She gave me a funny look. "I didn't know how to. Patrick is so close with Riggs, and I wanted to be sure before I went and blew everything up. But now that school is over and we're moving in our own directions, I realize I don't want to stay with him. He's not my forever."

Chelsea patted her arm. "It's good to know before you end up sharing rent. I'm sorry, Ava. I know how hard this is for you."

I remained silent, my tongue stuck to the roof of my mouth. Irritation skittered through me, and another emotion I didn't want to name. Ava didn't look upset at all. I thought of how Patrick would take it, and wondered if she deliberately planned to do this around graduation. We'd just spent a great weekend together, and I watched while they made out and Patrick declared she was the one. Why didn't she seem uncomfortable? Why hadn't she given any type of hint this was coming?

Everything felt . . . wrong. But I couldn't challenge her, and wouldn't know how to ask. I wondered if she was secretly seeing other guys. But did I really want to know at this point? There was nothing to change the ending. Maybe it was better to be in the dark, even if it was on purpose.

I shook my head, refocusing on the conversation. Chelsea was talking. "I'm excited about starting my job at Wealth Planning Industries, and I have a three-year plan. The company will sponsor me while I study for the Certified Financial Planner and Securities exams. Meanwhile, I'm going to steep myself in work and learn everything possible to open up my own business." She gave a sigh. "I'm not sure where I'll want to settle."

Ava and I looked at each other. "Here," we both said together, then laughed.

Chelsea grinned. "I'd love to, but real estate here is too high for me to afford. I'll barely get enough of a loan to do the things I want."

"But the city is where the business is," I pointed out. "Do you want to run a financial firm in a small town?"

"I'll have to think about it."

"Unless . . ." Ava said, her eyes widening.

"What?" I asked.

"I invest in your business. With my backing, you can get a place perfect for traffic, and I can help with the media, which would support me launching my own business." As soon as the words were out, Ava jumped up from the couch, her face full of elation. "Oh my God, that's the answer! It's a win-win situation for all of us."

The possibility of us staying close and creating a business hit me full on. I thought of the scenarios and pictured the three of us helping one another, living in the city, and growing our brands. Most of all, being together. "That's brilliant!" I jumped up, too, and grabbed Ava. "Chels, what do you think?"

"I don't know." Shock reflected in her gaze, along with hope. "Is it possible? Ava, I can't ask you to invest money for me. What if it tanks and you lose everything? I could never forgive myself."

"You won't fail because this business addresses a niche that's been empty. Plus, I want to be a part of something bigger. It's exactly what I've been missing. Motivation. This is the first time I feel alive about a project. You'd be saving me, Chels."

I was struck again by Ava's generous nature and the way she freely gave of not only her money, but herself. She was our most dedicated cheerleader, never letting Chelsea or me let go of our dreams.

"I still have a lot to learn, so we couldn't do it now."

"I know, but that will give me time to research your world and make new connections." She tapped her lip thoughtfully. "I was offered a job at *Cosmopolitan* magazine. They want me to do a regular column and some consult work. I bet I could get you featured. Up-and-comer graduate looking to launch her own business helping women in finance? By getting you on the radar early, we can begin recruiting clients."

Ava dived into a brainstorming session, and our next few years began to take shape. I saw it all so clearly. All of us developing our own careers on our terms, and Ava helping to guide our way, like she usually did. "What do you think, Chels? Is this something you're even interested in? Because I understand if you don't want me involved. This is your dream."

I held my breath as Chelsea seemed to ponder the idea, and then with a whoop, she joined us in our circle, jumping up and down.

"I'm in!" she shouted. Usually the practical one in the group, her decision seemed to come from her gut and the belief we could do anything together. For the next few hours, we talked nonstop and sketched out ideas. Ava grabbed her laptop and we made a million notes, while Chelsea sifted through an Excel sheet of budgets and timelines. The future burned bright and hot.

It was almost 2 a.m. when we suddenly realized we'd all forgotten to wash off our masks.

We crushed together in the bathroom, scrubbing frantically at the particles now ingrained in our faces, laughing hysterically.

17

Graduation passed. I spent the day with Ava's dad and Chelsea's parents, celebrating at a lavish dinner. We shared our plans for the future, and I was surprised at the level of support received. Ava's father seemed to have a few words with her regarding Gabriella, but she remained stubborn. I think Ava believed if she kept denying the relationship, they wouldn't get married.

My parents sent a small check with a card but didn't make the ceremony. Ava included me like I was her sister, and told me I could share her dad, which made me burst into tears. She hugged me tight and promised I'd be fine without my parents.

I hated myself but ended up crying again in Riggs's arms that night. He stroked my hair and listened without trying to fix it. Being surrounded by everyone's support system was hard, even though I tried to say I didn't care.

Patrick and Brian moved out, and I formally moved in

with Riggs. Chelsea and her hot nerd, Ed, were still pretty serious but didn't want to live together, so she moved in with
Ava. Things between Riggs and Ava grew tense after she
broke up with Patrick.

My conversation with Riggs regarding them sowed the
seeds of disapproval I tried hard to ignore.

"She never intended to be with him long term," Riggs said
one night after visiting his friend. "I think she strung him
along just so she could hang out with you. That's fucked-up,
Maddie."

I hated having the two most important people in my life
at odds, and I tried to defend her. "You can't expect her to
feel the same way Patrick does. They had their issues, and
she tried, but it didn't work. I had nothing to do with it. I
wish you wouldn't blame her."

Riggs shook his head. "Patrick is a mess. All this time, she
was pretending to be on board with moving in with him.
And I swear, she was seeing other guys. He suspected, but she
never admitted it. Do you know if she was cheating on him?"

It was a pivotal moment for me. My throat tightened. "I
don't think so. If so, she never confided in me." I told him
about her taking the waiter's number.

Riggs swore fluently. "I knew it. Why do you always defend her? If you'd have told me, I could have warned Patrick, and maybe he wouldn't be so damn broken up."

"I couldn't break her confidence," I said quietly. "I'm
sorry, Riggs. But I also don't want to get involved with Ava
and Patrick's relationship. It's their business."

He stared at me moodily, and I went to him, taking his

hands. "I think you're being hard on her because Patrick is hurting, and I don't blame you. But she tried, I know she did. It just wasn't meant to be, and at least he knows now, and not after they moved in and got more serious."

It took a while for him to let the topic go, but afterward, I noticed he tried to avoid talking with Ava at all costs, along with shooting her the occasional glare. And Ava noticed.

"Riggs is pissed," she stated, walking beside me. We headed into Starbucks for our fuel before I needed to work on some social media posts and she had an appointment with Chelsea to see a rental space. "He looks like he hates me."

I blew out a breath. "He's just being protective of Patrick."

"God, what does he want from me? Just because you both fell madly in love within a year doesn't mean I can."

We ordered Unicorn Fraps with nonfat milk and no whip, and moved up the line. "It'll blow over. I promise."

"It better. And I hope he's not the type to control your social life, or we'll have a bigger problem. I hate men who get all judgy about their girlfriend's bestie. It's worse that I'm single now. He'll be imagining me luring you into cheating on him."

Ava was known to get paranoid about Riggs, imagining him ruining our relationship. I'd learned to balance between them both, understanding I was lucky to have two people who loved me that much. I refused to have either of them upset. "Riggs isn't like that. He'd never try to come between us."

She shrugged and turned away. "Whatever. I'm tired of defending myself to him. He can think what he wants."

I tamped down an inner groan and grabbed our two drinks. "Stop. You're getting upset when nothing has happened."

"Fine."

A gasp interrupted us, and I turned to find two women staring at us with open mouths. "Holy crap. You're Maddie Heart! Oh my God, you look better in person. Wait—and you're Ava, her bestie!"

I swept my gaze over them, noting their chic outfits. Jeans, cute T's, designer sandals, and embroidered jackets that screamed fashion find. One was a ginger, the other a blonde, and they were regarding us like superstars. I had to remind myself quickly that my picture had begun to circulate more widely and I'd be recognized on a bigger scale. I immediately smiled and fell into social Maddie, the persona I needed to create in order to keep my fans and momentum. "Yes, I'm thrilled you recognized us. How are you?"

Her gaze gobbled up my outfit hungrily, then switched to Ava's. Thank God I never left the house in sweats anymore. I'd learned that every outing was an opportunity, and I was never to go out without a trendy outfit and my hair styled. Today, I sported a high ponytail, a skimpy black cami, and retro flare Betty Blues jeans with seventies wedges in bright yellow. The blonde spoke up. "We love your stuff. We got the Betty Blues jeans and it's the best pair I've ever owned. I'm obsessed with the way you style outfits."

"The new store you tagged in SoHo? I found the cutest items there."

"Who does your hair?"

"Where did you get your shoes?"

"Ava, I follow you, too. I love the pics with both of you. It's just like us—we've been friends since the fifth grade!"

"Can we get a selfie?"

The chatter continued, and a few people in the line began to murmur curiously, pointing at us. Ava and I shared a look and smoothly answered their questions, taking pics and tagging them live with #fossilfueltime #unicorndreams #maddiefinds.

We left as their excited voices melded together and walked a block in total silence.

Finally, Ava glanced my way. Her face was dead serious.

"How fucking cool was that?"

I began to laugh, and so did she. We linked arms and everything was good again.

I BOOKED MORE campaigns and got better. Levi got promoted and became my full-time handler. We began to grow closer with the amount of time we spent together, and I started to treat him more like a friend than a business associate.

Trendsetters was strict with what accounts I could take on. My contract gave them most rights, so I had to be careful of who I fought to represent, trying to choose only items that would boost my stats and visibility. Ava helped guide me, using her vast connections to pick unique brands that kept me ahead of the other influencers, so I became the one to watch for trends. She also piggybacked on vintage and retro items and helped me begin a series where I took older items and made them modern. I'd even made a few mentions in *Cosmopolitan* due to her support.

Combining work with pleasure kept me and Ava tight. She'd become a staple in my various shoots. The crew adored her when she stopped in, and my stylist already admitted she had a major crush. Ava would glide in looking fabulous, gifting out lattes and bits of gossip that fueled the tedious hours of camerawork.

My time became a shrinking commodity more important than money. There was little of it left. Riggs was also working nonstop, staying late to show his initiative, and got bit by the law bug. After diving deep into supporting the legal division, he was talking about going to law school to pursue a more dedicated career. Between our endless work hours and contradictory schedules, evenings together were few and precious. But we were dedicated to each other, and I never felt truly, deeply satisfied the way I did when I was with Riggs. He was my safe place. I longed for him if we spent too much time apart. He calmed me by the touch of his hand, but also elicited excitement. Being with Riggs was like a gentle roller coaster, lots of easy curves, better than average speed, and the occasional dip that kept things sexy and new.

My life was everything I'd dreamed it to be. We were young, passionate, and focused on our future. The most vibrant city in the world was our playground. When I imagined the girl in her bedroom, lonely, lost, while scrolling endlessly to connect with a world of beauty and light to finally feel alive, I wanted to go back and hug her. I wanted to tell her it would all work out in the end, even when things got hard. That Riggs and Ava and Chelsea were on the other side. That a career where people recognized and admired her was going to happen.

Looking back, I laughed at my naivete. I was so damn young; I didn't understand how fast things could change. How life could take away everything you treasure without warning. I was ill-equipped to deal with the fallout, but the years beforehand were so perfect, maybe it was silly to believe I'd have it forever.

Maybe that's exactly what youth was about—belief in happiness and immortality.

"THEY WANT ME to go to LA."

I watched Riggs's face with dread. I'd been keeping the news to myself for a bit, trying to figure out the best way to handle it. When the agency told me about an opportunity for a role in a movie, I thought they were joking. I was no actress. But then they said I'd be playing a fashion diva influencer, and they wanted to combine my walk-on role with an ad campaign. The movie was about a famed fashion model who went a bit mad from social media and began to kill people. It was horror and black comedy, and the director was an up-and-comer who wanted to create a parody regarding the current FOMO status of young people who didn't know what was fake and what wasn't.

I'd be out there for a month, and it was a huge opportunity I couldn't pass up. But the idea of leaving Riggs behind for so long hurt. I couldn't imagine not coming home to him, or sleeping wrapped in his arms. My days were a long tangle of incessant activity and being "on" constantly, which drained my energy. Riggs had a way of refilling my well, reminding me of what was real and what wasn't. Kind of like this new role I was supposed to play in the movie. It was actually ironic.

"What are you talking about?" He was getting undressed for bed and turned to face me in his black briefs. I admired his muscled body, my gaze greedily taking him in, happy he belonged to me. I never considered myself a jealous person, but I knew he was probably hit on at the firm. He looked too damn good in a suit for women not to want him.

"They want me to be in a real live movie, Riggs. I have this cameo and then I'd do an ad campaign for Ray-Ban, which is a sponsor for the movie."

He sat down on the edge of the bed, looking slightly shocked. "Babe, that's fucking amazing. I can't believe how big you've grown in the past months. Tell me everything."

I shared all the details, sketching out the movie and the schedule. "It's for a month, though."

"Well, it sucks for me, but it's a no-brainer for you. Besides, I'll be working nonstop. You might as well go and have some fun."

I reminded myself I wasn't asking for his permission, but I couldn't hide the relief his support gave me. Overcome with excitement now that he was on board, I pulled him down on top of me. "Have I told you lately I adore you?"

"No, but I'm ready to hear it now." He grinned, and we

began kissing. The usual spark lit and caught fire, until we were pulling off the rest of our clothes, and I arched in demand, frantic to feel him inside me. He whispered my name and I clung to his shoulders, tearing up as I looked into his beloved face. "I love you," I whispered, gazing deep into his eyes.

"I love you more. You'll always be mine, Maddie."

And I knew he was right.

We may have found each other early, but he was my soulmate.

THE NEXT DAY, I told Ava and Chelsea at lunch.

"Are you kidding me?" Chelsea shrieked in the middle of the restaurant. "Oh my God, you'll be a movie star!"

I laughed. "Not even close." I told them about the role. "I'll also be doing some photo shoots for Ray-Ban. Do you believe this is happening to me?"

"Yes," Ava said, her face glowing with excitement. "I'm not surprised. This movie is the perfect vehicle for you and you'll kill it. When do you leave?"

"Next week. My head is spinning."

"What did Riggs say?" Chelsea asked, picking up her fork again.

I spoke between bites of my grilled chicken Caesar salad. "He was so sweet. Didn't get upset that we'll be separated for a month."

Ava arched a brow. "Hope not. That would be a dick move."

I ignored her, knowing things were still strained between

them. "He's working his ass off and finally began applying to law schools. It's a good time for me to go."

Chelsea seemed to sense my hesitation. "You and Riggs are solid. You support each other, which is amazing. A month away isn't going to make a difference."

"Yeah, I know. I'll just miss him." I gave a sigh. "I'm a little freaked-out. Being alone in LA, on a movie set? Levi's coming with me, but he's paid to be there. God, what if I mess it all up? What if I suck and blow up my career?"

"Stop. You may make some mistakes but then you'll learn and nail it," Ava said firmly. She gazed at me for a few seconds, then slowly smiled. "I have an idea."

"What?"

"I'll come with you."

My jaw unhinged. "Excuse me? Are you kidding?"

"No, I mean it." Her blue eyes lit with fervor. "I'll be your support system. I'm not tied to the city—I can work anywhere, and I know a few people in LA I can catch up with. It will be amazing!"

My head spun, imagining my best friend with me. It would be an adventure instead of an intimidating experience. She knew how to calm me during shoots and could be my cheerleader. "Ava, this is unbelievable. Are you sure you can leave for a whole month? What about Chels?"

Chelsea gasped. "What about me? She needs to be with you! I'm copying Riggs; all I do is study and work. I'm boring as hell."

I cocked my head, concerned. "Are you and Ed still okay?"

"Yeah. It's kind of cool because we're both working toward the same goals. There's nothing sexier than spending a date studying for exams and drinking Red Bull. We've bonded more than ever."

I relaxed. "Good, you two are perfect together."

I caught sight of Ava's expression, a mix of judgment and doubt, but I swept it away. She'd always been vocal about not letting men dictate our lives, and consistently reminded us our core group was the most important relationship. I agreed on some level but also knew Ava wasn't madly in love like Chelsea and I were. Being the only single member in our group must be difficult, so I gave her tons of leeway and understanding. I never wanted her to feel left out just because she wasn't coupled up, but it was also hard knowing she was critical of Riggs.

"So, we're doing this? Taking over Hollywood?"

I turned to Ava, filled with gratitude and a sense of anticipation. Everything was better with her by my side, and once again, she planned to drop all she had going on to support me. Emotion lodged in my throat. I was so damn lucky.

"Hell, yes," I said.

Ava grinned.

"You better bring me back something epic," Chelsea said, shaking her head. "I'm talking impressive. Like Scott Eastwood's underwear. Okay?"

We laughed and began talking about what we were going to pack.

18

LA was a bit of a shock after New York.

I was used to a certain vibe being a New Yorker. There was a hurried purpose I'd perfected, amid the buzz of knowing you needed to cultivate your own persona and style in order to be recognized. Seasons dictated outfits and attitudes. Wealth was restrained and elegantly ignored. New York was the cool girl who reserved judgment until you proved yourself. From fashion, to politics, to business, you were used to being surrounded by the best, and what was said or promised better be delivered. Competition was ruthless but understated.

LA blasted me right from my comfort zone.

The weather was sunny and hot all the time. Everything was loud, from the endless sea of blonds, to the parties, to the conversations. Mansions were ostentatious, outfits were skimpy, and no one said what they meant. The first week passed in a blur of cocktail parties, meeting people who all held important titles, pitched me multiple ideas, and promised me the world. Then they'd press a business card in my hand, float away, and I'd never see them again.

Here, business was done by the pool in bikinis, and everything ran an hour late. Without Ava, I sensed I would've fallen apart. Imposter syndrome kicked in as I questioned my ability to run with so many well-known people and hold my own on the movie set. Sure, I was doing a small role, but I practiced nonstop, rehearsing my lines with Ava, and tried to pretend I was comfortable with the other actors and actresses.

Ava was once again in her element. She was a true chameleon, studying the room and becoming what was not only needed, but wanted. Her wardrobe became less severe and more Californian, with short, tight dresses and glittery accessories. She returned from a salon appointment with gorgeous blond streaks in her hair and a burnished golden glow to her skin. I moaned over my red hair, freckled white flesh, and awkward silences I still struggled with, but Ava reminded me I needed to be different here in order to stand out and that I had her to help.

And she was right. Under her protection, I began to navigate the LA social scene better. Ava moved among the parties with a big smile, making nice with everyone yet giving off a distant aura that attracted men to her by the masses.

We were at the director's house when everyone began murmuring about the new famous actress that just stopped by, but I noticed Ava's circle of admirers never budged. The actress eventually left in a bit of a huff. We giggled about it later by the pool.

"I heard she kept asking who you were," I said, perched on the end of a lounger. The infinity pool reflected the moonlight, and the view was stunning from the rooftop. The city was laid out in front of us, luxury homes scattered amid the hills. Eclectic groups merged in various circles, drinking cocktails, dressed to outdo, whether in glamorous evening wear or trendy activewear, a who's who list of important people looking to either use you to excel, or be used for a future IOU.

Ava rolled her eyes, stunning in a red jumper with a Chanel belt and matching shoes. She paired it with a puffer jacket from Rag & Bone, combining glamour with street wear brilliantly. "Like I care. She's got a reputation for being needy and you know how I hate that. How did today go?"

I lifted my chin with pride. "Nailed it. I have the next few days to breathe a bit, and now that my part was filmed, we may be able to go home early."

An odd expression flickered over her face, but it was gone too quickly to analyze. "I think we should stay the extra week. This is a great opportunity for you to get ahead of socials and connect with some new people. Who knows? Maybe LA will be bigger for you than New York."

I wrinkled my nose. "Hope not. I can't wait to get back."

"For Riggs?"

I shot her a look, but her tone was innocent. "Yes. I miss him. But more than that, I feel like the city is my home. This is a bit too much for me."

"Too?"

"Fake."

Ava nodded. "Yeah, it's a lot. But there are still a ton of possibilities we shouldn't leave behind. Plus, we need to play a bit and enjoy the beach. Have some fun."

I motioned to the trendy mansion we were partying at. "This isn't fun?"

Ava grinned. "It's still work. I'm talking me and you unleashed on our own terms."

"What did you have in mind?"

"Everything."

I laughed. A shadow fell over us, and I looked up to see Levi. He handed each of us a glass of champagne. "Ladies. Are you cooking up trouble?"

"Always." I slid over to make room, and he sat next to me. His thigh brushed mine. "Ava and I were just talking about staying till Friday instead of heading home. Would that be okay?"

"Of course. You have the hotel until then. Might as well take advantage of the sunshine and rest. Your schedule has been demanding, and you never complain." I studied him in the moonlight. We'd gotten closer this past month. With his new role, he was in charge of making sure my career was flourishing at the agency, being my go-to for bookings, travel, social calendar, and everything in between. He stopped wearing the fancy suits and adopted a more casual look, favoring rich fabrics such as cashmere, silks, or linen, mostly in black. Stuck for too many hours together waiting on photographers or companies, I began to depend on him more for support.

"Will you go back?" I asked.

Levi shook his head. "I'll stay. Button up some things here. Get you invited to a few more parties. Have you seen your last post? It went viral."

Ava gave a whoop and a high five. "Told ya."

I'd created a mock video where I did a fashion show on the diving board and Ava pushed me in. When I stripped off the layers, I was in the newest bikini from Beverly Beach, who I tagged even though they weren't an official sponsor. It was a free boost because I loved their swimwear. I'd brainstormed the idea, and Levi helped carry it out, using Ava as the catalyst. Ava took out her phone and looked at it, whistling low. "Holy crap, over a million views already. You're on fire, girlfriend."

Levi lifted his glass. "To fire. And the future."

I clinked glasses and he held my gaze. A tiny shiver raced down my spine at the sudden intensity, feeling trapped, and then I drank and turned, catching Ava's thoughtful stare. There had never been anything intimate about me and Levi, but I felt strange. I cleared my throat, then got up with a quick smile. "Excuse me for a sec. I'm going to call Riggs before it gets too late."

I walked away and didn't look back, but felt them both watching me.

I dialed his number. His voice was husky with sleep when he answered. "Hey. I'm sorry if I woke you. I just missed you."

"Hey, babe. It's okay, you're worth a little less sleep." I felt his smile, and my whole body relaxed and hummed with contentment. I pressed the phone closer to my ear like I could touch him. "What's going on?"

"At my director's party with Ava and Levi. We're finishing up soon."

"Good. You still flying back next Friday?"

Guilt stirred knowing I could be home earlier, but I pushed it away. "Yep, that's the plan. How's school?"

He filled me in on the details of his life. Usually, it helped make me feel closer to him, but tonight, I only felt a strange distance, more than the physical miles. As if he was steeping himself in his routine that had nothing to do with mine. I was used to reconnecting every evening, allowing our bodies to touch and share space, but each day that passed, it seemed like a piece of me was taken away. I couldn't share my thoughts or fears with Ava when it came to Riggs, so I just ignored them. But talking to him now, I longed to run my hand over his rough jaw, press my forehead to his, lean into his strength. Instead, I concentrated on his words and told myself it was only one more week apart. He spoke about school and the other students he bonded with amid the challenges. Patrick had also decided to go to law school, and spent the past week crashing at our place, both of them studying till late. I didn't like the idea of Patrick in my space, his voice in Riggs's ear, but stayed silent. When it was my turn, I spoke of fashion shoots and social media and parties in mansions where promises were made but never kept.

There was a short silence between us, heavier than usual, and then we said good night.

THE LAST WEEK in LA gave me a new appreciation for the West Coast as I discovered hidden treasures with Ava and Levi.

We hit the beach in Malibu and sunbathed on powdery sand, being entertained by volleyball games with half-naked men that gave me vibes of the old *Top Gun* scene. The ocean was completely different from the rough, hard edges of the Jersey Shore or Jones Beach. The place buzzed with activity, from bike riding to surfing, and beachgoers ranged from wearing fancy gown-like cover-ups and jewels, to tanks and denim shorts.

The three of us walked Malibu Pier and rode the Ferris wheel, while we indulged in cotton candy, then watched the sunset. We drank wine and held our breath as the dazzling colors merged and exploded while the waves crashed beneath. Days blurred into evenings as we dined in expensive restaurants and ate artfully plated health food, ending up either at a club or hosted party with night swimming, dancing, and pretending we didn't care about the celebrities standing in the same rooms with us.

Actually, I doubted Ava and Levi cared. It was definitely hard for me not to gape when I spotted Kendall Jenner and Timothée Chalamet in the crowd, though they weren't together. Eventually, I felt as if the limitless supply of alcohol, fabulousness, and sun affected my brain. Things were a bit fuzzy, and my usual nerves melted away with Ava and Levi flanking my side. I missed calling Riggs two days in a row, the time zone and my partying making me forget, but I'd be home soon, so I told myself not to worry.

One night, we hit a popular club where Paris Hilton used to DJ, seeking to lose ourselves in music and strangers and expensive drinks. I wore leather pants, a chain belt, a corset, and red boots, crimping my hair and painting my lips black. Sexy, animalistic sounds roared from the DJ, whipping the crowd into a fervor. The dance floor glowed like we were underwater, and at various times in the evening, waves of mist would explode around us, mixing with our sweat and creating a howl of approval.

I'd never allowed myself to be this free back home, and I took advantage of it by throwing myself into the experience.

Levi tipped his head back and laughed from the current wave of mist. "Have you ever been in a mosh pit?" he yelled into my ear.

I shook my head. "Never."

"It's sick. You lose yourself in the frenzy of people until only the music matters. It's like merging into the consciousness of the group."

"That sounds a bit scary."

He grinned, grabbing my hands and pulling me close. "Sometimes the best things are scary at first. You strike me as a risk-taker."

I snorted, but the sound got swallowed up from the music. "Not even close. Ava's the one who takes chances. I just follow her."

"I don't think so. I can't believe your creativity. That stunt with the pool and the way you're able to do things differently from everyone else? That's why you've become a sensation. People want to be around you."

I opened up my mouth to dismiss the compliment, but he surprised me by wrapping his arms around my waist and lowering his lips to my cheek. Stubble rubbed against my jawline, making me shiver. His voice was a rough demand. "Don't say it. Stop underestimating yourself."

I went to pull away, but the crowd pressed in tight and Levi made me feel safe. I leaned toward him instead and changed the subject. "Where's Ava?"

"Hooked up with that guy at the bar."

I'd suspected. She had her eye on him from the moment we walked in, and she got any man she wanted. "Good choice."

"Ava always makes good choices."

I smiled, noticing he was slurring his words, but so was I. A lovely, light fog enveloped me like the mist that floated down over us. I wondered how Levi could smell so good after all our dancing. His black T-shirt clung to his chest, slightly damp, but a delicious warm spice rose from his skin. A few inches separated us, and his fingers settled on my hips, guiding me into a small spin. I bumped into him, laughing. "What other good choices has she made?" I asked, teasing.

"Picking you as her best friend."

I poked his chest. "And Chelsea."

"And Chelsea," he repeated. "Also, she knows who can't be trusted. And she's able to pinpoint the right people to talk to in a room. It's like she has a sixth sense for success."

I agreed wholeheartedly.

"I mean, she knew you'd be famous even though you had no previous experience. When she called to have me reach out, I knew immediately you'd be special. And I was right!"

His words penetrated my mind but didn't make sense. Everything kind of spun together. I tried to grab onto a thread from his declaration, but then Ava joined us, handing out more drinks. "Guys! This is Max." She introduced him quickly, then pulled out her camera. "Get close!"

We smooshed together, and Levi had his arm around me, cheek pressed to mine, and I felt a goofy grin curve my lips as I stared into the camera. Then we drank more and danced more and Levi had to get me into the car, helping me back to the hotel. Lights flashed in my vision and I quickly shielded my eyes before the door slammed shut.

"Ava okay?" I asked with a groan, feeling everything spin.

"Yeah, she went with Max. Do you have to throw up?"

"Not yet."

I don't remember the car ride, or how I got into my room. I had a fleeting image of collapsing onto the bed, drinking some cold water, then falling into a pool of blackness where nothing existed.

I liked it there so I stayed a while.

WHEN I WOKE up the next morning, my head throbbed and even the silence felt loud.

I blinked and looked around. I was in my room, but not alone. Slowly, with growing horror, I turned and saw Levi in my bed.

The moan that escaped my lips hurt my ears. I stared at the large body under the covers, noticing his bare muscled chest, and his handsome face relaxed in sleep. Soft puffs of breath emitted from his mouth. His hair was mussed and stuck up in the back. The scene seemed to hit me all at once, and I fell into a panic, my hands patting my body to make sure I still had my clothes and underwear on. It was only when I confirmed nothing had happened between us that I fell back in relief.

God, what a mess. My memories of last night were a series of fleeting moments and snatched snippets of conversation. Ava had gone home with that guy and left us. Levi was probably so drunk he collapsed next to me.

Gingerly, I got up and hit the bathroom. I brushed my teeth, took some Tylenol, slipped on a robe, and trudged to the kitchen to make coffee. No room service right now. I didn't want to see anyone until I got myself together.

I used the powder cream they provided and sat down, sipping the hot brew. I grabbed my phone to text Ava, then noticed I had several missed calls from Riggs last night.

Shit.

I bit my lip, deciding to check in with Ava first. Hookups were fine, but safety was key. I typed out You ok?

I got the three dots right away. Yeah, a bit f—d up. You?

Same. Levi crashed here.

Thumbs-up emoji.

I finished my coffee then opened up my social media

feeds to check in. It was too early to call Riggs back, anyway. A headline caught my eye on the Gossip OK site, and I paused to read it. Then froze.

No. No, no, no.

I was there in the photo, shielding my eyes as Levi gripped my shoulders, holding me close. My corset had dipped so low one of my boobs was practically hanging out, and my hair had that tousled, messy look that looked freshly fucked. I was obviously drunk. **Influencer Maddie Heart parties hard with Ava Aldaine and new boy toy.**

My mouth fell open as I scrolled down to read the brief post, speculating on our affair and hinting I'd taken LA by storm since being cast in a movie. It was bad, but then I saw a bunch of other sites posting the same, along with a brand-new pic that made everything worse.

Ava, me, Levi, and the other guy on the dance floor. We looked high, though we hadn't done any drugs, and it definitely looked like Levi and I were dating. My ridiculous smile and Levi's lips on my face practically screamed hookup.

Fuck.

It got worse as I dug further. My feed was overrun with comments and speculation, and my follower count had risen dramatically. I prayed for the Tylenol to hurry up and work so I could come up with what to do next.

Footsteps echoed. I looked up to find Levi framed in the doorway. He'd put on a shirt, but his pants were unbuttoned and hung low on his hips. As he peered over his glasses, rubbing his bed head, I was surprised when my stomach jumped in a too-familiar way. Guilt snapped my gaze away.

His voice was husky with sleep. "Hey. Do you feel as crappy as I do? I need pancakes. I'll order room service."

I half closed my eyes. "Levi, forget pancakes. We're in big trouble."

He stared at me in alarm. "What happened? Is Ava okay?"

"Yes. Go look at your phone. Start with Gossip OK."

A tiny frown creased his brow as he grabbed his phone and began scrolling. I watched his face change while he read the story, wincing and shaking his head. "Damn. You've officially arrived, Maddie. The press is now following you around and you're clickbait. Congrats."

I gasped. "Levi, have you lost your mind? I have a boyfriend! Oh my God, Riggs is going to freak—this looks like we hooked up! And the pics are awful. I look drunk."

"Well, we were, and Riggs will understand if you tell him the truth. Hell, did you see how many followers you gained? You're on all the entertainment sites. This is huge, Maddie. You need to look at this differently."

I shook my head hard, then stopped from the sharp pain. "I don't know how you can think this is a good thing. It's not the truth!"

Years later, I remembered his response, and counted it as another turning point for me; the knowledge that life didn't necessarily fall into line with what you wanted. Sympathy flickered in his dark eyes, and his tone was grave when he spoke. "I'm sorry, but you need to get used to it. There's no truth to being in the public eye, Maddie. There's only perception." He paused, allowing his words to penetrate. "And if you want this career, and all that comes with it, you need to be okay with the bargain."

I sat silent, in shock with this statement I hadn't really thought of. How stupid. He was right, of course. Celebrities paid the price by dealing with paparazzi and a loss of privacy. I'd sought fame out, wanting more, and I got it. Just not in the way I imagined.

"I'll call up for breakfast."

I dropped my face into my hands. "What am I going to say to Riggs?"

Levi shrugged. "Tell him what happened. He'll either believe it or not. But he better get used to it, because this is what success looks like. This is what you've been working toward."

He walked back into the bedroom and left me alone.

A few minutes later, Ava called. "Did you see the press? You're blowing up—it's insane."

"I know. Ava, how did they get that picture you took?"

A few beats of silence. "I posted it last night."

I groaned. "Ugh, I wish you hadn't done that! Riggs is going to be upset with the way everything looks."

"Sorry, I was drunk and not thinking. But you have to admit it's great for your following. This is what you want, Maddie. With the part in the movie and this new campaign in LA, you're the new it girl. You should be excited and not worry what Riggs thinks."

I tried not to get annoyed, because I saw her point. But

she didn't understand how close Riggs and I were. How much I loved and needed him on a level she refused to accept. Ava was the one I went to with my problems, so it was hard she wasn't here to help or listen to me. She'd definitely taken on Levi's philosophy.

I wondered if I was the one not accepting reality. It may be time to have a serious talk with Riggs and warn him of what could be coming.

"Yeah, I know. I'm just a bit overwhelmed," I said.

"Totally get it. Did you have fun with Levi, at least? I'm glad he was looking out for you while I hung with Max."

The image of him waking up in my bed, half-naked, hit me full force. I reminded myself again nothing had happened and never would. I loved Riggs. "It's always nice to have someone hold your hair back when you vomit," I said, trying to lighten the mood.

Ava laughed. "I'm glad. He's good for you, Maddie. Not just for your career, but as a friend. He understands what you want to accomplish and wants to support you. It's hard to find that in a guy."

"Levi's great," I managed to say. "But I don't want anyone to think we're dating. It's not fair to Riggs."

"I get it. Hey, I'll come over in a bit and we'll talk. It's going to be okay. You're not used to this much attention, and it takes getting used to." Humor laced her voice. "Now, my stock is going up by being your bestie. I know the pics aren't the best, and you're stressed, but this is a good thing. Trust me."

"I do. Talk to you later."

I hung up. The sound of the shower echoed through the quiet room. I thought about what Ava and Levi said; I thought about what Riggs would think; I thought about my parents who didn't give a crap that I was on the home page of a famous site. Images of the girl I was mixed with this new identity. It was time I owned who I was becoming, and it was part of the world. I'd never truly belong to myself anymore, because I made a choice and wanted more. It was time to stop apologizing or worrying and fall into this fame hard. God knew how long it may last. I knew how fickle the public was, and to stay on top, I needed to keep upping my game.

A tiny part deep inside me began to slowly wither. That shy, scared girl couldn't exist any longer. I'd replaced her with a grown-ass woman who was taking the world by storm, on her terms. With that came payment.

So, I'd pay.

I picked up the phone again and called Riggs.

19

When I got back to New York, I felt like everything had changed.

We drove home from JFK Airport in darkness and drizzle. I was quiet, listening to the dialogue between Ava and Levi. A part of my brain kept circling around a comment from Levi on the dance floor that night, but it was still foggy. I sensed it was important, though, and had to do with Ava. But since the media storm blew up, things had been chaotic and I hadn't had time to really try and remember.

When I got home, Riggs was waiting. Our phone call had been strained while I explained the pictures looked misleading. He said he believed me, but his voice had been distant when we finally hung up. I decided to fly back home a day early and deal with my relationship.

Ava didn't fight me.

I dropped my luggage and moved across the room, and he held out his arms to me. The moment I was wrapped in his embrace, all the parts of my soul took a breath and exhaled. A sweet protectiveness flowed around me, and I snuggled close, inhaling the familiar scent of cotton and soap. "I missed you so much," I whispered against his chest.

"Me, too." He cupped my nape and kissed me, long and sweet, and I melted against him. My lips parted under his, and I moaned when he picked me up and walked into the bedroom. Pressing me into the mattress, I cherished the excitement he coaxed from my body, and surrendered to the sensations of his mouth and tongue and teeth, until we lay together naked, panting, and clinging to each other.

"I planned to talk first," he said, and I laughed, trailing my fingers down his carved bicep.

"I'm glad we didn't," I teased back, hooking my leg around his thigh. "This month was hard without you."

"Was it?" He lifted his head and looked at me. Uneasiness curled in my gut. "Because I didn't realize you finished up early and decided to stay."

Crap. I had been hoping he wouldn't find out. I kept my tone light. "It wasn't a big deal. The hotel and airfare were booked, and when Ava suggested staying, Levi said it would be easier rather than changing all the arrangements."

"Ava, huh? Why does she always seem to be in the middle of any problem we have?"

I sat up, pressing the sheet against my breasts. The melty, giddy state seeped away, and I stared at him with concern. "She's not. You can't blame Ava—I was the one who decided to stay. And I did miss you, Riggs. I'd been working nonstop and thought it would be nice to actually visit the beach and do some touristy things before I got home. That's it."

He gave a tight nod, but his gaze held a moodiness that made my heart clutch. "What about the club? Whose idea was that?"

"Why does it matter?"

He sat up, too, and rubbed his head. "Because Ava is single, and I think she'd rather you be, too. She's always the first to go with you anywhere, whether it's a weekend getaway or to LA. She's involved with your friends and your work and gives you the guilt trip if we try to spend time alone."

"Ava is one of my biggest supporters. I honestly think you're a bit paranoid. She hooked up with a guy at the club, but I stayed with Levi. It's not like we hang together and court strange men to buy us drinks. I like to dance and have fun, that's all."

"I'm not trying to take that away from you!" Irritation flickered over his hard features. "What about Levi?"

"He's my rep for the agency, but we're also friends. I told you on the phone there is nothing romantic going on with me and Levi. I love you."

"I bet Ava wants you to hook up with him. That way, she'd be able to have you to herself."

The flash of memory from our dialogue that morning hit me full force.

He's good for you, Maddie.

Still, that didn't mean Ava wanted to make trouble with

Riggs. She had her questions but had never tried to force me to date anyone else or set me up. She knew I wouldn't allow it.

Riggs continued. "Patrick told me how she works. She's manipulative. Do you know she used to find excuses not to go out alone with him when they were dating? She said it was more fun with all four of us. It's weird. And then she broke up with Patrick when the two of us decided to move in together. Like she realized she'd no longer have full access to you via him."

I gave a long sigh, shaking my head. "I should've known Patrick got in your head! He's been bitter since the breakup and hasn't moved on. How is that Ava's fault? I don't like you constantly hanging out with him."

"Well, he's my best friend and we're both in law school together. Plus, I can trust him."

"Ava's my best friend and has always had my back. You just can't see it."

We stared at each other for a while, the tension in the air thick. I hated fighting. A thick lump settled in my throat, and I wanted to reach out and touch him to make things right. But I wasn't about to sacrifice Ava because he wasn't comfortable. She meant too much to me.

Riggs muttered a curse. "I guess we can only try and respect each other's opinion. I'm not dumping Patrick and you're not dumping Ava. We'll all have to find a way to get along."

Relief blew threw me. I cuddled up to him and kissed his frowning mouth. "Exactly. I don't want to argue over something that's not going to change." He took my hand and pressed my palm against his cheek. "I need for you to understand, Riggs. Things might get intense now that those photos leaked. It means the press is following me."

"Isn't that what you wanted?"

I gave a half laugh. "Thought so. Just didn't realize they'd be up in my business over everything I do. I don't want you to get upset if we're out and followed, or if you see something that looks dramatic. Paparazzi love to use clickbait and false stuff. Will you promise you'll always check with me first?"

He studied me for a while, his green eyes somber. Then nodded. "I trust you. Don't you know you're the only one for me, Maddie?"

I leaned in and whispered I loved him. He pulled me close and the fire ignited all over again. A rush of confidence and joy hit, and I surrendered to the embrace. We were ready for any challenge thrown at us, and the month apart had proved it.

Riggs and I would only grow stronger.

"I MISSED YOU both so much!" Chelsea threw her arms around us and squeezed tight. We laughed and pretended to choke from her boa constrictor hug, then fought our way free to get to serious business: opening up the wine.

I'd decided to stop by Chelsea and Ava's apartment for a catch-up. It was a whirlwind week and I barely had time to check in with either of them. I watched Ava effortlessly uncork the bottle and pour into three crystal glasses etched with Swarovski crystals. "We hated being without you, too, Chels," I said. "We desperately needed some grounding."

Chelsea grabbed her full glass and settled on the stylish white couch that Ava had insisted on. Their place was trendy and comfortable, with high ceilings, polished wooden floors, and an open floor plan. There were two large bedrooms upstairs. They'd decorated the rooms in white and gold, and no one was allowed to eat Cheetos or drink red wine on the couch per Chelsea's strict instructions, so I'd brought Riesling.

"Ava filled me in on a lot, but I want your take. Tell me everything."

I spent the next half hour catching her up, and dropping some names that made her squeal. She asked about the pictures that were leaked, and I filled in my part of the story. "But it's a good thing, right?" Chelsea asked.

"Well, I wish I didn't look drunk off my ass."

Ava grinned. "You still looked hot! Gossip is all good in this business. How did Riggs take it?"

I studied her face but she looked honestly supportive. "We had some issues to discuss," I said carefully. "But we worked it out."

"Good," Chelsea said. "You two are relationship goals. A future lawyer and current movie star—the perfect match."

I choked on my sip of wine. "I had a walk-on role in a B movie."

"Did you like acting?" Chelsea asked.

I shrugged. "Kind of? It was such a small role, but I found it was a lot like modeling. Tons of time to set up, get everyone in place, with a lot of breaks in between. I was nervous, too; I didn't want to be the one to screw up. But it was very cool to be on a movie set and meet the actors and actresses. No one gave me a hard time for being an influencer and trying to act."

Ava spoke up. "She was a pro. We ran her lines nonstop and she stayed on set to watch everything. Who knows? Maybe she will be a movie star and we'll all walk the red carpet together."

We laughed and gossiped. Another part of me came alive surrounded by my friends. It was a part a bit separate from Riggs—different but just as important. Many people swore that a great marriage was based on marrying your best friend, but I wasn't sure. Maybe those people never had an Ava and Chelsea to fill in the gaps.

"How was it being with Levi for a month? You seemed pretty close in those pics."

I rolled my eyes at Chelsea's statement. "We definitely formed a bond. He's an amazing support system, and handled everything for me—I had nothing to worry about other than doing my work." I paused, thinking back on that morning when I woke up next to him. I was keeping that detail to myself. "He got close with Ava, too."

"He's a doll. I adore him."

The words brought up a memory, and suddenly, Levi's remark hit full force. What had he said about Ava? That she'd made a call to him about me? A tip? My stomach sank in dread at the possibility, but I had to confront Ava about it. I had to know.

"Levi actually said something to me in LA that I wondered about," I said slowly. "I meant to ask you about it, Ava."

She tilted her head. "Sure. What's up?"

I pinned her with my gaze. "He said you called him about me. That he knew you were talented at picking out successful people. Did you set this whole thing up? Did you call Levi and ask him to take me on as a client?"

I knew the truth immediately. She turned a bit white before blinking hard, as if trying to settle herself to answer. Disappointment crashed through me, along with shame. All this time I'd been insistent I'd succeed on my own, but it was a setup. Ava had used one of her connections to hook me up after all. She'd betrayed me.

"I can't believe it," I whispered, slamming down my glass. "Why? I told you I didn't want help!"

Distress poured from her figure. "Maddie, please listen to me. It's not what you think."

"Oh, how is it? Explain how you didn't lie."

Chelsea turned her shocked gaze to both of us, confirming she didn't know, either.

"I ran into Levi at a restaurant. We met a while ago and are friendly, so we ended up grabbing a drink together and he told me about this agency he works for and how he's on the lookout for new clients. Once he told me the vision, I knew you were perfect. But you've been so damn stubborn about me helping I didn't know what to do! So, I told him where you worked and gave your social media handle. Levi said he'd check you out but not introduce himself unless he sensed you'd be a good fit."

She paused, but I stayed silent, arms crossed in front of my chest.

"He loved you immediately—said you were the perfect client he'd been searching for. I knew you wouldn't even listen if you thought it came from me, so we agreed to pretend not to know each other beforehand. I'm sorry I lied."

My voice was tight when I finally spoke. "You knew how I felt about this! God, why can't you ever listen to what I want and respect my decision?"

"Are you really going to sit here and blame me for helping my best friend? I know you have pride, but that's just plain stupidity. You did it on your own, Maddie! All I did was give him your name. The rest was all you."

In some part of my brain, I knew she was right. But all I could think of was her and Levi keeping this a secret from me, making me feel stupid. "You should've told me the truth."

"I know, I made a huge mistake. I wanted to, but it never felt like the right time, and I knew you'd be mad. But can't you see? What if I had never mentioned your name? All of these opportunities from the agency helped get you to the next level. Are you saying you'd rather have me stay silent?"

I didn't want to think about it. Right now, all I wanted was to hang on to my anger and work through it on my own. I got up, ignoring both of my friends' protests, and walked to the door. "I need some time. The whole thing is fucked-up."

Chelsea jumped between us. "Guys, you can work this out. I understand how you feel, Maddie, but Ava was only doing it to help. She didn't want to hurt you."

When I looked back, I saw tears in Ava's eyes. I swallowed hard and shook my head. "Not now. I gotta go. I'll talk to you later."

I ran out of the apartment. All I wanted to do was talk to Riggs.

RIGGS WATCHED ME pace back and forth as I told him the story. My nerves were jagged as I tried to sort it all out and decide what part upset me the most. I kept going back to Ava's decision not to tell me, whether she thought it was for my own good or not. Riggs agreed.

"Look, her intentions were good. She wanted to help you. But you had a right to know how this all came about. How can you ever trust her again? Or even Levi?"

"Exactly. How could she keep this from me? She had plenty of opportunity to tell me, even when we were in LA together." I blew out a frustrated breath. "I kept telling Ava not to use her contacts because I wanted to do this myself. Did Levi really see something in me or did he just decide to do Ava a favor? Has this whole experience been preplanned? Am I really getting these jobs myself?"

He cut his hand in the air. "Babe, I don't think that has anything to do with it. I'm sure Ava only got you an introduction. You did the rest on your own."

"How do you know?"

His smile warmed my heart. "Because I've seen you in front of a camera. You come alive. You're drop-dead gorgeous and smart and fun. No way are they giving you pity jobs to make Ava happy."

I began to relax. He sounded confident and calm, which helped take me down a level. Ava was texting me nonstop with apologies and memes, begging me to call her back. Chelsea did the same, obviously trying to defend Ava. I ignored them.

"What should I do?"

Riggs got up from the couch and snagged his arms around my waist, pulling me close. I rested my head on his shoulder. "I think you should take a break from Ava. Don't you wonder what else she's lied about?"

I tried not to stiffen. Yes, there were things I'd questioned before.

Yet . . .

I remembered those nights where I wanted to give up, feeling out of my element and lost. Ava never let me stay in that headspace. She knew exactly how to lift my spirits, consistently supporting and pushing me in the right direction. She'd leave me inspiring text messages and force me to do brand-new posts. She'd accompany me to new stores and go exploring with me, making me laugh. Chelsea had always helped, too, but Ava was my core person, the one who showed up daily to say she believed in me.

I'd had no one else. Did she deserve to be judged when she only wanted to help? And she'd run into Levi coincidentally—it wasn't as if she sought him out or made specific phone calls trying to find me an agency. It was a twist of luck and fate and Ava's determination to see me succeed.

Yes, she lied, but I understood trying to avoid conflict. Would I have done the same?

Maybe. I'd never know.

I leaned into his strength. "I'm not sure. But I don't want to punish her, either."

"Give yourself a little time. God, she's always pushing. She's already texted you a million times. Sometimes, I think she's only happy when you're under her control."

I pulled away and tilted my chin up. "That's not true. Why do you sound . . . jealous?"

Irritation flickered over his features. "I'm not jealous, I'm concerned. You have no idea how you are with her. She calls and you jump, no matter what you have to drop to obey."

I took a step back. "That's ridiculous! Why are you acting like this now?"

He held my stare, then shook his head. "Forget it. I didn't mean it, got carried away."

I still felt uneasy from his verbal attack. "Look, I know you're not a fan of Ava, but I wanted to talk this out. I need a neutral opinion."

"Okay, sorry. But my advice still stands. Take some time to be by yourself. I'm not saying drop her as a friend. I think a little distance may put things into perspective."

Slowly, I nodded. "You're right."

He reached out to touch my cheek. "We need to spend more time together. Our schedules suck. Why don't we go out tomorrow morning? I don't have study group until the afternoon. Breakfast?"

I wrinkled my nose. "Brunch?" I loved sleeping in on a Saturday, and he loved being up at sunrise.

He laughed. "Sure, I'll pay extra for eggs and bacon since it's a few hours later and they serve champagne with it."

I hit him playfully on his arm. "It's still better."

He kissed me. "Come to bed. But first send your text."

I watched Riggs disappear into the bedroom and scooped up my phone. The messages verged on desperation, and even though I was still mad, my heart twinged a little at causing her to be so upset. I quickly drafted a text to both of them saying I was okay, and that I just needed some time to think and that I'd contact them when I was ready. I even put in a heart emoji so they didn't freak out.

Chels texted a thumbs-up. She knew it wasn't about her anyway.

Ava remained silent.

I bit my lip, waiting a minute for her response, but nothing came. After a while, I pushed the issue out of my mind. I'd listen to Riggs and take a break from Ava's drama. I'd also have a heart-to-heart with Levi and tell him how I was hurt he didn't tell me the truth. Eventually, it would work out.

I went to bed and lost myself in Riggs's body, his taste, his smell. It was my favorite place to go because there was nothing else to think about other than pleasure.

I was learning some addictions were well worth the price.

20

When I was in high school, I lived a lonely existence with only my dreams for company.

In college, I was introduced to a brand-new life. Suddenly, I had best friends, a vibrant social life, and a burgeoning career that held endless possibilities.

What I didn't account for was how things changed with age. Being in school gave me direction and a goal to focus on: graduation. It was exciting and free but there was still a level of comfort and security in knowing you had to show up for classes, complete homework, and pass tests. I liked the structure of it all.

Afterward, we created our own set of rules, and sometimes, it caused confusion, chaos, and occasionally, pain.

Chelsea passed all of her exams and made a name for herself at Wealth Planning Industries. They asked her to stay on and offered a promotion, which she decided to take until she was ready to open up her own business. Ava tried to convince her to jump sooner, but Chels wanted to have a bigger nest egg behind her and more experience. But she worked on preliminary ideas with Ava and decided to name her company Freedom Finance.

She'd also changed her mind about focusing solely on work. Chelsea announced her engagement to Ed over dinner, flashing her diamond while Ava and I bawled. They'd set the wedding for August at the South Street Seaport. We reminisced about the night in Italy where we skinny-dipped and made a blood pact. Now, the first of our group was getting married, and we were just as tight as ever.

I finally forgave Ava after she showed up at my place and tearfully begged for my forgiveness. I just couldn't keep being mad at her when I knew she had my best interests at heart.

Ava moved into her own place—a trendy loft in Tribeca—and exploded her business. She was in continuous demand for her consult work on leveraging social media, and would take over stagnant brands to revamp their platform. She was constantly dating new men who made the home page of most Internet sites—from actors to Wall Street finance moguls and the occasional politician. Gabriella had moved in with Ava's father and wore an engagement ring, but Ava refused to visit. The strained relationship with her dad made me sad for her, but she was too stubborn to see reason. He'd visit her in New York and they'd go out, but she said it wasn't the same since he'd been hijacked by Gabriella the Hun. In her words.

Riggs and I began having issues. Law school was more demanding than we imagined, and when my career took off after the movie released, neither of us knew how to handle it. Suddenly, paparazzi followed us, blinding our vision with photos, and shouted questions that were rude. Magazines still ran articles on Levi being my secret lover. Riggs hated every moment and said he felt stalked.

I'd curated a bit of a cult following after the fashion movie and commercials that flooded digital media. I was offered a cover shoot at *Cosmo*, and Ava laughed and said she had nothing to do with it. She'd left the magazine years ago and swore she didn't use her contacts, but I didn't care because it was another bucket list item. My agency had me on constant jobs, moving from social media to modeling to new offers for movies I still didn't understand. I guess my part made the audience laugh and want to be me, the perfect combination for profit in Hollywood.

Riggs and I worked hard to see each other and manage our calendars, but it was getting more difficult. Our different worlds had begun to put a crack in our solid foundation. He spent a lot of time with Patrick, the other law students, and the business partners he was trying to impress at his company. It was a buttoned-up type of environment, with suits and legal jargon and too many handsome, charismatic white males.

My career brought me into a more eclectic world, spanning diverse people I learned from and fascinating icons who'd created fashion or social media empires. When Riggs and I were alone, I still felt he was the other part of myself. But when we got together with his friends or mine, we found ourselves on opposite sides, even slightly mocking the other for our staunch opinions. We began to fight. To blame each other. To accuse.

He still didn't like Ava, and I still believed Patrick poisoned his mind. Levi added another layer to our problems.

Riggs didn't trust him.

The trust deteriorated over time. Too many late nights spent at parties with Levi and Ava. Too many phone calls and trips and comments from me about Levi. I'd begun to lean on him for all my needs at the agency, until even I admitted I'd be lost without him. We built a friendship from the ground up, and I began to be a part of a new foursome—me, Levi, Ava, and Ava's latest boyfriend. Unfortunately, Riggs said it was suspicious, and blamed Ava for the maneuver, even though I told him she couldn't have manipulated the situation.

I began to feel uneasy around the man I loved, waiting for a comment, phone call, or gossip site to stir up a fight. I fought to get back to the ease we had before, but it seemed the more effort I put in, the more distant we became.

It began affecting my job. I became distracted on set, and moody at events, snapping occasionally at my followers or people wanting something from me. I was drained from my very heart and soul and didn't know what to do.

One day, Levi told me to come into the office for a meeting. I was surprised at his formality, but when I got into the conference room, I noticed he had a serious expression on his face, and not the usual affable smile. He wore a casual suit with red suspenders, tailored black pants, and the newest Chuck Taylor All Star sneakers that cost big bucks.

I tried to break the tension. "You look hot," I teased, leaning back in my chair. "Are you here to tell me I scored the new Nike campaign?"

He didn't laugh. Just gave a sigh and sat next to me, tapping his finger against the polished mahogany. "Madison, I'm worried about you. Your head hasn't been in the game for a while, and we need to fix it."

"Madison, huh? This is serious."

His brow creased in a deep frown. "It is. We got an offer for you that's life changing. But it won't work like this."

I cocked my head with interest. "An offer? What kind?"

"A movie. A part specifically created for you. It's a comedy where you play the best friend of Amy Schumer."

I gasped as shock waves vibrated through my body. "Are you kidding me?"

"No. It takes place at a big fashion house—kind of a spoof on *The Devil Wears Prada*. You're the fashionista in charge of makeovers. It's an amazing role, but there's a lot that goes into it, and I'm not sure you can handle it right now."

I shifted in my seat and tried to focus. "Tell me and I'll make that decision. Not you."

A ghost of a smile hit his lips. "That's who I need, not the mopey, sad version of you these past few weeks. You'll need to go to LA for six months. We got you another booking for XOXO fashion so you'll be busy. We're also hoping for the cover of *InStyle* with a shoot in LA." He paused, considering. "This can launch you to a whole new level. If that's what you still want."

I stared at Levi, my brain madly clicking over all the possibilities. A real movie. LA. Another cover shoot.

More fame. More fortune. More . . . everything.

I shook from the inside and wondered if it would be enough for my parents to call. A hot flush of shame hit me at the thought. Still desperately trying to get them to love me was pathetic. I needed to move on.

This would help.

I cleared my throat and dragged myself back to the present. "I want it."

Levi finally smiled. "Thought so. We have a lot to talk about." He reached in his briefcase and removed a fat folder. "Here's the script. You'll need to fly out for a test shoot, and if that goes the way they expect, you go in a month. I sent it digitally, too. I'm assuming Riggs will understand?"

I wanted to hang my head with defeat because I already knew the answer. Could this be the straw that finally broke us? But didn't all couples go through challenges, especially when they were working on advancing their careers? It was a temporary block we could push through if we both wanted it badly enough. I know I did. I just had to be sure he did.

I couldn't lose him.

"He'll understand. We'll make it work."

"If he loves you, he will." My gaze caught and held with Levi's. For one brief moment, I caught the flare of want in his eyes; a raw hunger that thrilled me on a feminine level as much as it terrified me. But it was quickly banked and he was back to being my friend and business representative.

And I pretended I didn't see it.

I left the conference room, sensing I was at a crossroads. I just needed to be careful about which road I chose.

21

I can't believe I'm getting married this weekend!"

I laughed and hugged Chelsea, loving the way she practically glowed with happiness. The three of us were gathered at Ava's place for a cocktail before the weekend festivities began. The rehearsal dinner was tomorrow, and the wedding on Saturday. Then she was off on her honeymoon in Mexico for the week. When I asked her why not two, she'd laughed and said both of them were too busy at work. But she didn't look sad when she said it. There was a camaraderie between her and Ed that was truly special. They were both proud workaholics and had a shared vision for the future. Throughout the years, they'd managed their calendars and fun time, sticking together.

The way Riggs and I used to be. I mourned for it, missing him so much sometimes it became a physical pain. Too many nights he came home late and didn't reach for me. Too many nights I allowed it, feeling resentful.

I needed to fix things.

Ava brought out a charcuterie board filled with goodies,

and we dived in, sipping rosé and going over every detail of the wedding. Ava and I were co-maids of honor, and Chelsea had mercifully picked black dresses, sleek and classic with a low, sexy back. It was actually a dress I could wear again which made it . . . priceless.

We gossiped and chatted and got wonderfully tipsy. Chelsea turned to Ava. "Are you still taking Xavier as your date tomorrow or did you change it again?" she teased. "I've had to cross off names three times so now I just put GUEST."

Ava laughed. "No, I'm still with Xavier. Except I'm not sure how long it will last." She pursed her red lips. "My father would adore him. He keeps mentioning your wedding, Chels, and how I need to settle down and get serious. Like I'm about to get married because he expects it." She rolled her eyes.

I looked at her with sympathy. "Are you both still having trouble?"

"Gabriella the Hun strikes again. He refuses to see how she's ruining our relationship. I may need to push him a little harder to see the truth."

Chels shot me a concerned look and quickly changed the subject. I spoke up. "Why isn't Xavier the one to settle you down and impregnate you with lots of babies?"

Ava laughed. "He's way too good for me. He helped fund a charity for kids with disabilities, and does tons of pro bono work. Eventually, he's going to find out the only help I've given to the world is decorating it with fashion."

I bumped her elbow. "Stop! You help anyone you encounter and you're a treasure."

"Agreed," Chelsea said. "He's lucky to have you."

"You guys are the best. I swear, I'd be lost without you both." We stilled at the catch in her voice. She shook her head and dabbed at her eyes. "Sorry, I'm so emotional. It's our first wedding in the group, and I feel like it was just yesterday we made our pact. We were so young."

"We're still young," I reminded them. "And we have two weddings ahead of us, so let's just enjoy this one for now."

Chelsea cracked up. "Maddie, what's going on with you? We both noticed you've been a bit down lately, but we didn't want to push." Sympathy flickered in her eyes. "Anything you want to talk about?"

In the warmth of a rosé buzz and flanked by the two people I trusted most, I decided to tell all. "I'm going to LA again. I think I got a part in a new movie. And I'm terrified I'm going to lose Riggs."

And then the words poured out of me in a torrent. I told them about how my relationship was having trouble, that I was terrified if I left for LA we wouldn't make it. When I was finished, my entire being felt lighter. They both grasped my hands and I didn't feel alone anymore.

"I can't believe all of this is happening to you," Chelsea said. "No wonder you're a mess. But I know you and Riggs will work this out. There's no way you can turn down LA, and I'm sure he'll agree."

"Chels, how do you make it seem so easy with Ed? I feel like I'm not doing something right. You both work constantly and pulled it off."

"Sweetie, it's different for us. We work in the same business and want the same things. Both of us lead a pretty boring life and it's exciting for us. You have a different challenge—you're in the public eye, you travel, and law school is one of the most demanding things a person goes through. Riggs is stressed-out and probably scared. You need to give yourselves a break."

"Yeah, maybe you're right. I'm in my head way too much." I forced a laugh, then looked at Ava. "What do you think?"

She took a while to answer, and I could tell she was thinking hard about what to say. The whole time, she squeezed my hand, and I leaned into the comfort. "I'm afraid what will happen if Riggs doesn't understand," she said softly. "Believe me, I want to see you both happy. But if he gives you an ultimatum, what will you do?"

I sucked in my breath. Tension tightened my muscles. "He wouldn't do that."

"And if he does? God, Maddie, I'm sorry, but I just don't want to see you give up an amazing opportunity for a guy who's still in law school. If he's meant for you, he'll be supportive. It's only a temporary long-distance relationship. I want you to know this in your heart before you talk to him. That's all."

Shocked, I processed her remarks, and though my initial instinct was to lash out at her for doubting Riggs, I saw where she was coming from. I also knew Riggs would never do that. He'd see the big picture and we'd fight for each other. That's what our relationship was about.

"I appreciate it, Ava. I do. But I know Riggs, and he'll always have my back."

She nodded and released my hand. "Good. That's all I wanted to say. Now, let's focus on having the best weekend of our lives! To Chelsea!"

We clinked glasses and kept our talk to happier things.

I WALKED INTO the bedroom and stopped. Riggs stood in the mirror, and I froze at his reflection.

God, he was sexy. He was trying on his suit for the wedding. The sharp navy blue pinstripe tailored material emphasized his broad shoulders and strong thighs. The red tie was a narrow silk. Cuff links sparkled at his wrists. He turned to the side, checking the fit, then caught my reflection in the mirror and smiled.

My heart stuttered on cue. It always amazed me how easily I responded to him, as if I'd been made to be his. "Hey, baby."

He reached out his hand and I walked over, standing close to him. I studied our mirrored image, noting how well our bodies melded together, hip to hip, feet turned toward each other, my hair brushing his cheek, his clean scent rising to my nostrils. "Hey. You look good."

He laughed. "Wanted to make sure all those nachos I've been indulging in didn't cause me issues. This is my favorite suit."

"Mine, too." I enjoyed the simple peace of the moment and how the energy flowed between us. I wanted to steep myself in it and enjoy him, but it was time to tell him everything. "I was hoping we could talk before you head out. I was going to wait until after the wedding, but you deserve to know now."

His face tightened. "Doesn't sound good."

"It just depends on the way you look at it," I said lightly.

Riggs took in a deep breath. "Go ahead."

"I have an opportunity to do a movie in LA." I told him the details, then walked over to the dresser drawer and pulled out the script. "It's really good, Riggs. I'd love for you to read it."

He glanced down but didn't pick it up. His voice was controlled yet distant. "You're right. Sounds like it can be great if I look at it like you."

I tried not to wince. "What does that mean?"

He rubbed his head and muttered something under his breath. "Maddie, I don't know what to say. Am I happy as hell that you got a movie and more work? Yes. Am I thrilled that your career has exploded and your dreams are coming true? Yes. But forgive me if I'm not jumping for joy that we'll be apart for months again, when we barely see each other now when we live in the same apartment."

"I know, but it's temporary, and maybe it will give us both time to focus on our work without feeling guilty?"

Ice chilled his tone. "I didn't know I inspired guilt in order for you to see me."

"Don't do that! Don't twist my words; you know what I mean." I'd meant to hold my temper and be calm. I was going to be the most understanding, patient girlfriend ever, but the weeks of stress and worry made me snap. "Why are you doing this? I know it sucks—I don't want to be away from you, either—but can't we just agree it will be hard for a while but we'll be stronger when I get back?"

"Is Levi going with you?"

I jerked, then glared. "Yes. Of course."

"Then I guess you won't be lonely like me."

"Thanks so much, Riggs. For all the support. And the trust."

"Maddie—"

I stormed out and didn't look back.

THE WEDDING WAS magical.

Chelsea floated down the aisle in a gorgeous Vera Wang gown with a big-ass train that confirmed she always secretly wanted to be a princess. She sparkled in pearls and bling without apology, and I loved the way our own classic dresses complemented her look.

My heart was full of joy for Chelsea. Their vows still echoed in my mind, their promises to each other. Riggs and I didn't talk about LA. We dropped the subject and got ready for the wedding in silence, occasionally chatting with politeness until we merged with the wedding crowd. Then our social faces were firmly on, and no one could tell our relationship was slowly dying for every minute we didn't try and talk to each other.

I forced myself to dance and laugh and drink. Ava showed up at the wedding alone, much to Chelsea's distress, saying they'd gotten into a horrible fight and broken up the night before. With Ava, you never knew, but after checking in on her mental state, we both agreed she was fine.

Better than fine. She seemed almost gleeful, taking on her maid of honor duties with relish. Before long, she was being sought out by Chelsea's cousin, who looked half in love with her, and Ava danced with almost every male at the wedding. Married and single.

I watched Riggs from the corner of my eye. He sat at the back table, smiled, and chatted when people came over to him, but kept his perch. His glass was always full, and when I noticed he was drinking tequila instead of his usual beer, I knew trouble was on the way. Every time Ava floated in his line of vision, his gaze narrowed with a resentment that made me slightly sick.

The thought of another fight tortured me. I kept my distance and did an occasional check-in to make sure he was okay.

Everyone had booked local hotels for the night, and a bus picked us all up after the wedding to bring us there. Chelsea and Ed had already made their exit and were on the way to the airport for a red-eye to Mexico. I squeezed on with Ava and Riggs, ignoring his moody silence, and trying to tune in to Ava's drunken chatter. When we got to the hotel, everyone scattered, but Ava dragged both of us toward the bar.

"One last drink to celebrate," she sang. Firmly linking her arms in ours, she ignored my weak protest and sat us at a set of lounge chairs. "On me. Maddie, wine?"

I made a face. "Just seltzer, please."

She rolled her eyes and looked at Riggs. "Tequila," he clipped out.

"Nice choice."

She was at the bar ordering our drinks when I leaned over. "Can you at least pretend to be sociable? God, it was my best friend's wedding and I had to spend it fighting. Why are you acting like this?"

I waited for a cutting remark, but instead, he held his hands to his temples and stared at me with a raw devastation that stole my breath. "Because I'm losing you." His voice caught. "Because I already did."

"Here we go!" Ava set down the drinks and took the seat next to me. "So, what'd you think of the wedding?"

Riggs took his tequila and stood up. He swayed on his feet. "I can't do this right now. I'm getting some air."

He walked away. Ava looked taken aback. "What happened?"

I was drained. Everything inside of me surrendered and hurt, and all I wanted was to crawl into bed and sleep and figure it out in the morning. The pained way he'd said those words haunted me. I couldn't let him think I wanted to break up. I needed to show him how important he was to me. I needed to choose him.

"I may say no to LA."

Ava's jaw dropped. "What are you talking about?" she hissed. "Did he threaten you? God, Maddie, I knew it. I fucking knew it."

I shook my head. "You don't get it. He's upset, but it's not about LA. It's about how things have been lately and how he's dropped to the bottom of my list."

"That's how it's supposed to be when you're becoming famous! Why can't he let you shine for a while? Why can't he take a back seat and do the heavy lifting?"

I couldn't think or defend. I took a gulp of seltzer and faced her. "I love him, Ava. With everything I am, and he needs to know that. He needs to know I'll choose him, and then he won't need to ask me."

"That makes no sense."

But it did to me. I opened my mouth to try and explain, but her sudden words held an edge of venom, making me freeze.

"I knew he'd destroy you because of his selfishness. But I didn't think you'd let him take away everything we worked so damn hard for this easily!"

The word *we* shot out at me like a cannon.

I waited a few beats, then leaned over, gave her a kiss on the cheek, and stood up. We were drunk and emotional, and now wasn't the time to hash it out. Besides, it was between Riggs and me. And my final decision. Somehow, she'd need to accept it.

"I'm going to bed. I'll talk to you about it tomorrow, okay?"

She let me walk away. I got to my room, undressed, and crawled into bed. I'd wait for Riggs and then we'd talk the way we should have. I'd make it right for both of us.

I fell asleep.

22

When I woke up in the morning, Riggs wasn't there.

I grabbed my phone to check for messages, but he hadn't contacted me. Rolling out of bed, I tried to clear my head and think of where he could be. Did he come back last night and I never woke up? Maybe he just left early this morning? God, I hope he didn't wander around drunk somewhere and pass out.

I texted him and called. When I got voice mail, I left him a message saying I was worried and just to call back.

I brushed my teeth and got dressed, but when I still heard nothing, I decided to go look around. I'd start with the breakfast buffet.

I closed the door behind me. Maybe I should check with Ava quickly since she'd been the last one to hopefully see him. I stopped at her room and knocked but no one answered. Probably still asleep.

I bit my lip, then fished out the extra key she'd given me

just in case. Ava told me she'd once gotten drunk and lost her key, so now she always gave someone a copy in case she needed it rather than having to go to the front desk. I slipped the key card in the reader and saw the light go on. Then I opened the door.

A heavy scent filled the dark room. I shook my head, seeing the tiny bottles from the minibar laid out. Poor Ava, she'd continued the party late into the night. I wrinkled my nose and stepped farther in, noting the sprawled figure underneath the covers. "Ava," I called out softly. "It's me. Are you awake? I want to ask you something."

The figure moved. A low mutter rose in the air.

I moved closer to the bed and noticed there was another body next to her. Of course. Only Ava would be able to pick up a hot guy at a bar at 2 a.m. I decided to back up slowly, not wanting to disturb them, and caught the familiar waves of blond hair against the white pillow.

It was as if I was watching my body from above, taking in every detail of the scene.

The tiny steps closer. The flash of a naked leg. The glimpse of a bare, hairy chest lifting softly up and down. The way I peered over the bed for a closer look, knowing who was there, knowing what I'd see, screaming from outside myself to turn back and run and pretend I never went into that room.

But of course, it was too late.

Riggs was in Ava's bed.

The full realization slammed through me at the same time his eyes fluttered open.

I met the jeweled green of his stare. He blinked. Groaned. Reached out to touch the sheets, as if he had forgotten he was there. Ava moved, and the blanket fell, revealing her naked breast. I kept staring at Riggs, wondering what would happen next, wondering why I still couldn't move.

"Maddie?"

He sat up. I saw the exact moment he realized I knew.

His eyes widened with pure horror. My vision pulled back from him, and I noticed the other things in the room. Ava's black lace panties. Riggs's pants crumbled on the floor. The scent of sex wafting in the cramped room. The littered bottles stained with Ava's lipstick. One stiletto peeking out from under the chair.

"Oh my God, Maddie—wait! Let me explain!"

I walked backward, stumbling, but as he began to move, the silence broke through me and I screamed. "Stay away from me!"

Ava woke up and jumped halfway off the bed. Her gaze caught me and she gasped, and then a savage cry ripped from her lips, almost like an animal in pain, and she was yelling my name over and over.

And then I was out the door and running and running until I couldn't run anymore.

23

AFTER

I stared up at the familiar villa.

Sunlight seeped into the pale yellow structure and bounced off the arched windows. Colorful flowers exploded in full bloom, dripping down from the multiple wrought iron balconies and encircling the foundation. People milled about the grounds, busily trimming the landscape, setting up furniture, and rushing back and forth with hands full of large platters.

Ava invited me to stay in her home with Chelsea, but I insisted on checking into a hotel. I couldn't pretend things were the same, and I refused to sleep in the same bedroom where she and I had once laughed and held hands and shared secrets.

I'd been invited to lunch with both of them before the official wedding activities began. It'd be a jam-packed few days, but I'd already decided if it was too much, I'd just stay at the hotel and keep my attendance only to the wedding.

I took a step forward, and memory dragged me back to the first time I was here, sandwiched between my best friends, excited to spend the holiday weekend at Ava's family home. It felt like a lifetime ago, and it was, because I didn't recognize the girl I'd been with Ava and Riggs; the girl that looked at the world with stars in her eyes, secure she'd found everything she'd been looking for.

I was surprised at the pain. Mostly, the past was firmly put out of my mind, and any reminders brought numbness; a scabbed-over wound that held the occasional pinpricks but no real teeth.

But now, I almost doubled over with emotion, standing by the dock, waiting for Antonio to come rushing out to greet us, caught in the past and present like a spider crawling to freedom before getting stuck in a web.

I dragged in a shaky breath and reminded myself I'd chosen to come. Besides the shitstorm I left behind in New York, my soul was too bruised to go on. I needed to heal, and there was only one way to do it.

Face Ava.

Face my past.

Tilting my chin up, I walked along the path, nodding to the workers who called out *ciao* in greeting. My palms grew damp with nerves, and as I neared the door, I almost turned back and ran away. Almost.

Because Ava was suddenly in front of me and everything else fell away.

We stared at each other. My breath caught at her beauty—somehow, she'd grown even more stunning. She'd gained some weight, and her body took the extra pounds and transformed them into lush curves. Her hair was a few inches shorter, framing her heart-shaped face in gentle waves that gave off a softer look. Golden brown skin glowed with health, but it was her eyes that held me prisoner, a hypnotizing cerulean blue that used to flash a myriad of intense emotions, but now reminded me of the lake—calm, deep, with a clear crystal light that reflected a quiet joy.

I stood, frozen, trying to accept this new Ava who was now a stranger to me. Her red lips opened, and I heard my name whispered in the breeze, carrying gently to my ears.

"Maddie."

She raced forward with her usual grace, and before I could decide how I wanted to react, her arms were around me, holding me in a tight hug.

One second passed. Two. Three.

Of their own accord, my hands lifted and I embraced her. The scent of rosemary mint tickled my nose from her hair along with her earthy cologne, wrapping me in memories. I held her close, shutting my eyes, and allowed myself to remember.

When she pulled back, her eyes brimmed with tears, but she furiously blinked them back, letting out a half laugh. "I can't believe you came. I'm so happy. You look amazing. Like a true movie star."

I'd chosen my own outfit carefully, needing a proper amount of armor. My sleeveless wrap top was in my signature color of emerald green, emphasizing my toned arms, obtained from too many hours at the gym. Slim white pants kept the look clean and classic. I'd done my hair in a French twist with a few strands framing my face. I looked grown-up and composed, as if the drama of the past couldn't touch me.

I shook my head. "Not even close, but thanks. You're the one who looks beautiful."

She flashed her signature smile, full of warmth and ease, waving her hand in the air. She wore a long maxi dress in bright yellow floral that hugged her bust and hips. Her feet were clad in gold strappy sandals. She looked chic and elegant. "Not even close! I gained a bunch of weight, which doesn't surprise me, because all Italians love to do is eat, drink, and nap."

I smiled back, and for a little while, it was just like old times, and there was nothing bad between us. I wished I could live in denial, but my conscious mind knew it was temporary.

As if she sensed my thoughts, her smile faded. "I missed you, Maddie. More than you can ever imagine."

My throat tightened. The truth was on the tip of my tongue, though she didn't deserve to hear it.

I'd missed her, too.

I was saved from my response as Chelsea came up to us, a familiar squeal emitting from her lips. We couldn't help laughing as she jumped up and down and surrounded us with her bear hug. "We're back, bitches!" she screeched, kissing us both on the cheek, beaming with happiness.

I drank her in with greed, noting the differences. She'd

dyed her hair a lighter blond and straightened out all those curls. Fringy bangs gave her a stylish look. The casual denim shorts and cute blue polka dot top accented her petite figure, which looked amazing considering she had a one-year-old.

I pulled back and gave her a shocked look. "I can't believe you did it," I said.

Chelsea frowned. "Did what?"

"You got bangs."

She cracked up, touching her head. "I'm a woman steeped in diapers and bottles. I had to do it."

"You look gorg," I said, touching her arm with affection. "It's been way too long."

"For all of us."

Silence descended as we stared at one another, Chelsea's words echoing in the wind. Ava broke the sudden tension. "I've got lunch for us on the back patio where it's quieter. Sorry for the madness—all of these final details before the families descend. I thought it would be nice to have time alone."

"How's your dad?" I asked, following her through the gardens.

She beamed. "He's wonderful. He can't wait to see you. Of course, he had to squeeze in some last-minute business at the office. Here we are."

A wrought iron table set with flowers, crystals, and Tuscan yellow china was set out under a small grove of olive trees. I breathed in the scents of citrus and took a seat. A red pitcher held sparkling water. A wooden bowl of salad was in the center, surrounded by crusty bread, with tiny plates of prosciutto, melon, roasted peppers, and fragrant oils with fresh herbs. A bottle of prosecco perched in an ice bucket. My stomach rumbled. I hadn't been able to eat today due to nerves, but I guess Italy demanded an appetite. It was a visual feast.

Chelsea gave a sigh of pleasure. "This is heaven. I'm used to chicken nuggets and applesauce. I'm not going home."

I grinned, and Ava began to serve the salad. "I give you a few hours before you're saying you miss your kids."

"Absolutely not." She poured glasses of champagne for each of us. "Give me till morning. I definitely won't miss them tonight. Do you know how often I fall off the bed because the four of us are in it? With the dog?"

Ava and I laughed hard. "I can't imagine it," I said. "When you'd fall asleep in bed, if either of us rolled close, you'd get all grumpy. You hated people even breathing on you."

"Oh my God, remember the artist? He liked to snuggle after sex, and you'd have to pretend to fall asleep so you could push him away," Ava said.

Chelsea groaned. "How do you remember this stuff? Well, Ed never tortured me with clinginess, but the whole family broke me down. I literally sleep with dog breath in my face."

"How is Ed?" I asked, forking up a piece of leafy green.

"He's great. Got another promotion at the firm and working on partner." I caught the shadow that flickered over her face, and looked closer, but it was already gone. "Thank goodness, because who knew children were so expensive? Plus, the dog ended up having a tumor, so he needed surgery, and Ed hit a deer last week, totaling the car." She shook her head, the smile returning to her lips. "Lord, I don't even want to talk about it—life's ridiculousness."

Ava gave her a concerned look. "You didn't tell me all that was going on."

"That's what this trip is for. Not only a chance to celebrate your wedding, but to share the real crap. Like we used to."

The fork froze midair. No matter how bad I wanted to pretend this whole situation wasn't fucked-up, the truth hovered constantly just beneath the surface. We weren't just best friends reuniting to catch up. We were broken and smashed to bits by lies and betrayal. A fancy lunch or even a wedding could never change it.

The weight of reality crashed over me, and I stared at my plate, wondering if I should just leave now.

This whole thing had been a mistake.

I opened my mouth to announce I couldn't do this, but Ava interrupted.

"You're right. I can't expect us to fall back into the way things were, no matter how bad I wish we could." She stared at us, her gaze calm, but I caught the swirl of emotion there: a mixture of pain and regret; a cocktail that had made up the fabric of my life these past five years without them. "This weekend is a gift to me. I know how much pain I've caused, and I'm not trying to run away from it. All I want is to face the truth and to talk to you about . . . everything. That night. Afterward." Her voice broke, but she gathered control and forged on. "I want a chance for all of us to heal and move forward, in whatever way we need."

"I want that, too," Chelsea said.

I stared at them both. The familiar bitterness rose up and demanded to be spit out. "Convenient, isn't it? You're about to embark on a marriage and decide to tidily button up the past, like it's something you can rewrite. What about us? We've been here in the fallout trying to piece stuff back together, and now we're on your schedule? It doesn't work like that, Ava. Not anymore."

I braced myself for an emotional outburst and usual drama, but she only inclined her head in a regal sort of nod. "I know. I'm sorry, I'm probably expressing this wrong because I'm a mess. Seeing you again makes me nervous and happy and so sad, because I no longer have the right to hear you laugh or hold your hand or be the one you trust."

I sucked in my breath at the sheer honesty, but couldn't speak.

"I tried so many times over the years to talk to you, Maddie. Did you read any of my letters?"

I refused to get defensive. I took a long sip of champagne to relax. I remembered the stream of letters that came regularly, scrawled in familiar writing, my name a flashing beacon on the envelope warning me of the emotional bomb contained within. No, I hadn't wanted to be detonated on all over again. I only wanted silence in an attempt to find a shred of peace.

"No."

"I figured. I don't blame you. But you blocked me on all outlets, didn't read my letters, and refused to take my calls. Chelsea said if she mentioned my name, you'd hang up on her." I winced, but it was the truth, and I wasn't going to deny it. "All I want is a chance to really talk and share . . . some important things. Maybe reach some kind of peace. You're here for a reason, Maddie. Don't you want the same?"

I wondered if I did. I wondered if the price for acceptance was too high to pay. Would I have to rid myself of blame and rage and bitterness to get there? And if I did give it all up, what was truly left of me? The past five years had morphed and defined me, and my excuse was the same over and over.

That night I found Riggs and Ava in bed together.

It wiped out all the good and stole my precious memories. But God, I was so tired of the anger. Could I try and listen and find another path? And if I did, would Ava be lost again forever, or was there a chance to salvage something?

"I don't know," I said honestly. "I don't know why I'm here. Sure, it would be wonderful if I can hear some magic words that make it all better, but how? How do we even try to get there?"

"By listening, I think. By trying to be open. And if at the end of all this there's no forgiveness, I swear I won't bother you again, Maddie. No matter how much it tears me apart. I'll understand."

Chelsea blinked, obviously fighting back tears. I measured Ava's words and slowly nodded, knowing I had to try. For myself. For us. For the future.

"Okay." I dragged in a rough breath. "How do we start?"

Ava gave a wobbly smile and swiped at her eyes. "Tomorrow everyone will arrive and we have a few excursions planned. We can go off on our own and talk."

"Why not now?" I asked. Not that I wanted to dive into a mess of emotion hours after arriving, but I was curious.

"I wanted to ask for this one lunch together. Like old times. If we can maybe pretend for a little while, I would truly love to hear about your lives now. All the details I've missed so much. Do you think—do you think it's possible?"

A few days ago, I would have mocked her request and stormed off. But sitting here now with them, the two people I loved with my heart and soul, it was all I ever wanted. I forced the words around the lump in my throat. "I can try."

Chelsea reached out and snagged our hands, squeezing tight. "I'd love that."

Ava laughed and lifted her glass, and automatically we raised our own and the glasses tinkled merrily.

"To Ava's wedding," Chelsea said aloud.

I repeated the words and we drank.

THE NEXT FEW hours, I wrapped myself in a cocoon and became the girl I was when surrounded by my besties.

We chose our memories carefully, leaving out Riggs and Patrick, keeping to neutral and beloved topics such as our trips and sleepovers and college years. We tiptoed into the present like you'd test ice to see if it was truly frozen and safe, eventually finding a sweet spot.

"Tell us how you met Roberto," Chelsea prodded. "You never shared your love story with me."

I tilted my head, curious. Ava had never easily settled down, but I'd noticed how she'd glance at her sparkling diamond ring and her face would soften. "Yeah, I'd like to know more about him."

"Roberto works for my father. He's a software engineer and one of Dad's close friends." She wrinkled her nose as if embarrassed to tell us. "We'd actually met before—he's five years older than me so we were never interested in each other romantically. Dad would have freaked."

We all laughed.

"But other than him coming to the house now and then, we had little interaction. When I came back to live here, he invited me to lunch, and there was an instant connection."

"That's romantic," Chelsea said with a sigh. "You were always meant for each other. It was just the timing."

"I think so. I never would've looked twice at him before—he definitely wasn't exciting enough—but now I feel more . . . whole. I can't explain it. This space inside of me that always felt incomplete, or empty . . . that I was so desperate to fill; it's no longer there."

I watched a brief darkness settle in those brilliant eyes, then clear. She drank some of her champagne, but her fingers trembled slightly around the glass. I felt there was more to the story, but hearing her talk about him with such emotion moved me.

"You seem to really love him," I said quietly.

"I do. He's my rock. I can't wait for you to meet him."

"We can't, either," Chelsea said. "Your father is happy, I'm assuming?"

"God, yes. He's over the moon."

I hesitated to mention the name but had to ask. "What about Gabriella? Did they ever end up marrying each other?"

I prepared for the usual bitter resentment she'd always felt about the woman, but Ava lit up like I'd mentioned a close friend. "Yes! Oh, the wedding was beautiful, and they're really happy."

Chelsea didn't look surprised, so I assumed she'd known already about Ava's change of heart. "You don't think she was using your dad anymore?" I asked carefully.

She waved her hand in the air. "Lord, no! She adores Dad and they make a wonderful couple. I got mixed up and believed my mom and I wouldn't matter to him anymore. I was extremely jealous and insecure back then. About a lot of things."

I nodded, my mind flashing on those instances Ava seemed to act out, wondering if there was a bigger hole inside her I'd refused to see. She'd always been my savior and I put her on a pedestal. But the problem with pedestals is they all eventually break, and it's easy to resent the ones you stuck up there. I thought of cultivated public image. How my followers now hated and judged me by that one bad moment.

I understood things a bit better now.

"I'm really glad, Ava. Your dad deserves it."

"He does, thanks." She nibbled on a slice of prosciutto, looking at me with a slight hesitancy. "I've been watching your career explode, Maddie. The last movie you did? I saw it half a dozen times. Seeing your face on the big screen never gets old."

Pleasure coursed through me at the compliment. There was no one left in my life who truly celebrated and cared about my success. Most of my new friends were more acquaintances who liked to hang out for the glamour and free ride. The men who I briefly indulged with seemed more interested in my persona than in getting to know the real me. Not that I blamed them. I refused to show any part of my true self, so all they had to deal with was the superficial. It was a vicious cycle I repeated over and over, because to break it I'd need to be vulnerable.

I forced a smile. "Thanks, but honestly, they're nothing parts. I got lucky with the first movie hitting big, so I keep playing the same type of role. I'm mostly hated in Holly-wood because I have no acting experience and never dreamed of being an actress. There's something about an influencer that's easy to mock."

"Don't."

I regarded Ava with a roll of my eyes. "Don't what? I'm just being real."

"No, you're pretending what you accomplished isn't important. But, Maddie, look at what you've done! Movies, huge ad campaigns, and 1.4 million followers! Women buy anything you recommend. That is insane."

Chelsea jumped in. "Ava's right. When some of the pre-K moms found out I knew you, I became the most popular in the group!"

My laugh fell flat. "Not anymore. Better denounce me so you don't get dragged into the mess I made."

They shared a glance, and it was like the old days, the three of us joining to support one another. My insides clenched with sweet agony; the sheer relief of temporarily being around people who knew who you truly were; who understood your past and the demons you'd fought; who loved you anyway. Once, we'd had it all. I wanted to relive that feeling, even for a little while.

"It wasn't as bad as you're probably telling yourself," Ava said softly. "It'll pass."

"That's exactly what I told her," Chelsea added. "You can't be this big without some missteps. You were obviously drunk. Look at the celebrities who were forgiven after scandals worse than yours. Chrissy Teigen, and Ellen, and, well, so many others!"

The reality of my career blowing up forced me to grieve in stages. Denial had helped at first, but after the press kept feeding on the video and sharing, it seemed to get louder rather than quieting down.

"Your apology video was a good move," Ava said. "Though it pisses me off women are always held to a higher standard. If a guy said that crap, the world would laugh it off."

My video had mixed reactions. Sierra had read me the riot act about getting her approval on everything since many of my contracts had ethics and moral clauses. Many commentors offered support with the popular hashtag #mentalhealthfirst, but I was still being dragged and mocked by the press. I'd even been mentioned on *The Late Show* in a skit where the actress dressed in designer clothes drank wine and told everyone to eat cake because she was depressed and they weren't her problem. Like that hadn't been done to death from poor Marie Antoinette.

"Maybe. But it doesn't matter. Some of my sponsors canceled, and Maybelline stopped our negotiations to launch their new mascara line."

They nodded in sympathy, but no one seemed to ask why I'd gone on the rant to begin with. Yes, I was drunk. Yes, I was being pushed and prodded by paparazzi, who were being particularly obnoxious, screaming things in my face and shoving cameras at me, asking over and over about my feud with Kameron Divinity, the other social media influencer.

Ava leaned forward. "Who cares? You'll get better accounts later. Maybe more interesting movie roles where you get to play deeper characters."

"Change is good," Chelsea said. "Sometimes what we didn't plan for are the best surprises."

I sighed, but their words had affected me. There'd been too many people around in panic mode, rushing to force me to beg forgiveness and acting as if the cracks in my popularity would shatter and drag them down to mediocrity. My friends reminded me this may not be the end of everything but the beginning of something else. Because if I admitted the truth in my deepest, darkest part of my soul, I knew I hadn't been happy in a long time. I needed a change from the endless grind of photographers, and judgment, and fast-paced culture that sought shock and bliss and numbness by picking up their phones or putting on the TV.

The ridiculous part was I'd emanated that exact person. I'd transformed into my dreams, but along the way, it had stopped meaning anything valuable.

What I was going to do with that information and my latest fallout would determine my new path.

"I don't know what I'm going to do next," I finally said. "Even worse? I don't think I care anymore what happens."

My words fell into the wind and scattered. Ava opened her mouth to respond, but her name was called, and then she turned and our intimate circle broke.

Ava exchanged rapid Italian with a young woman, then sighed. "I have to go. I'm sorry, I wish we had more time together. I need to help with some last-minute details for the wedding."

I rose to my feet. The spell had been broken, and now all I saw when I stared at her was my best friend's betrayal. Ava seemed to sense the change. Her shoulders dropped. Grief flickered briefly in her blue eyes, then cleared. "Thank you. There are no words to tell you how much this afternoon meant to me. I love you both so much. I'll see you later."

She turned and disappeared through the lush gardens, leaving us alone in the silence.

"How do you feel?"

I drew in a shuddering breath. "Beat up."

Chelsea laughed and linked her arm through mine. "I bet. It's hard to love someone who you still want to hate."

Startled, I stared at her. She'd managed to define my exact feelings. "You should've been a writer, not a finance genius."

She rolled her eyes. "You were the one who tutored me on Dickinson, remember? Besides, I'm not a finance anything anymore. I'm just a mom."

I frowned, wondering at the slight edge to her voice, but she was already leading me away from the table. "Chels—"

"No more heavy stuff—I can't take it. Let's go for a walk and clear our heads. Then I need several hours to morph into someone fabulous for the party tonight. I can't wait to see your outfit."

I took her lead, agreeing I didn't have the brainpower to process anything more today. We walked around the property and by the lake, talking, and allowing me to remember again how it felt to have a true friend.

24

The party transformed Ava's villa into a glittering diamond shimmering against the water and cliffs of Lake Como.

I caught my breath as I took in the twinkling lights, bathing the pale lemon structure in a warm glow amid the night. There was music played by a live band, and the scents of flowers and citrus and musk hung heavily in the air. People swarmed the grounds wearing elegant dresses, holding champagne, chatting in casual groups beneath white tents.

I paused, overwhelmed at the number of people for an intimate pre-party, and almost decided to flee. I didn't know anyone, and my relationship with Ava had fallen into obscurity. I certainly didn't know who she loved or lunched with; knew nothing about her life in the past five years. But just as I was about to turn, Chelsea came down the walkway, waving with her usual enthusiasm, and I relaxed, moving toward her.

"Isn't this incredible?" she exclaimed in wonder, waving

her hand in the air. "Maddie, you look like you came from a movie set! This dress is a dream."

I'd chosen a classic Dior in seafoam green, a tricky color for many to pull off, but the perfect shade for me. It made my eyes glow deeper, and accented my hair, which I'd braided into an intricate knot and allowed to hang down my back. The diamond choker and matching bracelet were real. My one ring on my index finger was a square-cut emerald, given to me by an admirer a few years ago.

I'd discarded him but kept the ring.

"Thank you, Chels. But you win this contest. I hope you took a picture and sent it to Ed. He'd drop dead on the floor—you went sexy."

She mock posed in her short black dress beaded with so many sparkles she lit up the place. Her shoes were sky-high Jimmy Choos with a peekaboo toe that had me salivating. Chelsea always had classic good taste with clothes, choosing pieces that never went out of style and actually became pricey vintage. I recognized the pair immediately. "Is it wrong I'm happy Ed isn't here? I'm looking forward to not needing to have sex tonight."

I cocked my head. "Uh-oh. Is sex with your husband getting boring?"

"Hell, no. It's just whenever we leave the children, we feel like we need to do it. And sleep is so much better than sex right now, Maddie. It's like . . . five orgasms."

I cracked up, loving her humor, pushing away the regret I hadn't been able to enjoy her wit for too long. We entered the crowd, grabbing some champagne and getting used to the flow of things. It was the type of party I dreamed of being invited to when I was young: timeless and magical, like a Disney movie. I'd been ruined by LA parties and their ostentatious hunger to be better than the others, resulting in the very one-note events they tried desperately to avoid. But I was back in Italy, and even under the awkward circumstances, it was a place that seemed to welcome me.

"Oh, there's Ava and Roberto! Aren't they a beautiful couple?"

I stopped and stared. They looked like royalty. Her fiancé was tall, his muscled body clad in a black suit reminding me a bit of James Bond. Leaning over to whisper in Ava's ear, his face was full of interesting lines and craggy features—a large blade of a nose, sharp cheekbones, and bushy brows. His coal black hair had a bit of a curl and gave him a touch of softness. But it was the look he gave Ava that held me arrested.

Love. Not adoration, or admiration. No, this man looked like he met her on a higher level, and it was exactly what Ava needed. Someone who already knew he was worthy. Someone not seeking her approval. He stood on his own, and that's what finally made me see how this man was different.

She grabbed his arm, laughing up at him with her usual zest, inviting everyone to study them with greed. Her dress was white—a bold choice before her wedding day, but she pulled it off. The baby doll style had a scoop bodice and layers of delicate fabric that floated and danced around her body. The barely there jacket was pale pink, matching her strappy sandals. Her hair was caught in a low bun at her nape, emphasizing her long neck and delicate collarbone. Diamonds winked at her ears. Her lips were painted the same color as her accessories.

I drank them in, my heart beating painfully in my chest. They held hands with the ease of a couple comfortable with intimacy, moving from group to group to bestow greetings. In that place tucked safely away, I mourned not being by her side, not being able to hold her other hand or gather in her bedroom later on, drinking wine and giggling as we analyzed the party.

Chelsea's soft sigh hinted at the same regret. The two of us stood together, separated by too many years and too many lies and too much pain. But God, I wanted to cross the barrier and be able to love Ava again.

I'd thought Riggs was the great love of my life.

Now, I knew it had always been Ava Aldaine.

On cue, she spotted us and tugged on Roberto's arm. I pasted on my smile as they closed the distance. "Roberto, this is Maddie, and of course, you remember Chelsea."

His grin reached his beautiful dark eyes. He clasped my hand in a warm shake, genuine interest reflected back to me. "I've been wanting to meet you for a long time. Welcome, Maddie. Good to see you again, Chelsea. You both look stunning."

"Thank you for having me."

"Antonio mentioned you this morning. Said he always

remembered Thanksgiving weekend and how all of you burned brighter than a firecracker together. Ava was lucky to have you both."

The words stung like bees, but I knew he wasn't doing it on purpose. How much had Ava really told him about our relationship? How it ended? How she'd bedded the man I loved and threw away years of friendship and trust?

I kept silent, nodding.

"This weekend has already exceeded my expectations and I just arrived," Chelsea said. "What's on the agenda for tomorrow again?"

"We set up boat rides throughout the day for any guests who wanted a tour around the lake. Everyone has tomorrow to explore on their own, and then we're hosting a dinner at Trattoria Baita Belvedere in Bellagio. It's a wonderful restaurant on the lake," Ava said.

"And where's the wedding again?" I asked.

"Villa Pliniana. It's an eighteen-acre estate with waterfront gardens. Both the ceremony and reception will be held there," Roberto said. He leaned over and kissed Ava on top of the head. "But I'm sure you'll want to sneak away for some alone time. Dealing with relatives can be challenging. Especially my mama."

Ava waved off his comment with a genuine grin. "I love your mama," she teased back. "She raised her son right. You know how to cook, take out the garbage, and do laundry. Most Italian men are too spoiled by their mama."

"Correct. She also taught me to make enough money to hire those services out. I did right by her." Ava punched his arm lightly. We all laughed. "Seriously, why don't the three of you sneak away for an hour or two? Grab cocktails in Varenna."

I watched the look they exchanged with each other, communicating with only their eyes. The air between them grew heavier. Ava nodded slightly. When she spoke, her voice had lost some of its lightness. "I'd like to talk to you both. Share some things."

Chelsea waited for my answer, but I knew it was time to face the truth. "Sure."

"Good, I'll text you with the time. We can meet here." I heard Roberto's name called. "Sorry, we better keep moving. I'll see you later."

Roberto grasped our hands again, but I noticed the way his gaze prodded mine. Again, I wondered how much he knew. Maybe she had told him. Maybe he was hoping I'd forgive her and clear things up before the wedding. Maybe he was wishing I'd never come to stir up trouble.

Either way, I'd find out tomorrow.

We watched them leave. I turned to Chelsea. "He seems really nice."

"I know. Have you noticed how she's changed? Even her demeanor has this eerie calm now, when before she always seemed to be turned to the highest volume."

I couldn't help my laugh at her description. "Yeah, I noticed. Maybe he taught her meditation."

Chelsea snorted. "As if Ava would ever sit for longer than ten minutes. No, it seems deeper than that."

"I thought you kept in touch enough to know what was

happening in her life. Speaking of which, I never asked why you aren't in her wedding party? I assumed you'd be the maid of honor."

Chelsea shook her head. "Not without you. It would feel too weird for me to stand up there alone. Neither of us wanted that."

Shock vibrated through me. Was it wrong to feel slightly glad they valued me? That my loss had been bigger than simply a number, and Chelsea and Ava didn't continue their friendship without me? I'd never taken the time to analyze my role in our threesome. Through the years, I'd imagined Ava and Chelsea moving on without me. Chelsea had confessed it had taken her a long time to forgive Ava and begin to rebuild the friendship, but I'd never been part of those conversations. It was easy to picture them laughing and lunching happily without me.

Maybe it was time I stopped looking for my value in others and started finding it in myself.

"Come on, I see Antonio. Let's go say hello before he gets mobbed," Chelsea said, interrupting my light bulb moment.

We weaved our way through the glittering, happy crowd and stopped beside him, waiting politely for him to finish his conversation with someone. He glanced at us, then stopped in mid-sentence. His face broke into a joyous smile, and he threw out his arms, our names booming from his lips in rich, Italian song. "Maddie! Chelsea! How beautiful you are, exactly as you were from so many years ago!"

The gentleman he was talking with drifted away. Antonio

gathered us in a close hug, the comforting scent of cinnamon and cloves rising from his skin. A rush of emotion hit me hard, but I blinked back the tears, refusing to give in. I allowed myself a few precious seconds in his embrace before stepping back, my face carefully composed. I'd lost Ava's father in the betrayal, and it was another blow. Though I hadn't seen him often, when he'd visit New York, he'd take us to a play and dinner, regaling us with dramatic tales from his business and making us laugh. He treated us like substitute daughters and always said Ava was better because of us. He was everything I dreamed of having in a father, and Ava had told me he could be mine.

Until she took him away, too.

"You look wonderful," I said, smiling. "How is Gabriella?"

"She has made me happy," he answered. "You will see her a bit later. Watching her and Ava together heals my heart."

Chelsea sniffed. "That's so beautiful. Could you tutor my husband on being romantic for me, please?"

We laughed. "Ah, he must know what a treasure he has in you, *cara*. Maddie, I'm so proud of what you accomplished. You are a star, and I brag about you constantly."

I felt my cheeks flush with pleasure. "*Grazie.*"

We fell into easy chatter. The party buzzed about us, but I steeped myself in the moment, enjoying Ava's father and the bold way he showed his heart. It was amazing how such a successful businessman who'd created an empire could have such tenderness toward the people he loved.

Finally, he was called up to give a toast, and I stood back

with Chelsea to watch him praise his daughter and future
son-in-law, raising his glass for their happiness and future.

I drank, but the bubbles were a tad bitter.

I got through another hour before it was too much. The
past had hit harder than my defenses could hold. "I'm really
tired, Chels. Going to head out."

She took one look at my face and understood. "Want me
to take the ride back to your hotel with you?"

"No, honestly, I'm fine. I just need to sleep. It's been a
long day."

"I understand." She hugged me tight. "Maddie, thank
you for giving this a chance. For our lunch. For being here,
willing to listen."

I took a deep breath. "I can't promise how things will
turn out."

"I know. But that's enough for me. It will be enough for
Ava, too."

The trip to the hotel was short at this late hour. I got undressed and climbed into bed, but my thoughts were spinning. After trying to sleep for over an hour, I finally walked
out to the balcony and sat, my feet propped up on the
wrought iron rail, staring out at the dark water. Scattered
beams of moonlight bounced off the surface like they were
hitting glass. The cliffs in the distance were shadowed peaks.
A gentle breeze kissed my face as I tilted my head up and
closed my eyes.

Tomorrow, I'd finally hear the whole story. The whys. I
couldn't keep going on slapping Band-Aids on a wound that

cut too deep. I sensed it needed to bleed freely in order to finally heal. And that meant confronting the past and the truth.

I'd run for too long, refusing to hear from Ava or Riggs about that fateful night. I cut them out like a cancer that would destroy me, and never looked back.

I thought it was a good way to cope. I focused on my career and moved ahead. But I'd been lying to myself, and eventually, no matter how hard or long you run, the only thing you end up with is yourself.

I didn't recognize who I'd become. The fame I'd worked so hard to achieve didn't fulfill me like I imagined; my numerous followers weren't true friends but fans. My heart hadn't been part of my work because it shattered that night, and I'd done nothing to heal it.

God, I was tired. Tired of an identity I'd carefully created that now seemed to have grown separate from my true self. I'd thought I was in control, but I never looked deep inside to find what would make me happy. I'd never found inner peace, and that's what I craved the most.

I picked up my phone and scrolled quickly through. My huge drop in followers had leveled out after the apology, but gossip about me still clogged the feeds. My inbox held pages of unread mail, which I ignored. I had a missed voice mail from my agent, so I quickly played it.

I'd lost not only the Maybelline account, but a few others we'd booked. My agent talked about trying to push back, but I knew the morals clause would cause an issue. The company could easily cite my video as a loophole to pull out. I texted back, instructing her to let the contracts go. I had no desire to work with clients who didn't want me.

Guess my schedule was wide open for the next few months—something I'd never experienced. I waited for the rush of depression, for the tears and anger and bitterness, but I felt oddly calm. The idea of not having to push myself to put on a fake persona, to be able to step away from social media and take a break, began not to look so scary. I'd confessed in my apology I'd be retreating from the public eye, and maybe it was exactly what I needed. Some time to really figure things out, not just with Ava and what happened, but with myself.

I pondered the thought and the view for a long time.

25

BEFORE

never really stopped running.

Outside the hotel, I took off into the streets of Manhattan and called Levi. I frantically told him to come pick me up, that I was in trouble, and he said he was on the way.

I told him what happened in short bursts, taking time to gulp in ragged breaths in between the horror of my story. Immediately, he demanded we go back to talk to Ava and Riggs, to find out what the hell had really happened, but I went completely hysterical until he swore he'd keep driving.

I got to the apartment, threw things in a bag, grabbed my passport, and headed out.

I arrived in LA the next day, ready to start work.

Grief is a funny thing. I thought I'd be laid out, unable to talk or think or cope, but I used my job as a lifeline to pull me through, gobbling up extra hours of acting classes, sponsored posts, and anything else that kept my brain engaged in the present.

Ava called. Texted. Wrote letters and emails. I knew she was ready to get on a plane to see me, but I told Levi to make sure she knew I never wanted to see or talk to her again. I pressured him with all the skills I learned, convincing him if he chose to allow Ava back into my life in any way, I'd walk away from him and the agency.

Eventually, the calls stopped.

The same thing happened with Riggs, and I chose the same route—complete banishment from my life. There was nothing to discuss or go back to, and I knew any type of dialogue would only destroy me further.

It was harder with Chelsea. She returned from her honeymoon and discovered our friendship had been destroyed. I sobbed with her on the phone, giving all the details, but whenever she tried to force a confrontation or conversation, I turned cold. For a while, she hated Ava along with me, but I noticed over the next year how she'd sneak in mentions of her, hinting at forgiveness. When I confronted her, Chelsea told me the truth: that they'd made a tentative peace. Something broke inside me after hearing it. Eventually, our calls began to lessen, trickling to an occasional check-in.

I think we both knew it was too hard to pretend. It was like a death had occurred but there was no grave or way to properly grieve.

I fell into a romantic relationship with Levi because it was easy. We lasted awhile, and with him I experienced a level of comfort, buffering me from the pain. He loved me, but I couldn't love him back. I'd given it all to Riggs and Ava, and there wasn't enough left of me.

The press adored us together, so we fed the beasts with gossip and pictures until Levi found someone else who could love him back. We parted amicably but didn't stay friends. He was the last tether to Ava I watched walk away.

I stayed in LA. I started and ended dozens of relationships so I didn't have to be alone. I scored some minor movie roles, and cover shoots, and soon, I'd become everything I ever wanted. I was famous. Fans wanted to see what I wore, or ate, or read. What parties I attended. What people I hung out with. I bloomed into what they wanted and was safe for a while, but it was all a mirage.

Inside, I was rotting away. I'd pushed the mess so deep, it began to bleed, escaping from tiny bouts of temper with my clients; snottiness with the press; dismissal with my fans. I picked men who were slightly cruel so I could discard them more easily and feel justified about the hurt.

When an up-and-coming influencer, Kameron Divinity, tried to partner with me for some TikTok videos, I scoured her feed and froze on a face I recognized.

Patrick.

His cheek was pressed to hers in the cute selfie. They were both dressed up at some type of formal function, and I automatically scanned the background for a glimpse of Riggs.

I immediately turned her down without explanation or apology.

She took to social media, calling me out for my rudeness, and the press took hold and blew it up. I sent her a mean message. She screenshot it.

The night I was coming from a club, I'd already noticed the slow cracks in my facade; sensed I wasn't too far from the breaking point. There is only so long one can deny or ignore the past before it comes rushing back in a tidal wave, demanding to be dealt with.

When the press got in my face, berating me for being bitchy to her, asking me a million questions, pushing, pushing, pushing, I finally broke.

And spilled my guts to the world on camera.

Maybe Ava's invitation was a gift.

Life happens for me, not to me, just like Tony Robbins said.

It was time I met it full on.

26

AFTER

Today, our lunch had a completely different tone.

We were quiet. Chelsea had lost her giddy excitement, and we walked into the restaurant together with shadows chasing us. The owner or host from Al Prato greeted Ava with kisses on both cheeks, leading us to our table outside, tucked back for privacy. The view was stunning. Boats cut through the water, and the mountains were framed in the distance. Bright sunlight soaked the lake, and trees turning all colors cast vibrant hues. I noticed there were hardly any tourists here, which was nice since we were about to have such a private conversation.

I remembered being here that Thanksgiving. Remembered how free I felt exploring the hidden streets of the small fishing village, admiring the pastel-painted homes as we walked by the water; climbing endless steep stairs while we gossiped madly about topics that had seemed important. As

I laid my napkin on my lap and quickly ordered a prosecco, I knew this trip was completely different, and we sat together more like strangers than intimate friends.

I ordered the tuna tartare, and we agreed on grilled octopus for our appetizer. For the first few minutes, we chatted about the party, and the wedding, keeping it light, but soon we fell into silence and stared at one another with a touch of discomfort. My palms were damp with nerves. I couldn't take anymore, but then Ava began to talk.

"I feel like I'm going to throw up."

A half laugh escaped my lips. "Me, too."

"Me, three."

Ava dragged in a breath and placed her clasped hands on the table. I noticed they shook slightly. "I have so much to say I don't know where to start. I'm afraid I'll say it wrong and you'll leave and that will be it."

I shook my head. "I won't leave the restaurant no matter what you tell me. I only want the truth, as bad as it is. I need to know everything, Ava. All of it."

"Okay. The night of Chelsea's wedding, I was in a funny place. I'd been trying to hide my unhappiness for a long time. On the surface, my life looked perfect. And I was grateful, knowing I had so much, but maybe that made it harder to admit I felt completely lost? I watched everyone around me scramble for money and work, and though I wanted to carve my own path out, I always felt like an imposter. I mean, I had plenty of money and didn't have to do anything to deserve it. Meanwhile, you were killing yourself to make your dreams come true, along with Chelsea, and

Riggs, and Patrick, and most men I dated. I floated around and pretended I'd do something important. That's why I was so excited to be involved with your and Chelsea's businesses. It gave me purpose."

I dug my nails into my palms and nodded for her to continue. There were a million ways I could cut her down; shredding her excuses with bitter judgment as a poor little lost rich girl. But I knew it went deeper than that. I'd glimpsed Ava's pain multiple times, and the way she shook it off like a cloak, leaving it behind. But she hadn't left it anywhere. Pain followed, and I'd just begun to realize it.

"What started as purpose began to change for me. Maybe I noticed that first time I went with you to LA, Maddie. When it was just us, and you were on the cusp of breaking out big." Her eyes half closed, as if seeing an image in her brain. "God, I loved every moment of that trip. Loved watching you come so far from that girl who told us she was awkward and shy and could never make her dream come true. I felt like I'd had a part of that transformation. It made me feel valuable and happy."

"You were, Ava," I said quietly. "So was Chels. I'd never had anyone in my life give me confidence before. Or make me feel valued."

She gave me a grateful glance. "Thank you for that, though it's not true. You would've found your way without us. I just want you to understand what was in my head to lead up to what happened."

The waiter dropped off our plates. I tried to take a bite, but it was only Ava's words that I wanted—not food. I drained my prosecco, and Chelsea halted the waiter, pointing to my glass. "We're going to need a bottle of this."

He nodded and returned quickly, filling all our glasses, then drifted away.

Ava continued. "I never thought I was trying to live my life through yours. I'm not sure when I got mixed up and began to believe all of your choices affected me. Looking back, I can see now that I used you as my own identity. When we were all together, I felt powerful and in control. Not of you, but of me." She glanced at Chelsea. "It wasn't like that with you, Chels. I'm not sure why, but you seemed to not need me as much, or more likely, I didn't feel as needed by you. You seemed to know what was coming next, and you'd get there on your own. Does that make sense?"

Chelsea smiled gently. "It does." Sadness flickered in her dark eyes. I hesitated, wanting to probe deeper, but this was about Ava right now. I swore I'd take Chelsea aside later and find out what was really going on in her life.

Ava abandoned her fork, too, and lifted her glass to drink. "The night of the wedding, you told me you were going to turn down the job in LA. I'll never forget what that did to me. I was so angry, Maddie. To think of you throwing away your dreams for a guy? To think of how hard you worked to get where you were to suddenly give up and wait around while Riggs finished law school? I don't know—I went completely nuts. It was like my deepest fears were coming true, and all I wanted was to shake you out of it and make you realize it would be the biggest mistake of your life."

My heart knocked crazily against my chest. It was as if

the story was building and I knew what the ending was, but like any story, anticipating didn't change it.

"I was so drunk." Her voice broke, but she held my gaze as she spoke. "It's not an excuse. But I need you to know if I'd had a shred of clarity left, it never would've happened."

"You're right. It's not an excuse. For either you or Riggs."

She dipped her chin, gracefully taking the hit. Almost from a distance, I noticed there was a light of acceptance and deep resolve in her blue eyes, as if she'd made peace with her actions. I wondered how long it took. I wondered if she struggled or if she was able to forgive herself easily enough by using rationalizations. But now wasn't the time to ponder, because the story was finally being told.

"You took off and wouldn't listen. After you went to the elevator, I intended to follow you and finish our conversation, but I heard a commotion, and when I glanced at the glass doors, I saw Riggs had fallen and knocked over a chair. I went out to get him and bring him inside. He was half-gone, mumbling stuff about how he'd lost you, how I made you hate him, terrible, rambling junk that I hated. I helped him into the elevator and to his floor, intending to take him to the room, but he kept trying to turn around, saying he couldn't see you yet."

She paused. I swallowed.

"You took him to your room instead?" I finally asked.

"Yes. He was a mess. I was a mess. He opened up the minibar and kept drinking, glaring at me, and then we got into it. Started fighting and saying mean stuff to each other. It was awful."

Meanwhile, I'd been trying to wait up for him down the hall. Hoping to save us both by being the martyr and giving up LA to support him. Looking back, I saw exactly why Ava had been so upset with me. Would I have missed my opportunity and always resented Riggs? Or would I have been happy, married to the only man I'd ever loved? The questions whirled in my mind. I kept picturing them in that hotel room, yelling at each other over me, and asked the question I needed answered.

"When did it turn?"

She didn't flinch, and I appreciated the way she finished, refusing to hide from my stare.

"He started crying. Just sat on the edge of the bed, drunk out of his mind, and began sobbing that you were the love of his life and he'd never be able to keep you. Said you were meant to belong to the world and not one person."

The pain exploded inside of me like shrapnel. I braced myself for the rest.

"I sat next to him, and suddenly we were hugging each other, and I said I was afraid I'd lose you, too, and that I loved you and didn't know who I was without you. And I have no idea how it happened, Maddie. I'm not trying to rationalize any of it—there's only what I did, but I began to kiss him and he kissed me back and suddenly we were having sex. But it wasn't regular sex; it was this horrible release of pain and sadness and confusion, all tumbled together. I hardly remember it—I just grab these faded, flashing images—and then it was over, and we both passed out. The next thing I knew you woke me up."

The breath released from my lungs in a shudder. I noticed a tear running down Chelsea's cheek, but she remained eerily silent, allowing us our own time and space to process.

The low noises of the restaurant rose around us. I looked past Ava to the rocky cliffs and rolling hills; to the flash of sunlight on the water; to the world outside of this table where no one knew what was going on inside me.

"Was there any passion? You both seemed to hate each other. Were you hiding deeper feelings I didn't know about?" Over the years, I'd half convinced myself they'd been hiding their lust behind resentment and I was the naive girlfriend.

The expression of horror on her face told me the truth. "God, no! Neither of us felt any of that. And I know this is fucked-up, but all I remember between us in those flashes was . . . anger. As if we were both using each other and trying to grieve you. It was physical, but it meant nothing to either of us."

I pictured the whole thing so clearly now. How the hate and blame turned. It was a horrible image but different from what I'd expected to deal with. In my deepest fears, I'd imagined his mouth on hers, and between her legs, whispering her name in the night while they indulged in each other. I'd imagined pleasure and orgasms and secrets. Instead, she described an exorcism that held no softer emotions.

It didn't make it any easier. But oddly, a piece of me gained some calm by hearing the truth, no matter how brutal.

"What happened after I ran?"

Grief ravaged her elegant features. "We both fell apart. We were frantic trying to get in touch with you and find out where you'd gone. He tore the apartment to pieces, and called everyone. Levi refused all my calls for two whole days, and when he finally answered, he said I was not to come after you under any circumstance. He was so cold. Said he wouldn't talk to me again, either. Not that I blame him. It was just another reality check showing me exactly what I'd done. I tortured myself with what-ifs until I went a bit mad. If I'd only forced him to go to his room. If I hadn't seen him outside. If I hadn't kissed him." A choked sound of emotion escaped her lips. "If only I hadn't been so weak and needy."

I closed my eyes for a few seconds, finding my center. The wound throbbed, but was finally clean. "I didn't know." Ava tilted her head in question. "That you felt like that inside. About yourself. About me. I thought I was the one who depended on you two for everything, and that I wasn't enough."

"Oh, Maddie, don't you remember what I told you that weekend in Saratoga? It was always me who needed you. I just hid it better."

Chelsea leaned forward, her arms outstretched on the table. "I got back from my wedding, and everything was gone. It was hard for a long time. I froze out Ava the first year because I was so mad you could do that to Maddie. And then more time went by, and I was so damn lonely. You were my sisters, and nothing was the same after the wedding. I finally began talking to Ava, and slowly, we rebuilt a relationship. It was never the same, of course. It couldn't be. But it was easier for me to forgive her than it was for you."

I sighed, watching the past events flicker in front of me and the million ways I could have handled them better.

"When you began talking to Ava again, it was too difficult for me to process. Knowing she was back in your life haunted me. I decided to back away from you, too."

"I understand," Chelsea said softly. "I'm not blaming anyone. I just know from these last two days how much I missed you both, how I need you. But the biggest thing we owe ourselves is some type of forgiveness. If we can get there. This is about you, Maddie."

"I don't know." I could only offer my truth. "I need time to process. To accept. I've kept the past shoved down for so long, I'm not sure how to go about making peace with it." I looked at Ava. "Have you spoken with Riggs?"

She shifted in her seat, and suddenly, my senses spiked. There was something else she was about to tell me. Something big.

Something that could change everything all over again.

"Ava?"

She dragged in a breath. "Yes, Maddie. I've spoken to Riggs."

I gasped. Shock vibrated through me at her confession. The familiar numbness threatened to creep back in to protect my ravaged heart. "You're telling me you continued your relationship?"

"God, no. It wasn't like that at all. When you left, Riggs had a mini breakdown. He had to drop out of school for a while because he went into a deep depression. He blamed himself and wanted to go to LA and force you to talk to him. But Levi stopped him, saying he'd ruin you and your career if he tried to come back into your life. Finally, he gave up."

"I reached out to him a few times," Chelsea said. "At first, I wanted to punish him for what he did, but I realized quickly he was a mess. He disappeared after that, so I assumed he left New York."

I couldn't help the flare of satisfaction, quickly replaced by sadness. We had all suffered for that one bad moment. I'd always wondered if Ava had set it up to deliberately show me that Riggs wasn't right for me. I suspected Riggs always had a secret crush on Ava and needed to be tipsy to act on it.

I was glad I was wrong, even though the end hadn't changed.

But the story plot had.

"So, did you keep in touch afterward to see how he was doing?" I asked curiously.

"No. You see, something else happened that night. Something that was even bigger than losing you, Maddie."

We waited. She opened her mouth, and fear froze me in place, waiting for the plot twist.

"I decided to come home to Italy for a while. Figure things out. Find a way to make you forgive me. Then I got really sick and Dad forced me to go to the doctor to find out what was wrong with me. I assumed it was stress, but the doctor ran some tests and came to a different conclusion."

A roaring settled in my ears. The world seemed to tilt on its axis. My entire focus shrank to a pinpoint, watching Ava's face as she spoke.

"I was pregnant."

27

A strange noise came from Chelsea. My hand pressed against my trembling lips.

"I had a baby girl. Riggs's child. That's why I got back in contact with him."

I stared at Ava, dimly noticing her wet lashes, the ravaged emotion carved into her features, the hard tilt of her chin.

"Y-y-you had a baby?" I whispered.

"Yes."

I swiveled my accusing gaze to Chelsea, but she looked just as stunned as I did. I realized she hadn't known, either. "Wait—what? I'm staying at your house! I haven't seen a baby!" Chelsea burst out.

A faint smile curved her lips. "Diana's staying with Roberto's parents until the rehearsal dinner. There's too much activity in the house, and workers coming and going. I felt more comfortable having her at her grandparents' place. And, of course, I wanted the time to have this conversation and tell you the truth. I didn't want to spring her on either of you."

"How didn't I know?" Chelsea asked faintly, looking as shell-shocked as I felt. "All those times we spoke, you never told me."

"I couldn't. I couldn't tell anyone for a while. I ran away from New York to hide, and suddenly, there was the possibility of a baby." Her voice shook. "I thought about not keeping it. But . . . I couldn't go through with an abortion. I already felt like we were a team." I watched as her hand automatically lay on her stomach, as if she still carried the baby. "I was so damn scared, but my dad backed me up, and Gabriella was wonderful. She was calm, and loving, and listened to me. Instead of treating my pregnancy like a tragedy, they celebrated."

My throat scratched like sandpaper. "Did you tell your dad about what happened?"

Ava nodded. "I told him everything. We cried together, knowing how badly you were hurt, Maddie. I spent the year at home, thinking about all the actions that brought me here. I talked with a therapist, and let my baby grow, and when I had her, I swore I'd be different. Braver. For her."

A wobbly smile curved her lips as she glanced at both of us. "I can't wait until you meet her. Roberto loves her like his own. She was only one year old when we began our relationship, so he's the father she knows."

"What about Riggs?" I asked, shaking my head and trying to clear it. It was like trying to grasp smoke that disappeared through my fingertips. My mind refused to compute all the things she was telling me. "When did you tell him?"

"Not until she was born. He wasn't ready to deal with my pregnancy, or a baby. He blamed me, I think, and then he was focused on finding you. But once I had Diana, I knew I couldn't keep her a secret. He deserved to know and decide if he wanted to be a part of her life."

"How did he take the news?" Chelsea asked.

"At first? Not well. But then he flew to Italy and met her. We talked. Worked things out." She stared at me, as if waiting for me to either freak out or burst into tears. But I was still processing the idea that Ava had a child with Riggs, and kept the secret for five years. Ava continued. "We decided it was best if he wasn't part of Diana's life. It would be too confusing for all of us. Riggs met Roberto and was happy she'd have a stable family. We'll tell her when she's older, but all she knows is love and a father who adores her."

"That's wonderful," Chelsea said, shooting me a concerned look. "What is Riggs up to now?"

"He's back in New York and opened up his own law firm."

"Did he get married?" I asked casually.

"No," Ava said. She gave me a look that told me I hadn't fooled her with my fake ease. The idea of Riggs marrying someone else still hit hard. I'd refused to think of him for so long, but instead of healing, the image of his face only haunted me more. "As far as I know, he hasn't had any type of serious relationship. Not since you, Maddie."

My stomach clenched. I hated how happy the fact made me, but there was nothing I could do but face the truth.

I still cared.

"There's one thing left you need to know."

I gave a humorless laugh. "I'm not drunk enough for all this, Ava. I can't take any more."

"I know." Raw emotion ravaged her face. "There aren't enough sorrys in the world for you. I hurt and betrayed someone I loved so much. Living with it almost tore me apart, but I had to put myself back together for Diana's sake. She deserved so much more from me."

"What is it?"

"Riggs is coming to the wedding."

For the second time, my chair seemed to tilt and dump me off the edge of gravity. I blinked, staring helplessly into her blue eyes. "Riggs is coming to the wedding?" I repeated.

"Yes. He'll be here tomorrow."

"Why?" I burst out. "I thought he didn't see Diana?"

"He doesn't. Maddie, I don't know how to say this, but Riggs is coming to see you. He asked if you'd attend, and when you RSVP'd, I texted him. I can't speak for him. But I think he's spent these past five years desperate to talk to you. I'm not sure if it's closure or forgiveness or something more."

"And you let him manipulate this situation? Without telling me?"

Regret flickered in her gaze, but her voice remained strong. "I know the hell I went through living with my actions and not being able to face you. He needs to see you. And I think you need the same. To finally be free."

We fell into silence, at the fancy table with our past and future mingled together, taunting us with images and what-ifs. Finally, Chelsea stood up. "I'm gonna go. I think you two need a bit of time alone. I'll meet you back at the house and see you tonight."

I couldn't accuse her of running away, because I knew Chelsea wouldn't budge if she felt either of us needed her. She kissed us both and disappeared, leaving us frozen in our seats.

"She always did know how to make an exit."

I shook my head and laughed. My nerve endings felt raw, my temples throbbed with the onslaught of a headache, and yet a tiny flare of hope ignited within me. I was with Ava again. The familiarity and bond between us still burned bright, even with everything that had happened to us. How were we able to connect after all this time? After so much pain?

"I don't know how I feel about all this," I finally said.

A small smile touched her lips. "I don't blame you. Maddie, why did you decide to come to my wedding? Was it the pact? To finally tell me off? Or something else?"

I hesitated. What was the real answer? There were so many things I'd be able to cite, but it was time to dig deep and be truthful myself. "I wanted to see you again. Half of me imagined this big scene from *The Real Housewives*—where we'd have this dramatic confrontation and I'd scream in front of your guests and relatives and you'd drop to your knees and beg forgiveness." Ava gave a half-choked laugh. "The other half hoped I'd learn it was all a big mistake. That you never truly slept with Riggs, and we'd be able to go back to our friendship after clearing it up."

"I'm sorry you got neither of those things."

"Both were illusions. Looking back, we had bigger issues never dealt with. You said you were obsessed with my life, but Ava? I was just as dependent on you. I wonder if I ever made any real decision without taking your opinion into account. Somehow, along the way of our friendship, we got lost with each other."

Ava let out a long breath. "Yes," she said slowly. "I tried to get in the middle of your relationship because I was convinced it was for your own good. That he'd mess up everything. But I was just looking out for me. I wanted you to myself."

The truth jerked me back in my chair. There were so many layers in our friendship I'd never poked at because I was afraid of losing her. I relied on her opinion and love because I was desperate to experience such attention and care. God knows, I'd never got it from my parents or anyone else. Not until Ava.

But what I hadn't counted on was how much I'd changed her, too. It was a dual experience, but neither of us had bothered to look deep enough. Riggs had only complicated us further, as the one standing between us. "Can I ask you something?"

"Anything."

"Did you date Patrick just to be with me?"

She met my gaze head-on. "Yes. I liked Patrick. I liked having sex with him, and the way he made me feel special. But I never loved him the way you loved Riggs."

"You asked me something at the club that night. If I'd be happy with the four of us being together."

Ava winced. "Yeah, I guess I did. It was a way to make sure we stayed tight. The four of us had a blast, but when Patrick pushed for us to be alone, I realized I wasn't interested in him like that. It was just fun to hang out with you."

I'd sensed the truth, but hearing it straight helped put the doubts to rest. "Riggs knew."

"I figured. Another reason I disliked him. I couldn't hide."

We drained the last of our champagne. Paid the bill. Then walked out and headed toward the water.

"Did you ever think of telling Chelsea so she'd let me know? About the baby?"

Ava stared out at the lake. The sun played on her glossy dark hair, deepening the cerulean blue of her eyes. Her voice sounded far away, like a misty fog drifting over the cliffs. I studied her familiar profile, and my heart tugged. My hand almost reached for hers out of habit, but I kept my fingers in a tight fist. "Why would I? To hurt you even more? No. I never planned to tell you about Diana. But the moment I got engaged, the only person I wanted to call was you and Chelsea. And I cried and told Roberto I didn't think I'd ever be whole until I got a chance for you to forgive me. He encouraged me to reach out. He said he believed you *could* forgive me." She paused. "But I know you never really will."

Startled, I tilted my head to study her. "How do you know?"

When she looked back at me, her eyes shone with unshed tears. "I can never regret that night, Maddie. Not like you'd need me to. Because then I wouldn't have Diana."

The breath left me in a rush, and I bent over, clutching the stone wall for support. God, she was right. And what could I do with that information? Was there a place for either of us to go from here?

"I have to get back. I need . . . time."

She took a step away from me, nodding. "Of course. Will you come to our dinner tonight?"

"I don't know, Ava. I simply don't know if I can handle it right now."

Her hand reached out to me, then fell flat between us. "I understand. You've already been through so much. Thank you for listening to me. No matter what happens, to see you again was the greatest wedding gift I could ever imagine."

Emotion choked my throat. I wanted to touch her, too, to reassure both of us, but I couldn't manage to take the necessary step. Instead, I walked away, practically running down the cobblestone streets, leaving her behind.

Just like I had that fateful night.

28

Hours passed in a haze.

I walked, losing myself in the crooked, narrow streets of Varenna. I climbed steep steps and passed brightly colored houses and various shops, the lilt of Italian rising to my ears. I walked the red-gated path along the lake, where couples held hands and kissed passionately, hypnotized by the romantic allure Italy was known for. The sun shone bright, and fluffy clouds drifted in the sky. Boats cut across the lake, from sleek paddleboats like Ava's to luxury yachts where the rich sunbathed on decks and took in the stunning views.

I walked and allowed my surroundings to soothe my numb brain as I searched for answers. I waited for the justifiable rage to soak into my blood and spit outward; the knowledge Ava had ended up with it all. A baby she adored. A husband who loved her. A family who supported her. She had betrayed me yet she'd won.

But nothing happened. Not anger or bitterness or a desire for revenge. Instead, there was something so much worse.

Nothing.

I could blame the past five years on Ava and Riggs. God knows, it had been my story I clung to, even as I pretended I'd buried the pain and moved on. But the story ran deeper, and if I didn't pull it out piece by piece and examine how I got here, I'd spend the next five years doing the same.

God, I was tired. Tired of living my life off one event and letting it define me. Now that I'd heard the details of that night, I realized there were shades of gray amid the clarity I'd once known. I still blamed them both. Their actions had ruined all of us. Yet . . .

There was a baby in the mix; a child Ava said changed her life. There had been no evil intentions, only a buildup of events exploding into bad choices. They hadn't wanted to hurt me. Could I find a way to some type of peace and forgiveness? Didn't I owe it to myself to try?

I didn't want to keep hiding. From the past, or in a career that had gone flat. Somehow, I needed to find myself again, and I sensed this weekend was the beginning of the journey.

I'd spent five years running full circle. All roads always led back to him.

My heart squeezed in my chest. Yes, it was a mess I never expected to deal with, but that her child was safe and happy, that Riggs knew the truth and made his own decision—all of it helped me accept the consequences of that night. We had all changed. I had every right to walk away and remain bitter. Diana was a constant reminder of their night together. Yet, I wanted to meet Ava's daughter.

And I wanted to see Riggs.

I went back to my hotel, got dressed for the evening, and headed to Trattoria Baita Belvedere. The ride was not for the faint of heart. Ava had sent a van to take me there. The driver climbed the twisty, winding road hugging the cliffside at top speed, but with a deftness that told me he'd done it a million times. The restaurant was small and rustic, situated high on a cliff in Bellagio, with an open balcony. The view made me catch my breath with wonder; it was like floating in the clouds, looking down at the tiny boats in the lake, and being part of the mist surrounding the cliffs. Brightly colored flowers spilled over the edges around the terrace. One large table had been set up with pristine white cloths, low vases of fresh flowers, and candles. The breeze carried the scents of flowers and herbs and perfume.

Chelsea was waiting for me. "I love your jumpsuit," I said, giving her a quick hug. "Red is your color."

She wrinkled her nose. "More Ava's color, but I was getting tired of black. I love your pants—is that linen?"

I'd gone with another classic—cream-colored wide-legged pants with a short matching beaded jacket and a lace tank. It screamed elegant and at ease. My hair was in a basic low ponytail held with a pearl-encrusted clip. Hoop earrings and a simple choker made me look polished. "Yeah, I actually got this in Milan."

"Good. I can hop on over there later and get my own."

I laughed. "It's a smaller crowd tonight."

She frowned with worry. "Ava said there's only going to be about twenty people here. How are you? I wasn't sure you'd come."

"I walked all afternoon, thinking about things. Decided I'm here for a reason, and I need to face it all. Which means meeting Ava's daughter. And Riggs."

Chelsea bit her lip. "Do you feel ready?"

"No. But I think it's important."

She let out a breath. "I agree. I still can't believe Ava had a baby and we both had no clue. It feels so wrong. That we weren't a part of such an important event. That we were the last ones to know."

I nodded. "It's a lot to process. I'm going to take it moment to moment."

I was interrupted when Ava came in with Roberto. Everyone clapped. She beamed with happiness and that new calm she now reflected, then tugged her left hand a bit, looking down.

My heart stopped.

Diana took a step forward, peering around her mother's legs as she took in the people crowded at the table. Ava bent down and whispered in her ear. The little girl smiled.

Chelsea gasped. "They look so alike!"

They did. Diana was Ava's mini twin. Her hair was a thick, dark cloud hitting above the shoulders. Chubby cheeks couldn't disguise the elegant bone structure of her face, the natural curve of her lips into a familiar grin; the way she clasped her mom's hand with tiny fingers. Every movement and feature reminded me of Ava, except for one thing.

Her eyes.

Instead of blue, they were a piercing sea green, wide and clear, staring back at the crowd with curiosity but no shyness. It was like looking straight into Riggs's gaze, and for a moment, I swayed on my feet, my brain unable to make sense of what was before me. Chelsea sensed I needed the support, because her hand gripped my arm hard, keeping me balanced. Emotions slammed into me from all sides, and I shuddered, staring helplessly at Diana.

In slow motion, Ava's gaze swung around and met mine.

Everything else fell away. Within our connected stare was a heartfelt plea for understanding. Acceptance.

Forgiveness.

I swallowed hard and reached deep, managing to nod.

A sad, grateful smile curved her red lips. She pressed against Diana, as if unconsciously needing her support the way I needed Chelsea's.

In that moment, we moved into new territory, because she knew I wouldn't hold Diana against her.

Relatives rushed to their side, fussing over Diana and chattering merrily. I gulped in a breath, and Chelsea shoved a champagne flute in my hand. "Drink. God, I feel like I'm in one of those Netflix dramas. Ed has no idea what he's missing."

And then I was laughing and so was she, and the tension mercifully eased.

Ava did her rounds and finally stood in front of us. Her

hands rested on her daughter's shoulders. I noticed they were slightly shaky. "Diana, these are my very best friends in the whole world—Chelsea and Maddie. Mommy went to school with them."

Diana's eyes widened, and her brain seemed to try to compute how old we'd have to be to reach such a milestone. "I have a best friend in school, too," she whispered, her sweet face beaming with excitement. "Her name is Melinda. I call her Mindy."

A reluctant smile stole over me. Chelsea and I knelt down to get on her level. "My real name is Madison, but I'm called Maddie. It's nice to meet you," I said.

"I love your dress," Chelsea said.

"Thank you. It's like Mommy's."

They did match. They both wore sleeveless polka dot A-line dresses that swirled at the knees. Diana reminded me of a little Minnie Mouse with her red glittery shoes and tiny red bow in her hair. Ava kept it grown-up with black stilettos and a wide-banded red belt that cinched her waist tight.

"Are you excited about the wedding?" I asked.

She clapped her hands. "So, so excited! I get to stay up late and have extra dessert and even dance and I get to go up the aisle with Mommy."

"That sounds so cool," Chelsea said with a wink. "Maybe we can dance together? We love to dance."

Diana nodded seriously. "I will dance with you."

My heart skipped in my chest. She was too cute for words and had charmed me within minutes.

Just like Ava.

"Okay, sweetie, let's go talk to Papa and Aunt Sophia and then we'll sit down and eat."

"Do they have pasghetti?"

"Yes," Ava answered. She shot us a brief smile, then walked off with her daughter. Chelsea and I faced each other. "She's beautiful," Chelsea said. "I can't believe Ava's a mom."

"She has Riggs's eyes."

Chelsea jerked, worry creasing her brow. "I know. How are you doing? I know this is a lot, Maddie. I didn't know what to expect with your reaction, but you've been really strong. Are you okay?"

I hadn't been okay for five long years. But right now, meeting Ava's daughter, accepting the past instead of denying it and pushing it away, my chest loosened, allowing space for me to breathe. I welcomed the lightness and knew I needed to walk farther down the path. "Surprisingly, yes. I'm not sure if it will last, but I'm taking it slow."

"I missed you, Maddie."

I blinked at her sudden emotion and hugged her. "I missed you, too."

Dinner was a special event. I was introduced to more of Ava's family, and sat next to Roberto's parents, who seemed smitten with both their future daughter-in-law and grandchild. Diana ate her pasta while Roberto teased her, and when I caught the fierce look of devotion in his face, I realized Diana truly did belong to him. By choice.

By love.

We feasted on a multicourse meal. Crisp lettuce dressed

with fragrant olive oil and lemon; salami cured in oil amid delicate cheeses; creamy polenta paired with tagliolini in a light tomato sauce; stewed wild boar, the salted, earthy meat dancing with flavor on my tongue. The Valtellina Superiore was a fine, light-bodied red wine that complemented each course. Dessert was a latte cotto tart, combined of milk pudding and honey; chewy chestnuts with cream; and tiny cups of bitter espresso. I devoured the meal with gusto, falling in love all over again with food the way it was supposed to be prepared: simple, clean flavors with the freshest ingredients.

When we left the restaurant, the moon was full, suspended above the lake like a silvery, glowing dome. Before climbing into the van, I heard my name called.

Ava rushed over, slightly breathless. "I'm staying at my father's tonight. Roberto's taking Diana, and Dad and Gabriella are staying late with friends from out of town. I wondered if . . ."

I tilted my head, curious. "What?"

"Would you—want to take a ride with me? To the beach?"

I stilled. I knew she spoke of the beach where we made our pacts; the beach where we skinny-dipped and floated with hands entwined and made promises we believed we'd keep. I opened my mouth to say no, too beaten by the events of the day, but something else rose up inside of me.

"Okay."

Ava let out her breath. Excitement glittered in her blue eyes. "Really? I'm so happy—Chelsea's coming, too. Wait here—we'll come in your van."

Guests trickled to their vehicles, and I watched as she said goodbye to Roberto and Diana. The three of them stood tight in a circle, already a fully formed family. My eyes burned. I blinked the sting away and got in the van.

Chelsea and Ava joined me, and soon we were driving down the cliff, around the bends, the windows down and the wind tearing through our hair. We didn't speak, just enjoyed the ride and the way Lake Como came alive at night around us.

We walked to the small strip of rocky beach where we'd once stood. I kicked off my shoes and trudged into the water. The cool water caressed my ankles, my toes curled into the smooth pebbles. The night was full of sounds and scents, from the gentle wash of waves over stone to the screech of a night owl, the stillness of night enclosing the cliffs and swallowing up the lake. The moon whispered and beckoned fools to fall in love and make vows of forever. The light bewitched, dancing over Ava's smooth skin, getting lost in her blue eyes.

They joined me in the water. Chelsea threw her head back and opened her mouth, like she was about to swallow the moon whole.

"What happened to us?" she asked the sky, her voice carrying on the wind.

"We grew up," I said.

"I fucked up," Ava added.

"I miss who I was back then," Chelsea said.

I jerked in surprise. We turned and stared. "What do you mean?" I asked. "You have everything you ever wanted."

She slammed me with the truth of her gaze. "I love being

a mom. Being a wife. But I never accomplished my dreams. The one thing I've always been sure of is opening up my business, and now I'm thirty years old, and I never did it. I'm a failure."

Ava gasped. "Chels! That's not true. Sure, you took a different path, but you always had goals. You worked with Ed while you were pregnant—you're literally the poster child of mom perfection. What are you talking about?"

Her laugh was full of self-derision. "Not even close, Ava. You have no idea, do you? How I hate watching my husband come home from work and talk about his clients, while I have throw-up in my hair, and cookie dough under my fingernails and stupid *PAW Patrol* playing on the television. That wasn't supposed to be me! I was going to do more!"

I spoke in a gentle tone. "Babe, you accomplished so much. It's not over—you just had your kids earlier than expected. You got a degree and passed all your tests and worked for one of the most prestigious firms in New York City. You are a powerhouse."

"Was. I was. God, I was going to make such a difference for women. I had such a clear vision, and then I got pregnant on my damn honeymoon. Do you know I was looking at properties with Ava? I was ready for the leap. I'd worked so hard to prepare, and when I got back, Maddie, you were gone, and Ava was gone, and I was pregnant. Ed said it wasn't a good time to open up a new business. And sure, I agreed, but then I guess I thought after Brady turned one, I'd circle back and get it done."

She blew out a hard breath, her voice edged with frustration. "And then I got pregnant again. I'd switched from the pill to the IUD and it didn't take. So I delayed opening my business again, still thinking I'd have something to give afterward. But it's gone. And God help me, I can't get it back."

"What's gone?" Ava asked, reaching out to touch her arm.

"Knowing who I am. I feel like I lost my whole identity."

I shuddered. Pain exploded through my body along with a sharp empathy. It was so easy to lose yourself in each step toward the person you dreamed of being. I wasn't a mother, but I felt Chelsea's grief deep in my bones. The grief for how it all turned out; from my choices and acceptance in what I got dealt.

"I don't have the certainty I used to. I'm terrified I'll never follow through, after years of sacrifice and focus! And now I have these beautiful children, but I stare at them and mourn everything I gave up. Not Ed. Me, always me."

Then, suddenly, a primitive cry exploded from her lips and into the night. I watched, stunned, as my friend who'd always been the most balanced, the surest of everything, suddenly began tearing off her jumpsuit in a frenzy, throwing her bra and panties to the ground and running into the water. I watched as she screamed up at the moon from a primal place inside of her; the part that no one liked to talk about or acknowledge because it was ugly, and judgmental.

I looked at Ava and she nodded. We stripped down and followed Chelsea into the water.

Because that's what friends do.

Splashing out to meet her, I grabbed her hand and joined my voice with hers in a howl. The sound broke through the last of my barriers, and I didn't even notice the tears running down my face. I was caught up in the power of the moment. Ava's cry mingled with ours, and suddenly, we were laughing and crying and howling in the lake, naked and free.

"I love being a mom," Chelsea said. "It's hard to explain how these little humans broke me into a thousand pieces of pure emotion. It's the most difficult, rewarding job I can imagine. But I'm tired of wondering why it's not enough. For me, I need more."

Ava turned on Chelsea with her typical fierceness. "Don't apologize for it. You want to run your own business. You want to use your talents for more. It's who you are. And guess what? We can be a mom and a wife and a businessperson. Just don't believe that crap where they say you can have it all without sacrifice. We do sacrifice; every day we make choices. But isn't that okay?"

I watched my two friends try to explain a place I hadn't visited yet, but could still relate to. I'd dealt with those choices with Riggs, trying to decide if I had to give up love in order to gain fame. Maybe we were told wrong all this time, by too much of the world. Maybe it was better to be honest about what you were choosing and what was being given up, rather than in denial that there were no consequences.

Maybe consequences made the choices we *did* make more precious.

Maybe loss was the greatest lesson of all.

"I don't want to do this anymore."

They faced me with matching frowns. Ava bit her lip. "Being with us? Trying to forgive me?"

I shook my head, my wet hair slapping against my shoulders. "No. I meant, me. This career I chose, the one I wanted so badly I couldn't see anything else. I'm so . . . tired."

Chelsea's eyes softened. "Over the fallout? I know it's hard, but it will pass. I bet you'll begin getting jobs again shortly, if you can ride it out a little longer."

"I don't want the jobs anymore." A wild laugh escaped my lips. "I don't want to model anymore. Or do daily videos for my followers. Or act in roles that mean nothing to me. Or pretend my heart is in it. I'm burned-out and lost. I don't know what I'm doing it for anymore."

They shared a glance. "What do you want to do?" Ava asked curiously.

I raised my hands in the air, then let them drop. "I don't know. I've spent years wanting one thing for myself. To be seen. My parents never did that. But suddenly there were both of you who somehow cared about me, and Riggs, and then all these strangers who gave me value. I had everything I ever dreamed, but I never had the one damn thing I needed most of all."

They were silent, as if sensing I was on the verge of a huge realization I'd been burying.

"I never valued myself. Somehow, I'm still trying to make up for the little girl who was never wanted. And I'm done.

With all of it. I just want to figure out who the hell I am without the noise or endless need for approval and attention."

I waited for them to soothe me, or brush off my speech. I figured they'd chalk up this emotional outburst to all the truths of the day that had been lobbed at me like fastballs thrown by a baseball pitcher in a World Series game.

Instead, Chelsea grinned. "Sounds pretty badass to me. And overdue."

"Agreed," Ava said.

I laughed, at their easy acceptance and the way they were able to make me feel better no matter what I shared. "You both are seriously weird."

They laughed with me, and we swam under the full moon.

Memories rushed past me as I floated on my back; the past and present fused together.

Ava's husky voice rose in the breeze and drifted to my ears.

"Thank you for spending the night before my wedding with me."

Her hand eased close. I didn't answer, but took her hand, and then Chelsea's, until we'd completed the circle.

And didn't speak for a long, long time.

29

⁂

walked through the elaborate wrought iron gates of Villa
Pliniana, and my breath caught in my throat.

The broad pathway was carved like a bridge over the water, spilling into a giant terrace lined with bright lanterns
and fresh flowers. Sunset had just begun, and the sky was
streaked by a brilliant array of colors—umber, burnt orange,
mustard, sienna—casting a rosy glow over the estate. A
tuxedo-clad musician sat at a grand piano, his fingers dancing over the glossy keys, spilling a haunting, gorgeous melody into the breeze. The rolling hills and lake were a
backdrop to the three-story square villa surrounded by cy-
press trees.

It was a scene from a movie set, and I was part of the cast.

I nodded to various guests, thanking the server who offered me a glass of champagne, and was led into the main
room where the ceremony was taking place. Ava had told

me the small chapel only fit a handful of people, so they'd chosen a bigger space to invite everyone.

The groomsman, Roberto's brother Salvatore, escorted me to my seat near the front row. I took in the room in awe, admiring the elaborately painted wooden ceilings, the Venetian terrazzo–styled floors, and the heavy velvet curtains pushed back from the large windows to let the last rays of sunlight stream in. Six-foot pedestals of flowers anchored the archway in soft lavenders, cream, and lemon yellow. The buzz of chatter rose when Roberto took his place at the front. His tuxedo was deep maroon with a paisley jacket, emphasizing his dark Italian looks and trim body.

I chewed my inner cheek and looked around but didn't see Riggs. The idea of him showing up to see me made my stomach twist with nerves. Half of me wanted to run away and not face him. The other half craved his presence after all this time.

Chelsea suddenly squeezed by me, taking her seat. "Sorry I'm late. I was crying. Wait till you see her."

"Oh my God, I can imagine. Did the paparazzi invade yet?"

Chelsea shook her head. "Nope. Ava said she was pretty much out of the spotlight these past years so attention has dropped. Which is great for you—I was worried those vultures would sniff you out here."

I was relieved. I'd been sick with worry about photographers showing up to harass me at Ava's wedding, driving me away. "Oh, it's starting. Here comes Gabriella and Roberto's parents."

A singer began softly crooning with the harp player, creating the perfect blend of emotion. Salvatore escorted his parents up to their seats, and Gabriella walked down the aisle with a big smile. The priest patted the groom's arm, then made the announcement to stand.

My belly fluttered. Diana appeared in the doorway, and everyone gasped in unison.

She was a mini bride, dressed in a gorgeous concoction of lace and tulle, her white shoes sparkling with pearls as she slowly walked down the aisle, dropping yellow rose petals on the runner, a shy smile curving her lips. A tiara-type crown perched on her head. Her hair was in ringlets.

I stared with wonder at this child Ava had created with the man I loved, wondering how the hate and bitterness had edged toward forgiveness. Even bigger?

Acceptance.

Ava's daughter was a miracle.

The little girl stopped at the front, waving to Roberto, making everyone laugh. Then the music changed and Ava appeared, her arm linked with her father's.

I'd learned a lot about photography through the years, and what aspects made the lens either love or dislike you. Ava practically demanded every gaze as her right, and none of it came from ego or a desperate need for attention. It was a quality that beat from her very aura; an innate surety of self, even though she questioned it with us. The world only saw stunning beauty and craved to be in her orbit.

She floated down the aisle in a lace dress that spilled into an elaborate train of feathers. The simple bodice balanced the intricate crisscross beadwork at the back, dipping low in a sexy goodbye. Her hair was caught up in a stacked bun surrounded by a diamond crown that attached to a veil matching the long train in the most delicate of lace.

I heard the oohs and aahs, mesmerized by the joy sketched on her face; the full tilt to her stained red lips; the gleam of hope in her cerulean blue eyes as she made her way to Roberto and Diana.

I couldn't speak, caught up in the overwhelming emotion of the moment. Ava joined her husband-to-be on the altar, and when their gazes met, they reminded me of teenagers, giddy and smiling and obviously madly in love.

The pain hit hard and low. I'd experienced those same emotions with Riggs. I wondered what it would have been like if we'd stayed together and had our own wedding day. Maybe it wouldn't have lasted. Maybe it would've been my biggest regret.

But God, I wish I got to choose. Ava had taken it away from me, and that was the biggest obstacle to fully moving on from the past.

They recited their vows and Diana joined them, completing the circle.

And then they were husband and wife.

The cheers rose for the first kiss, then Ava turned to face the crowd, her gaze going directly to me.

"Thank you," she mouthed, eyes gleaming with unshed tears.

I nodded.

In minutes, she was gone and the ceremony was over.

Chelsea sighed. "Ugh, my mascara is a mess. I gotta clean up."

I laughed, trying to compose myself. "You go ahead. I'm going to hang here for a bit."

"You okay?"

"Yeah. I need a minute."

She squeezed my arm and left.

I sat in my seat, staring at the flowers, watching the musicians begin to move their stuff. I listened to the animated chatter and laughs from the guests behind me. And I thought of what was next for me. After today.

Was I going home to New York?

The thought gave me a sour taste in my mouth. I needed a break from the madness to figure out what I wanted to do. I had enough money to step away and take time off. I'd been going nonstop for the past five years, and had never paused to reflect on anything other than how I had been betrayed. All that anger and bitterness had nested inside me for too long. This past weekend had leeched much of it out, but I knew there was still work to do.

On myself.

With a sigh, I got up and began walking back down the aisle.

Then froze.

Riggs stood in front of me.

Time stopped. The world tilted. My breath got stuck in my lungs.

I studied him with greed. He wore a royal blue pinstripe suit cut to his trim frame. His hair was shorter and better tamed, but the stubborn curl in the front still threatened. I crimped my fingers into tight fists, fighting the urge to slide those thick strands back like I had so many times before. His face held a few more lines, but it was his eyes that had me spellbound. A misty sea green like Diana's. His gaze drilled into mine, turbulent and restless, nothing like the calm focus or laughing mischief from before. No, these were eyes of someone who'd seen and done things I didn't know.

"Maddie."

His voice saying my name made me jerk, the familiar lilt like a long-forgotten song. He was the same but different. Caught between two worlds, I remained still, unable to speak for a while.

A ghost of a smile touched his lips. "I'm afraid to say anything more in case you run."

I broke the spell, shaking my head slightly. "Sorry. It's been . . . a long time."

Shadows crossed his face. "Yes. Yet, seeing you now, I feel like it was yesterday. Isn't that strange?"

I felt the same so I nodded. "I like your suit."

We both laughed and seemed to fall apart at the same time, remembering how I used to be all over him when he put on his favorite navy blue classic. Remembering how it was the last time we were together, the night before Chelsea's wedding.

"Well, that was an icebreaker," he said, easing a few steps forward. "I've been wanting to talk to you. When Ava said you were coming . . ." he trailed off.

"I know." I paused, searching for the words. "I couldn't, Riggs. It was all too much."

"Yeah."

We locked gazes. I was surprised at the raw bite of hunger that tore at my insides. Even with all that had happened, I still wanted him. Wanted to close the distance and slide my arms around his shoulders and lean into his strength. He had been my home for so long. I'd been searching for another one for five years and never found it.

"Will you talk to me now? Please?" he asked gently.

"Yes. Ava warned me you were coming. I know about everything."

Resignation was in the set of his shoulders. He regarded me from under thick eyelashes. I wondered how he'd dealt with all that had happened, and for the first time, I was curious to hear his story. I was ready to unlock Pandora's box and deal with what sprang forth.

"She told me she planned to tell you. I know this isn't the best place to have this conversation, but I was desperate. Can we go into the chapel while they're taking pictures?"

I nodded and followed him out. Guests gathered for the cocktail hour, spilling onto the open-air terrace, holding drinks and eating from the various plated appetizers. We passed by and entered the chapel, a small stone sanctuary. A fountain took up the center between three columns, and fresh flowers were strategically placed. It was a quiet and reflective space. We sat down on a bench next to the altar and faced each other.

"You look beautiful," he said, his voice slightly gruff.

I'd dressed with him in mind. The dusty rose gown accented my skin tone and red hair. The fabric was a luxurious blend that clung to my figure in a wraparound cut, emphasizing the curve of my rear, the gentle swell of my breasts, the straight line of my hips. The dress was backless, offering an onlooker a shock of bare skin. I'd learned by being in front of the camera sometimes less was more, and had gotten used to letting clothes adorn my body instead of trying to wear the clothes for my own purposes. My fans called it my stoic period, where I moved away from sparkle and various bling I'd loved in my early twenties. It offered a more sophisticated palette, which suited me. My hair had been left loose to fall in a tumble of waves. My only jewelry was a drop diamond necklace and cocktail ring that shimmered under the light.

I watched him as he took me in, the familiar light of lust flaring in his eyes. My body softened, still well trained to respond under a look, a touch, or a word. No matter what had broken us, the physical connection still burned bright and hot. It was both a thrill and a disappointment that with us, nothing had changed.

"Thank you," I said. "Ava mentioned you're a lawyer now."

He nodded. "I took a year off from law school after you left. I couldn't focus. Nothing made sense or had worth for me. I chased after you for a long time, Maddie. Even after Levi told me to leave you alone."

"You broke me. The only way to keep going was to forget you and throw myself into work."

His jaw tightened. "I know. Believe me, I know. What we did—what I did—was unforgivable. No apology was going to fix it. I think I wasted that year convincing myself I could explain my actions away and it would all work out. But of course, it didn't. I eventually got my shit together and went back to law school. I opened up a small firm in Westchester recently and I really like it."

"Good. I'm glad you found your passion."

"You've done amazing for yourself. Not that I ever doubted it. I saw your movies several times. You're a wonderful actress."

"All three," I joked. "I played the same exact character—the best friend in the fashion industry. It wasn't much of a stretch."

"Don't do that, Maddie. Undersell yourself. In a few years, you were on television, on the big screen, and on New York billboards. You made the impossible happen just like you dreamed."

I should have been annoyed he was giving me a pep talk after sleeping with my best friend, but I only warmed under his praise. No matter what he did, Riggs had always seen the real me, including my insecurities. My belief I wasn't worthy; wasn't enough. He'd held me when I cried about my family, and encouraged me when I'd been terrified of facing the camera in case I failed.

I crossed my arms in front of my chest, slightly defensive.

"You're right. I'm not dismissing my success. I did work hard. Unfortunately, things are a bit challenging right now."

"I saw the video. You looked—" he broke off.

I waited but he never finished. "How?"

He seemed reluctant, but the word shot out like a cannon. "Angry."

I let out a breath and examined my painted rose-tinted nails. "Yeah. I was. That was another reason I came to Ava's wedding. I'm tired of trying to forget what happened. Instead of letting it go, the bad stuff festered until I blew up. I need to move on, Riggs. Ava told me her side of what happened. What's yours?"

His voice was as tight as his muscled body. "I knew we'd been drifting apart, and it was haunting me. Each time I felt like we got closer, something would jerk us back apart. When you mentioned LA, all I could think of was you hanging with Levi nonstop, and meeting all these big-name actors and models, and how my life revolved around studying law for the next few years. I got in my head."

I looked up. "You didn't trust me?"

His smile was sad and resigned. "I didn't trust the world, Maddie. It wasn't about you cheating on me; it was about growing apart and wanting different things in life. I didn't know how to stop that from happening, so I was a selfish ass and figured if I put on some pressure, maybe you wouldn't go to LA. I convinced myself you could become just as big in New York City and still be with me. There's no excuse. It was just the way I felt back then."

I nodded. It hurt, but I also understood. Raging against what-ifs didn't help.

"I got really drunk at Chelsea's wedding. When you told me you were leaving, I lost control. I remember passing out, and Ava dragging me to her room. I was so mad at her, for what she did to Patrick and the way she manipulated you. We got into it, and there was yelling and things got nasty. I wanted to go back to our room and wake you up, but I also knew that we'd only fight, so I drank some more from her minibar. And then Ava said I had no right to keep you from your dream, that I was a selfish bastard, and I started to cry because I already knew you were lost. I knew you had to go and it would be over between us, because you were always meant for bigger things than me."

I held my breath, watching the emotions flicker over his face. His fist curled, then uncurled.

"And then we were just kissing. I felt her pain, and it was like we were grieving you together, as ridiculous as that sounds. I don't even remember the sex. I only remember wanting to stop that empty, awful feeling inside. Then I passed out, and I woke up when you were at the door."

His hand rubbed his forehead. "I tried everything to get in touch with you. So did Ava. Within weeks, I had fallen apart and dropped out of school, and Ava disappeared to Italy. I never heard from her until a year after Diana was born."

My heart felt raw and heavy. The memory of finding Riggs with Ava hit me all over again, and I shuddered, my muscles aching from reliving the trauma. But this time, I had context, and I dragged in a breath, holding in air as I settled back into present day.

Neither of their explanations erased the pain, or changed my ability to move on with our relationships intact. We'd never be the same. But maybe there was a tiny crack open to wriggle through. To rebuild on. In whatever capacity I wanted or chose to pursue.

Having control of my story helped. This time, I wasn't the one running. I was the one in power, to decide how much I wanted them back in my life, or if at all.

"What happened when you heard about Diana?" I asked.

"God, I lost my mind. I tried to deny the possibility, but I knew Ava wouldn't lie about that. We talked. She wanted to stay in Italy and raise Diana with her family. I flew out to meet her, and I finally agreed. I figured I'd give it some time and see what would be best for Diana.

"Then Ava met Roberto. I knew immediately they were meant to be a family. There was no reason to tear them apart. I was her blood father, but Roberto was her real father. It was easy to see how much they loved each other when I went to meet him. Diana's face lit up when he was around. Why would I try to shove my way in? To be acknowledged as her real father? To be across the world and see her on summer vacations and confuse her? No. Diana deserved more. She deserved love and stability and a beautiful life I couldn't give her."

Passion emanated from his sea green eyes. I had wondered how I'd react to his decision not to be Diana's father, but hearing his explanation made sense. Stepping back wasn't a selfish move; it was actually the opposite.

"Will you ever tell her the truth?"

"Maybe. When she's eighteen, or if she begins to ask questions. I'll let Ava and Roberto navigate what they feel is best. And I'll be here if she ever wants to get to know me. But not now." The muscle in his jaw ticked. "God, that little girl is beautiful. She looks exactly like Ava."

"Except her eyes." His gaze swiveled around and drilled into mine. My palms grew damp at the growing intensity sparking around his eyes.

"Yeah. She has my eyes." He leaned forward. His breath hinted at mint and coffee. His skin was clean-shaven, and his lips looked full and soft. Desire stirred low and dipped. "Maddie, I'll never be able to apologize enough for that night. I know you've moved on. But you have the right to know one thing. There hasn't been another woman since you."

I jerked back as if burnt. My whole body trembled. "You can't be telling me the truth."

"I am. I've tried to be interested in other women. Hell, I've even tried a one-night stand to get you out of my head, but it's always been you. I just feel you deserve to know that."

I hated his declaration.

I loved his declaration.

Not knowing how to respond, I remained silent, pondering his words. I chose mine carefully. "It doesn't make anything right again."

"I know. I came tonight with no expectations—I only

wanted to talk to you. I've tortured myself for too many years, and it's time I find a way to live with my mistake."

"Ava can never think of it as a mistake," I said softly.

"Because of Diana." Riggs blew out a breath, nodding. "Yeah, it will always be complicated. The past. Our actions. How we hurt you. But Diana is special. Somehow, she was a little light that came from it all, only . . ." he trailed off. Stared at the thick white columns of marble where sunbeams danced and played.

"Only what?" I prodded.

Sadness wrapped his tone. "Only for you, she's a constant reminder of what happened. I can't imagine how that must feel."

A sigh escaped me. "I don't look at her like that. Yeah, I have a ton to process, and I'm not going to lie and say everything is suddenly okay because enough time has passed, or you both explained what happened in a way I can accept. But with Diana, I only see you and Ava and how much joy she brings. I can separate it." I tilted my head, thinking hard. "Maybe because you weren't having this affair behind my back. You didn't plan it. Maybe I'm able to look at Diana and only see the good, of how much we all tried to love one another, even when it got fucked-up."

I let out a half laugh. "Or maybe I'm just exhausted and overly emotional and trying to figure shit out."

"Maybe that," he said with a smile. "Whatever it is, you're a gift to me, Maddie. You always were."

He stood up and offered his hand. "Will you join me?

Ava said she wasn't assigning seats. I'd love to talk more, if you're up for it."

I swallowed back the hard ball of need that gathered in my throat. "Chelsea's here."

"Of course. I was looking forward to seeing her, too."

I nodded. He quickly dropped his hand, realizing I wasn't ready to touch him, and we joined the guests in the main room where the reception was being held.

The next few hours flew by. Chelsea, Riggs, and I sat together, keeping conversation light. We feasted on plates of truffled pasta, fresh roasted lamb with rosemary, crusty breads, antipasti, and an array of vegetables. The band played songs in both Italian and English, and everyone danced throughout the rooms, under the painted wooden ceilings of the ballroom, under the beaming moonlight on the terrace, and wherever the mood took hold.

Ava floated over to me halfway through the evening, her cheeks glowing. Her train had been bustled, but her veil still trailed behind her, a remnant of the ceremony she didn't seem to want to let go of yet. "Did you talk to Riggs?" she asked, leaning close.

"Yes. I'm glad we did, Ava. It was time for both of us to face the past."

She nibbled at her plump red lip. "Are you . . . okay? I didn't want to get married without you at my wedding, Maddie. I know that was selfish, but it wouldn't feel real without you and Chelsea. Can you understand?"

I noticed she didn't ask about forgiveness. I knew she

had her own demons to face; a pregnancy she bore alone, a child she loved and raised while the past shadowed her actions; hard choices to make moving forward. But she'd gotten her happy ending—she'd found love and had a beautiful daughter. She was facing her future with a calm focus I'd never seen before. Ava had changed.

I wanted to change, too.

"I understand, Ava. And I'm glad I came to your wedding."

Her smile was heartbreakingly hopeful. "Thank you," she whispered, hugging me close. The scent of musk and sandalwood drifted from her skin. "I love you, Maddie."

Then she drifted away, pulled into the crowd who shouted her name for a dance, and I was left alone, staring after her.

A shadow fell across the floor. I looked up. "Will you dance with me?"

My breath stopped. I opened my mouth to say no, but instead, I gave him my hand and we moved to the dance floor.

The song was low and sweet, a melancholy melody that spoke of great love, and the fragility of it; the woven threads crisscrossing to create a strong bond to stand the test of time. The violin played, and people danced close around us, holding each other tight.

Our bodies remembered and fell back together effortlessly. My arms slid up to his shoulders; his hand splayed across my lower back, bare where my dress ended. Goose bumps shivered up my spine. My breasts brushed against the hard wall of his chest. His cheek hovered near my temple, his breath stirring my hair, rushing past my ear. Our thighs shifted inches at a time, right, left, center. Again. Again.

Time stopped. I got lost in the music and him, in the scent of cotton and lemon; in the touch of his fingers on my body; in the raw need to get closer, always closer, until we melded back into one, where we'd always returned.

"I still love you."

The softly spoken words broke me into tiny pieces. "I can't go back to who I was. She's gone. So are we."

"Not looking to reclaim what we lost." His hips bumped mine and I shuddered. "I'm more interested in now. Seeing if you'd want to get to know each other again."

"You don't think that's dangerous? Trying to rewrite or reclaim the past?"

"Like you said, we're not the same. I'd like to learn about who you are now. But it's on your terms—all of it. I've told you my truth, and you need to honor yours."

A tiny laugh escaped my lips. "I don't know my truth any longer," I said honestly. "Maybe I never did."

"Maybe you can find out." He tipped my chin up and met my gaze head-on. I sucked in my breath at the heat in those beautiful green eyes. "Maybe I'm desperate or insane, but I still have hope. For us."

"Riggs—"

"I know. I won't say anything else. I just want to hold you for a little while longer."

We finished the dance. I surrendered it all to those last precious refrains of song, melting against his hard chest and savoring his presence. When the music ended, and I pulled away, I only knew I had to go. My heart was cracked open and couldn't take anymore. I needed to retreat and be safe.

Riggs was no longer my safe place.

"I have to go. I can't do this right now."

"Can I reach out? Maybe text you?"

I didn't answer because I had no answer. Retreating a few steps back, I took in him standing there, sexy in his blue suit, with Ava in her white dress and Diana beside her dancing in the background, and Chelsea off to the side at the bar, chatting with a few people. I took in the joyous fervor of the moment and the glittering lights bouncing off the terrazzo painted floors, and then I ran, out of the reception, out to the terrace, and into the night, leaving the wedding and my past behind me.

30

I didn't sleep. Instead, I perched on the large windowsill in my room, staring out at the night. I thought about Riggs and Ava and Diana. I thought about Chelsea's struggles trying to rediscover herself after motherhood. I thought about my choices to mistake adoration and likes for love. I thought about how I waited for my mother to call after every film shoot, after every magazine cover, and only received the same heartbreaking silence. I thought about chasing fame and how empty I felt inside.

By the time dawn struggled over the horizon, my eyes felt crusty from staying up. Tired but resigned, I called my agent.

"Thank God. How are you? How was the wedding?" she asked in a rush. I'd signed with Sierra at the peak of my career, and she'd done well, intent on growing my fame with a gutsy and ambitious focus I admired. She was a female shark, which I'd desperately needed since my background as an influencer was looked down on a bit in both Hollywood and the inner circles of high fashion and modeling. I pictured her trademark worried frown, which regular Botox injections smoothed out, her trendy glasses pushed up high on her nose. She was no-nonsense and preferred streamlined tailored suits, minimal makeup, and a pulled-back, sleek ponytail. Unfortunately, Sierra wasn't going to be happy with my decision, but it was the first step I needed to take in order to grasp back control of my life.

"The wedding was good."

"Fantastic. I have decent news. Yes, we lost the other contracts—fucking morals clause I tried to negotiate back then came to bite us in the ass—but things are beginning to quiet. Did you see what happened?"

"No, I've been out of touch here."

"It's poetic, Maddie. You know those two hot costars from that new Netflix series about the teen addicts? They had an affair! Even better? One of them broke up their marriage over it! You're pretty much old news for now. Isn't that wonderful?"

I almost laughed but recognized I felt sorry for both celebrities. Unfortunately, the world was there to capture every misstep. Distaste curled on my tongue. This was the career I'd flung myself into, hoping to recruit young girls like I'd once been. Now I realized I'd done it all wrong.

"Well, I guess it's good I claimed some breathing room."

"Good? Darling, this is better than we hoped for! Already, I have Belle cosmetics interested in hiring you for a lipstick campaign. Guess what they said?" I didn't need to answer because she was already talking. "They said even though the video crushed your reputation, your lipstick looked divine! They're going to build something a bit humorous and edgy into the new ads, featuring you screaming at the camera—isn't that genius? So, I need you out here right away. Get on the next plane and we'll meet with them and hammer out details."

"Sierra—"

"Once you're back in everyone's good graces, other companies will want in. I bet those bastards will circle back and beg you to wear that new mascara, but we're not going back, even if they double the offer. We need to show them we don't run scared. Don't you agree?"

"Sierra—"

"I'll have a car meet you at the airport—when do you get in?"

"Sierra!"

"What?"

"I'm not coming back to New York. Not for a while."

The silence crackled with tension. "What are you telling me?"

I rubbed the back of my neck. "I'm tired, so I'm staying in Italy for a while. I need to get my head together and figure out what I want to do next."

I imagined my agent pursing her lips, madly computing what she needed to do to get me home. "Okay, you want movies, right? Of course you do! I'll call Santiago and see if he can find a decent script. We'll say no to fashion for a while and hit it hard—I bet we can score a few commercials while we wait to see—"

"No, Sierra. You have to listen. No movies, or ads, or social media videos. I'm taking a real break. I'm getting off my phone and figuring some stuff out. I'm unhappy."

Her voice softened. "Darling, of course you are; this has been a lot to go through. I'm here to help you navigate things, but doing nothing will ruin everything you've built. We need to strike when things are cooling down but you're still relevant. I promise you will have more fans and followers than ever before!"

A choked sound escaped my throat. "That's exactly what I was afraid of. I know you can't understand this, but I'm telling you how it's going to be. I'm taking a break. If I get any offers, just email them to me, and I promise to look at them. But no phone calls."

"Wait—what? For how long? Is this some digital detox? Are you addicted to drugs and going to rehab? Oh my God, Maddie, are you okay?"

I couldn't help laughing, realizing the world would probably assume that's exactly where I was. My apology had hinted at it. Getting clean to go back to the madness.

What was even more amazing? I didn't care. It didn't embarrass me or scare me. Everything I'd worked so hard for was built on smoke and empty promises. Yes, I loved fashion, but I'd gotten so far away from that girl who really wanted to help other girls score gorgeous fashion for low prices. The joy had been sapped out and replaced by dollars.

"I'm fine. I'm not on drugs. I just want to disappear for a bit and see what happens."

"What about Belle cosmetics?"

"Say no."

"Movie scripts?"

"No. Tell everyone I'm taking a mental rest or whatever you feel is best. I don't care as long as I'm not bothered and you don't tell anyone where I am. Understood?"

I knew it was taking Sierra a lot to swallow my demands, but she eventually grumbled out a yes. I made arrangements for her to hire someone to take care of my apartment, and when we hung up, I felt lighter.

Now, the fun part.

I brought up my laptop and began to poke around. I wanted to be close to Milan so I could steep myself in the fashion I truly loved, without the filter of how to gain likes. Along the way, the purity of that love was lost, and I wanted to see if I could recapture some of my passion. I didn't want to stay in a big city like Florence, either, and Lake Como and Bellagio were crowded with tourists.

I settled on Nesso, a small, quiet town on the lake that was known for its steep steps; for its quiet solitude and peaceful atmosphere. A good place to find myself and settle in under the radar, with gorgeous surroundings that promoted peace and self-reflection.

The rest came easily. I secured reservations at Tra Lago e Montagna Baita la Morena, a guest home high up on a hill with simple decor, a farm restaurant, and stunning views. By the time Chelsea buzzed my phone, I was satisfied with my plans.

"You left without saying goodbye," Chelsea said.

"I'm sorry. I danced with Riggs and I got hit with all this emotion so I ran off."

She muttered a curse. "He pushed too hard, didn't he?"

"No, he was just honest. You were having such a good time, I didn't want to interrupt. When are you flying out?"

"I took this extra day to recover, so not until early tomorrow morning."

I smiled. "Good. Come over so we can spend the day together. I made a decision that's going to blow your mind."

"Oh no, I can't wait to hear! Okay, I'll shower and get dressed and head over. I haven't seen Ava yet, but they're supposed to leave for their honeymoon soon."

"I never asked her if Diana is going?"

Chelsea laughed. "Yep, they're taking a toddler on their honeymoon. Who would've thought? But I guess the cruise ship has a lot of amenities for kids, too, so Diana will have fun and they'll get alone time."

A bittersweet happiness flowed through me. My friend had truly found her happy place, and it ended up being her family. "That's really nice, though."

"I know. See you soon."

An hour later, I met Chelsea in the lobby and we headed to the villages of Lake Como, passing the time popping into the shops and walking by the lake. We ate gelato, and stopped for an aperitif, lazing the day away under the hot sun. I told her about my plans to stay, and loved that she was supportive rather than questioning my motives.

"This is the best move for you," Chelsea said, licking the

last of her pistachio gelato from the spoon. "For the past few years, you've been caught in a whirlwind, and you never slowed down. I'm sorry you're not happy anymore, but this is a way you can find that peace again. Will you do anything in Milan?"

I shrugged. "There's a lot of fashion houses I've done work for, and some up-and-coming designers I can contact. But first I want to figure out what to focus on. Modeling? Movies? Being a straight-up influencer? Or maybe none of it? Maybe I want to try something completely different."

Chelsea nodded. "Makes sense. Are you going back to New York? I know that's where Riggs is."

I pondered her question. "When I think of home, I still think of New York. I think that's where I'm supposed to be eventually. LA has never captured my heart, and I don't want to set up residence in Italy like Ava."

Chelsea gave a longing sigh. "Not a lot of women have the means or time to do what you are doing right now. Take advantage. I can't imagine being able to take time off to figure crap out. Too many people need me."

I winced. "I know. I've lived strictly with one goal: to not have anyone care about me. Guess I won, huh?"

Chelsea slapped her hand over her mouth. "Maddie, I'm sorry—that came out fucked-up! I only meant to treasure this time and use it for what you need. And I care about you, idiot! So does Ava. And it seems Riggs has never stopped, after what you told me. Do you think you'd want to see him again?"

I bit my lip. "I can't believe I'm saying this, but when we

were together, it was like all the time spent apart dropped away and we seemed to still . . . fit. He asked if he could text me, but I ran off. I wasn't ready to make that type of decision."

"Maybe that's another thing you'll figure out here."

"Yeah. But I want to talk about you, Chels. I've been thinking a lot about what you said. How you're juggling all these roles and feel lost. Is there any way you can talk to Ed about what you feel? Find a way to move forward and build this company you dreamed of for so long?"

She shot me a look, and I stopped walking. "Actually, Ava asked me the same thing. And offered to put up a stake, just like she did five years ago. With her backing, I'd be able to get the loan from the bank."

I gripped her hand in excitement. Her dark eyes sparkled with hope. "Babe, that's amazing! Please tell me you're thinking of doing it."

She nodded. "I am, but it depends on Ed. He's a little stubborn about taking help, so I'll have to show him spreadsheets of how we can return Ava's investment and make her money. That's the way to sell it."

"You know the way to an accountant's heart," I joked.

"I learned the hard way."

We laughed. "I know this may seem like overkill, but I'd love to be involved, too, Chels. For any portion you'd be willing to give."

"You don't have to do that, Maddie. We'll have enough now."

"No, hear me out. When I look around at all the things

I've done and invested in, nothing feels real. The idea of holding a small part of a company that will help women be empowered with finance is exciting. It's not about wanting to help my friend. I believe you can make this really huge and important, and it would be an honor if you let me invest."

She blinked hard, and I noticed tears fill her eyes. "You are the best friend ever."

"I'm not. I'm the worst friend. I froze you out along with Ava, and it didn't have to be like that. I'm sorry, Chels. Sorry I haven't been there for you, but I will be now. I swear it."

We hugged and laughed and did a little more crying.

We lingered over dinner, nibbling on pizza topped with salty prosciutto, drinking prosecco, and enjoying the view of the lake. When she was ready to leave, I knew we'd gotten back on track with our friendship and she was once again part of my life.

I returned to my hotel with a full heart.

31

Over the next few weeks, everything in my life changed. I woke up to the sun and a beautiful silence instead of the constant ringing of notifications on my phone. At first, it was hard to remain off social media sites. I craved finding out how my follower counts were and what the press was currently saying about me. The life I'd created revolved around the Internet and my sponsors, but stripping it all away caused a sharp jolt of anxiety, as I struggled to find out what was important and what wasn't.

Until my anxiety gave way to a new type of peace I'd never experienced.

Suddenly, it was just about me and what I was going to do for the day. I'd eat breakfast at the main table and chat with the owners, Claudio and Morena, while I nibbled on fresh pastries and fruit, and sipped rich roasted coffee. The two-bedroom chalet was situated on a mountain, so I'd take the funicular down depending on where I wanted to explore.

Most days, I walked for hours. I ended up investing in some good walking shoes, and my body began to morph into a more muscled model from old-fashioned steps rather than fancy gym equipment. The endless walkways were fit together in a maze of uneven cobblestones and steep inclined steps. The small village consisted of red-roofed homes scattered on the hillside, with brightly painted doors, crushed into odd corners due to the uneven, sloped landscape. The lake was the main center, the view that pulled everyone consistently to the edge of balconies or beaches, pressed against the stone walls or perched on curved bridges to drink in the deep, rippled water. But it was surpassed by my new favorite spot.

Piazza Castello was the main square in Nesso. I stood on the small, flat surface and looked down at the mighty waterfall that raged between a steep gorge of carved rocks. The sound of rushing water pounded in my ears, the noise echoing to many hidden corners of Nesso, a constant reminder for me to stop and breathe. The gorge was named Orrido di Nesso, and sometimes, I was drawn to my window late at night, closing my eyes and smiling as I listened to the rumble of the water. The vibrations were felt in hidden corners of the village, under my feet as I walked, and I always began my day with a long walk and visit to this magical place.

At first, I itched for my camera, not knowing how to look upon such beauty without sharing it, or posing before it, or trying to sell it to unknown masses for constant likes. Then, I became greedy about beauty like this, and loved the early morning when no one was around and I could enjoy the view all by myself, in quiet. I peered behind the protective mesh, taking in the split streams that melded into one; the moss covering the damp, slippery rocks; the power as water merged into one giant rush and raced down the gorge in a mighty roar.

I crossed to the lakeside road and stared down at Lake Como in its early morning glory. The water was still and empty, and the light bathed the villas and houses in a rosy glow, accenting the colors.

I made my way down the steep, uneven steps, treading carefully over loose gravel, shaded by the tall buildings that blocked the view around me. I arrived at the harbor where small boats were enclosed by stone walls, and gazed across the lake at Brienno, a beautiful town painted in vibrant colors.

I felt myself changing each day. With every step of effort my muscles grew. With every new view my soul quieted. For the first time, I became comfortable with the silence and no one around me. The first few days I only felt fear and a grieving loss of myself. Then, I was rebuilding into someone I didn't know, but who was maybe there all along. I just needed to still myself in order to find her.

My walk concluded at Civera Bridge, an arched stone structure curving over the water. I passed my favorite yellow house covered in moss, with dark purple shutters. I gazed at the bridge, and studied the crumbling facade of another building with sloped red roof and crooked angles merging with one end of the bridge. The light played on the scene before me, and I caught my breath from the naked beauty of nature showing off; of time passing; of people before me taking this same path, holding the same dreams, searching for the same peace.

As I stood on the bridge, I gazed at the lake before me, while I listened to the rumble of the waterfall behind me. Yesterday, I watched a group of teens jump from the bridge into the water, screaming and laughing and daring one another to do it. Now, the place was empty and belonged only to me.

It had been two weeks since I spoke with Riggs. Or Ava. I had been checking in with Chelsea on a regular basis. She said Riggs called asking about me, and I told her it was okay to give him my number. I'd run away from the question the night of the wedding. But being here alone made me realize I still wanted to talk to Riggs. I had no end game, nothing I wanted to accomplish except to spend some time with him. Perhaps, I needed a bit more to settle things within myself. I didn't try to analyze and went with my gut.

I made a promise to do that more. Listen to myself instead of looking to others. It was time to break that habit and truly grow up.

I started my walk back.

I was smiling.

I ENJOYED GOING to Milan to steep myself in fashion and reconnect with the things that I loved about the industry. The Cormano Flea Market was streets filled with stalls selling every secondhand item imaginable, but it was the silks that made my head spin. Colorful, expensive fabrics tucked amid used clothing like buried treasure. I swiftly purchased a ton of fabric to have custom clothes made—a huge bargain and new way to beat the high prices of designer clothing. With so many up-and-coming brands fighting for attention, I noticed a new phase of scoring the fabrics, then having new designers create outfits for influencers to wear and grab consumer interest. Again, I reached for my phone and stopped myself, a bit sad I wouldn't be able to share with my followers, but also a little giddy at the total freedom of experiencing a moment without worrying about an audience. It was an interesting realization about my lifestyle.

My new favorite place to shop and lose myself was Brera, a cool boho district with amazing shops. There were interesting handmade crafts to discover, trendy cafés to sip an espresso, and I loved losing time at the Pinacoteca di Brera, a public art gallery of Italian paintings.

Sometimes as I wandered and pondered the artwork, I'd think of Riggs and our first date at the Met. How we laughed about our weak art knowledge and picked our favorites; the easy connection formed immediately that allowed me to truly be myself without worry. I wished I hadn't met him so young, and that I could have had time to develop into a grown woman. Then again, maybe the ending wouldn't have changed anyway.

I took up writing. One afternoon, I brought a notepad into the garden. Nibbling on juicy figs and creamy cheese with bread, I began to write. It was more like journaling— my odd thoughts and impressions of my childhood, the dreams I had when I was young—and soon I became hooked. I wrote for long clips at a time daily, putting together a map of myself, until the journal entries turned more into essays. I wrote about fashion and history, and how young girls were connected to the way they looked and felt in a way the world still judged.

The days drifted by, slow and lazy, and eventually Ava called.

"You're still in Lake Como," she said breathlessly, her voice more demand than question. "Chelsea said you're taking some time off."

"I am. How was the honeymoon?"

"Heavenly. Diana loved the cruise and met a few friends, and she's already asking if they can come visit." Her laugh was bubbly. "I gained five pounds from the food and don't care. Where are you staying?"

I told her.

"I adore Nesso. It's perfect for some R & R." She paused, and the silence held deep undertones. "I won't bother you, Maddie. I'm assuming you don't want to see me anymore. I just wanted to check in and make sure you're okay, and say that I'm here if you ever need anything."

I closed my eyes at her voice, the quiet pain threaded within it. "I'm still unsure of how to move forward, but I can't say I never want to see you again. Can we just see what happens? I'm learning about myself. I need to stop depending on people around me so much. I sacrificed everything for this career I no longer want. These past two weeks? I feel like I'm learning to breathe again. Does that make sense?"

"Yes. So much sense. You deserve to be happy and find your way. How was your talk with Riggs?"

"Good. Chelsea gave him my number."

"You'll talk to him?"

I smiled. "Yeah, I will. There's still something there between us. I just don't know if we can find a clean slate with so much junk in the past. But I'll talk to him."

"Okay." Her sigh was wistful. "You know, when I came back to Italy and found out I was pregnant, I went through such a depression. I wanted to be back in New York where I felt more at home. I missed you and Chelsea and my life. But once I surrendered to knowing life was taking me somewhere new, I became happier in simple ways. I'd walk, and eat, and nap. I was less in a hurry to be something or do something. And along the way, I realized Italy was really my home; I just hadn't been ready for it."

"Are you telling me to move permanently to Nesso and be your neighbor?"

She laughed. "No, I'm telling you that Italy has a special magic that heals people. There's nothing wrong with being fast-paced, and ambitious, and wanting it all. But it all got away from me. Sometimes, we need to take a step back in order to take the next step forward."

Yes. I agreed with her and, once again, found myself wondering at this new Ava who seemed more in touch with her inner self. "Thanks for the advice. I'm not sure how long I'll stay. Maybe until my agent threatens to jump off a cliff if I don't return?"

We both laughed. "Well, again, I'm here if you need me. Have fun, Maddie. Love you."

She hung up. I cradled my phone against my chest.

I loved her, too.

Still.

I just needed to figure out if there was a new path to our friendship, or if it was healthier to let it go.

32

I'd been in Nesso for three full weeks when Riggs called.

When I picked up and heard his voice, my heart beat crazily in my chest. My reaction was proof I hadn't gotten over him. Instead of rage and pain, I was filled with a hesitant excitement. "Hi."

"Chelsea gave me your new number. Is it okay I called?"

His deep, husky voice gave me shivers. I hugged myself and walked out to my balcony. "Yeah, it's okay. A little weird but okay."

He chuckled. "I know. There's no rules for this. I feel more nervous now than I did on our first date."

"Me, too." The pause gave me time to drag in a deep breath. "How's New York?"

"Muggy. Feels like a hundred degrees. I had to make sure I brought spare shirts to change into this week. Where are you?"

"I decided to stay in Italy for a while. With my life blowing up, I wanted to take some time to figure things out."

"Are you in Lake Como?"

"Nesso. I rented this chalet on a mountain. Every day, I go for long walks, then eat in the garden. Then I go explore, eat some more, and sleep. I've never had so little to do in my life. Yet . . ."

"Yet?" he prodded.

I decided if I was going to take his calls and try this, I would be honest. Even if it was uncomfortable. "Yet I feel like I'm doing more than I've ever done before. Who would've thought inner work or getting to know yourself could be this hard?"

He didn't laugh or try to tease. His tone was reflective and serious. "It's damn hard. After I lost you? That year was a blur for me. But I realized I had to learn to accept some things I didn't want to about myself. I did therapy for a while and that helped. I think it's great, Maddie."

I liked this new intimacy over the phone, hearing his voice tell me things about himself without his presence interrupting us. Our physical connection always trumped conversation because it was so primal. But now, I felt free to explore other pieces of him. "I haven't done therapy yet, but I've been writing. I'm learning a lot."

"You always liked to write," he said thoughtfully. "Everyone seemed to complain about the English requirements the most, except you. Remember when your story got picked from that creative writing class you took when you were younger?"

I'd forgotten. The class had to write short stories based on a personal narrative and they went to a pool of judges who were professional writers. I'd written about the Mother's Day tea in elementary school where everyone's mom showed up all excited, taking pictures, fussing over their children. My mom hadn't come. I'd been paired with Eliza, whose mom had passed away, and spent the afternoon trying not to cry.

I'd won the contest with a prize of fifty dollars.

When I proudly presented the check to my parents, they lectured me on saving rather than spending and never asked to read the essay.

"Yeah, that's right. I'm surprised you remember."

"I remember everything you tell me, Maddie."

The words wove an intimate spell that made my breath catch. "What do you want from me?" I asked straight out. "Are you calling me for a particular reason?"

He didn't get defensive, which helped me relax. "When I saw you at the wedding, I knew I still had feelings for you. I also know I can't expect you to immediately give me another chance after everything that happened. I wondered if we could just talk again? Get to know each other? See if there's anything to salvage? I don't want to hurt you anymore."

My eyes half closed. Emotion choked my throat. This is what I'd been led to. Deciding to leave Ava and Riggs in my path, or rebuild a new relationship. There was no going back, only forward. And the choice was all mine.

"I still feel things for you, too," I finally said. I needed to be ruthlessly truthful with myself and him. That's why I was in Italy. I had to stop running from all of it. "I told Ava I wasn't sure what comes next, and it's the same with you. But I do want to talk to you, Riggs."

"Good. I simply want to know you again, Maddie."

A smile curved my lips. Hope stirred. "I'm good with that."

"Then let's get started." He paused, dropping his voice. "What are you wearing?"

And then we laughed for a long time. And started talking.

RIGGS AND I talked every day.

We'd chat during my walks, and I'd describe the scenery, reaching to evoke the sensations of taste, touch, and scent for him to experience with me. I held the phone up so he could hear the pounding water of the falls, or glimpse a piece of art from the gallery where I liked to roam. It became a lovely ritual for me to describe my meal of the day, and how it tasted. He said he felt like he was there with me.

I learned about his love for the law, and how he viewed it as the biggest equalizer if used correctly. He was both a realist and dreamer, noting the multiple times law failed people and helped the rich, but his position at the firm allowed him to take on smaller cases he believed made a difference for the working class. He worked with teens who got thrown into the system due to lack of knowledge or proper defense, and became passionate about educating the younger generation about their rights. I loved the way he spoke about his work, and began to see a new side of him.

I wrote furiously, filling up notebooks with ideas and essays. I took back my phone on my own terms and began taking photographs again. I loved being able to record things that moved me without worrying about hashtags or likes. Sierra set up a few meetings with beloved designers I admired, but when I was asked to model some newer pieces, I hesitated. I still didn't know if modeling was something I wanted to continue. I explained I was taking a hiatus and that Sierra would be in touch, but I liked the idea of working with one company I believed in rather than jumping from campaign to campaign.

I found myself changing. I woke up calmer and excited to start my day. I paid attention, and simple things stirred joy—the quiet moments amid the chaos became my focus rather than a thing to avoid. I visited church regularly, seeking out the stillness as others prayed around me, surrounded by statues and murals of Jesus, and Mary, the symbol of grace and forgiveness.

I prayed for Ava. Chelsea. Riggs. Diana. My parents.

I prayed for myself.

And slowly, step after step, my solitude became more like a gift than a tool for growth. It had started as a punishment, a forceful way of stripping away all I'd depended on to see what else was under the surface. Now, I was at ease with my company and my thoughts. I no longer needed social media to validate my choices. I needed nothing else but . . .

Me.

I decided to forgive my parents and stop chasing a love and approval that would never come. When I reread some of my journal entries back, I was shaken by the level of loneliness threaded within my narrative; of my endless search for someone who'd love me, and I allowed myself to cry for the little girl who'd never gotten what she craved. I grieved for her, but knew I was grown up now, and had the ability to love and be loved by the people I chose. I didn't have to chase. I didn't have to be scared. I had everything I needed.

On the seventh week of my hiatus, I called Ava and invited her to lunch.

We met in Milan at Via della Spiga, the upscale shopping center of the city. Ava had reserved a table at Paper Moon, and we sat on the terrace surrounded by gardens and designer stores that were spoken of in awed whispers. Armani. Prada. Gucci. Versace.

I may have worked on my inner self, but I'd always revere the fashion gods that made this life more beautiful.

Ava looked like her usual goddess self, clad in a toasty oversize sweater the color of terra-cotta, and matching suede skirt, with boots made of supple leather I craved to touch. "You look fabulous."

She waved her hand in the air. "A present from Antonio—one of the new collections from D&G. Maddie, I swear, you are glowing! You look so . . . different."

I smiled at the compliment. I was wearing jeans, boots, and one of the new sweaters I'd snagged in Brera—a gorgeous sage green cowl-neck that was as soft as it looked. My hair had grown a bit, and I'd left it loose, enjoying when the wind made the strands dance around my face. I wore little makeup lately, and found the simple food and daily exercise had strengthened my body and given my skin a healthy tone. "Thanks. I feel really good. I'm madly in love with Nesso. It's my spirit town."

Her laugh warmed my ears. "One of our best-kept secrets. I'm so happy you called. I admit I screamed like a kid and Diana wanted to know if she could come play with us."

I grinned. "How is she?"

"Wonderful. Active, curious, and spoiled rotten by Roberto."

The waiter glided by and uncorked our prosecco, pouring two glasses. She put her hand up. *"Mi dispiace. Dell'acqua, grazie."*

I lifted my brow. "We always drink at lunch."

"I can't." Her cheeks flushed. "I'm pregnant."

A rush of happiness cut through me. "Ava! Oh, I'm so happy for you, congratulations!"

"Thank you. I can't believe it. I've never been so happy to throw up in my life."

We laughed together. "Did you tell Chelsea yet?"

"No, I'm going to call her tonight. How is she?"

"Good. She found the location for the business, and Ed is completely on board. I'm happy she's moving forward with this. I hated seeing her so torn up about not feeling like motherhood was enough. It sucked."

Ava nodded. "I know, especially from her. She was always the one we turned to when we needed grounding. She said you also wanted to be an investor?"

"Yeah, I think it's going to be the best thing I've done

with my money in a while. Other than buy more clothes. Milan has been hell on my wallet."

Her blue eyes sparkled wickedly. "But what a way to die, right? I better look drop-dead gorgeous in my casket."

I snorted. "That's awful!"

"Maybe, but I know you agree. Who do you want to wear on your final day?"

I bit my lip to stop the giggles. "You'll think I'm psycho."

She leaned in. "Never. Tell me."

"Well, I always thought it would be sickly cool to be buried in a Vera Wang wedding gown."

Her jaw dropped. "You are definitely psycho and I love it."

"What about you?"

"Versace, all the way. A sexy, in-your-face, the world will grieve me forever, outfit of the decade."

This time, the giggles fell from my lips and we screeched like teenagers. It was then that I knew I'd forgiven her. The idea of not having Ava in my life was too much to bear. We'd never be the same, but that was good. Our relationship hadn't been healthy; we'd gotten lost within each other, searching for things we should have had inside of us. But we were different now. We could be the best for each other.

"I love you, Ava."

She stilled. Her cobalt blue eyes widened, and teared up, and she reached across the table to grasp my hand. We stared at each other for a long time, the past and present and future melding together in a whirlwind of memories and moments and dreams.

"I love you, too, Maddie."

We smiled at each other.

The afternoon passed in the best way possible. We talked and laughed and shared. "Are you thinking of going back?" she asked, reclining in her chair.

"Yeah, it may be time. Even though I'd love to stay here forever and live my best life."

"You could. Nothing says you need to go back to New York. You can build a new place for yourself here," Ava said.

"I considered it. But when I picture the future, I see myself there."

"With Riggs?"

I stilled. We hadn't mentioned him, but his presence was always around us; a reminder we'd never be able to forget. I picked my words carefully. "We've been talking. A lot. I told him I had no expectations of what we could be, but lately, I'm drawn more and more to going back and seeing if there's a chance for us. What do you think? For real?"

Her opinion was no longer crucial to my decisions, but I was curious to know where Ava stood. I watched the emotions flickering across her elegant features and waited. "I think you never got your real chance," she said softly. "I think you deserve a second shot at this."

"Yeah. What about Diana? And us? Do you think it will be . . . messy?"

She laughed then, but it wasn't self-mocking. "Maddie, life is a mess. But I learned that nothing worth fighting for is easy, or clean, because love is a gigantic ball of uncertainty, and chaos. And God, it's fucking awesome, too. Isn't it?"

I grinned and shook my head, because only Ava could describe it like that—so perfectly.

"Riggs will always be Diana's father, but we've all agreed on how we want to move forward. If you had decided you never wanted to see me again, I'd still consider you my best friend. I'd still love you. That could never change. If you and Riggs are able to have a relationship together again, I would be happy for you both."

I nodded. Knowing she had zero reservations about Riggs helped me resolve some of my lingering doubts.

"Do you want to go back to modeling?" Ava asked, tapping her nail against her lip. "I know you've been doing some soul-searching about your career. What did you come up with?"

"Well, I was having difficulty deciding exactly what I did want, so I began by making a list of what I *didn't* want. It helped me gain some clarity."

"Okay, read me the list."

"I memorized it. I don't want to be an influencer anymore. Social media is a wonderful tool, and I'm not saying I won't use it, but I really don't want my career tied to followers, or likes, or societal opinion."

"Got it."

"I don't want to model full-time. Besides my age and the fact that booking campaigns will only get harder, it doesn't fulfill me on a deeper level. The pleasure has burned out."

"Do you want to be behind the camera?"

"I thought of that. I love photography, but I don't think I want to build a career doing that right now."

"Okay, so scratch that off, too. Movies?"

I made a face. "Nope. Leaving my short Hollywood stint behind me."

Ava tilted her head, studying my face. "What have you done in the past two months that you really love?"

A smile curved my lips. "Writing. I love writing about everything. Fashion, society expectations, young girls coming up in the industry—I feel like I have so much to say on the topic and it keeps bubbling up like a fountain of content."

"Ooohh, I love that image! What if you created a blog?"

"I literally wrote that down as a possibility. But I'm thinking bigger. I began drafting some pieces of content I was considering sending to Sierra. Remember when you did your *Cosmopolitan* column?"

"Yes, it was a blast but not something I wanted to do long term."

"Well, I'd love to be able to contribute to the fashion industry. I have a lot to say and share." I hesitated, then told her my plan. "I'm going to approach *Vogue* about writing for them."

Ava gasped. "That's fantastic! I love that idea, Maddie. Hey, I have this contact I can get a hold of and . . ." She trailed off, eyes widening in slight horror, and then our gazes met.

"I think I'll handle this on my own," I said, deadpan.

We broke into laughter.

That's when I knew we were truly beginning to heal.

33

I returned to New York on a rainy Friday evening.

As I made my way out of JFK Airport, I was recognized at baggage claim by a few people. Within minutes, I smiled at cameras and took a selfie with a sweet young girl who gushed about my clothes and said I'd gotten a raw deal with the press. I thanked her and hurried out, hoping no one found out about my return until I got back to my place.

Sierra had a car waiting for me, so the trip to my apartment was uneventful. I dropped my luggage and looked around the large, empty space. Shadows darkened the sleek rooms. The air still had a faint scent of lemon polish, probably from the cleaners who'd freshened up the place before my arrival. I noticed a bouquet of cut flowers on the table. I leaned over and sniffed the fragrant blooms, smiling. The card read: *Welcome back, we missed you! Love, Sierra.*

Slowly, I walked around my place, feeling like an outsider rather than an occupant. A pang of longing hit hard. I missed my simple place in Nesso, with the chipped walls and rusty pipes; I missed the sounds of rushing water and laughter from the terrace; I missed the fragrance of citrus and earth and sunshine. Somehow, this no longer felt like the home of the woman who came back, but instead of mourning or getting frustrated, I realized it was my opportunity to find what I truly wanted.

I ordered takeout from my favorite Thai place, and sat at my table with my notebooks and laptop. I created a plan, then dipped into my social media feeds. The results didn't sting like before. My followers had drastically dropped, but comments had slowed. Most of the posts revolved around my absence and meanderings on where I'd disappeared. A picture popped up of me walking in Milan, with a caption *Hiding Amid High Fashion?* that had run in *Us Weekly*, but not much since. My meeting with Sierra and the *Vogue* style coordinator on Monday would be key in moving forward, but I'd already focused my vision and my next steps. I'd scale down my expenses and dig into my new love for writing. If *Vogue* rejected me, I had a list of contacts to reach out to, and if that blew up, I was ready to begin my own curated newsletter. I had tons of ideas to include essays, photos, and fashion inspiration. The years of influence within the fashion industry had left me rich with lots of contacts, and I was no longer stubborn about doing everything on my own. After all, looking back, everyone had contributed to my success. Ava, Chelsea, and Riggs. Levi. My followers. It was the content I chose to bring forward that counted.

I finished up and went to bed. I stared at my ceiling, excited for the future, grieving Italy and the joy I'd found. I thought of Ava and how much it meant to be with her again. I thought of Chelsea and her new business I'd be able to share in. I thought of the pain we'd gone through, the choices we made, and how it all ended up. I wish I could tell my younger self that no matter how bad it got, there was one thing to cling to.

It would all be okay.

Finally, I slept.

THE NEXT MORNING, Riggs called. "Are you home?" he asked.

"Yep. Got in last night."

"Big meeting Monday?"

"Yep."

"Things good?"

"Yep."

His laugh was a husky caress. "Want to go to bed?"

"Stop!"

"Can't blame a guy for trying," he teased.

I laughed with him. We'd managed to find a new balance between us. Some of the old banter had been easy to fall back into. The new stuff was the honesty we shared, facts given without worry about how the other took it. No more excuses or defenses—we learned to listen better. It had helped us build a more secure foundation and get to know each other again. "What are you up to?"

"Wondered if you would like to get coffee with me today."

I thought about it. We hadn't been face-to-face in three months. Every day that we spoke on the phone gave us an opportunity to see if we'd fit; if the past could be resurfaced and rebuilt on. My stomach danced at the thought of seeing him again, to allow that physical connection breath and space and new life.

Was it too soon? Then again, would I ever be ready to test this again? Either way, I'd learned my life with or without Riggs would be what I made it. And I intended to make it beautiful again—on the inside and outside.

"I'd love to get coffee," I said slowly. "Want to meet at Bryant Park?"

"Yeah."

I grinned and clicked off. Our first meeting spot so many years ago. Everything coming full circle. How appropriate.

I dressed casually, bundling up for fall in corduroy stretch jeans, high boots, and an oversize cocoa brown sweater with a pink heart stitched on it. I took a wool shawl painted in earthy colors, wrapped it around my shoulders, and headed out.

I enjoyed the click of my boots on the concrete; the rush and madness of the crowds walking with and against me. I breathed in the smells of smoky grilled meat from the hot dog vendors, and wet from the last rainfall, and grit from the people who fought for success every day in one of the greatest cities in the world. I weaved in and out, hurrying through flashing walkway signs and dodging the occasional screeching cab. By the time I reached the steps of the park, it was packed with people sitting at tables reading, shopping at the stalls set up for vendors, or in line to grab food from the various parked trucks. I looked around, breathing calmly, and gave myself a lecture.

Coffee didn't mean a promise. I'd changed, and just because we spoke daily, it didn't guarantee a happy ending. Stuff like that only happened in the movies or in books.

But maybe, just maybe, I was ready to take a leap of faith anyway.

I blinked, recognizing the figure walking toward the steps.

He was in a black wool coat. His strides were long and purposeful as he increased his pace, those sea green eyes pinned on me. With each step the distance between us closed, and I noticed so many things. The square jawline shadowed with stubble. The full curve of his lower lip. The loose curl that escaped his hat and flopped over his brow. My heart beat faster and my ears roared and then he was in front of me. His familiar scent of cotton and soap wrapped around me and squeezed. I fell into his gaze, his wild, emotional, beautiful eyes so full of everything I ever asked for, vulnerable and raw, all for me. And then he smiled, and time simply stopped.

"Maddie."

My name like music. The past roaring up, then disappearing like fine mist, to a future that wasn't written yet. My response hung in the air, heavy with anticipation.

"Riggs."

Slowly, he leaned in. I pressed my forehead to his. "I missed you," he whispered. "I missed us."

My whole body shuddered. The voice from deep inside me sighed.

"Me, too."

And I knew it was so much more than just coffee.

AUTHOR'S NOTE & ACKNOWLEDGMENTS

There are no words to describe how thrilled I am to offer you another book set in Italy. I remember visiting Lake Como years ago. We sailed around the lake, gawking at the gorgeous mansions lining the water, then spent the day exploring the shops, feasting on delicious food, and falling into a magical world I never wanted to return from.

I knew when I decided to explore the intricacies of female friendship, Lake Como would be the setting for Ava's family life and the girls' pact. I imagined both a retreat and a healing place as I wrote.

There are so many thanks I need to give to the amazing people who constantly surround me. My Berkley editor, Kerry Donovan, for allowing me to chase my story on my terms and helping it get to the best place on the page; the talented team at Berkley who promote my books, Jessica Mangicaro and Tara O'Connor; and Mary Baker. Thanks to Kristi Yanta, who took an early peek at the book as it was being formed and helped me tweak. Hugs to my agent, Kevan Lyon, who has helped guide my career to wonderful places. Gratitude to Nina Grinstead at Valentine PR and her incredible team for their constant hard work on my books. Thanks to my amazing assistant, Mandy Lawler, for all that you do to keep me sane.

Thank you to the readers who keep showing up, book after book, year after year. You are the reason I am here and why I do this!

A
WEDDING
IN
LAKE COMO

Jennifer Probst

READERS GUIDE

DISCUSSION QUESTIONS

1. Both Ava and Maddie experienced difficult relationships with their parents. Do you think this affected the intensity and role of their friendship in their lives? If so, how? Discuss.

2. *A Wedding in Lake Como* provides only Maddie's perspective on the story. How do you think Ava's would differ? Chelsea's? Did you wish to have anyone else's point of view shown?

3. Italy becomes a backdrop for both Ava's and Maddie's personal growth. Discuss how their second trip to Lake Como varies from their first. How have they changed with each other and within themselves?

4. Chelsea was one of the first two people in the girls' friendship circle, but many times she seemed to take a more distant perspective in the story. How would Ava and Maddie be different without Chelsea? Would

things have gone on a different path, or do you think they would both still have made the same choices?

5. Maddie wants to be a social media influencer. How does this choice of career affect the story? Do you know anyone who is an influencer? Did you learn more about the influencer world through the story?

6. Riggs and Maddie fall for each other quickly. Do you think they were meant for each other? Do you think it was their ages that gave them the biggest challenge? Do you think they'd still be together if Ava hadn't been in the picture?

7. When Riggs and Ava sleep together, it is five years before Maddie is able to deal with the fallout. Did you agree with her decision to go to Ava's wedding? Why or why not?

8. Forgiveness and growth are themes in *A Wedding in Lake Como*. Discuss how each of the characters experiences both forgiveness and growth in their individual character arc.

9. Do you think Riggs and Maddie end up together? Do you think Ava and Riggs's baby will always be an obstacle between them? Why or why not?

10. Female friendship is shown in many intricate layers as the young women transition to adulthood. Do you consider Ava a toxic friend? Have you ever experienced difficulties in a close friendship in your past? How did it end up?

11. Who do you feel the most connected to—Maddie, Ava, or Chelsea? Why?

12. Do you believe Ava was cheating on Patrick the entire time? Do you believe Maddie should have confronted her?

13. Do you think Maddie should have stood up to Ava? When? How do you think the story would have changed if this had happened?

14. Do you blame Ava for not telling Riggs or Maddie about the baby? Do you agree with the decision for Riggs not to be involved in his child's life?

15. Ava made choices along the way that hurt other people. Were you able to forgive her like Maddie and Chelsea did?

1

PRISCILLA

Priscilla Hampton wondered if every daughter who buried her mother suddenly became swamped with regrets.

She'd never been one to question her decisions or linger on actions she'd taken that couldn't be changed. But staring up at her childhood home, facing the task of cleaning out her mom's personal belongings, she was pretty much sick with what-ifs.

The overly large Tudor house still seemed as if it was judging her as she walked up the curvy pathway leading to the sweeping arched doorway. Pris had never liked the way the two giant windows gave off an eerie yellow glow from the sage-green stucco, like eyes stuck in a deep-set face. The balcony dead center reminded her of a flat nose and had been the bane of her mother's existence—a perfect escape route for teen girls to sneak out at night. The lower brick should have lent an elegant, timeless tone, but it all ended up looking like a mishmash of old and new. Still, it was the only family home she'd ever lived in. After the divorce, Dad had given the house up without a fight, moving on and moving in with his newest love interest. She'd blamed him, of course, until she realized her mother hadn't seemed to care, which somehow made Pris angrier with her than with Dad.

It would've been easier if Mom wanted revenge, or insisted her daughters hate him. Instead, she'd snatched Pris's right to bitterness and swept all the messy emotions away with her usual sunny smile, encouraging them to have a healthy relationship with Dad and not worry.

Did her mother ever get exhausted by the endless pursuit of perfection? Always having to be nice, and forgive, and put everyone else first without resentment?

Pris trembled as she thought of her beloved mother alone in her hospital bed. Once again, refusing to ask for help, hating to bother anyone with her issues, even sickness.

And dying alone.

A wave of emotion battered her body, so Pris held her breath, sensing she was on the verge of either a breakdown or a breakthrough worthy of an *O Magazine* feature article.

Her sister bumped her from behind and Priscilla stumbled forward. "Dude, you're blocking the pathway. Why do you have that dumb look on your face?"

Pris shot her an annoyed look. Her fleeting come-to-Jesus moment departed faster than a conservative trapped in a room with liberals. "I was thinking."

Bailey rolled her eyes and kept walking. "No time to think. I've gotta be at open mic tonight."

The sound of her middle sister's voice floated in the air with a tinge of annoyance. "Really, Bae? We cleared this day to pack up Mom's stuff and be together. You can't even hang with us for one lousy evening?"

"I gave you my day. Don't pretend if you had one of your important meetings that you wouldn't ditch us without a thought."

"Maybe for a job I get paid for," Devon said. "Not to read some crappy excerpt of another poem you'll never publish."

Pris tried not to wince, but once her sisters got going, not even a naked Jason Momoa could stop them.

They stepped through the carved mahogany doors together, their shoulders deliberately bumping, while Pris trailed behind.

"Real nice," Bailey said. Her sleek golden ponytail bobbed in protest. "Go ahead and judge my life, but at least I'm not pretending to be someone I'm not."

"And I'm not wasting mine doing nothing worthwhile while I pretend to search for meaning," Devon retorted.

They'd just arrived and it was starting already. Her temples throbbed with the beginning of one of her migraines. Not today. She refused to let them hijack this day for their familiar arguments. When they'd been younger, Pris had been jealous of her younger sisters' close relationship. Being five years older than Devon forced her to be the leader, even though Devon had always been bossier. But like everything else, Pris had taken on the role believing that was what was needed. It also erected an invisible barrier between her and her siblings she'd never been able to overcome.

"Guys, can we just focus? The estate handlers come tomorrow, so all we need to do is Mom's bedroom. They'll take care of the rest."

"Feels weird to think nothing will be here," Dev said with a sigh.

"Did you ever wonder why Mom never sold this place?" Pris asked. "She always complained it was too big for one person."

Bailey waved her ink-stained fingers in the air. "Us, of course. She told me once there were too many memories to ever give it up. Maybe I'll move some stuff in and live here."

Devon snorted. "Don't think so. You'd turn it into some hostel for your broke friends. We'll sell it and split the proceeds like Mom wanted."

Bailey huffed with her usual drama. "Mom always said I could have the house if I wanted. I bet she'd rather have it stay in the family."

"Did you get that intention in writing?" Dev asked, her gaze sweeping over the spacious foyer to the crystal-dripping chandelier. Pris could practically hear her brain clicking with how much they could get for the place. Her role as tenured professor in the finance department at NYU was impressive, but she had a tendency to see things in stark black and white. Money was serious business, and Devon had made sure they all agreed to sell so everyone would get a fair share.

"Seriously? That's messed up," Bailey said.

"So is this." Devon's gaze cleared, her hazel eyes glinting with a new hardness Pris had never seen before. Like there'd been additional layers that crusted over during the years they'd grown apart. "Let's not pretend this is what any of us want right now."

"Mom's death?" Pris asked, her insides clenching at the rising tension in the air. They formed a semicircle together. A memory flashed of the three of them ready to play hide-and-go-seek—squeezing into a tight knot while they picked who'd be it, back when they not only loved but liked one another.

"No. Being together. I'm not playing the role assigned to me, okay? So, let's just agree to tackle the house piece by piece without getting all sentimental for things that no longer exist."

Even Bailey sucked in her breath, a shadow of pain flickering over her delicate features. "Why are you so cold?" she whispered.

The air shimmered; softened; quieted. Pris waited for the answer too, wondering when the real turning point had been, when they'd decided being apart was better than trying to make the fragments of each of them fit into one clear puzzle. Two years ago? Five? Or had their relationship deteriorated so slowly no one had cared enough to count?

For a second, Dev opened her mouth and the words hung unuttered in the air, like an overfull balloon ready to pop.

Then she turned and the moment floated away.

"We better get started," Devon said.

They watched her climb the grand staircase and disappear.

Bailey muttered something under her breath. "I need to use the bathroom," she said, marching down the hallway. Left alone, Pris looked around, wondering if her mother's presence would show itself. A brush of cold air. A sound. A wave of charged energy that announced Mom's arrival to help smooth all these jagged edges between her children.

But nothing happened. Just a terrible empty sensation in the pit of her stomach and a familiar tension behind her eyes.

Pris dragged in a deep breath, set her shoulders, and headed up the stairs.

2

DEVON

Dev muttered a curse under her breath and opened the first empty box. Why did she have to act like such a bitch? At least when Bailey lost her temper, people accepted it as her artistic streak. She'd grown up with her parents shaking their heads at Bailey's tantrums as if they were amused. But when Devon lost it? She was called ugly and out of control.

And right now?

They were right.

She yanked the top drawer of her mother's nightstand and began to sift through an array of junk, making neat piles. One for garbage. One to sell in the estate sale. And one for treasures she or her sisters wanted to keep.

She heard Bailey's stomping footsteps echo up the stairs and tried to push the sliver of guilt aside. Bailey was too old to be treated like a child. Why did everyone cater to her? If

Devon hadn't taken control, this house would still be sitting on the market, rotting away like all their potential money. Pris had her rich husband, and Bailey still relied on their father's generous handouts, but Dev made sure to make her own way.

Living in New York was damn expensive. Sure, being a tenured professor at NYU was a respectable career, with a decent salary. But there was still so much she craved—like scoring that elusive dean position and gaining a spot on the board. Being respected by her bosses, colleagues, and students on a higher level. Dev had a voracious appetite for success and sensed the victory she craved was close.

Dev refocused, finished the top drawer, and started on the next. Most of the stuff was throwaway remnants of cast-off makeup, holiday cards, empty notebooks, broken picture frames, and a mishmash of collectibles that had meant something to Mom once. The calming scent of lavender drifted in the air, soothing some of the jagged edges of a grief she'd not been willing to steep herself in. Not yet. When she got back to her place, she'd take some time to cry and mourn.

Alone.

"Nice going," Pris drawled, sitting down on the edge of the bed. Crossing her long legs with a natural grace that spoke of all those days she used to dance, her oldest sister gave a deep sigh, clasping her hands on her knees. Dev took a moment to study the large, glittering rock on her finger, her French-manicured nails without a chip. Even at forty, she held a youthful beauty, from her swanlike neck and long blond hair to her wide powder-blue eyes that still shaded an onlooker from her secrets. Pris was the peacemaker but also the most secretive. Dev wouldn't have been surprised if she'd learned her sibling danced in the fairy world when everyone went to sleep and had never breathed a word to anyone.

Both her sisters had inherited Mom's looks—light hair, blue eyes, fair skin. Dev resembled her father with his dark hair and hazel eyes. He was a handsome man, always had been, but somehow the features she'd inherited didn't work on a female as well. Dev always felt a bit too stocky in the hips and bust, a bit awkward in her gait, and a bit dull with her coloring. It was hard growing up with the golden sisters and the constant comments about how Dev looked so different. Sometimes, she'd had to grit her teeth to keep from slugging those nice old ladies who gave her a slightly sympathetic look.

She refocused and shrugged. Time to defend herself for being cruel to Bailey. "Sorry, but we all need to be grown-ups now. It's not good for her to depend on Dad, or have grandiose ideas of keeping this house for fun. Can you work on the closet? I've got some not-for-profits coming to collect her designer labels, but the rest can be donated."

"Don't you want anything?" Pris asked. Her gaze flicked around the room as if cataloguing every personal item. "I'd like some pieces of jewelry she wore. And that red-gold sweater."

Dev lifted a brow. "I think we should all take what means the most to us. I won't fight anyone on it. Why would you want that sweater, though? God, it was awful."

Bailey interrupted their conversation, her ponytail bouncing as she walked into the room. "For once, I agree with Dev. I begged Mom to throw it out every time I saw her, but she'd only wrap it closer. It's old as dirt and ugly as sin. So bright I couldn't even look at her when she wore it."

Pris laughed, walking to the closet to search. "I know, but there was something she loved about it. I think she treasured it more than the few diamonds she owned."

"Can I have her wedding ring?" Bailey burst out. At Dev's sharp look, her pixie face turned stubborn. "Not for the value—because it reminds me of when we were all together. And happy."

The slice of pain surprised her, along with her sister's words. When was the last time they'd felt happy together? Holidays were now strained affairs, with all of them desperate to leave as soon as the turkey was eaten or presents opened. Dad had his own family and always looked uncomfortable when his old and new families collided. As the youngest, Bailey was stubbornly optimistic, seeing the tension through rainbow-colored glasses, which was part of her nature. If only Devon could blot out the bad stuff as easily. But it lay in wait every night, whispering in her ear. Taunting.

"Sure," Dev said. Her sister relaxed, the tension between them slowing from a burn to a slight simmer.

"Thanks."

"Found it!" Pris pulled the sweater from the closet with a triumphant grin. The fabric was worn—once a wide, loopy-type knit that reminded Dev of a handmade afghan. It was oversize, and the pattern was a swirling mix of bright sunset colors that was overdone, making an onlooker a bit dizzy. Pris slipped it on. The sleeves stretched out over her delicate hands, and the large rust-colored buttons only added to the clownish image.

Dev and Bailey burst out laughing. "It's just as horrible as I remember," Dev said with a grin.

"I don't care, I'm going to take it," Pris said.

"Enjoy," Bailey said with a wave of her hand. "I'm sure Mom would be happy someone actually wanted it. We'd better get working—I need to shower and change before my reading tonight."

Dev swallowed her retort and reminded herself to relax. It was a short weekend and then she'd be back to her busy life. For Mom's sake, she'd hold her temper. "Why don't you work on the bureau?" Dev suggested.

They focused on the work, mostly in silence. Each object Dev touched was like a sharp memory bursting into her brain, leaving shimmers of grief trickling through her body. She pushed forward with the methodical precision that had served her well. A lone silver-handled hairbrush. Mini albums filled with wallet-size photos collected over the years, mostly stuffed with awkward school pics. A bottle of travel perfume still in its box. Dev removed it and took a deep whiff, the floral scent light, with notes of citrus. Definitely a scent Mom would wear. Perhaps it'd been an extra, thrown carelessly in a drawer for later, because wasn't there always a later? A tomorrow?

Her fingers gripped the smooth glass tighter. If only

Mom had told them she was sick. Why couldn't she reach out and ask for help? Why did she have to die alone in a hospital when all of them would have been there if she had told them?

The words escaped her mouth before she could bite them back. "Mom should have told us."

Pris kept her back turned as she gathered clothes off the hangers. "It happened fast, Dev. No one knew it would turn into pneumonia."

"No, before that. She'd been sick for a damn week and hadn't even seen a doctor. God, why couldn't she just have called for broth, or Mucinex, or anything?"

"Because she was afraid no one would come."

Bailey's voice whipped her head around, shock barreling through her. "What are you talking about? I'm under two hours away—I would've driven here right away. And you're under an hour! Why didn't she contact you?"

Bailey's shoulders stiffened, but she refused to meet Dev's stare. "Not sure. Probably afraid we were all busy, which we were. She was stubborn like that."

"She didn't give us a chance." The frustration writhed in her belly like pissed-off cobras. "Not to say goodbye, or that we were sorry, or anything."

Pris cocked her head, a frown furrowing her brow. "Why would you need to be sorry? Did you guys have a fight or something?"

Or something. Like the thousands of patronizing questions she'd ignored, hating always being compared to perfect Pris and adorable Bailey. And God knows she despised her whining mind, which tortured her, but the truth was too terrible to avoid.

Somehow, her mother had made her feel completely unworthy.

And now there was no more time. No hope they'd finally have an honest dialogue about why Dev had been the one to disappoint her. Life wasn't a chick-flick rom-com with a neat ending.

It was more like a shit show.

"No fight," she said, dumping the perfume and shutting the last drawer. "Just a random thought. I'm just mad at the way it happened."

Pris gave her a sympathetic look. "Can't blame you. Getting a call from the hospital that Mom died was like a nightmare. I kept thinking someone would jump out and say, 'Kidding!' and I could hate them for a terrible prank."

"I didn't believe you," Dev said. "When you called me. It was too much."

Bailey's voice trembled. "I ran. I was in my pajamas at the hospital because I didn't stop to even change. I think I figured if I got there fast enough I could prove it was a terrible mistake."

The memory of Bailey in sleep shorts and an old black T-shirt, hair unbrushed, with those blue eyes wild with grief, would haunt Dev forever. Her sister had collapsed on the floor and let out a wail that brought goose bumps. Was it easier for her to pour out her emotion at all times? To empty herself like a vessel until it was filled up again with feelings, and then tip it over and spill them out—like the little teapot song? Dev had always wondered. Because her insides were like a devastated forest—quiet, dehydrated, with perished trees standing in even lines.

Silence settled over the room. Everyone seemed lost in their thoughts, so when Pris called out their names, Devon jumped.

"What is it? Did you find the Gucci suit?" Dev asked, trying for some sarcastic wit to break up the heavy sadness thickening the air.

"No. I found a trunk."

Dev watched her sister drag out a cedar trunk with beautiful gold carvings. It was medium-size, with pedestal feet and an intricate lock. A shiver raced down her spine as they all gathered around the piece, staring at the object as if it held the answers to something instead of some carefully preserved blankets or linens.

Dev was the first one to speak, ignoring her suddenly racing heart. "Open it up."

Pris hesitated, her hand like a fragile bird, hovering midway in the air. A strange foreboding swept through Dev.

Then the lock clicked and she lifted the lid.

The scent of must and cotton and wood drifted to her nostrils.

They stared down at a quilt.

Her shoulders relaxed. The quilt was ivory colored, hand stitched, and quite beautiful, but still a boring reveal after such anticipation. It was obvious from her sisters' relieved sighs they'd done the same thing. Expected something else.

Bailey smoothed her hand over the soft material. "Pretty. I would've saved my dibs for this, Pris. Better than the sweater."

Pris grinned. "You and Dev can fight over it, or we can donate it. I certainly don't need another quilt in my life."

Dev lost interest and turned back to the second bureau. "Not sure why Mom needed a trunk to store bedding. This place has a huge linen closet that's only half full."

"Maybe she liked the beauty of it," Bailey murmured. "I'm always attracted to those pretty hatboxes, but I've never owned a hat in my life. It's kind of romantic."

Dev gave a snort. "Mom was the least romantic person I've ever known."

"Why would you say that?" Bailey asked. "She probably had dreams and fantasies like everyone else."

"I agree with Dev on this one," Pris said, her voice a bit brisk. "Mom was practical. She preferred stability and smart decisions over passion. She wasn't the type to date a bad boy or ditch a logical plan over an impulse."

"Well, I disagree," Bailey said.

"What's new?" Dev muttered. She practically felt Bailey's glare, so she concentrated on her task. A rustling rose in the air, along with her sister's voice.

"Um, guys. I found something."

Dev turned, expecting to see more quilts, but Bailey was holding a fat manila envelope in her hands. "It's probably copies of important financials or old pictures," Dev said, peering over her sister's shoulder.

Bailey opened the clasp and pulled out a stack of letters tied with a purple ribbon. Dev watched as her sister tugged on the ribbon and flipped slowly through the papers. No envelopes. Just one letter after another with dates at the top and the same salutation repeated.

Livia, amore mio.

"What is it?" Pris asked, turning from the closet.

"Letters. A lot of them," Bailey said.

Dev picked up the envelope and slid her hand inside. "Nothing else in here. Are they to us?"

Bailey shook her head. "They're from someone named R. And they look like love letters."

The sudden silence seemed to crackle with electricity. They shared a look. Pris shook her head. "Impossible. She wasn't dating anyone after Dad. And she got married at twenty-three, so there wasn't tons of time to have love affairs."

"Maybe they were from a college boyfriend?" Dev suggested. "Maybe she forgot they were in there."

Bailey's fingers tightened around the papers as she scanned through some of them. "These seem kind of intense."

Pris reached inside the trunk. "I found something else. It looks like a certificate."

Dev waited while her sister examined the document. When she looked up, shock carved out the lines of her face. "It's a deed for a house. That Mom owns. In Italy."

Bailey gasped. "Wait—Mom has a house in Italy? That's crazy! She would've told us."

Head swimming, Dev tried to focus. "Can I see that?"

Pris handed it over. "Oh my God, Pris is right. Mom owns a place in Positano, Italy."

"Is that on the Amalfi Coast?" Bailey asked, frowning. "We don't even know anyone from Italy. Has she ever mentioned it to either of you?"

They shook their heads. "There has to be some explanation," Pris said. "I'll get in touch with her lawyer and see if he knew about it."

"And Dad, of course," Bailey added. "Maybe it was Dad's and he gave it to her in the divorce?"

"Doubt it. Don't you think we would've taken a trip there?" Dev asked.

"I don't know what to think," Bailey said in a strangled voice. "It's so weird."

"Maybe she left us a letter?" Pris suggested.

Bailey split up the papers. "Good idea, let's look. I only glanced through them."

They each shuffled through their pile, but Dev found nothing addressed to them.

Pris sighed. "I don't see any letter to us. They're all from this R guy. But we need to go through the rest of her things. Maybe the explanation for the house is somewhere else and we missed it. Did Mom keep a diary? Journal? Special folder of personal items?"

"We found those already, remember? We needed all that stuff for the funeral and death certificate," Dev said.

Bailey waved her hand in the air. Her voice sounded highly pitched. "Guys, you need to hear this."

She began to read.

Livia, amore mio,

Today, I climbed onto the roof and watched the sunset and thought of you. The way you smell like lilacs, and the way your blue eyes light up when you smile and the way you say my name in a whisper after I kiss you. I count the days until summer and wonder if you will think of me the same. If another semester at college will cause you to realize you can have so much more than this simple life I can offer here. Yes, it would tear me apart to lose you, but can I be enough? This woman who sets my heart on fire and brings the world to its feet with just a smile? And even worse—I am too selfish to warn you away, dolcezza. If you will have me, I will wait for you. I will make sure you find the type of happiness you deserve by the way I love you, and I will force open the cities like an oyster to give you the things you need. I'm not surprised you are at the top of your class, especially in art history. There are many museums and art curators who will be lucky to have you. Soon, you will arrive with Aunt Silvia and my life will truly begin again. Until then, the fish and the tourists keep me company during the day. And you keep me company in my dreams.

Il mio cuore sarà tuo per sempre,

R

Bailey finished reading and lifted her head.

Dev had never heard such words from a lover—the way the raw emotions seemed to wrap around her and squeeze. Who was this woman who'd inspired such heartfelt vows? Certainly not the mother she'd grown up with. And why hadn't she ever spoken of him—even as an old boyfriend?

Her thoughts knotted into a tangle. Pris looked like she'd been sucker punched, her face dangerously pale. Bailey had that dreamy expression, like she'd been carried far off somewhere outside reality. Probably romanticizing the whole thing, when there had to be a rational explanation. Dev just needed to find it.

"It's just a silly college crush," Pris said firmly. "We all keep memories of old boyfriends. She probably hid them from Dad and forgot they were even in here."

Dev bit her lower lip. "This guy was from Italy! What about the house? And who's Aunt Silvia?"

"I don't know," Bailey said. "It sounds like she traveled there every summer. Why wouldn't she have mentioned this to us? Grandma and Pop Pop never said anything about Aunt Silvia either. Was she some type of secret? A black sheep or something?"

"Don't know. But they both died when we were young so we never got a chance to ask," Dev said.

Pris kept shaking her head and murmuring under her breath, like she refused to accept their discovery. "There must be an explanation. Mom is not the type to hide a secret life and an Italian getaway. It's not possible."

"Anything's possible," Bailey pointed out. "This must've happened before Dad, though. Do you think she looked this guy up after the divorce?"

Dev lifted a brow. "Well, Dad was the one who had an affair. Maybe she got back in touch with this guy for revenge? Or from loneliness?"

A strange sense of anger made Pris snap. "I think we're overreacting and there's a rational explanation. Let's read another letter. The latest one. What's the date?"

Bailey flipped to the end of the pile, careful of the ink on the crisp white paper. "No date." She hesitated. Dev held her breath, sensing they were all caught on the precipice of knowing too much. Once they fell off the cliff, there'd be no turning back or pretending it didn't happen. Did they want what they knew about their mom to change forever?

But it was already too late to turn back. They had discovered these letters, and Bailey had already begun to read.

Dearest Livia,

For too long, I was unable to accept your letters. It was best for both of us—to finally let go of a past that was so beautiful, it may have ended up destroying us both. I had done my best to keep those summers locked away. Even that one precious week when I believed you'd come back to me is a memory best not to revisit. I convinced myself our time together was a dream, but when I saw my name on those envelopes, I realized I alone could ruin a life that I'd rebuilt after you left. I couldn't do that, dolcezza. Not even for you.

But now, I find myself at a crossroads. I still think about you. I still wonder what could have been. I still want to gaze upon your face one more time.

So, yes, I will meet you here for your 65th birthday.

R

Bailey dropped the pile of papers. They gazed at one another in stunned silence.

Dev's mind clamored to understand, and she stumbled over the timeline. Her mom had passed in February. Her birthday was in May—which meant she'd died before this meeting could have taken place. After the funeral, her sisters had taken time to settle paperwork and the will, putting off the house to the last task.

Had this man been waiting for Mom in Positano on her sixty-fifth birthday? Did he know she passed? Or was this a secret kept from everyone?

Dev was the first to break the silence. "I think we need to read all these letters and figure out what's going on."

Bailey slowly nodded. "I think I'll cancel my reading tonight."

Pris gave a long sigh. "I think I'll run out and get us some wine."

Photo by Matt Simpkins Photography

Jennifer Probst is the *New York Times* bestselling author of the Billionaire Builders series, the Searching For . . . series, the Marriage to a Billionaire series, the Steele Brothers series, the Stay series, and the Sunshine Sisters series. Like some of her characters, Probst, along with her husband and two sons, calls New York's Hudson Valley home. When she isn't traveling to meet readers, she enjoys reading, watching "shameful reality television," and visiting a local Hudson Valley animal shelter.

CONNECT ONLINE

JenniferProbst.com

🐦 JenniferProbst

📷 AuthorJenniferProbst

f JenniferProbst.AuthorPage

Ready to find
your next great read?

Let us help.

Visit prh.com/nextread

Penguin
Random
House